The Last

By

Paul Howe

*To, my friend Jo
I hope you enjoy the read.*

Copyright © 2019 Paul Howe

ISBN: 978-0-244-44916-2

All rights reserved, including the right to reproduce this book, or portions thereof in any form. No part of this text may be reproduced, transmitted, downloaded, decompiled, reverse engineered, or stored, in any form or introduced into any information storage and retrieval system, in any form or by any means, whether electronic or mechanical without the express written permission of the author.

This is a work of fiction. Names and characters are the product of the author's imagination and any resemblance to actual persons, living or dead, is entirely coincidental.

PublishNation
www.publishnation.co.uk

About the author

Paul Howe lives in Weston-super-Mare, England. He has pursued successful careers in teaching, entertainment, film work and as a hypnotherapist. Even though he has written various newspaper articles, The Last Lama, is his first book. As a hobby, Paul has a passion for investigating anything mysterious and seeking the truth. From ghost hunting, to UFO's and religion, all, he believes *"deserve looking at with a sense of adventure and an open mind."*

Acknowledgements

A special thanks to both my wife, Grace and my good friend, Clive Pardoe for their continual inspirational support when I needed it. Also, thanks to Darren Bane, another friend and author for his help with my editing and advice. Finally, thanks to Jim MacRoberts for his painting of the book cover and to Perry March for the donation of one of his wonderful photos which became the background for my back cover.

Chapter One

Tibet, 2029

The door banged open, splintering the rotting, slatted base of the old wooden hut. The shock of the entrance had just begun to register on the outer edge of Simeon's mind when a barrage of bullets splayed out from left to right, the high-powered Uzi machine gun discharging its full load, pulverizing the soft wooden inner walls and ramshackle furnishings and punching through the young couple and their two-year-old son. The boy sagged in his mother's limp, blood-spattered arms. Within seconds, the colour of the walls had changed from a dull, damp grey to a dark, glistening red.

In those few seconds, as the shock finally registered, and blackness overcame him, Simeon had a dawning realization – it was the end of days.

Ignoring the carnage, splashing through the pools of blood, Sergeant Ling marched determinedly forward to what remained of the toddler's torn corpse. Ling was a small, muscular man with a scarred face that gave him a mean, countenance matching his perverse and cruel nature.

Carefully, he bent down to examine the child's arms and shoulders, wiping away the warm blood with his sleeves. The markings were there as promised. He had had little doubt, having spotted the two crows perched on the roof of the hut as he had stepped over the crest of the hill. The prophecy was accurate, and the target was now confirmed. An arrogant smirk spread across Ling's face as he reflected upon his torture of the high lama. Even a lama of the highest ranking from the Lhasa Monastery itself hadn't been able to withstand the torments inflicted upon him. He'd had to talk eventually. He did. Ling's smile grew wider. His orders had been not to harm a single hair on the lama's body, and he hadn't. But no man could endure the torture he had brutally inflicted, and the strengthened, jagged, plastic shaft violently forced through the man's rectum, chased by a red-hot poker finally broke the lama. The screams had been heard more than a mile away. The answers to his questions had taken only seconds to fall from his captive's lips, and there had been absolutely no doubt as to their credence. The man had answered truthfully.

Just as the exhilaration of what he had accomplished began to fade, as his thoughts wandered briefly to picturing his promotion to captain or even major, and as he contemplated his coming riches and renown, he heard a distant thud followed by a singing pain in his back. A swirling wave of dizziness overcame him, his vision blurred and then faded. Then nothing.

And a fourth soul left a body. But this one was heading for a different place.

Chapter Two

Twenty-two years later. Sitting in the University's union bar,
Amalialad pondered once again on the extraordinary twists and turns his life had taken. Even now, he had some difficulty in understanding how he could quite naturally master such extraordinary human feats. All his teachers had been good, brilliant in fact but privately admitted to each other that Amalialad's abilities had even surpassed their own. They were amazed. He was accepted de facto as a child prodigy in virtually everything he studied. But there was one question he could not come to terms with. Why? Amalialad's intuitiveness was extraordinarily astute. He could not remember a time when his 'gut feelings' failed him. It was akin to a sixth sense Over the last few days he'd felt a strong foreboding. With it came a strong sense of urgency to recognise and accept something. But what was it? In his quiet moments the question began to haunt him.

"You're always in deep contemplation. What is it this time? How to dematerialise an inanimate object, send it halfway across the world and materialise it again?" Ben spoke with his usual good humour and mild sarcasm. He had taken an instant liking to him when they'd met at registration on their first day at university. He reflected. He saw a man of muscular stature, not too tall, probably 5' 8" with an oriental complexion, He displayed a placid and gentle air. Yet Ben felt a hidden element of mystery about this young man and sensed he masked a powerful inner strength and wisdom that very few, if any, of his age could boast.

Amalialad smiled brightly at him. Ben had just returned from a week's field trip in Wales. Ben was tall, extremely fit and possessed a never-ending spiel of sarcastic humour that made him one of the most popular characters in the university. Amalialad remembered his first meeting with Ben. It was at the university registration. And he'd quickly taken an instant liking to him.

"Well, actually that's already been scientifically demonstrated and proven, my good friend," said Amalialad. "But regardless of such worldly machinations, it's good to see you Ben. How'd the trip go?"

"Well, if you mean from an academic perspective, great! We managed to uncover some real interesting bones dating from the early Jurassic period. Dr. Johnson was beside himself. But, blimey, his usual stuttering is bad enough but when he gets excited, he takes a lifetime to explain things. Honestly, his description of the bones took us less than a page to write from an hour of verbal diarrhea."

"He's brilliant in his field, Ben. It's worth waiting for," Amalialad suggested.

"Yeah, I know." Ben smiled to himself.

"How was it from the social level then?"

Ben brightened and smiled briefly. Then his face darkened.

"Amalialad, you just wouldn't believe it! It was disastrous. We were stuck in the middle of nowhere. There was one small pub, about a mile away in an isolated village full of old codgers. I didn't see anyone under fifty."

"Ah, but then it was surely a most positive trip, my friend. You could focus more on your studies. Consequently, you will surely benefit from your written assignment and raise the sorely needed marks to achieve a respectable result."

"Hmm, I suppose so." Ben had his doubts. He'd spent most of his free time moping around the pub waiting for some gorgeous Welsh lasses to show up.

"Hey, there's an 80's night here tomorrow, fancy coming?" Ben wasn't expecting his friend to say yes. He knew Amalialad attended the Buddhist Temple every Friday evening, without fail. But it was worth a try.

Amalialad smiled broadly. "You know the answer to that already my friend, but thanks for the invitation."

"Yeah, ok. But you've been going to that temple for three years now and you've never missed a single week. Please tell me, what do you find so compelling about it?"

"Ben, there is so much to learn about life and I want to learn as much as possible, especially about people and why we all behave so differently. Some people are logical yet so many others are so illogical and I find this perplexing. Just imagine, if you can, that all wisdom is the equivalent to a bucket full of sand. Then imagine, if we reach the age of one hundred, we would at best have only reached the measure of a single grain. I simply want to spend as much time as possible learning about life and about the mysteries of our universe. I want to delve deeply and understand as many of its intricacies as possible. So, in answer to your question, my spiritual beliefs and practices help me to do this. I fervently believe that if I study hard enough I may, at least one day, accumulate a single grain of understanding. I may then find just a few answers to so many unanswered questions which I have. I also attend the temple because I believe in the Buddhist philosophy but more than that," Amalialad thought carefully, "I feel spiritually drawn towards the temple. I simply can't explain this." Amalialad paused. Why had he always felt completely at home in the temple? Why had he immediately felt so wonderfully comfortable and happy within its walls?

"Anyway," he continued, "in simple terms, Buddhism teaches that we are all as one, united in our creator's essence. We passionately believe it's incumbent upon all of us to continually try to help others and to do each other no harm. That, Ben, is something I truly believe. Something which I feel is paramount if people with their diverse religions and beliefs are to live in harmony, side by side. But, of course, everyone has the free will to choose his own path. I believe individual destiny will be determined accordingly." Amalialad smiled. "Anyway, I have to go and catch up on a bit of studying. How about we meet up at the dojo tomorrow morning, ok?"

"Yeah, ok, see you tomorrow, but you know you can go blind studying too much, don't you?" Ben grinned.

"I'll risk it."

As he watched his friend leave, Ben thought, Hmm, only a single grain? Something at the back of his mind was telling him that his friend was due for a bucket full.

essence that saw, thought and felt. He had felt himself possessed by an extraordinarily light, colourful body, buoyant, joyful and somehow four-dimensional. But most of all he remembered feeling so very wide awake with a wonderful sense of absolute freedom where everything was more bright and vivid than he had ever experienced.

His starting point was above the roof of his house. He then gently floated over the rows of neighbouring houses and roads, looking intently for signs of suspicious movement. He was looking for a small person in dark attire. Not much to go on, but he was also relying on his astute intuitiveness to play its part in identifying the assassin. Just a few minutes into flight, Amalialad sensed a dark presence below. He suddenly felt fearful as the foreboding returned. It was stronger this time. He hesitated in going further. But he was angry. No, damn it! I need to find out who tried to kill me! Amalialad sped forward to continue his search. He flew lower. Suddenly, he saw movement under the boughs of an old elm tree in the rear garden of an almost derelict house, a house he recognised as being deserted. So, who was the trespasser hiding under the tree? He went down to investigate.

The voice came from nowhere in particular, but its intrusion into Amalialad's consciousness was forceful and urgent. "Leave now, Amalialad! Please, just trust me. Leave now and return to your physical body. Your life is in grave peril if you continue!" It was Lopsang.

"What's the danger, Lopsang?" he responded tele pathetically. "This man tried to kill me. I need to know his identity."

"Please, just trust me on this and return immediately. I will explain later. Return to your body now and come and meet me at the temple. And bring the knife."

Reluctantly, feeling frustrated, Amalialad retreated.

Chapter Four

The Buddhist temple was set back from the road, occupying the far corner of Church Avenue. It was a twenty-minute walk from Amalialad's lodgings.

As he entered, he thought back to the first time he'd visited the temple. The serene atmosphere was still the same. It was so wonderfully peaceful and tranquil. The fast-paced London life subsided as he walked down the central aisle and onto the foot of the wide, wine carpeted steps which, in turn, led to the feet of the marble statue of the Buddha. In quiet contemplation, kneeling to the left of Amalialad was an elderly monk. He was dressed in a bright red robe decorated with yellow, thick seams. Lopsang. Silently, Amalialad knelt next to his friend and mentor…and waited.

After several minutes of prayer and quiet contemplation, Lopsang spoke.

"Please be patient, Amalialad, and I will explain. First, I ask you to follow me, if you will?" Lopsang stood and, turning to his left, walked slowly down to the end of the aisle to a large iron door. Amalialad followed. His curiosity was aroused now, but with it came a strong intuitive feeling that some profound inner awakening was about to be revealed to him. He felt giddy. Were all his questions to be answered at last? He had very little knowledge of his roots, but his intuition told him that something of the utmost importance was about to be disclosed. What was it?

Lopsang opened the door. Inside was a large rosewood table covered with an assortment of what seemed to be ancient artefacts. They were certainly old. Lopsang walked around to the opposite side of the table. He said absolutely nothing; he simply stared hard, gazing intently into Amalialad's eyes.

It was inexplicable. It was confusing. Yet what happened next somehow felt perfectly natural. Looking closely at the table, Amalialad recognised some of the artefacts. Then just as abruptly he felt, quite uncannily, an overpowering feeling of love and affection towards three of the objects. The affinity grew even stronger. It enveloped his entire being, until finally he was overcome with tearful emotion. The revelation hit him hard. These things belonged to him. He reached for the old silver knife with the ivory handle.

"That's mine." Amalialad was confused. He knew he never wanted to lose or part with the knife again, but he didn't know why. After all, wasn't this the very first time he'd seen it? Then he reached for the Holy Book. "That's mine, too." He felt an overwhelming sense of possession that he couldn't account for. His emotions just didn't make sense. Finally, Amalialad reached out and grabbed the old walnut staff. "And that's mine." He realised he was shouting, and looked up at Lopsang, embarrassed.

Lopsang reached across the table and grabbed Amaliad's shirt sleeve yanking it aggressively upwards.

Amalialad stepped back in horror. Lopsang seemed to be possessed.

"Forgive me!" Lopsang said. "But look at your arm."

Amalialad lifted his shirt sleeve higher to reveal his birth mark. But he noticed nothing unusual himself and looked back at Lopsang in dismay, waiting for an answer.

"Look at your birthmark. It's the conch - the mark of the Dalai Llama! You must now accept. It is meant to be! You are, indeed, the Dalai Lama, the Kundum! The Oracle was right." Lopsang fell to his knees and kissed Amalialad's feet.

"My Holiness, I hope you will forgive me".

Amalialad was momentarily stunned. Why was he being referred to as 'Your Holiness'? And what was there to forgive? Other than, he thought, the embarrassment he was feeling at Lopsang kissing his feet.

"Please, Lopsang. Are you ok? What's wrong? Why do you call me such and why are you kissing my feet?"

Tears of joy ran down Lopsang's cheeks. Then he smiled.

"Your Holiness, you were lost to us but now returned. But forgive me. It must be so confusing for you and I am being selfish in revealing these emotions. Let's be seated. I have much to tell." They sat down on two chairs in the corner of the room and

Lopsang lowered his head and pressed his hands together as if in prayer.

"My Holiness."

"No, please, Lopsang, for now please still call me, Amalialad. I wouldn't feel comfortable with anything else."

"As you wish, my Hol…. Ah, my apologies, I mean, of course, Amalialad. For some time now, I have had suspicions about your real identity. But now you have confirmed them. The three artefacts you chose are, indeed, yours. They've belonged to you for over six hundred years."

"What the …"

"Please! Please." Lopsang urged. "There will be questions, but firstly, it's most imperative you hear me out."

"You are the fifteenth Dalai Lama. You are the reincarnation of fourteen others before you. You are the temporal spiritual leader of all Tibet. You are the Kundum. Indeed, you are the only possible savior of the world and you have been lost to us, presumed dead, for more than twenty-two years. You must have wondered why you have such extraordinary gifts? Most of them were developed in your lives over centuries. In this life you have almost mastered and finely tuned them. What you can do only a few individuals scattered around the world are able to do – but even they can only accomplish one or two of the talents you have and never to the same degree. The chosen studies, with which you've excelled, philosophy, psychology, world religions, daemonology and metaphysics were no coincidence. Similarly, your attraction to our temple was predestined. You were lost to us twenty-two years ago. The Chinese forces have ravaged our country since they invaded our lands over seventy years ago. When our last Great Dalai Lama, Lhamo Dhondup, was assassinated twenty-two years ago it caused a great sadness. It was the day you were born. However, two years later, just as our sources had discovered your whereabouts, we received grave news of your brutal murder. We thought that you'd been murdered by Chinese military forces. Our suspicions about your death arose about two years later. We'd received no signs as to the whereabouts of the birth place of the next Dalai Lama.

Normally when the Kundum dies the next is discovered within two years. We decided to send scouts back to your village to find out more about your past and it was then that we discovered that you had an identical twin. The Chinese had mistakenly identified your twin as the Dalai Lama and slaughtered him instead of you." Lopsang bowed his head solemnly, looking briefly away, and swallowed hard. He then looked back at Amalialad and continued. "We discovered that, at the time of your family's murder, you were in a nearby village where you were treated by the local physician for measles. An old seer told your uncle of a dream he'd just had in which it had been explained that the Chinese had slain your family but would soon discover their mistake and search for you. We later discovered that, after a period in hiding, your uncle managed to smuggle you out to the West, to England, where he felt you would be safe from Chinese assassins. Your uncle was very intelligent and with cunning, careful planning and a lot of quiet subterfuge he finally managed to get you to London. Unfortunately, within a year, your uncle suffered a heart attack and died. You were then taken in by Barnardo's Children's Homes. We think they did a fine job in helping to bring you up.

"Yes, they did a very good job and I have very fond memories of my time with them. This sounds so unbelievable, Lopsang, and yet I instinctively know that what you say is true. There is much that has happened in my life that I have found confusing, but it is now, finally, beginning to make sense." Amalialad thought back to a time when he was about eight years old, when he had woken up to find himself levitating three feet above his bed. Terrified, he'd suddenly felt his 'astral body' being swiftly drawn down into his physical body which was lying comatose upon the bed. He awoke in pain. He felt like he'd been punched in the solar plexus. Finally, the pieces fitted. Amalialad turned back to Lopsang. "There are things that you say that disturb me greatly. For instance, you say I am the hope of the world?"

"Please, let me continue, for I think when I've finished much of what has happened to you over the years will become clearer."

"Whilst living under Chinese domination the Tibetan people have, for many years, been oppressed and very cruelly treated. Currently, they feel lost, forgotten and abandoned by the world because they have no Dalai Lama to lead them, yet they wait patiently, always praying for his eventual return. However, it seems that the perpetual cycle of conflict and suffering grows rapidly worldwide. Indeed, as it has always been since time immemorial, the battle between the forces of good and evil continues. Until now, most of humanity had kept the spirit of goodness and love within their hearts, and this has kept the evil forces in check. Amalialad, I must tell you with great sadness that the tide is beginning to turn against us. Evil, daemonic forces are gathering. And they are determined to conquer the world," Lopsang explained.

"There is now a malevolence afoot, the evilness of which we have faced only once before. The Nighthawks have returned. They have come from the bowels of the earth. From the very depths of Hell itself, they have returned to challenge us. It is written that 'One man, pure of heart, true to himself who has risen from the East, but grown in the West must lead the quest to overcome this mounting tide of evil.' A man older than seven generations of men! That man is you, Amalialad."

"Please, hold on a minute, Lopsang, I really don't think that can be me!"

"But it is you! You see, the Oracle was also right in its advice in finding you, the chosen one.

"What's that supposed to mean? It doesn't sound like much of a clue to me."

"Well, if you remember, you found us first, three years ago, by deciding to come to our temple of your own free will. Do you agree?" Amalialad nodded. "Look at your name. You are Amalialad. Spell your name backwards?" Lopsang looked sadly at Amalialad, as he realised what a great burden he was about to put on his shoulders.

As these thoughts were passing through Lopsang's mind, Amalialad stood motionless, yet not shocked, as the penny dropped and the truth, the final realisation, sank in. His name, spelt backwards…D..a..l..ai L..a..m.a. Dalai Lama! How had he not realized this before? But then, perhaps he wasn't meant to, maybe he hadn't been ready. But he'd always felt there was something special about him and now he knew, at long last, the relief of knowing overwhelmed him.

Lopsang broke through his thoughts. "I'm sorry, Amalialad, but I must also tell you," Lopsang's features suddenly became forlorn as he turned, with tears in his eyes, to look directly at Amalialad, "we have so little hope of defeating this entrenchment of evil. In fact, most of the high lamas are saying it's impossible. I am so very, very sorry, Amalialad, but it is my duty to tell you this and hand this mission to you. You must do battle with this mounting tide of evil. You have been chosen by destiny to be God's gladiator against the devil and all his dark forces."

Amalialad smiled. Now, at least, he understood Lopsang's apology.

Lopsang spoke again.

"Even with all your talents, you will need help. The Oracle's prophecy is somewhat vague and obscure, but one part is clear. 'There will be six to face the Demons and the Hawks of the night'. You must find five more 'good souls.' You must find five more individuals, stout and pure of heart and mind. It won't be an easy task, for some may have their own quests to fulfil. You are young in this life, but you have the wisdom of many within your reach if you look deep enough within yourself. Use that wisdom. Use your talents. There is one final thing. It's something that is puzzling me, but it's an important part of the prophecy. It is said, 'Look to Abraham and the Gospels for help for they will provide the final light to vanquish the wanderers and demons of the night'. I must simply leave that with you. And, finally, about the assassin … it was a Shadow Runt, a servant of the Nighthawks. They do the bidding of their masters by day when the Nighthawks are at rest. But the one you must eventually face is their leader. We don't know who that is yet, but we know that never has such a creature had such malevolence towards humans. An evil exists which grows daily. Your life is already in danger; you must tread your path with great care. Had you continued to follow the warrior, your 'astral cord' may have been severed. You would have been instantly separated from your earthly body and doomed to existence on the Astral Plane for all eternity. I must let you go on your quest now but take your belongings with you. They can help."

"My thanks, Lopsang, but I find myself in a dilemma. For me to overcome this evil you say I I must destroy this malevolence but that goes against our whole philosophy, never to kill. Killing anything goes against the fabric of my whole being."

Lopsang smiled sadly. "My dear friend, on that score you have no worries – you are fighting an abomination of beings that are already dead."

"Then that leaves me with a bigger problem. How do you destroy something which is dead already?" They looked at each other for a few silent moments.

Lopsang shook his head. "May Buddha's words of wisdom, and the aid of the gospels, guide you. I can give you no other advice."

Amalialad gently nodded his head, turned and left. Quietly, he walked back out of the temple, contemplating the almost impossible task with which he had so suddenly been burdened.

Chapter Five

Ben enjoyed the Monday morning sessions at the dojo. It was the day the club welcomed beginners, and he looked especially forward to the close physical bouts with the female trainees. It was a great opportunity to try out his best chat-up lines. Nevertheless, he realized that his friend was late. That was very unusual as Amalialad was a stickler for punctuality. As those thoughts faded, he caught a movement on the periphery of his vision and turned to see Amalialad standing in the doorway. Ben didn't miss the troubled expression on his Amalialad's face. He knew then something was amiss with him even though Amalialad, noticing Ben looking towards him, suddenly presented a beaming, wide, engaging smile. Ben, still in full swing, finished the Crescent movement with a side roll, gave the customary bow, whispered his phone number once more in her ear, and walked towards Amalialad.

"That yellow belt you keep wearing still never fails to make me smile," laughed Amalialad.

"Well, it's refreshing to see you laughing, but you know that if I wear my black belt I'd be expected to coach nearly all men, since they are mainly the ones who need training above the yellow grade and we both know we only have two here with black belts so I'd be denying the young trainees my invaluable experience." Ben said, smiling.

"I see, so it's just a coincidence that all the trainees are female is it? Hmm…" Amalialad said smiling, "I think there will be a time when you may regret this subterfuge."

"Nope, I value your advice and admittedly you're rarely wrong, but on this occasion, I think I know best."

"And so be it." Amalialad answered amusingly.

"Anyway," Ben said, "forget about my idiosyncrasies, something's wrong. What is it?"

Amalialad looked hard at his friend, momentarily wondering if he had made the right decision. He knew Ben would want to help him in his quest, but in doing so, his life would be in grave danger. Could he live with that responsibility if anything happened to Ben? Damn it! He had wrestled with these same thoughts all night and had decided he owed it to his friend to be honest. The alternative would be to simply disappear from Ben's life without any reason, and that would be even more cruel.

"Let's sit down." Amalialad's tone was quiet and the humour had gone. They walked over to an isolated table in the corner of the hall. Out of earshot of the others, they sat down and Amalialad explained the previous day's events. A few seconds of silence followed.

"Wow! My best friend is the spiritual leader of all Tibet? And he must conquer the greatest of all evils to save the world. Ben said sarcastically.

Amalialad looked Ben directly in the eyes as he spoke.

"It's true Ben. Unfortunately, it's true." And it was the way in which Amalialad spoke that convinced Ben it was true. "

"I see." Ben's tone changed, and he became serious. "If it was anybody else telling me this, I'd be doubled up laughing. What do you plan to do? How will you go about achieving all this?"

"You don't have to get involved with this, Ben. Your life, like mine, and anyone else who helps me, will be in great danger. You're my best friend, and if anything, bad ever happened to you because of this, I would find the burden unbearable and ..."

"You just stop right there! Stop thinking about how you'd feel and think about how I'd feel if I allowed my best friend to wander off and face these 'things', these 'creatures' of the night, alone. Just think how I would feel if anything happened to you and I hadn't been there to help you. But if what you say is true, and you fail, then there's no hope for me or any other person on this earth, is there?"

"I'm sorry." Amalialad looked directly into Ben's eyes. "But you're right."

"In any case, how could I not help you defeat these ... what did you call them? – Nighthawks? When we've defeated them, just imagine – I'd become a hero. Every woman in the world would idolise me. They would be queuing up to date me. Yep,

I'm sorry, my friend, but I'm coming with you whether you like it or not. Where and when do we start?"

Amalialad felt a mixture of relief and sorrow at Ben's decision. He had a true and capable friend at his side, but there was a good chance that he would get him killed. A further thought crossed his mind. He knew that even if they succeeded, they wouldn't be able to tell anyone. Knowing that such an evil malevolence existed, even if defeated, would still stir fear and panic. Some might question whether the creatures had truly been defeated. Society wouldn't be able to live with the repercussions. But he would explain this to Ben when the need arose, when they had defeated the Nighthawks. For now, the odds were stacked heavily against then. There were two to meet the challenge. Four more were needed. Where would he start looking?

Sometimes in life the answers are never too far away, and this was one of those occasions, Amalialad later reflected. Then his neck twitched and with a start, he became alert and his senses immediately tuned in to his immediate surroundings.

"What's wrong?" asked Ben, aware of the change in his friend.

"Shh." Amalialad looked slowly around the hall, studying the aura of every individual until his eyes finally rested upon one person.

"You're looking at their auras, aren't you?" Ben has seen his friend doing this many times before when he'd helped sick friends recover by simply caressing their limbs and foreheads, but on this occasion the gaze was somehow different.

"You see the girl in the opposite corner? The girl with long blonde hair who's staring out of the window?"

Ben turned to look. "Yeah, but she seems absolutely rooted to the spot. What's wrong with her?"

"There is a presence next to her. A dark entity stands by her side. The girl's emanations are changing rapidly. They discolour her aura. The black of the malevolence's intrusion is disturbing her normal bright exuberance of red and orange. We must act quickly. Even from here, I sense its penetration. We have only seconds to avoid the girl becoming permanently, psychologically impaired. Ben, it's risking your safety, but I want you to go straight to her – talk to her, say anything. The fact that you are physically next to her, touching her, if possible, will distract the focus of the force and allow me to approach it undetected."

Ben flew across the hall and, finding his momentum too fast to control, went sprawling into the woman, knocking her to the floor. He quickly reached out and grabbed her while simultaneously rolling to one side, allowing her to fall on top of him, so that he managed to break her fall.

"Wow, what move is that?" shouted a young trainee.

"It was a special move," said Amalialad, walking up to Ben, smiling. "It broke the force. Indeed, a classic manoeuvre and far more effective than I could ever have done."

The girl stirred.

"Where am I?" Her voice was shaky, but as she began to take in her surroundings a semblance of normality gradually came to her. The she heard a gentle voice in her head. It felt most reassuring. You need not be afraid now. You're in safe hands. Please follow us out of the hall and we will talk further in private. She sensed security in the voice and her intuition urged her to do as instructed. She looked at Amalialad, who smiled reassuringly and gave her a gentle nod. And strangely, she felt compelled to surrender to his request. Amalialad and Ben calmly and slowly turned and walked out of the hall. She followed.

Chapter Six

Amalialad led them to a corner table of the cafeteria. It was likely to get busier and he wanted some privacy.

"Three strong black coffees please," Ben said to the waitress.

Smiling, Amalialad spoke first.

"My name is Amalialad and this is Ben. Do you mind telling us your name?"

The girl was extremely attractive, quite stunning in every way, wearing a short, white cotton blouse and a woolen, black skirt. She had blonde hair, blue eyes and perfectly symmetrical facial features, which were highlighted even more by her soft smile and gentle demeanor.

"Of course," she said, "in view of the circumstances, its the least I can do. I'm Tara." Her warm smile widened displaying a perfect set of teeth and Ben, after being temporarily mesmerized by her beauty, answered. He guessed she was a model or something like that. Ben spoke.

"But I just ran straight into you, knocking you over! I'm so very sorry. I hope I didn't hurt you too much. I'm glad you're not angry with me."

"Angry with you? Far from it – I owe you my life!" Her warm and sincere smile brought a lump to Ben's throat and moved him close to tears.

"If I may?" Amalialad broke in, patting Ben gently on the back. "Could I perhaps say something?" He looked sympathetically towards Tara.

"Please do." Tara held the smile and instinctively knew the man facing her was no ordinary individual. Perhaps at last she had found the person she had been seeking. Her premonitions had foretold that she would, but they'd been wrong before.

"How long have you known about your psychic abilities?"

Tara was taken aback.

"Well, I suppose since I was five, but I was too scared to tell anyone.

"You have a rare gift and, if it's any consolation, I share it with you. You were able to receive my thought transmissions earlier, and I yours. How long have you been able to do that?"

"Hmm, that's a puzzle. I've been able, on occasion, to pick up other people's thoughts, but never has anyone been able to read mine."

At this Amalialad smiled.

"The explanation is simple. Since we both have certain psychic abilities, we can read each other's thoughts, but you will be pleased to know, only if we both choose to do so, since it normally requires intense focusing." He smiled, and reddened slightly, as she attempted to control her blushing.

"But in the hall, I wasn't focusing."

"Ah, but you were in great danger and in the process of being possessed by a malevolent entity. We found you in a trance state. It was your subconscious that came to your rescue. The subconscious is there to protect you and is much stronger than anything we can achieve at the conscious level. It allowed you to communicate with my thoughts."

"Please, you must help me!" Tara suddenly became concerned. Ben quickly broke in.

"Of course, we will. Please, don't worry. Try to calm down," Ben reassured her.

"Tara, please listen very carefully. You will be fine, and we will help you, but you must listen carefully. Your life depends on it, ok?" Amalialad spoke gently but there was urgency in his voice. Tara's hands were trembling, but his reassurance calmed her. She felt a great strength emanating from him. She instinctively knew this man was true to his word, and from that moment felt the heavy burden lift from her shoulders. She broke down with relief.

"Please don't upset yourself. My friend means what he says. If anyone can help you – he can." Ben said He reached out and reassuringly touched her hand. "Please trust us. Whatever is threatening you, you'll be safe with us."

"I believe you. I sense the truth in your words, but I'm crying with relief. I've known my life's been in danger for weeks now, but nobody understands. People think I'm mad." She tried to smile again. She looked at Amalialad.

"I'm listening," Amalialad spoke softly. As the words were spoken the waitress arrived with the coffees. She carefully placed the tray on the table and left.

"Ah, that's excellent timing. I think we could all do with a strong coffee right now, don't you?" Amalialad said. "Tara, when we saw you, you were experiencing the beginnings of demonic possession and if Ben hadn't intervened when he did, it would have resulted in a complete takeover of your whole personality, indeed, your very soul, by a diabolical force of the evillest intentions. It would have dominated you completely."

"What do you mean by dominate?" Even though she barely knew them, she had absolute trust in the two people facing her. There was a strong intuitiveness deep within her telling her she would be protected.

"There are stages to a demonic possession. When we first saw you, you were at the point of experiencing the first stage. That is the actual point when the actual entity first starts to take control of the victim. Over the coming days, you would use erroneous judgements and make unethical choices in all vital matters. You would then yield control of everything and completely submit yourself to the invading entity. Even though you may have been aware that everything you did was totally alien to your personality, you would be helpless to do anything about it. Finally, you would be totally possessed. You would have become a lost soul and at the complete beck and call of the demon!"

"Bloody hell!" Ben interjected. "Was that a Shadow Runt?"

"No, Ben. It's malevolent, but totally different. I fear we are dealing with the black arts from a different source."

"Is that possible?"

"Indeed, it is." Amalialad looked again towards Tara. She returned the gaze questioningly. He understood her thoughts.

"Tara, I will explain about Shadow Runts later, but for now we have more pressing matters to contend with and I think it's time for you to tell your story." Ben stared at his friend in disbelief. What in hell could be more pressing that the advent of assassination attacks from shadow runts and the imminent build-up of an army of Nighthawks? He thought. But he kept quiet.

"Until a week ago my father was the reverend at St. Mary the Virgin Church, Clapham." Amalialad looked worried. "My father had only been there for six months, and although he was initially very excited at the prospect of being its Vicar, he quickly became disillusioned. His usual emails to me lost their bright, optimistic tone and became negative in outlook. I knew something was wrong, but I decided not to say anything about my feelings to him. ..." Tara burst into tears.

"It's ok," Amalialad answered. "Whatever happened wasn't your fault. Please continue."

"Well, I wanted to visit him, but he pleaded with me not to, and suggested I wait a few weeks until the summer, when the weather would be brighter, and we could enjoy a woodland walk together but I just knew something was wrong. He'd never spoken to me in that way before, but I didn't want to upset him any further, so I agreed. I shouldn't have done, should I? But ..."

Amalialad spoke again. "I would have done the same thing. Please try not to blame yourself. You obviously found out something afterwards that greatly upset you about the decision you made, but unfortunately, it's so often only in hindsight we realise which actions may have been the best ones to take. Even with your psychic abilities, when families are involved, we often choose a direction we wouldn't otherwise have done."

Tara took a few slow deep breaths before she continued. Ben looked on. He was always amazed at his friend's ability to speedily read situations and the eloquence with which he could then explain them to everyone.

"Well, a week went by and I still hadn't heard from him. I'd called every day and left messages on his answer phone. I even called the bishop, but he seemed unconcerned and suggested my father may have gone to the Church House in Westminster, London. It was the Church of England's biggest meeting and administrative base, but I didn't believe any of it. My father would never go there unless he really had to. "Too much time wasted in eating and drinking," he used to say. So, I decided to visit him at his home for myself. I plan to go tomorrow. I must find out exactly what's going on. We're very close and there's no way my father would have not contacted me within that time. He knows how much it would worry me."

"Tara, please listen carefully to what I'm about to say. I don't want to frighten you, but I know that you have the strength and resolve to cope with this. I also sense that you prefer us to be straight with you, and I'm not one to beat about the bush. My personal interests and the subject of my doctorate is the paranormal. I'm telling you this because I know the diocese in which your father works is well documented as the former base of operations of one of the most devilish covens of the Black Arts that this country has ever had. They're called The Friends of Hecate."

"I'm sure I remember reading something or other about Hecate," said Ben. "Wasn't she a Greek goddess or something?"

"Indeed. She was supposedly the most feared of all the Greek deities. She displayed no mercy for her victims and relished death. She's often depicted as having three heads. One is that of a frenzied witch, the second a manned horse, and the third a savage snake. She was chiefly regarded as the divinity of the Underworld. However, she's known by many names: Mistress of Ghosts and Spectres: Goddess of Untimely Deaths: Suicides and Epilepsy: Goddess of the Underworld: Queen of Magic: Queen of Witches. Shall I go on?"

"I didn't think I'd ever say this, but that's one Greek goddess I wouldn't mind giving a miss!"

"Ben, we must hope you're right because now, the odds are it's the one we shall meet, albeit in the guise of her infernal servants." Amalialad looked directly into Tara's eyes as he continued to speak, and for the first time since meeting him she felt the despair in his voice. She, too, involuntarily shook as the realisation of what they potentially faced began to sink in. "If your father is somehow involved and threatened by this, and I'm sorry, but my instincts tell me this is so, then we have no choice but to enter the lion's den and face our adversaries head on."

Amalialad looked at Tara. "By the way, what brought you here?"

"A dream."

"I see." Amalialad seemed satisfied with the answer. Ben was confused but decided not to question Tara any further.

"Do you have somewhere to stay tonight?"

"Yes, thank you, I'm staying with a friend."

"Great, I want you both to go home, pack enough clothes for a few days, and get a good night's rest." He looked straight at Ben. "That means no clubbing tonight".

"Yeah, yeah, ok." He can read minds, Ben thought, rather disturbed at the prospect.

"Then I want us all to meet here again at nine tomorrow morning. Any questions?"

"Where are we going?" Ben asked.

"We're going to Clapham."

Chapter Seven

Amalialad knew he wouldn't be getting any sleep. He had his packing to do, but he also had other far more important preparations to make. He knew it would be prudent to do a little more research about the 'Friends of Hecate'.

Two of his bookshelves were near breaking point with the weight of books, magazines and newspapers. As he perused the array of disorganised literature, he had a rough idea where to find what he was looking for and eventually found it sitting between two large volumes of books entitled, 'Demonic Arts'. He picked the first one up. 'The Demonic Connection'. He remembered the primary author, Charles Walker, and scanned through it. It gave him crucial background to information about the powers of Hecate – the powers with which they would have to contend. He read the text slowly. 'Honoured by Zeus who gave her a portion of the underworld, the earth and the air, Hecate was to be held very powerful in all these areas. She could give men riches, victory and wisdom, and sat by kings in judgement, helped speakers in the assembly and granted favours in games, sea fishing and cattle breeding. She was the goddess of enchantment and magic charms as well as presiding over purification and expiations and could be invoked by any who made suitable sacrifices to her.' He paused here and considered the implications of this last sentence. It was no surprise that the 'Friends of Hecate' were the most feared and powerful coven of the black arts. With such a powerful deity on their side, what chance had he, Ben and Tara of defeating them? He read on. 'She was renowned for sending demons to earth, to torment men or ghosts from Hades to drive people mad or cause epilepsy by her assaults on them.'

The sacrifices made to her were usually of a dog, her favourite animal, and the places she haunted most frequently were crossroads, spots near tombs, or the scenes of crimes.

Known also as 'she who meets', Hecate, as mistress of ghosts and spectres and everything uncanny, was said to appear to travellers and walkers by night in lonely places as a frightening apparition, and to especially haunt the places of those who could join her host of ghoulish followers in darkness. This host or rout of followers was known as the 'Wild Hunt.' He read on for a few more minutes, then sat down to collect his thoughts.

They were disturbing, very disturbing.

Chapter Eight

Ben was almost half an hour late, his mind racing to find an excuse. He spotted Amalialad and Tara, sitting at a table, waiting for him, both grinning widely at him. Both were grinning like Cheshire cats, not what he'd expected to see. It was disconcerting.

"What's so funny then?"

"Sit down, Ben, enjoy your coffee and read the piece of paper under your saucer."

'You will arrive in the canteen, LATE, at precisely 9.25am where you will find a hot black coffee waiting for you. We know why you were late so please do not give yourself a headache by coming up with excuses.' Ben began to blush. 'Enjoy your coffee now and then we shall talk about other, more serious, matters at hand.'

Ben looked up at his friends and then started to say something.

"But …" he started to speak when Tara abruptly interupted.

"Don't worry, Ben, I'll explain another time. Please enjoy your coffee." Ben felt embarrassed and looked away, pretending to be interested in the comings and goings of the other students as they finished their breakfasts and quickly headed off to lecture theatres and seminars. Amalialad couldn't help but notice his friend's behavior; it was the first time he'd seen Ben feeling so uncomfortable in female company. Hmm, he thought, it was very unusual.

"There is no easy way to dilute the dangers we face so I'm going to come straight to the point." He looked at Tara. "Our objective is twofold. We must find your father and ensure his safety. Amalialad's eyes then focused steadfastly, first on one, then separately on each of the other two companions. "And then we must set about the destruction of the power which the Friends of Hecate possess." He allowed his words to sink in.

"Sweet, Jesus! I hope you have a great plan of attack? And how many others are coming with us?" asked Ben.

"What do you plan?" Tara was far more composed.

"In searching for Tara's father, we will undoubtedly be threatened and hampered by the coven members. Indeed, our very lives will be at risk. There is only one way to defeat them. We must find The Book of Shadows."

"The Book of Shadows, what's that?" Ben asked.

"In contemporary witchcraft ..."

"Witchcraft – where's that come from!" Ben cut in.

"I'm sorry, Ben, but I assumed you understood. We are dealing here with a coven of witches who follow the worst of the Black Arts. They worship Satan, the devil. But they are not just any coven. They follow one of Satan's most devilish partners, Hecate. To defeat them we must fight fire with fire. We must use the craft's own acknowledged spells to counter their power. And to do this we must find The Book of Shadows. The original Book of Shadows."

Chapter Nine

Amalialad saw the Clapham Station sign glide slowly past the window of their carriage. The train came to a halt at Platform One. It was precisely 2:30 p.m. and the train was exactly ten minutes late. Amalialad once again felt a strange sense of foreboding. Leaving the station, he couldn't help noticing how changeable the weather was. One moment it was bright and sunny and the next the sun was suddenly obscured by black, threatening clouds. The abrupt change upon their arrival was, he thought, most unusual, especially when he knew that the weather forecast for this area predicted clear, blue skies all day. Indeed, the sun had been shining brightly for most of their two-hour journey. Although Amalialad felt something very strange about the change he kept his thoughts to himself and, with a little tweeting, also from Tara. The three of them, he thought, had enough to contend with.

"I'm going ahead. Are you two ok with that?" Ben and Tara nodded. Then in unison said, "yes." But both looked perplexed.

"Good. Follow me shortly." Then Amalialad left.

"Shortly?" Ben queried. "I hate it when people say that. What's shortly supposed to mean? Is it one minute, ten minutes or what?" But Ben's frustration was broken his sudden awareness of a creeping but deepening darkness that was suddenly enveloping the area.

In alarm, Tara turned to him. "Quick, Ben! Follow me! Amalialad's in danger." The wind picked up. It rustled, swirled and churned the litter on the pavement, hurling it across their path. Thunder rumbled aggressively above them, growing louder, unnaturally louder. And more frequent too. Dark, threatening clouds were growing larger and massing together. A blackness took shape. Slowly, materialising above them, three ghastly, luminous heads appeared. They could only be described as fearsome. The heads of a boar, a snake and a horse barked, hissed and whinnied maliciously at them. Tara and Ben were rooted to the spot. And then the rain came. It poured down from the sky in a torrent. It bounced and hissed as it hit car roofs and cascaded onto the pavement forcing traffic to a standstill. Walking ahead, Amalialad felt a sudden ache at the base of his neck. Something was wrong! Instinctively, but only a fraction of a second before the jagged bolt of lightning left its source, Amalialad ducked down and rolled to the right. The mighty lightning bolt struck the exact spot where Amalialad had been standing. The second onslaught was almost simultaneous, but Amalialad's instincts were yet again just ahead of the threat. In the blur of time he rolled again. He spun his body violently to the left and hit the ground. He stayed down, spread-eagled on the floor as the second bolt also narrowly missed him and pounded into a delivery van parked on the side of the road. The metal split and twisted leaving a gaping hole in its side. Then the contents caught fire and started to emit plumes of dense, black, putrid smoke. There was an eerie silence. Then the most haunting voice that Amalialad had ever heard shook the ground beneath him. Amalialad lifted his head and turned, to see that the people around him were silently screaming, rooted to the ground in absolute fear. Amalialad looked up to confirm his worst nightmare. The diabolical vision of Hecate in her most hideous form had appeared. The ghastly faces glowed brightly in the sky above them and the spittle from their contorted jaws flowed to the ground, forming green puddles of stagnant liquid. The animals looked to be in a state of hysteria and tried to jerk forward but were mysteriously held in check. Then their hoarse voices bellowed in fury.

"Be warned. I am the dark Goddess. I am Hecate.

I am the darkness behind and beneath the shadows,

I am the absence of air that waits at the bottom of every breath,

I am the queen of all witches,

Seek me, man of many pasts and futures, and you and yours shall know my wrath.

I am she who is at the beginning and at the end of all time and cannot be vanquished."

Then the vision disappeared leaving the people below in a state of panic. They ran shouting and screaming in all directions. Car horns honked and vehicles collided in desperate efforts to get away. Amalialad was helpless to do anything. He knew that when the mind was so saturated with confusion, madness stepped in.

He looked up. As quickly as the storm had come, it had gone. The clouds had dissolved. The sun shone, and the sky was clear and blue, just as forecast. Although dishevelled and shaken, he managed to appear calm as his two friends ran forward to meet him.

"We saw it all from the path. It was terrible. We just couldn't move. Those poor people. Are you okay?" Ben's face was ashen and still.

"Well, let's just say I've had better welcomes, but, yes, I'm okay, thanks." Amalialad's calm composure didn't fool Ben. Ben knew that his friend was deeply worried. He knew that the most powerful witch that had ever existed had just threatened all of them. Then, Tara looked hard at Amalialad. She'd just felt all the emotions Amalialad had experienced, but her face was pale and drawn and she felt lost and helpless. Amalialad was just a twenty-three-year-old student, wasn't he? Tara thought, how could he possibly cope with such enormous pressure? Yet it hardly seemed to faze him.

She walked forward slowly and put her arms around Amalialad's neck. Sobbing, she whispered in his ear, "I'm so sorry. This is my fault, isn't it? If I hadn't asked for your help, this would never have happened."

Amalialad felt a little uncomfortable, but he held her for a few moments. You have no need to apologise. We decided to help willingly. We knew there would be dangers ahead. Please, don't upset yourself. You must remain strong. I promise you we'll find your father and bring him back safely. Now, dry your eyes."

Amalialad had never broken a promise before and he hoped for Tara's sake he'd never break the one he just made to her.

"Look!" Ben said. "The station has a café and it's still open. Let's get a drink, shall we?"

"Yes." Tara attempted to smile at Ben. "That'll be great." She looked in her bag for a tissue. Ben stepped forward.

"Can I help?" He offered her a small packet of tissues. Tara looked at him with warmth and pride. She'd really grown to like Ben. Ben momentarily looked into her eyes and felt very uneasy as she returned the gaze with the most radiant smile. He wasn't used to receiving such genuine warmth. "Well, I keep them, just in case of emergencies," Ben said, bashfully.

"Thank you, Ben. I'm so glad you do." She knew Ben felt embarrassed at her gaze and changed the subject. "Come on, let's get that drink now, shall we?" She held out her arm for Ben to take. He took it gently, relishing every moment of her touch, as he led her towards the station's small cafeteria.

Amalialad was in deep concentration as he followed. He knew now that what had just happened was no natural storm. It was the cunning collaboration of Hecate and her Satanic forces. He recognised now that the challenges ahead were far worse than he'd ever feared. Time was running out and unless they found the Book of Shadows soon it could be too late. He couldn't afford to let the thought linger long. He dismissed it and walked into the station.

Amalialad and Tara sat at a table next to a window, overlooking the platform. Ben had joined a small queue at the counter to order their drinks. Someone had given the table a cursory wipe over. Amalialad suspected the staff were all still in a state of shock from what had just happened. But, for now, it would do.

"I hope you're feeling a little better." Amalialad looked directly at Tara. Even though he sensed her apprehension, it was important that she remained as strong as possible about the situation.

Tara smiled. "I'm much better, thank you." Of course, he was reminded, she could read his thoughts. He needed to be careful in future. He decided to block them if he thought his thinking would alarm her. "What's the plan now?"

"Well, we're going to drink these coffees first," Ben said, as he placed the drinks on the table. "We're all going to relax a little, drink these and then we can talk business, ok?"

Then Amalialad spoke.

"My friends, it's time to be serious." His tone changed.

"I'm sorry," Ben interrupted, "But I'm still confused. Can you first explain what the Book of Shadows is?"

"In contemporary witchcraft, The Book of Shadows is a book of beliefs, rituals, witchcraft laws and ethics along with incantations and spells. It is the witches' bible. It serves as their guide in practicing their craft and religion, whether it's for good or evil. In this case, it's Satanism." The silence became more intense. But Amalialad continued. "Each coven has their own Book of Shadows, which can be added to or adapted by separate covens over the years. In effect, it's a book that, if used by White covens, can provide the secrets to performing what we would consider to be miracle cures and spells - it enables infinite healing powers. However," Amalialad briefly considered what he was about to say, "It can also provide the rituals for obtaining absolute power over others. The rituals can force people to do their masters' bidding, turning them into despicable entities, slaves, if you will, for their evil mistresses and masters. The Egyptian priests used to protect their tombs by creating such poor creatures. Unfortunately, years later, our curiosity and our selfish desire for either fame, fortune or prestige, persuaded us to open these tombs without exercising containing spells. It was the équivalent of opening Pandora's box. The opening of the tombs released a devilish and noxious hoard of destructive entities upon the world, entities willing to execute the commands of their cruel-minded masters." Amalialad paused briefly to allow what he'd just said to sink in. "My good friends, The Friends of Hecate possess such a book of spells which was copied from the much more ancient and original Book of Shadows. The very first and original Book is said to contain the entire magical knowledge of the Roman philosopher and magician, Maximus, and is believed to be connected to Clapham."

"Are all entities like this? Evil?" Ben asked.

"No," said Amalialad. "Some are good and employed by white magicians to protect or help others and some are like what are referred to as 'evergreen children'. For short periods, these children often interact and play within our own world. You might have heard of them as the Little People."

This book they possess contains the most secret Rites of Hecate. It is said that the book was brought to Britain by devotees of the Roman emperor Maximus after the fall of Rome. It's recorded as having safely reached here, in Britain, in AD484."

"Sweet Jesus!" Ben exclaimed.

"Although its actual whereabouts remains a mystery, scholars of magic lore believe it's located somewhere in southern England."

"So why do you think it's in Clapham? After all, southern England covers a vast area," Ben enquired.

In unison, Amalialad and Tara replied. "Intuition!"

Ben smiled. "I see. Well, I mean, I don't, but you two obviously do. Ok, where do we go from here?"

"We go to a small village called Findon. From there we go into Clapham Woods. It's claimed to be the most haunted and sinister place in the whole of Europe."

Ben sighed. "Why am I not surprised?"

The others couldn't help but smile at Ben's remark. It helped, as Ben hoped it would, to relieve the growing tension.

Chapter Ten

This time, their journey seemed uneventful. About a mile from Findon, Amalialad stopped the silver Peugeot 307 they'd hired. He parked the car well back from the road, hidden by large bushes.

Amalialad discreetly removed a plastic bag from the glove compartment and then sat up and faced his friends.

"I want you to listen very carefully." He removed some blue and white medallions from the bag. They were hand-shaped and about five centimeters in diameter.

"There's something you must both be aware of. We're about to walk into the lion's den. We're walking straight into the witch's lair to face occultists of the most diabolical coven that's ever existed. They will use every evil incantation at their disposal and it's fairly certain they will use the evil eye on us."

"But what…" Ben cut in.

"And before you ask, Ben," Amalialad said, "the evil eye is a way of cursing you by 'staring'. The technique will have been thoroughly mastered by all the occultists. Some will be better than others in its use. They can influence your thinking and distract you and you're unaware. While in this state of vulnerability you could be either physically or mentally attacked." He then showed them the medallions. "I want you to wear these at all times. It should significantly ward off their ability to curse you."

Ben broke in again "Should? You mean they may not work?"

Amalialad smiled, not at all surprised by Ben's questions. "I have it on good authority, from a dear and trusted friend, that they will work but I've never used them before. All I can say is that this medallion," Amalialad held it up to show them, "is called the Hamza Hand, or the Hand of Fatima, by Muslims and it contains the Eye Motif that wards off the evil eye. Virtually every culture has something like this to fend off the effects of the evil eye. The same sort of amulet is called the Hand of Miriam among Jews."

"Wow, do you think this is how Tara became so transfixed in the dojo, because someone used the evil eye?" Ben was incredulous.

"Yes, Ben, I think that's exactly what happened." As he spoke Amalialad glanced at Tara. "But it won't happen again." The steel tone in his voice allowed for no doubt in Tara's mind that everything would be ok, but Ben, on the other hand, even knowing the strengths his friend possessed, still had his doubts.

They passed an old wooden sign displaying the words Findon. The road led into the small High Street and a few hundred yards further on the Findon Manor Hotel came into view on the left-hand side.

"We'll be staying here for the night," Amalialad said as he parked in front of the large ivy-clad hotel.

They walked through the entrance into a large, brightly-lit hallway. The walls were covered with paintings of seasonal country scenes from the past and a thick, red carpet. The area was furnished in a Georgian style, and the reception was surprisingly small.

The old man behind the reception frowned as the three approached. Amalialad observed that his bulky, blue blazer hung too loose from his shoulders. However, the gold-plated buttons on his chest shimmered and finely complemented the gold braided stitching on his sleeve cuffs. His demeanor was casual, and his pose seemed nonchalant. That was until he saw Tara. He then suddenly became momentarily transfixed and looked totally lost in thought for a split second. The moment passed quickly, but Amalialad saw it. Then the man's dark eyes narrowed, and he stared at her.

"Do we know each other?" Tara asked. She looked straight back at him.

He jumped, startled at her words.

His left eye twitched.

A large suite was booked consisting of a twin room next to Tara's adjoining single. The rooms were all fitted out elegantly in the classic Georgian style.

Tara made coffee as Amalialad and Ben sat at a table illuminated by the light streaming through the window, which overlooked the near empty car park below.

"What do you think?" Amalialad asked Ben

It was at that point that Tara's life changed!

It started very faintly at first. In fact, it was almost inaudible. She heard a gentle voice in her head. As it grew, she sensed a strong physical feeling of overwhelming love combined with the emotional pain of a deep sadness. She sensed someone was trying to reach out to her. That someone had a friendly intent. She sensed goodness. So, she focused intently on her effort to pick up the vibrations which suddenly started to pour through. Words gradually started to build up in her mind. Then suddenly she knew. Everything became apparent.

The tray fell from Tara's hand and crashed to the floor. And the cups, saucers, milk, sugar and spoons scattered across the carpet. She clutched at her heart to quash the sudden stabbing pain in her chest. She shrieked loudly in agony, an agony not from physical pain, but from the surety that her greatest fear had now become a reality. She knew that this day would become the most unforgettable and devastating one of her life.

"Oh, my God! Oh no, no, no…please, no!"

Ben and Amalialad both felt the surge of invisible energy which swept the room and touched all their hearts. They felt her grief. They knew at that moment, for Tara, the worst had happened.

Then the words her father struggled to say suddenly echoed through her whole being.

"Forgive me, Tara! I love you so very, very much. I had no choice…" They were full of desperation. Other words came but then trickled quietly, incoherently away…then there was a deathly silence.

Tara's body suddenly jerked and shook. She sobbed loudly and uncontrollably. The grief was unbearable. She fell heavily to the floor, almost crashing onto the broken crockery beneath her. But Ben instinctively rushed to break her fall and just managed to catch her before she hit the jagged shards of china. He didn't notice the sharp cut to his leg as he caught her; he had felt her loss and pain and his feelings and concern for her were paramount in his mind. Nothing else mattered. He focused solely on saving her from more hurt.

"Oh, Daddy, why? Why? I love you so very much!"

Distraught and clutching her tear-stricken face in her hands, Tara wept. It was heartbreaking to watch and both Ben and Amalialad could only look on helplessly.

Ben whispered. "I'm so sorry, Tara. If I could bear this hurt for you, I would." Tears streamed down his cheeks as he spoke. He knew too, in that moment, that he could never imagine being without her. He looked at Amalialad, hoping somehow he could help console Tara. Amalialad sat next to her. Tara opened her eyes.

"I've lost him forever, haven't I?"

Amalialad wiped a tear from his own cheek before responding. "I'm so sorry, Tara. You had a very loving father. These moments are the worst of life and there are no words I can give which could possibly describe your loss. I remembered once when I went to my local temple a monk was there to meet me. I'd gone to him for words of comfort. As I entered, he came forward and gently took my arm to lead me to a wall in the corner of the temple. Carved on the wall was a poem called 'Loss'. The poem had three words, but the poet had then scratched them out. Confused I looked up at the monk. The monk smiled before speaking.

"You cannot read loss, only feel it."

Amalialad looked at Tara and softly said, "I believe, in time, we will all meet again. But whatever you believe, I know this. The spirit of your father will always be with you. In here!" Amalialad touched his heart with the open palm of his hand. "I think your father would want you to move on in this life without dwelling on his physical passing too long."

Then, fleetingly, a most dreadful thought struck him. And Amalialad felt sickened at what he now had to ask of Tara in her moment of grief.

Ben saw the colour drain from Amalialad's face. He knew something was very wrong.

"What is it? he asked.

Amalialad stared at Tara. Then he spoke softly.

"I am so very sorry for you, Tara. I know your father was a good man and how very much you loved him but… forgive me now, please." He paused momentarily to get his words right. "I know you're suffering badly with your grief, but I must ask something of you, and if I don't, there are potentially thousands of lives at stake. I know this will come as a shock, but your father's very soul may also be at grave risk if we don't act. I'm sorry."

Tara shook her head in confusion; all this was just too much to take in. But time was running out and Amalialad knew he must act quickly.

"Please, Tara, you must trust me again. Please. You must use that inner strength, that amazing resolve you have and listen carefully to what I have to say. I'm asking that you try hard to focus on what I'm about to tell you, accept it for the truth, ok?" Tara cleared her mind and prepared to use all her energy and determination to do what must be done. It was almost impossible to blot out the torment of her pain and heartbreak, but she knew she must do as Amalialad requested and those emotions had to wait. She searched for a happy place deep within her mind then looked up at Amalialad and nodded.

"I'm going to ask you a question, Tara. And I want you think about it very carefully before answering, ok?

Tara nodded.

"Did your father kill himself?"

"What?" But a scene came into her mind. Tara saw a large group of black hooded people with scythes in their hands walking slowly but determinedly towards her father, who was cowering on the ground with his hands protecting his face. He had a look of stark terror. He was shouting. "I'll never tell you. Never!" It was at that moment she saw her father snatch a knife from his side pocket and stab himself in the heart. Then the scene disappeared. Tara shrieked and stepped back in horror. She realised then that, unbelievably, her father had indeed stabbed himself in his own heart.

Oh, God, no, that can't be true, she thought. Her father was so against killing. But she knew it was true.

"What's happening, Amalialad? What's going on? Why did he do it?"

"Forgive me for putting you through that ordeal but I had little choice"

Tara understood.

"But what did he possess that was so important? What did he have that could possibly save others?"

"Yeah, I don't understand either," said Ben. "What could he possibly have known or have which would have been so crucial?"

"It is my belief that your father found The Book of Shadows."

"You mean The Book of Shadows that had been hidden for centuries?" Ben asked.

"The very same. It contains spells which could effectively create anarchy and chaos across the world and law and order, as we know it, would cease to exist".

"Oh, my God. Can we stop this?

Ben spoke. "Don't worry - if your father did sacrifice himself, I think it was to take the secret of where the book is hidden to his grave. In which case the cult of Hecate, who I assume are the ones involved in this, won't be able to retrieve the information from him." He looked towards Amalialad for confirmation.

But Amalialad remained quiet.

Chapter Eleven

"I warned you of what this cult is capable of and the possible consequences to our own lives if we battled against them. Friends, we must win this battle or lose the war." Amalialad looked towards Tara. "Yes, I believe your father gave his life to save others; not just a few but thousands, possibly more. But I'm deeply afraid that the secret he kept with him concerning the whereabouts of the Book of Shadows can still be obtained."

Ben and Tara started to speak in unison.

"But that's imposs...... » "

Then slowly, it dawned on them. Tara spoke first.

"You mean...?"

"Yes, I'm afraid I do. I feel certain that one of the most despicable acts in the repertoire of Satanism is to be carried out tonight unless we can stop it. I think this cult will perform necromancy on your father to find the whereabouts of the book,"

"Necromancy? What's that?" Ben asked.

Amalialad looked grim as he spoke.

"The very word makes me shudder. It involves the most hideous act of human degradation. Only those who worship the darkest and most malevolent gods would consider its use and I'm afraid the coven of Hecate is one of those cults. Necromancy is an evil spell which, if performed precisely, can bring back the souls of the dead and force them, at the witch's bidding, to answer questions. Tara... the souls have no choice and must answer."

Tara fell to her knees and held her head with both hands. She cried uncontrollably. Then she pleaded. "But that's just a myth or a legend or something. Surely that's not true. It's not possible."

"I'm so sorry. Believe me, I wish it weren't true. During my studies of the Black arts there have been numerous accounts of this spell being carried out. However, it must be done in precise detail or those participating in the ritual risk being cast into hell themselves."

"Don't worry, my father will tell them nothing. I'm sure of that!"

"I'm sorry, Tara, but such is the power of the spell that he will have no choice but to answer. The spell decrees that should the soul resist, it would suffer torment and wandering thrice seven years.

"That's twenty-one years! That's unbelievable," Ben said.

Tara was aghast at the thought and felt sick again. Despairingly, she looked at Amalialad for answers.

"Can we do anything to stop this?" Her pale face and forlorn expression made Ben cringe, frustrated at his failure to come up with the solutions.

"If we can't I'm afraid the cult will find the book and then the world will have little hope of defeating the growing evil which shall most surely overwhelm it. Thousands of innocent souls will be raised to wander in torment and any opponents will be slaughtered without mercy for resisting the desires of the coven, and all Satanic groups will flourish to rule the world as they will."

Amalialad was silent in thought for a few moments.

"There may be a way," he was still thinking, "but we must act quickly. Their spell must be carried out at precisely midnight tonight, so they only have an hour. They will need most of that time to prepare."

He stared at Tara and sent her an optimistic thought. *There's hope yet.*

"Tara, you must focus hard again, ok? Your father's last words to you were telepathic but they should have left residual energy leading back to where he was. You must delve deep into your subconscious and feel for that. If you really focus you can do it."

Tara did as she was asked.

"I'm sorry, nothing. I can't sense anything."

"Tara, can't, is not an option right now. You must! Focus intensely and bring together everything you believe and everything you hold dear. You can do this. Just relax and allow your thoughts to drift down. Just let them drift deeply down."

Tara followed Amalialad's instructions and physically relaxed her body and thoughts. She eventually sensed a faint tinge of energy vibration touching her mind and focused harder to grasp more. She seemed to catch it somehow and felt its energy chord of intense light stretching out, leading far into a distant void. Suddenly, Amalialad appeared in her mind. He looked at her reassuringly and she sensed his words. 'Don't be afraid. You've done well, Tara. I've linked to your astral mind now and we are about to go on a journey together. Don't be afraid but just link arms with me and stay close, ok? Whatever happens, stay linked to my arm, ok?'

Tara nodded and they both flew, following a beam of thin white light into a black void of deep space.

Chapter Twelve

Tara grasped Amalialad's arm tightly. She worried she might slip and fall deep into the blackness below. But then she sensed he had somehow secured her to him and quickly relaxed. Moments later the blackness became light and she found herself flying over woodland. Findon Wood was below them.

She spotted a small copse in the centre of the wood and made out several people dressed in dark robes. They seemed to be carrying out some sort of ceremony.

"They're drawing the Pentagram." said Amalialad.

'What's that?' Tara asked.

'It's the most widely used satanic symbol in witchcraft. It actually represents the elements of earth, wind, fire and water and is the most powerful of symbols.'

Suddenly he gasped.

It was unusual for Amalialad to show fear of anything, so Tara became very concerned.

"What is it?"

"This is much worse than I first thought. They're now drawing the Hexagram around the Pentagram. The Hexagram is rarely used because only a handful of Satanists dare do so. It invokes enormous power when called upon but if one minor detail is incorrect, it backfires and simply annihilates all those using it.'

'What can we do?'

Amalialad looked at her and smiled.

'We can make it backfire! But to do so we must go back to our physical bodies and travel back here quickly and cautiously without detection by cult members or their other world servants. We don't have much time. Once they finish the incantation it will be too late.'

'Then let's get back'

Ben was sitting quietly in the armchair. He was trying to understand the events, when they re-entered their bodies and opened their eyes.

He smiled with relief when the two comatose bodies returned to normality.

"Wow, you're back." He looked at his watch. "I can't believe it. You seemed to have been ages, but you have only been gone five minutes."

Amalialad smiled. There was a reason for that, but he had no time to explain now.

"We only have thirty-five minutes to prevent what might be the most diabolical act to have ever occurred on humanity." Amalialad's tone was stern.

The strange man with the twitch was standing at the bottom of the stairs as they descended towards the hotel's reception hall to check out. As they got closer, they all noticed a menacing stare in his eyes. He moved in front of them, staring intently.

"Excuse us, please, we need to check out now," Amalialad said. The man's face relaxed a little.

"I'm sorry, sir, but if you could just return to your room and wait a little while longer, we will have your paperwork ready very soon." His false smile fooled no one.

Amalialad's reaction was swift and smooth.

His right arm forked out and his fist caught the man just below the chin, knocking him off balance and sending him flying backwards, to land, unconscious, on his side.

"Let's hurry. We've no more time to waste."

A mile down the road they pulled over into a layby

"This is Clapham Woods. It's renowned for being haunted and many walkers refuse to enter. They're right not to do so because it's plagued by the practising of spell casting by covens of the Black Arts. Many of the spells due to incorrect incantations and as a result weird and strange activities regularly occur here. However, we have no choice but to venture inside."

"But…" Ben said.

"Not now, Ben, later." Amalialad knew Ben would follow his earlier words with a stream of questions but now just wasn't the time.

"If we're to get out of here alive we must proceed with the utmost caution. Our lives, along with thousands of others, depend on how we act now." Amalialad looked at his watch again. "We have twenty minutes. Let's go!" But as he went to open the door, the engine switched itself back on again and the door he tried to open remained locked.

At that moment a message from Lopsang entered his thoughts. "Be warned, Amalialad"

And so, it starts, thought Amalialad. And as he looked at his rear view mirror, he was pleased to see they were wearing their medallions.

He turned the engine off and used brute force to open the door. He knew the spell had little power this far away from the centre of the wood, but conversely it would get stronger as they walked to the centre. Well, step by step then, he thought.

A fierce sense of foreboding hit them all as they passed the first tree line. The temperature suddenly dropped, and the atmosphere became oppressive. It felt eerie, more than that - sinister. A hundred yards in front of them a thick fog began to advance, threatening to engulf them. Prepared for this, they got their torches out and switched the power to full strength. Amalialad looked at his compass to check they were walking in the right direction. Then they proceeded, slowly but determinedly, in the direction of the ritual ground. Too much was at stake to worry now or even think of failure.

Suddenly, Ben stopped. He instinctively gripped his medallion tightly, closed his eyes and said a prayer.

Tara cried out. "Ah, my stomach! It's churning over and I feel sick."

Amalialad shouted to them. "Focus to resist. They're planting these thoughts in your mind. You must think about why you are here and resist!"

Tara simply felt the love she had for her father and the feeling she had left her as quickly as it came.

Ben thought of Tara and knew there was nothing that could overcome those feelings. He was right. The bear image quickly dissipated.

They slowly crept forward

The dense undergrowth became more difficult to walk through. It was almost impenetrable at times, but Amalialad used his sturdy, steel cutting knife to ruggedly plough on and clear away the tougher branches while ducking and climbing over what seemed to be a never-ending barrage of low-lying forest growth. He felt that even the life force of the forest itself was against them.

As they neared the centre, the sky suddenly darkened and Amalialad stopped suddenly in his tracks. He signaled by hand for quiet. They listened intently to what he had to say.

"The hard part is coming now, be on your guard."

Hmmmm, Ben thought. So we just had the easy part. He swallowed deeply. Oh well, let's get to it.

"From here on don't even breathe loudly. Not a whisper. Thankfully, the breeze blows against us and will carry any sounds away, but we must remain extremely vigilant. Tara and I can communicate with our thoughts, but Ben, I want you to remain in sight of one of us at all times and signal if you encounter any problems, ok?"

Ben nodded, and they cautiously continued.

"Stop!" Tara caught the message in an instant and felt the anguish in it too. She signaled Ben to halt.

Carefully looking ahead through the thick density of trees, they could just make out a ring of flames around a tall, gnarled, ancient oak. Amalialad signaled them to take care. As they got closer, they saw that the light was coming from a ring of thick black candles circling the tree.

"Stay well clear of the candles. At least twenty feet clear. It's a warning spell and any closer will trigger an alarm to the coven that we're here. It's crucial to take every step now with the utmost care."

Ben and Tara eyed each other. They knew the next ten minutes were crucial. There was just ten minutes left before the coven began its incantation.

Tara suddenly started to shiver. "Phew. Do you notice anything, Ben?"

"Yes, it's suddenly gone quiet. I can't hear any birds singing and for the past few minutes I've noticed a lack of animal movement. It's spooky."

"You're right and the temperature has just dropped rapidly. I'm freezing."

Just as they'd straddled a wide trench of broken branches and debris, scratching sounds could be heard.

Amalialad's face was pale as he turned to face his friends.

"They're drawing the Pentagram!" Amalialad's voice was urgent. "Oh, no! How could I have been so stupid?" He turned to his friends. His features twisted in frustration as he spoke.

"If things go wrong, I'm sorry. They're drawing the Hexagram around the Inverted Pentagram. The Inverted Pentagram represents a powerful symbol of witchcraft and occult rituals. This is the true symbol of Satan. Combined they are the most powerful and potent symbols of evil and conjure the most sinister powers of darkness. When together like this, these symbols have vast power and when used in satanic rituals they've never failed to be effective. Two hundred years ago even the most holy of monks in the church of Christ tried in vain to overcome their power."

Ben didn't have a clue who these monks were but was sure that somehow, they had to crack what the monks could not because the alternative was just too dreadful to contemplate.

"So, fellow warriors," he turned and looked at the others, "it's going to be difficult? Is that what you're trying to say, Amalialad?" His casual tone lightened the tension somewhat.

With everything happening so fast, they hadn't noticed the shallow grave beyond the black cloaked figures circling the symbols scratched out in the soil. Next to the grave was what seemed to be a blackened body and, as the scene registered, so did the realization that it was Tara's father lying there.

"It's ..." But before she could say anymore a hand had covered her mouth.

"Forgive me, Tara," Ben whispered, "But if they hear us now, we're finished."

The final incantation commenced.

They listened with dread and fearful fascination as the leading figure stood in the centre of the symbols and chanted loudly.

As he spoke, they trembled. They knew, assuming they lived through it, they'd never forget the words they heard that night.

Chapter Thirteen

The incantation was compulsive and mesmerizing. Strangely, the tall figure seemed to speak in Ben's own dialect and he somehow felt at home.

He found himself relaxing in his parents' garden. He watched the birds darting backwards and forwards across the flowering dogwoods and listened, happily to the sweet, enchanting, singing chirps of the blackbirds.

"Ben!" Amalialad's voice broke into his dream. "You're being hypnotized. Ben!wake up!" Slowly and with great effort, Ben began to focus on Amalialad's words. He started to slowly emerge from the powerfully induced reverie. But it took extreme effort. He felt himself sinking further into what seemed like a place of paradise. But then a vision of Tara flashed across his mind and feeling she needed help, he felt a jolt run through his body and finally, after further moments of what he could only later describe as a power struggle he became conscious of what happened and shook himself free of the mesmerizing cadence of the chant.

"Phew, what happened?" he whispered.

"Sorry, Ben, but I've no time to explain."
The tall hooded man was still speaking.
"By the virtue of the holy resurrection and the torments of the damned, I conjure and exorcise thee spirit of the deceased to answer my liege demands being obedient to these most sacred ceremonies on pain of everlasting torment and distress…"
The clouds above blackened and there was a thunderous roar from the sky, followed by a fork of lightning of dazzling intensity. The wind suddenly rose up. It increased in force, emitting a low eerie moan which mysteriously complemented the evil spell being enacted in front of them. The incantation continued and, as they listened, time seemed to stand still.

The incantation had started, and it was almost midnight. There wasn't long left until the spell was complete. And the world was unaware of its ending.

Like a torrent of water surging through a river, the thoughts came through fast. Tara focused, listening to every word emanating from Amalialad's mind. She knew that just a single mistake now could cost them everything, understanding only too well the dire consequences of getting it wrong. If any of the coven members picked up on them, they'd be finished.

When the coven members' thoughts were working together, Amalialad knew that nothing could break down their defense. Their minds, when linked, were too powerful.

"Tara," he said, "we must find a way to create a diversion. We need to locate an individual near the edge of the symbol. Then we can combine our strength and force him to step out of the sacred circle. If any one of them leaves the circle, they will destroy their own spell and it will backfire on them all. Do you understand?'

"Yes, I do," She knew their lives depended on this strategy being successful. Amalialad sensed her tension.

"Don't worry Tara, it'll be ok." Then suddenly, "Look! Do you see him, Tara?"

Tara nodded. The cloaked figure had stepped close to the eastern vertices of the Inverted Pentagram. He was standing just centimeters away from the edge of it. Close enough, Tara guessed, to allow them to pull him from the circle. It required a delicate, synchronized concentration of their telekinesis. "What suggestion do we throw at him to force him to move?" asked Tara.

"I sense he has children. We send a picture of his daughter drowning in water just beyond his reach. The thought that anyone should ever have to face such a situation disturbs me, but we have no choice. He'll have to step out of the circle to reach her. Ok, on the count of three send that picture to him."

"One, two, three, now!'

Never had Tara focused so much on anything. She channeled all her energy to link with Amalialad's mind and send the scene to the coven member. Her one focused, singular thought was 'push'. Simultaneously, Amalialad did the same and released a massive surge of mental energy. Their combined power was enormous.

The cloaked figure turned sharply and stepped forward onto the vertices, so that one foot was now in the circle and the other was outside it. Amalialad was surprised. The power they sent should have thrown the figure forward.

And they needed all of him outside the circle.

He desperately tried to muster more energy, but he was exhausted. But then the figure attempted to rise and Amalialad realized it was too late. They had failed! It was at that moment that he understood something else. He'd sensed it too late. The cloaked figure was no ordinary man. He was a warlock of immense strength.

The failed attempt registered on the warlock's deformed face and it slowly turned to face Amalialad. Its hideous, ghoul-like features twisted into a wicked smile of smug satisfaction and in the ten seconds that remained before the spell was complete, they both knew it was all over. Amalialad took one last final glance at his friends and saw them both lying unconscious on the ground.

He knew they'd tried their utmost, but their best was simply not enough. It was all over.

Chapter Fourteen

'Whoosh!' The sound was distinct. Amalialad, although still weak, wasn't yet accepting defeat. He stirred, as a gust brushed past him and he saw the cloaked figure at the pit's edge fly abruptly backwards off the edge. And relief swept through him as the coven leader landed on the ground outside the symbol.

Amalialad's mind was in turmoil. There was no logical reason for it. He heard a voice in his head.

"Lopsang thought you might need some assistance. My name's Chodon, I'll explain in greater detail later but for now we need to get out of here fast. All hell's going to break loose at any moment."

Without speaking they moved swiftly towards Ben and Tara. Without pausing, Chodon threw Tara over her shoulder, and Amalialad picked up Ben. They ran then, as fast as they could, away from the carnage that was about to happen.

The earth within the circle they'd just left behind collapsed and Amalialad turned to see the ground, with an unnatural moan, fall in on itself. Then the anarchy began. The members of the coven ran around in confusion, screaming and crying.

As the screaming stopped, the group followed Amalialad back to the outer circle's edge. They looked down. The scene below was terrifying. Tara stirred back to consciousness and tried to stand but then felt her legs give way as she did so. But Ben who had just come around to consciousness was there, and he threw his arm out to grasp her waist and pull her back. Below them was a deep and dark, open, stinking pit. There came a fierce trembling beneath their feet as the ground moved and shook. And the pit expanded.

"Quick, run back!" Amalialad yelled. They turned and began to run back towards the trees. But the pit seemed to follow them. It swiftly expanded, outwards and upwards, towards them as they ran. From its depths came fierce, scorching, flames. As these flames rose, each one became a solid human like form, each clutching a spear. They surged forward then threw their spears. And each spear pierced a heart of any coven member still standing. The horror continued and, as the ground opened still further, the shrieks of the coven diminished as they fell into the dark depths below. Long, black, bony arms, with serrated, vicious nails reached out from the pit's depth. And, as a whiplash, at lightning speed, the hands struck out like bullets from a gun. But there were no more coven members alive to grab and take back down to the depths of hell.

Suddenly, forked lightning appeared from nowhere and repeatedly thrashed and pounded the ground, illuminating the pit. Then, as fast as it came, it disappeared, except for one particularly strong surge which flew strangely, as if searching for a specific target. Then it struck out, narrowly missing Amalialad's right heel as he watched the fiendish show enacting before him.

"Run!" shouted Amalialad. And they kept on running towards the protection of the dense forest.

Once safe, Amalialad stared back at what they'd just run from. What had caused such devastation? Had the curse come true? If so, then all the coven members would now be in hell itself. Resting now under the relative safety and protection of the trees, Amalialad realised, with deep concern, that they had to go back.

Chodon looked at Amalialad and read the worry on his brow. She smiled warmly at him. Amalialad swallowed hard in embarrassment. Chodon was a beautiful woman. But her aura showed Amalialad she was something else too.The circular alignments of her aura were identical to those of the ancient Warrior Nuns. He vaguely remembered meeting them decades ago, in a previous life.

"Thank you, Chodon. I needed that. I'm not sure how you did it, but it was most welcome. How are the Warrior Nuns?" he asked.

She looked up at him in surprise. Chodon, whose name meant the 'Devout One' had been chosen by the leaders of her sect, The Warrior Nuns to serve and protect the Dalai Lama and her link to him was pre-ordained by the minor Gods who ruled humanity's fate. "My Holy Lord," she replied, "it's an honour to meet and serve you, but as you are fully aware, evil is in the ascendancy and those who are spiritually aware and are dedicated by honour to protect mankind have been the prime target of blind malevolent forces who are determined and cursed to create chaos and achieve the destruction of humanity. Should they do so, we will never recover."

Amalialad knew the terrible sufferings that the Warrior Nuns endured under the godless Chinese rule. He was aware of the cruel daily beatings, the rapes and torture. Yet he was always bemused at the name, Warrior Nuns, because it was their creed that they never physically hurt anyone, even their torturers, regardless of life-threatening duress. Their weapon was simply the truth. They extolled the truth no matter what cruelty fell upon them and even in death would not be swayed from being true to their creed and the liberation of any person from oppression, cruel dictatorial laws and practices. It was said they were even more moralistic and true than the high Lamas themselves. However, there was one exception to this. Tradition allowed just one warrior to use her fighting skills, to kill if necessary, to defend the life of the Delai Lama. That warrior wa alwayss selected by the high council of Warrior Nuns to guard the Delai Lama, no matter where in the future he lived. And it was a great honour to be chosen for the task.

"May the sisters persevere now that we have found you, my Lord."

Amalialad smiled.

"I'm unaware what fate will finally dictate, Chodon, but I sense Lopsang has updated you on the many and varied challenges we must face before we're able to ever consider returning to our homeland. Also, I'm aware of the rumours that flow through the void and have felt the negative energies there too. I may very well be the last Dalai Lama but it's important that the people will be able to vote democratically on whether they want me to continue as their spiritual leader. For now, however, we have much more important and immediate issues to contend with and unless we are able to resolve them, our homeland concerns will be meaningless." Amalialad glanced down at Ben and Tara, who were fast asleep.

"They're still exhausted but now's the time to wake them," he said. "We still have much to do and they will have many questions for you, Chodon."

She smiled sweetly, and sat down on a nearby grass patch, ready to answer them when they arose.

Hmmm thought Amalialad, Chodon will make an excellent warrior and become an essential part of their group in the struggle ahead. Her fighting skills were awesome, especially with the bow, and her skills in defense were second to none. Her telekinetic skills were also formidable, and he knew she would be a great asset to the group.

In a dream that night, Lopsang appeared to him and Amalialad brought Lopsang up to date with everything that had happened. They also digressed a little and touched briefly on the current problems still ongoing in Tibet but knew there was little they could do to help. The time together was joyful and refreshing and Amalialad was thankful for it. Then Amalialad awoke.

"We must return." Amalialad said.

"Return to where?" Ben asked. "To the hotel?"

"No. We're returning to where we've just been."

"But…" Ben began.

Amalialad interrupted. "Have no concern Ben, I'll explain on the way. Follow me." And with that they all slowly turned around and walked back to the ceremonial ground. Ben just shrugged to himself and followed. He resigned to just accept the wisdom of his close friend. Tara started to follow too, but suddenly stopped in her tracks when Chodon spoke.

"Tara, stop. This is not for us." She spoke with sadness in her voice and Tara, in that moment also felt, telepathically, the genuine sadness in Chodon's mind and realized in which Choden spoke was genuine and understood why.

"Oh, Chodon," Tara said. "I'm so selfish, I'd almost forgotten."

Chodon smiled in sympathy and put her arm around Tara, who, inexplicably, suddenly felt so remarkably at ease, simply rested her head into the crook of Chodon's arm.

"You've been through a lot. No one can blame you for momentarily forgetting about your father. They have gone back to give your father a proper burial so that his soul may rest in peace for eternity. Without your help tonight Tara this would not have been possible. As I arrived, from a distance I perceived the spiritual energy you were able to radiate in deflecting much of the dark force thrown out at you all and knew that without it we would, indeed, have failed. You made sure for now that the world is safe once again. Be very thankful and satisfied with that and know that nobody else could have done more to help in his hour of need."

Her words held such intrinsic truth that Tara felt a great weight lift from her shoulders and a warmth of enormous comfort stream through her body. She looked straight at Chodon.

"Are you an angel?"

"Ha, ha, if only I were. No, I'm afraid not, but I hope I've helped a little and that we can be friends."

Tara hugged Chodon tightly and began to cry. Chodon held her close to console her.

"Well, you're my angel," said Tara, as she wiped the last of her tears from her cheeks.

Amalialad and Ben saw that a gaping hole had filled the area where the symbols had been drawn. Everything within the vicinity was scorched. Trees were burnt and charred. But they were both stunned to see Tara's father's body still on the ground. It was unscathed.

"But that's impossible!" Ben said. "The whole area was devastated."

"His soul, until the very end, was protected by the sanctity of God. The good, on this occasion, overcame the evil, my friend. I'd hoped this would be the case." Amalialad took out a blanket from his sack and with Ben's help carefully wrapped it around the body. They quickly dug a shallow grave and Ben fashioned a cross from a fallen branch and placed it in the ground by the grave. They both stood quietly afterwards next to the grave, then Ben said a prayer and they slowly walked away from the carnage.

"How do you know so much?" Ben asked as they walked.

Smiling again, Amalialad looked up at Ben.

Ben continued. "You are without doubt the wisest person I've met but you're only my age, so how could you know so much? You seem to have the knowledge of a lifetime."

"Thirteen lifetimes actually."

"What?"

"Sit down, my friend."

They sat together on the edge of a mossy mound.

"I am the fourteenth Dalai Lama, reincarnated from the lives of thirteen others. That has gradually enabled me to take in all the wisdom and knowledge they'd all learnt themselves during each of their life spans. Remember they too were each wise in their own lives. Put simply, I have the knowledge and inherited a wisdom of a person spanning more than a thousand years."

"Wow! That explains everything."

"Hold on, Ben, I'm still only twenty-three, like you, and I only call upon that knowledge when I really need to. There are many things I care not to know about and will only be shown what I need to know when I need to know it. I don't want to feel old before my time. Does that make sense to you?"

"It's not easy to take in. It all seems so surreal but, considering everything you've told me very carefully, yes, it does make a kind of sense. But, I guess, I'll just need time to get used to it.

Chapter Fifteen

They left Clapham behind with a great sense of relief. Still tired from their ordeal, Ben and Tara soon fell asleep in the back of the car. Chodon and Amalialad took the opportunity to discuss the inevitable challenges ahead. While they were talking, Amalialad's mobile rang and Chodon answered it. Evidently, out of the blue, Peter, a friend of his from the time he'd spent in Dr Barnado's, had called asking for his help to 'up the ante'. When they'd lived together, Peter had had a way of manipulating people into joining him in his mischievous antics and often Amalialad would also find himself being reprimanded and losing his evening supper for getting involved. He agreed to meet Peter at the Science Museum in Kensington. It was close to where Peter was studying for his PhD in Archaeology.

"Hello, old chap, it's been yonks, how are you?" Peter spoke in surprisingly very eloquent BBC English which, Amalialad thought, he must have learnt over the past few years. Strangely, he pondered, it suited him. Peter was dressed in grey trousers and wore a black, blazer with gold coloured buttons. Under the blazer he wore a white patterned shirt and finally to set that off he wore black, prestigious Italian, leather shoes. Quite the toff, thought Amalialad, and smiled as he once again decided it suited him.

"Well, old fella, how's life?" Peter asked as they all sat down around a small table near the large book section. That was the million-dollar question, Ben thought as he and the others listened to Amalialad explain what had been happening.

"Blimey, old mate, you've been through the old ringer, haven't you?"

"You could say that, Peter, but now tell me about you. I've noticed you've developed a new accent."

"Yes, essential old boy, especially if I'm to make an impact in my field and mix with those in 'the know' as it were."

"Ah, I see," Amalialad answered.

Peter went on to explain how he'd eventually qualified as an archaeologist and was given the opportunity to go to Germany and bring back the Spear of Destiny, from the Hofburgh Treasure House in Vienna. When Amalialad showed an interest, Peter went on to explain the story behind it, how General Eisenhower had returned it following its retrieval from the Third Reich, by General Patton, after the Second World War. He explained the historic importance of the spear and told them how it was believed to be the very spear which the centurion, Longinus, used to pierce the side of Christ while he was being crucified. As a result, the lance was covered with the blood and water from Christ's body and from that moment on it was thought to be adorned with miraculous properties. Longinus himself, it was said, was almost blind because of deteriorating vision but evidently some of the droplets of blood and water covered his eyes and his sight was restored. Peter went on to say that the lance also seemed to have the power to make any owners of it successful in all their conflicts. Peter's excitement was passionate, and he went on to describe other accounts throughout history where proof of the spear's power was witnessed. It seemed even Hitler himself believed in its powers and was determined to acquire the lance since he'd first seen it as a child. And indeed, Peter continued, Hitler eventually did own it. He had it in his possession from 1939 to 1944, and he'd kept it safely hidden in a deep vault during that period.

"I've heard of that spear," Ben said. "But aren't there supposed to be several other lances around which others also claim to be the Spear of Destiny?"

"Jolly well done, old chap. You seem to know your stuff, eh? You're perfectly correct. There are other lances which people, over the centuries, have claimed to be the true spear, but it has now been narrowed down by the most renowned scholars to two possibilities. One of those is a lance which lies in St. Peter's Basilica, in Rome. The other is a lance which was last used by Pope John 1 to christen Otto the Great as Holy Roman Emperor. However, the one I'm talking about has been, following a great deal of painstaking work, officially authenticated as the genuine article. General Patton had a great interest in such relics and took great care as well. Furthermore, since then, many other leading authorities have authenticated it as the original."

"Really? Wow, that spear could be useful." Ben glanced at Amalialad.

Amalialad had thought, when Peter had called, that he could be useful. Now he wondered whether the Holy Lance could somehow help them.

Peter was aware of the growing interest and his own interest increased.

"Hmm, I sense mischief afoot," he said.

"Well, Peter, if you can tell me how I can help you, perhaps you may then help me?"

Peter laughed.

"Quid pro quo, eh, old chap. Always loved cricket you know." And his face beamed at the prospect of adventure.

Peter told them he was given a commission by a large charity to bring the spear back from Vienna, and it was, he said, likely that they would raise the funds for accomplishing the task. Evidently the prestige of bringing such a famous relic back safely would persuade them.

Ben was about to say that there was no way they could afford that much money if the charity refused to pay it when Amalialad spoke.

"I'll give you the money if the charity doesn't, Peter, but we need to borrow the spear."

The silence that followed seemed deafening.

"Ok, it's a deal old chap," Peter said, and he held out his hand towards Amalialad who smiled and shook it warmly.

"Well, the reason why it's so expensive is because of the heavy costs for transporting it. The Spear is in such a seriously deteriorating condition that it needs to be transported with extreme care. The shaft is virtually fully decayed, and the spearhead is eaten away with rust. It's simply been bound together with threads of gold, silver and bronze. However, a nail, which allegedly came from the True Cross, is still, supposedly, contained in the spearhead."

"The physical condition is of no importance to us, Peter," said Amalialad, "but its power and spiritual essence is. Yet I understand, we must try to keep it in tact so we can hand it over to the charity, if necessary, at the end. That spear contains the blood of Jesus Christ. There is nothing in or ever in existence since His death that has represented the power of good over evil more than that and if what is stated about the spear is true, well, but we need all the help we can get to transport it, which is a separate issue. I assume you'll help us achieve this since of course we'll have your spear. But we'll need to strategically carry this out in such a way that we can take it at any time during its journey without any suspicion but allowing all others to think it's travelling albeit slowly on a direct route, to you, back to London."

"Just one more minor detail you all need to be aware of." Peter coughed mildly, a pause to consider his next words carefully. "To lose the spear, legend has it, means death."

"Ah," said Ben. "We're used to that."

Chapter Sixteen

The hotel was very modern.

Ben had arrived a little earlier and was sitting at the table as the others came into the room.

"Morning, everyone," he said.

"Good morning to you too, Ben, and you, Amalialad," Peter answered, as he bowed his head slightly in the direction of Tara and Chodon, "and of course to the very fairest of our group, ladies." He smiled widely at them and before sitting himself he pulled out their chairs. He then sat next to Ben.

Amalialad thought the ceremony amusing but knew Peter seemed to love behaving as if living in an age of chivalry. He was simply like that. He was also very much like Ben. He tried to be a charmer with woman whenever the opportunity arose, and this was one of them. Nothing derogatory or insulting was ever meant by it and even though with some woman it may have been considered rude or demeaning, in which case Amalialad would have interrupted, he didn't feel it was here. In fact, he'd discreetly spoken to Tara and Chodon before Peter's arrival and they thought his character may be amusing and refreshing. Surprisingly, Ben and Peter got on well. and there was no competitive animosity between them, just a gentle, light-hearted, rivalry.

Just as well, Amalialad thought, they all had enough to contend with as it was.

"I spoke to Lopsang last night." They all stopped momentarily and looked up at him, mildly concerned.

"I hope you found Lopsang to be well," Chodon said.

"He was in excellent physical health, thank you, Chodon. However, psychologically, he is in deep turmoil, since he blames himself for sending us on what he still considers an impossible mission. Of course, I tried hard to comfort him, but it wasn't easy. However, on my return I picked up a strong signal from the depths of the astral plane. I felt such a close affinity with it. It could have been from one of my ancestors, I don't know, only that it was meant for me."

"What was it?" Ben asked.

Amalialad looked at them all and continued. He distinctly remembered the message and spoke the words to the group as they were said to him.

"Find the three most holy."

"What does that mean?" Ben asked.

"Well, ponder the statement, Ben."

Ben looked at Amalialad as the meaning gradually registered in his mind.

"Crikey, you mean we have other ancient holy relics to find too?"

"Precisely, Ben. And after very careful contemplation, as well as some guidance, I now know that after securing the Spear of Destiny, we will also need one of the thorns from the crown that was placed on Christ's head during his crucifixion. Further, we also need at least one fragment of the wood from the original True Cross, upon which Jesus was crucified. Only these most sacred of holy relics will give us the protection and power to help defeat the increasing benevolence that, at this very moment, is growing malevolently against us."

"But what you're saying is impossible!" Peter said.

"We really have no choice. We cannot afford to fail. To do so would be failing mankind. It would be failing our children and our children's children. Our quest is difficult enough, I know, virtually impossible, but you must also know that the demonic scourge of the nighthawks, and their human servants too, are afoot, and growing in power by the day. We must all be extremely cautious. We must not trust anyone or anything. Don't believe in coincidences and if you have any slight suspicions, act on them. Don't feel paranoid about this. It's all our lives at risk now. Our lives depend on extreme vigilance. For good reason now, I'm giving each of you an individual password. Should the time come when I ask for it, you will give it to me." His tone was pointed, and everyone knew it was a demand and not a request. "This is simply so that I can recognize that you are who you say you are. We have shape-shifting demons out there who can disguise themselves as any one of us. We can't risk confiding in an imposter."

"Are you saying the nighthawks can shape shift?" Ben asked.

"I'm not sure about them but I do know that many of the Demons we face can do so. We just need to make sure we're guarded against the possibility. Their powers are growing and I don't know what they're capable of right now."

"Crikey, old chap, what have I let myself in for here?" Peter said. "I'm an English gentleman. A true knight of valour." Peter spoke melodramatically and smiled widely. Then he paused to think more seriously about what Amalialad had just said, his cheerful demeanour deflating. "Anyway, old chum, just for the record, what's shape shifting exactly?"

Tara and Chodon laughed at his antics. They quite enjoyed his humour and being the centre of attention. It brought a sense of light relief which they could all do with right now, but they too now waited for Amalialad to answer.

"Well, it's basically as the name says. It's when a being can alter its physical appearance. The transformation may be intentional or not depending on whether its ability to do this has been the result of a curse or spell."

"You mean there's a difference?" asked Ben.

"The curse would normally create an 'unintentionage' like that of the popular werewolf myths, but a spell can often work to change with the intention of becoming any animal or being. I'm afraid what we're dealing with is that of the latter since only the evillest entities will have this terrifying power. In myth the usual animals they change into are those of great strength such as the bear, the wolf, the lion and so on, but don't be fooled. We can expect anything. Even if a cat jumps onto your lap and starts purring, expect the worst."

"They can really do that?" Peter asked.

"Well, is there any way of knowing the difference between a shape shifter and the real thing?" Tara asked.

"Yes." Amalialad looked at Chodon. "Chodon and I can focus on the animal or being and feel the negative energy, if you like, we can tell if the smell or stinkoff the entity is truly evil,

"Ah, well, that's just great." said Ben. "What about me and Peter, you know, the common guys?"

The others smiled at him. They knew there was no real anger there, but everyone was under a little duress. Tara felt some sympathy for him. He'd been there for her all the way and she warmed more to him each day. Suddenly, she felt a little disconcerted. She realised that her feelings for Ben were growing.

Amalialad gave his usual enigmatic smile and answered.

"Yes, Ben, there is something you can do. If you use that silver cross, attached to the small chain around your neck, or anything which represents a holy symbol for good and then touch the entity with it, it will feel great pain."

"Blimey, said Peter, "I'll have to get a bible or something." With that they all laughed.

"Perhaps," said Amalialad," but if we do it this way there may just be better odds than the alternative. Both of you go to the church tomorrow and get the crosses blessed with holy water. This will enhance their effect in protecting you against any evil."

Discreetly, Tara, looked at her companion's faces and noticed the growing despair in each of them. She was equally fearful of the future, but felt she needed to raise her friends' spirits.

"We can do this! Our faith is stromg and we have a brilliant and resourceful leader. I think that together we can tackle anything. So, my friends, can we cheer up a little bit? Please?"

The others laughed at her outburst and knew in their hearts Tara was right. They had no choice. If the world were to be saved, they had to move forward with determination. They had to simply fight with whatever strength and resourcefulness they could muster.

"Ok," Amalialad said, thankful for Tara's interruption. Even he was beginning to have some nagging doubts about winning this war.

"Let's get to planning."

The priority at this stage was to firstly bring back the Spear of Destiny safely. They decided to let it be known it would be returned by land, which would take a week, but they would transport it by air, which would mean they could hopefully use it for six days.

That was challenging enough but, in that same time frame, they needed to get hold of the other holy relics too. Amalialad didn't dare ponder on the potential obstacles ahead, it would have created too much negativity. Luckily, however, the whereabouts of the objects were known by Peter, who had a strong interest in such historical artefacts. Acquiring them was the biggest problem and they decided to sit down to work out the fine detail.

They arranged to meet Peter later that day, so he could make the financial transaction to secure his contract, with the authorities, to collect the spear. The administrations needed to process the official go ahead, which would take a further day or so, and they needed to leave for Vienna in three days.

Before leaving Peter gave them some more detailed information about the Crown of Thorns and the True Cross.

"The Crown of Thorns has become one of the greatest holy relics of medieval history. You need to understand of course that, in the context of faith, this thorn reliquary is unimaginably valuable and emotive. It not only touched Christ, the Savior, but also pierced his skin and drew his blood. You can perhaps imagine then, why Louis 1X King of France paid 135,000 livres for it in Constantinople in AD1239, which was nearly half of the annual expenditure of France at that time. It's now housed in Notre Dame Cathedral in a specially constructed container provided by Napoleon himself."

"Wow," Ben said. "They really did think very highly of it then?"

"That's an understatement, Ben. Many claim miraculous cures for a whole variety of ailments, diseases and injuries while simply visiting and observing the relic. As you know yourself, even today, people will pay exorbitant amounts of money if they think they can be cured of something which would otherwise be incurable. Just look at the numbers who travel thousands of miles to visit Lourdes, and you'll understand what I mean."

"That's true," said Tara. "My Aunt Hilda, God rest her soul, paid thousands of pounds to find a cure for her cancer, even though doctors told her it was incurable, but all her money, unfortunately, ended up in the hands of unscrupulous charlatans, who were pretending to provide cures, but of course, they were complete liars."

"There's a significant difference here though, Tara," said Peter. They all looked at him. "Many of the cures were genuine and witnessed. Even later, they couldn't be refuted and the reason for the cure was registered as unknown. The authorities weren't prepared to be ridiculed. They just couldn't accept, even with what seemed like overwhelming evidence from witness statements by people held in the highest regard, that such miracles were possible."

"C'est le vie!" said Ben.

Chapter Seventeen

His thoughts were suddenly interrupted by the loud screech of a car horn and he realised he was still standing on the side of the road. He quickly stepped back onto the safety of the pavement which led to the front entrance of the cathedral. Even though he hadn't been there before he'd memorised every one of the hundreds of photos of the building he had seen, both inside and out, and felt he knew it as well as anyone could. His confidence grew and tomorrow, if all went well, he'd be travelling back with the relics to the UK.

He felt a stab of guilt as he reflected on what he'd told Amalialad before he left. Of course, it was true he'd made the necessary contacts to borrow the holy relics but not in the official way he'd led the others to believe. He knew it was imperative to retrieve the relics in order to accomplish their mission. Equally, he knew that there would be no way at all to convince the authorities to release the relics. They were the most valuable, priceless, cherished items in the world today as far as the Catholic Church was concerned, and as such, no amount of persuasion would have got them released. Instead he'd meticulously arranged a plan to steal them with the help of one of the priests attending the cathedral. Phillip Alexander was deeply in debt due to his secret gambling habits, and he'd eventually agreed, after being offered 50,000 Euros, to allow Peter to the treasury on the day that renovations were to be carried out. And that day would be tomorrow, at 7am, when the cathedral would be closed to visitors and only a small group of visiting priests would be present. Two of these had been brought in from outside Paris to verify and collect some of the Vatican files, which were just temporarily kept at the cathedral. That made it easier for the ruse Peter had in mind. Peter thought back to the difficulty he'd had in finding a professional hacker to infiltrate the cathedral's administration and personnel computers, to find out the names of all the priests working inside the cathedral, and then, to investigate their personal banking circumstances. It was only by chance that he'd been told about a person who'd recently been freed from prison for managing to break into very secret files of MI5, that he'd eventually got lucky. He suspected the man would need money and went about tracking his whereabouts. He wasn't difficult to find. The newspaper article gave the name of the town in which the man lived, and the rest was simply a matter of searching the electoral role.

The hacker had explained that in exchange for keeping quiet about certain extremely secretive information he was offered an early parole, being freed after serving only six months. Peter paid £20,000 for the information. The hacker had discovered that there were two priests whose finances were poor, but one stood out from the rest. He gave the name of a priest who was very close to bankruptcy - Phillip Alexander.

As arranged, Peter drove up to the side of the road adjacent to the treasury block, at the north side of the cathedral at precisely 7am. He then waited. Five minutes passed before he saw a priest walking towards him, as if on a morning stroll. Peter wound down his window and greeted the priest.

"Good morning, Father."

Father Alexander smiled wanly and carefully looked around before surreptitiously handing Peter a small bag which he'd discreetly hidden under his robes. He then calmly walked on his way. For all intents and purposes any onlooker earlier would have simply thought that the priest had stopped to give someone information or directions. Peter quickly took the bag and jumped into the back of a prearranged parked van, where he speedily got changed into the priest's robes and shoes which were hidden in the bag. Then carefully but peeping out the windows to establish all was clear, Peter got out the side door of the van. Slowly, he retraced the priest's footsteps to the side of the treasury block. If any member of the public or another priest saw him, he thought, he was just a priest going about his daily routine. And if for some reason, the local priests didn't recognize him, they'd simply think he was one of the many visiting clerics from the Vatican.

As he approached, he saw Father Phillip standing quietly at a small door.

"Go through this door which will take you to the sacristy and that in turn will link you to the main treasury room. I've now done what you've asked of me and so I shall go."

Peter knew how guilty the priest must have felt in betraying his church and didn't expect any more than that. The stab of guilt he'd felt before came back with more intensity, but the world was in peril and that took precedence. He hoped one day, if all went well, the priest would understand and forgive him.

Peter gently opened the door, grateful that it didn't creak. Slowly, he walked inside and up to the sacristy which was straight in front of him. He opened the door and walked through, passing an old oak desk with four drawers and two chairs, as he did so. The wall of the sacristy housed a large brown wooden cross with the words 'Deus LoVult' printed onto its enamel base. Peter recognized it as pertaining to the Equestrian Order of the Holy Sepulchre of Jerusalem, a catholic order of chivalry and a shiver went up his back. Peter wondered what the words meant; he knew a little Latin, but he didn't have time to focus and instead he brushed the thought to one side. Before entering the room, he checked his pockets for the small tools he'd need to open the locks and disarm the complex security alarm systems around the glass containers in which the relics were housed. Then, feeling confident, he opened the door to the Treasury.

As he stepped into the chamber, he felt uncomfortable. He sensed a presence. Suddenly, a mass of bright lights lit up the large room, and Peter jumped back in shock at what the light revealed.

Chapter Eighteen

He saw their hands resting steadfastly on the hilts of their swords, and instantly recognized the crest indented there. Peter shuddered. He was facing the world-renowned Knights of the Order of the Sepulchre of Jerusalem. He knew these knights were the Catholic -Church's guardians of all the holy relics and the knights themselves were considered some of the best warriors ever to have lived. They had loyally defended the church's assets for decades. Indeed, their first charge after the Crusades was guarding the Holy Sepulchre and other Holy Places including the tomb of Jesus of Jerusalem and answerable then only to Augustus, the King of Jerusalem but now only to His Holiness the Pope himself, swearing a life of poverty and obedience. Later, in Rome, during the Jubilee Pilgrimage of 2000, Pope John Paul II said he expected all of them to continue, 'fostering and deepening the three characteristic virtues of the Holy Order, being, Zeal for Self-Denial in this society of affluence, generous commitment to the weak and defenseless and to courageously struggle for justice and peace.' The knights lined the walls and filled the chamber. Peter estimated at least a hundred of them. He looked closer and shivered. All were staring directly at him.

For the first time in years, Peter felt total despair. His thoughts spiraled. Then he felt both a deep anguish and a deepening sense of failure, as his thoughts finally rested on the idea of spending the next thirty years in prison, although he reflected, his sentence would be short lived since his failure in this mission meant the world was most likely doomed. And if that happened, evil would overcome, and the Devil would rule, then he and every 'good' person would be dead.

"Please follow me." The knight spoke with a low rumble which matched his size and Peter recognised an Italian accent. He followed the knight down the long aisle to the very end of the cathedral chamber. The knight stopped in front of one of eight chapels which radiated out from the apse. He then knocked slowly four times on the chapel door. Peter was completely confused. Considering his position, he was being treated with a considerable degree of courtesy.

The chapel door slowly opened, and Peter stepped back in disbelief as Francis, a very old family friend he'd recently approached for details about the layout of the Cathedral, walked through.

In shock, Peter was about to blurt out a barrage of questions, but Francis spoke.

"Please, my friend, don't be alarmed, your questions will be answered. Please, just follow me."

Had Francis betrayed him? Why were they being so friendly?

He followed Francis through the chapel doorway, then down some steps into a large bright room.

Francis led Peter to a large table at one end of the room. He pulled out one of the ten chairs.

"Please, Peter, would you sit here." Peter complied and was about to ask a question when Francis quickly put a finger to his lips.

"I'll return shortly, Peter. Your patience is most appreciated." He then left through a narrow, white door.

The waiting was frustrating and the quiet became intense. Peter had so many questions he wanted answers to and was eager to know exactly what was going on. For a second, just before the narrow door opened, he felt suddenly overwhelmed. His heart raced. It was inexplicable. Then he glanced towards the gentle sound of footsteps and his heart raced faster. Surely this can't be happening, he thought. It's just not possible.

Chapter Nineteen

He was dressed in his usual pure white cassock, adorned with a gold cross attached to a golden chord. But he was unmistakably recognizable by his face. Pope Francis II smiled warmly towards Peter as he spoke softly, but clearly, to him.

"God bless you, my son." With these words he gave the sign of the cross and said something in Latin which Peter couldn't quite make out. Even though he knew Latin these words must have originated on a slightly different or earlier version of the language. Immediately behind the pope followed Francis and two cardinals. Peter easily identified the cardinals by their coat of arms and their bright red, wide-brimmed hats which sat proudly on their heads, together with fifteen tassels which hung each side. The cardinals both quietly filed in and walked to the opposite side of the table he was standing by.

Intrigued, Peter waited in both wonder and anticipation while they sat down and settled themselves. The pope himself sat directly facing him and smiled slightly although Peter caught a note of sadness in his voice as he then spoke.

"May I call you Peter?" the pope asked.

Peter felt both honoured and humbled.

"Your Holiness, of course, the honour is most definitely mine."

"I hope, Peter, when I've finished talking with you, that most of your questions will be answered to your satisfaction. Firstly, I've known about your group's quest and your personal mission to take our holy relics for some time now." Take, Peter thought, 'steal' would have been more appropriate.

"Peter, you need to listen to me very carefully. Will you do that?"

"Yes, of course, Your Holiness"

"So I can meet you secretly and in person I'm here on the pretext of viewing the holy relics. For obvious reasons this visit was not publicized and only my cardinals and the chief administrator of the cathedral, a good and trusted man I've known for years, are aware of it. I convinced my cardinals that, for security reasons, it would be best this way. But, of course, in telling them I was just visiting here to observe the relics was not entirely true." For the briefest of moments, the pope displayed a slight smile. But he then looked at Peter directly. "Peter, the end of days is near, and we are losing the battle. We were aware of the changes in our fight against evil forces years ago but just assumed it was a short-lived change and that the goodness throughout the land with the help of the Lord would eventually prevail. However, this wasn't so, and we were forced to struggle hard in all areas to wipe out demonic entities and other elementals of evil which managed somehow to filter into our world. This intrusion of demonic malevolence has also required an immense task to change the attitude of so many people today who have succumbed to evil ways. Moral values have broken down. Wars have increased. Too many people now hold life with so little regard. Innocent women and children are slaughtered without remorse. Even the high moralistic values we, the Church once held have diminished amongst our own clergy." The pope lowered his head, as if in shame. Then he looked again at Peter. "We desperately struggle now to get it back. This growing evil is like a virus spreading rapidly from one to another. I believe this was mainly our fault and as head of the Catholic Church I must hold full responsibility. We have made some big mistakes - wrong decisions. But our biggest mistake has not been declaring them openly. We should have admitted to them and made them transparent. Instead, we chose to hide them. We have been hypocritical. We try to preach the doctrines of honesty, peace and justice, yet we have been guilty of being unjust and sometimes, although, indirectly, we've used violence to meet our own ends, to support our own agenda. Of course, we knew about some of these despicable acts but chose to do nothing about them. We should have declared the offenses publicly and immediately punished the offenders. But we didn't. We tried to hide the truth to protect the image of our church. We thought the revelations would destroy us. On reflection this now seems somewhat ironic.

In hiding our guilt and not bringing those offenders to justice, we made our biggest mistake. We should have recognized this. I, too, was arrogant in that I chose to be in denial that any of my clergy could act so evilly. Because of our actions we'd inadvertently allowed an influx of evil to creep deeper into the foundations of our own church as well as the world at large. I think, Peter, God himself was forced to teach us a lesson and now we find our own evil acts have provided the opportunity for Satan to cross the threshold into our world." Peter noticed that the pope's eyes were welling up. It was obviously both embarrassing and painful to admit. But Peter was also bewildered as to why the pope was confessing all this to him. "And Satan has taken full advantage of this. His forces have grown strong and they've crept into every small and isolated village, every small town and every city and we're now extremely fearful of the future. Wherever goodness is weak, his dominions make their home and try to manipulate and manifest evil. Satan is clever. His daemons have crept in surreptitiously. He's cemented a foundation of pure evil. Silently, at first, his soldiers came, but gradually, and through cunning and deceit, he's built up his hordes. Because of what we've done, we think we've brought forward the final battle. The End of Days has started. This final battle was not expected for decades, but our own stupidity has changed this, and, Peter," he looked at Peter directly again, and his face went pale, before continuing, "we expect defeat. And we need your help."

Peter felt the blood draining from his face. What could he say? He knew that the man in front of him had not even been a cardinal at the time of the scandals the church committed. Yet now, as the pope, the Supreme Head of the Catholic Church, he must take the blame. He must accept the responsibility. It was unfair, Peter thought. Anger suddenly flared up and flowed through Peter. The arrogance of Satan, to creep in like a robber to destroy his world. He made a personal promise. While he had breath in his body, he would do his utmost to change the odds and help defeat the diabolical incursion of evil. He would do whatever it took to change the odds. Do everything conceivably possible to defeat this satanic invasion. So, what, he pondered, could he now say to the pope? There really was only one thing to say.

"We must cling to faith, Your Holiness. We all must pray for forgiveness and cling hard to our faith."

The pope looked at Peter thoughtfully and gave a solemn nod.

"Thank you, Peter. Much of what I'm about to say is extremely confidential. Therefore, since I understand you are of no religious faith." Peter felt a warm surge of blood flow through his face at the embarrassment. How did the pope know that he had doubts about the existence of God? "I need your solemn word that you will not allow what we talk of right now to leave this room."

"I'm sorry, Your Holiness, and I really want to help, but I just can't do that."

"May I ask why?"

"Your Holiness, you know already I have come here on a vital quest on behalf of a special group of friends led by Amalialad. My allegiance has been promised to them just as we all promised allegiance to each other until our group's mission is fulfilled. My honour is at stake so I cannot agree with your request, but I will tell them everything that's happened here and ask for their consent."

The pope brightened up at this. "But, of course, of course, how remiss of me. Your friends, Peter, should know most of what we talk about here already. Because of this world crisis, we have been in close communication with the most trusted religious and political leaders around the world. In fact, for the past twenty years we've been in regular talks with each other to promote peace and harmony in the world. After all, we all have one definite thing in common; to overcome and defeat evil wherever we find it and to compromise, tolerate and respect all views so that together we can bring a lasting peace, justice and freedom to all people. One of these highly trusted leaders representing the Buddhist faith is Lopsang. I think Amalialad and you know of him?"

"Indeed, I do," Peter said, relieved, knowing now that Amalialad had a mentor and was confiding in a person held in such high esteem, and, more importantly, would be able to agree to the pope's request for total secrecy.

"As leaders, we are able to support each other in our planning and the development of strategies and in the building of our armies for the battle ahead. But, Peter, the outcome lies with you and your group of friends. This has been foretold."

Peter was aghast. "But how? We only known each other a few weeks and we're still unsure of the way forward."

"I know the outcome isn't certain, but we do know that if we win this battle it will be primarily due to you and your group. Yet, I know too, Peter, that the chances of you completing your quest are not in your favour. There will be extreme challenges ahead. You will be facing the full wrath of Satan and the full might of his daemon hordes. Even I cannot put into words the horror of the perils ahead of you. I'm so sorry to tell you this, Peter, but the fate of mankind depends on your small group succeeding."

What could he say to that? He knew it was likely they would fail, but he knew it wouldn't be for the lack of tremendous effort and sheer bravery on their part. He knew that they would all freely give up their lives to save the world.

"Have faith!" the pope answered, with a glint of humour in his eyes. "And God bless."

As Peter turned to leave, the pope called out.

"Peter, haven't you forgotten what you've come for?" Francis stood up and walked around the table to Peter. He carried a large package.

He looked up at the pope and saw sadness on his face.

"Thank you, Your Holiness."

"It's the very least I can do. Indeed, it's something I had to do for you and your friends to have any chance of completing your quest. Tell Amalialad he chose well in selecting these particular relics but, before you go, I have a little more to say."

Peter turned.

"I must firstly apologise to you. On my instructions, I told Francis to deceive you. He was, understandably, most reluctant at first because he considers you an honourable man and holds you in high esteem. However, he realised, after careful thought, it was the only safe and sure way to get you here without raising any suspicion. I'm sure you understand, Peter, secrecy here is paramount."

"Of course, Your Holiness, I understand completely."

"Have you heard of the Opus Dei, Peter?"

Peter certainly had. The Opus Dei, he'd read, was an ultra-secretive Catholic organisation particularly active in Italy, Spain and South America, although, he remembered reading they had members in most countries around the world. The group taught that everyone was called to holiness and that ordinary life was a path to sanctity. Most of its members, which now numbered more than 100,000, were lay people with secular priests, but under the governance of a prelate who was a bishop, appointed by the pope, the organisation, in general, had very high moral values and led a life of goodness. Peter also remembered reading that some of their activities were questionable. Most were expected to lead a life of celibacy but not all did since some were just ordinary family members who through their work helped to promote the values of the Opus Dei. However, their practice of the mortification of the flesh was criticized. Particularly the use of the cilice, which had a spiked ring and was worn tightly around the legs so that the person would feel the pain and bleed. In doing so, it was suggested, any sexual desire would be suppressed.

"Yes, Your Holiness, I have."

"That's good," the pope replied, but he looked quizzically at Peter.

"As a matter of the highest priority I have instructed the Opus Dei to assist you whenever they can with any help you seek during your quest. They can be trusted, Peter."

"Thank you, Your Holiness, we value any help we can get, but this will be a particularly great asset for us."

The pope nodded slowly.

"Also, I have instructed Francis and two of my knights to travel with you." Peter was concerned – Amalialad would have to approve this.

"Don't concern yourself, Peter. Amalialad has already agreed to this. Yesterday, in fact, when Lopsang spoke to him and brought him up to date on everything discussed here. However, the agreement is subject to your own consent since you weren't there. Are you happy with this arrangement, my friend?"

"I am, Your Holiness, and may I thank you on behalf of myself and my friends for your invaluable help. The battle ahead would, I'm sure, be most certainly lost without it."

"Please never underestimate yourselves, Peter. There is something very special about you and your friends. Although not all is crystal clear, your destiny is sewn into the fabric of time. Of course, I would say God has chosen you all for this task, however, I do know that the whole world is now standing on a precipice of annihilation, waiting to fall one way or the other, and so the more assets and support you have in your favour, then the more it will lean our way."

Peter nodded.

"One more thing I ask of you before you leave, Peter." The pope turned to the cardinal seated on his right and picked up a small, silver box. "I want you to give this box personally to Amalialad. Tell him he must take it with him on your quest. He must try always to keep it safe, even though he himself may not be the person responsible to open the box, since it could become your saving grace. Please, do not tell anyone else of this, Peter. Please do not tell anybody else at all. But I assure you, it's of no danger to any of you. I know you may think you have a duty to tell your friends about this, but I beseech you not to do so. Can I just say, I have my reasons for this and the safety of your journey could possibly be in jeopardy if you do so. Please tell Amalialad that if he ever feels, at any time ahead of him, that all is lost, when everything else has failed, when he feels that there is absolutely no hope at all left to cling on to, then he must use what is in the box. Will you promise to do this for me, Peter?"

"Yes, Your Holiness, I will." Peter didn't like the idea of keeping this secret from the others, but he trusted in the pope's judgement.

The pope passed the box to him across the table. It felt very light, no more than a few grams, and, as Peter looked closer, he noticed a tiny, almost indistinguishable, three-digit combination lock, fitted flush to one side.

"What's the combination, Your Holiness?"

"This may be completely confusing; but I don't know."

"Your Holiness, if it's something of such vital importance then we will need the combination. It's useless without it."

"I understand, Peter. I'm sorry. There is a combination, but that knowledge lies with three people and each person potentially has the answer, but only one will ever need to find that potential and use it. I don't know, and they won't know who it will be until the time comes. And none of them will hold that answer until that very moment time becomes necessary. It will be the precise moment when the lock must be opened. Faith, again, is needed here. I'm truly sorry. But I can tell you this; when the time does come, if the person is one of the chosen three, he or she will know the combination. They must answer the following riddle. 'The answer lies in the reflection'. I'm sorry, Peter but that's all I know. I have some ideas myself, but I've been instructed, by a higher authority, not to guess, but to completely refrain from aiding you further."

Peter was puzzled.

"Excuse me, your Holiness, if I can just clarify then, apart from having to decipher the riddle, you're also saying that if Amalialad is not one of the three people able to open the box, then the contents inside the box would be completely useless to us unless it gets into the hands of one of the chosen ones?"

"Yes, I'm afraid so. Amalialad could be one of those chosen but we just don't know. I'm sorry. However, we have strong reasons to think he may be. Researchers within the College of Cardinals have spent nearly five years researching this. But we're not completely certain, and as I said, our strong desire to help are restricted. We felt, in the circumstances, it would be better that you just take it."

Peter thought carefully about that and decided it made sense.

"I understand, Your Holiness."

"I'm so very sorry and regretful of our sins. My cardinals and I pray, every single day, for hours, for forgiveness for what we've done. We fervently hope that in the final hour, God will be at our side once more."

"I hope so too, your Holiness"

"We must part now, Peter, I pray we will meet again soon under a brighter sky and in better circumstances. May God always be with you and give you light to guide you through the darkness ahead." Peter knew his words were sincere. He also knew it was his cue to leave.

Francis brought the relics over to Peter, leaned down and spoke gently into his ear.

"Come, we have much to do." That was, Peter thought, an understatement. However, he gave Francis an appreciative nod and tapped him lightly on the shoulder as he walked by. He knew Francis had a wonderful, loving family, yet Francis was still prepared to risk all to help him and his group. The least he could do was to go back to his cheerful, jovial old self. If they were all to die, he decided, then they should die cheerfully together. The enemy should know that they would face them, and if necessary, accept their death without fear

"We've certainly got much to do, Francis. Let's go and sort these problems out, shall we?"

Francis then glanced across at his friend and wondered if in fact he'd heard exactly what the pope had told him, since Peter's sudden cheerfulness seemed out of place.

But then, Francis thought, considering what was likely to befall them, 'a stiff upper lip and a cheerful disposition' were probably their best weapons for that moment. It was most imperative, Francis pondered, not to become negative and defeatist. Not to let depression set in. No, a positive mental attitude was important.

Peter followed Francis back out of the small chapel and along the aisle of the cathedral, passing the knights along the way who were all standing, still and silent, and Peter assumed they were waiting for further orders. As they reached the door, a horrifying, screeching noise reverberated around the cathedral. A powerful blast tore the door of the chapel off its hinges and tossed it through the air to the opposite wall, almost decapitating the three knights standing against the wall. It splintered and smashed in two and fell heavily on top of the knights. Everyone turned to see what was happening. Peter wished he hadn't.

Chapter Twenty

He sensed it a second before he saw it. It was a creature most foul and its massive green, oval shaped head, with its large, globular, demonic blue eyes, sneaked out of the chapel door just as its green neck, undulating body and throbbing thick muscular arms reached out and charged. It came straight at him. And, as it came closer, Peter trembled in fear as he saw the creature's powerful biceps expand and grow further. They became a rippling, bulging mass of pure muscle, and they slowly jerked up and down as if pumping the arms for Peter's final death knell. Peter guessed the large hands would inevitably encircle and snap his neck and he trembled in fear. It was too late to run, and that final realization struck him as he felt the warmth of the creature's thick fingers touch his neck. He was stricken in shock and stuck to the spot and felt sure his life was about to be extinguished. The stench from the creature's body was nauseating and a last comical thought crossed his mind; if the grip didn't kill him, the smell would. Hmm, I'm funny 'til the end, he mused. Then he felt two strong hands gripping his shoulders. He found himself being thrown onto the lawn outside. Francis was hovering over him, catching his breath.

"It's a djinn, Peter. We must run for our lives. Just follow me." Peter followed him out of the cathedral grounds, adrenaline surging through his body. They finally stopped in a narrow side street, outside a small cafe. They hurried inside, collapsing at a table near the window, taking a few minutes to get their breath back.

"What the hell was that?" Peter said.

"It's from Hell and it's known as djinn," Francis replied. He was exhausted, trying to collect himself. Peter could see it was all extremely traumatic for him. They'd just had a monster from Hell itself chasing them, and the pope, with his cardinals, were probably, torturously, slain. Peter left Francis quietly contemplating and walked up to the counter to order two coffees, both with plenty of sugar.

"Drink this," Peter said. "It will help with the shock." Francis took the coffee and drank it down quickly.

"I'm sorry, Peter, but we're in dire straits. That monster we just escaped from, the djinn, what we might call a genie."

"A genie? But aren't they supposed to be friendly creatures who grant wishes in fairy tales?"

Francis gave a thin smile, his face serious. "Peter, I want you to trust me when I ask you to forget your normal beliefs. What I'm telling you about right now really exists. I haven't got time to dissuade you of your normal thinking about these things. But djinns exist, and don't grant wishes. They're supernatural creatures that live in a parallel plane that's like our own. The Quran describes the djinn as having free will, just like us. In other words, they can be good or evil. But if they choose to be evil, then they're one of the ugliest and most dangerous creatures there are. It looked muscular, didn't it? But their bodies are composed of a smokeless flame. You may have heard of Iblis?"

"I haven't. What is that?"

"I know you know much of the Bible, Peter, even though, sadly, you choose not to believe in much of it. So, Iblis was a djinn who was the Islamic equivalent of Lucifer. They believed that after the heavenly rebellion, which he led, Iblis was pardoned and allowed to live on Earth to lead mankind astray until Judgement Day. I wonder if you realise what this means, Peter?"

"Well, I could guess some of it," Peter said. "The pope and his cardinals have probably been killed. I imagine most of the knights were slain but I hope they managed to defeat it eventually. They have some of the best fighting men in the world. Also, if that creature was an equivalent to Lucifer, and there are more of them, then we're in big trouble."

"Well, you're probably right, Peter, but I hope not. I pray that His Holiness managed to somehow get out safely first, but, sadly," Francis briefly bowed his head, "the rest of what you say is probably true. Those knights are strong and include some of the best fighters we have. If anyone could survive that maelstrom and slay that thing, they could. You know what we must do now, don't you?"

"Yes. We must go back and find out precisely what's happened."

As they approached the cathedral, Peter simultaneously felt a chill down his back and a sudden, deep sense of foreboding. Something was wrong. Then he realised there were no ambulances or sirens. There was nobody. The whole place was as they'd left it after they'd closed the door behind them an hour earlier.

"Are you thinking what I'm thinking?" Peter asked.

"No. I don't think all the knights have been killed. That's inconceivable."

"That may be," Peter said. "I hope you're right, but haven't you wondered why none of the knights came running after us, to tell us the creature had been killed?"

"Perhaps you're right, but maybe the knights didn't venture out of the Cathedral to inform us since they're bound by an oath and therefore wouldn't risk any knowledge of what'd happened, including the Pope's appearance here, for risk of reaching the public domain. So, even if they were dying, they wouldn't step out of this building to seek aid."

"Ok," Peter said. "Then that's another reason why we should go in now and check. There may be some still injured who need our help. We must go in and find out."

"Of course, we don't have a choice, do we?"

"We always have a choice Francis. But I know you, of all people, would be aware that sometimes there is really only one direction to take." With that they walked up to the cathedral door.

Francis opened the door just a crack, trying hard not to make a sound. He peered inside.

He turned to Peter, his face agonized. His legs gave way. And as he knelt on the grass, he began to retch, then vomited. Peter took a breath, then walked inside.

It was horrendous. Limbless bodies littered the blood-spattered chamber. Decapitated heads lay bloodied, mouths left gaping, wide open shattered and twisted loose. Dented armour, broken swords and twisted metal visors lay scattered over the bodies. The awful stench of decay emanated from the dead, which was unusual within such a short time, but Peter guessed that the intensity of the evil had something to do with it, and Peter became aware of an eerie silence. It was quietly frightening. Francis brushed against him and stood silently, dazed beside Peter. For a few moments they were speechless as they took in the whole devastating scene. Then Peter spoke.

"We need to look deeper into the chapel, Francis, don't we?" His voice was trembling.

They carefully navigated their way down the aisle, through the mangled maelstrom of broken bodies, torn garments and congealed blood.

Peter hoped, and Francis had silently prayed, that the pope had somehow escaped the djinn and secured refuge in the chapel room.

Then, without warning, Peter heard an urgent voice in his head. Use the spear. Peter was momentarily confused.

But the warning came pounding back. Now! You must fight now for your life!

It was instinctive. Peter turned and took the bag of relics from Francis, tore it open and took out the spear.

"Run! Get out, now!" he shouted at Francis. Francis recognised the urgency. He grabbed the bag and fled towards the door. Before he got there, the djinn appeared in the doorway of the chapel, directly in front of Peter.

Intuitively, Peter stepped back and swiftly, using both hands, pointed the sharp end of the spear towards the creature. He felt his heart pumping as the surge of adrenaline accelerated through his veins. His hands gripped the spear tightly and, with all his might, his arms thrust forwards. The point of the spear was headed for the djinn's heart and Peter's body shuddered as it hit its target. But it simply pierced the skin. Damn it! He knew then that a return blow from the djinn would kill him. The djinn roared in pain and reared as Peter struck it again. But he misjudged the djinn's speed and missed his target completely. Peter knew now it was all too late. He closed his eyes tightly, ready to receive the death blow. He fleetingly felt sadness at not being able to say his final goodbyes but accepted his lot. It didn't come. The djinn didn't strike back. After a few agonizing moments, Peter slowly opened his eyes and looked up. He could see a green, thick, liquid oozing from the wound in the side of the djinn's stomach.

And as he raised his eyes to the creature's face, he was shocked at what he saw.

Chapter Twenty-One

The face of the djinn was distorted in pain. But Peter sensed immediately, it wasn't actual physical pain, caused by the wound in its stomach, but more of an emotional pain of anguish and sorrow, and tears were flowing freely down the djinn's face. Then it spoke.

"Forgive me, master. I'm so sorry. Please, forgive me." The voice trembled softly, and Peter knew the pleading was genuine, but he was still utterly perplexed.

Why had the djinn so quickly changed from a violent and brutal killer to such a gentle and sorrowful creature?

But then suddenly it came to him. Of course, he thought, how could he not have realised? It was the spear. The end of the spear had once touched the blood of Christ. The blood had come from Him, who stood for everything holy, righteous and good. Blood, he knew, which could never, of course, be totally removed from the end of the spear. He knew, too, that the aura of its presence there would always remain and anything that the blood touched would be transformed to goodness. Just as the Roman soldier, Longinus, who, after stabbing Christ in the side, inadvertently wiped his eyes with blood from the end of the spear and became good. It seemed unbelievable, yet it was so. Peter looked at the wound he'd made in the djinn's stomach. It was healing. The oozing was flowing backwards into the wound. The skin merged slowly back together and the wound, within seconds, was completely healed. Peter suddenly felt angry and wanted revenge for what the djinn had done. The djinn may be sorry now, but he still felt it deserved to die. Peter stared at it in anger and frustration. His dilemma was that he knew he could never just heartlessly kill it even though he desperately wanted to. It wasn't in his nature. But neither did he want to let the djinn go unpunished.

"Master," it spoke slowly, "I have committed great atrocities, including the killing of the knights, although I sense two are still alive if you search the bodies more closely." The djinn slowly raised an arm and pointed towards the far corner of the chamber and just beyond the door.

"I'm onto it." It was Francis, who'd returned to find him.

"I will kill myself, master. It is the honourable thing to do!" The djinn then bellowed and bent down to pick up one of many swords scattered on the floor. He grabbed it quickly by the hilt and flashed it through the air bringing it to a sudden halt just a hairs breadth from his throat. In lightning speed, he then pulled the sword back and forth to plunge the blade into his throat.

"Stop!" Peter shouted. "I command you to stop!" The djinn froze and looked down at Peter. Peter hated the djinn but something deep inside his very soul urged him to stop the djinn's execution. And without knowing why, it was a message he knew he must comply with.

"Why do you ask me to stop, master?"

"Because it's not for me to decide your fate, djinn. But I could do with your help. Will you assist me?"

"My life is now yours to command as you will, master." Peter was fascinated; the djinn had spoken in the same way he'd imagined a genie from a magic lamp would speak.

"Then I will. But firstly, djinn, tell me who sent you."

"The daemon Asmodeus sent me to kill the pope and his whole entourage, including the knights."

"You mean the one who is referred to as the president of Hell?" Asmodeus was one of the most feared and powerful demon lords that existed, one who hoped one day to be the king of Hell. It was told that he had more than forty legions of minor daemons and spirits under his command. Asmodeus was also responsible for travelling to other universal planes and manipulating the politics of the worlds for his own gain. He could disguise himself as man.

"Did you kill the pope and his cardinals?"

"No, master. Somehow they managed to escape before I stepped through into the Earth plane."

A flood of relief swept through Peter. He couldn't imagine how they could have escaped, but that was a question for later.

"Did the daemon say why he wanted them destroyed?"

"No, he just gave me the command."

"You mean you just did what he asked? Why?"

"Amodeus is clever and deceitful. One night, with the help of the minor daemons from his legions, our souls were possessed while we slept. When we awoke in the morning, we were all under demonic control. Amodeus also, somehow, gave us solid substance. Before, we were astral energies."

"I see. How many of your species still remain where you come from?"

"There were six hundred and seventy-one when I left."

"How did you get to Earth?"

"We simply willed our way through the astral plane by directing our thoughts on our intended destination."

"Do you realise, djinn, that you will now continue working for good, never to return to your evil ways?"

"Yes, I know this, and it makes me very happy."

"I want you to go back to your home and convert all of your species to work, like you now, for good."

"How can I do that, master? My own magic powers have no influence over my own kind. They all have evil intentions now, and though I'm considered a Warrior of Distinction in my world and may destroy some of them before they destroy me, they will eventually defeat me."

"But you do have a way, djinn. Your blood is now forever touched by the blood of Jesus Christ. If you take some of your blood and dip the end of a small needle into it, then prick the other djinns with it, they will immediately change as you did. Do you understand?"

"Yes, master, I understand."

"That's good. Can you find me wherever I'll be, djinn?" Peter asked.

"Yes, master. I'm now linked to your astral cord and can track you anywhere in this universe."

"So, when every djinn has been converted, will they follow you? Will they do as you command them?"

"No, master." That wasn't the answer Peter had been hoping for. He was hoping for the help of all djinns in the battle ahead.

"They will only follow your commands, master. But don't worry, my master automatically becomes their master."

"Ok, now I know you can reach me, but how can I contact you?" Peter asked.

"We will always be mentally linked. So, whenever you wish it, master, I will be there. You simply need to visualise me and wish it."

"Is that also how I contact all the other djinns too, after you've converted them?"

"Of course, master."

"Then I command you, djinn, go now and carry out my wishes. I will call you when I want you."

"Yes, master." The djinn vanished.

"They're alive, Peter!" The shout made him jump.

Peter had momentarily forgotten Francis was there, but he turned to see him helping one of the knights to his feet. The other knight had managed to struggle upright and was leaning on the open door for support. Peter was thrilled. Something good, at last, he thought, was going their way.

"Well done, Francis."

"Excuse-moi!" the knight burst out. Peter was confused.

"S'il vous plait, monsieur, apologise!"

"C'est bonne," Francis said to the knight, and then turned to face Peter.

"I'm sorry, Peter but I meant to tell you earlier."

"What is it, Francis?"

"You've always known me as Francis, an ordinary family man, Peter."

"That's true. I've known you for six years, your family too."

"Well, my friend, there is another part of my life you don't know about."

Intrigued, Peter questioningly looked at Francis, waiting for him to expand on his statement.

"I'm a Catholic bishop and the prelate of the Opus Dei and I've held this position for eight years."

Peter's heart sank. How many more surprises like this were in store, he wondered.

"Are you kidding me, Francis?" But as he spoke, Peter realized that it was true and knew why the knight was so angry. He had, from the knight's perspective, been extremely disrespectful when addressing his bishop. "Should I address you now as Your Excellency, then?" Peter asked Francis.

Francis smiled. "I'm sorry again, Peter. None of this is your fault. However, in order to protect us on our journey together, we need to act incognito, so please, do continue to call me Francis." Francis turned towards the knights.

"My loyal knights, Hughes de Payens and Godfrey de Saint Omer, do you understand that from now on you need to forget I'm a bishop and call me Francis?"

"Yes, Your Exc... sorry, yes Francis." The knight by the door answered in perfect English and Pete uncannily realised then, without knowing how, that they were the two knights which the Pope had referred to earlier, the knights who were going to travel with them. Wow! What an uncanny coincidence, Peter thought. From the one hundred knights slaughtered that day, the only two who had survived were the two who were delegated to travel with them. Or was it a coincidence? Had, somehow, a higher power become involved? At that point, nothing, he thought, would have surprised him. But he felt a sense of security in knowing that perhaps a divine power was keeping an eye on all of them.

"I'd like to introduce you to Hughes de Payens." Francis said, with his arm resting on the shoulder of the knight by the door.

"I'm very humbled to meet the distant relative of the renowned, most honourable, Knights Templar." Peter said.

The knight looked incredulously at Peter, and both somehow knew from that moment they would become good friends.

"What do you know of us Knights?" Hughes de Payeus asked.

"My knowledge of the legendary Knights Templar is fairly significant. From early childhood I read everything I could about their history. I would read for hours on end about their valour and heroics. Their Order first began in 1119 when a French nobleman persuaded the King to establish an Order of knights to protect pilgrims on their journeys to Holy Places. They became the first 'warrior monks' who used swords and who trained hard to eventually become the most elite fighting force of their day. The Knights Templar were well equipped, deeply motivated, chivalrous and skilled in all the arts of combat. They were highly respected by all and deeply feared by their enemies. I particularly remember reading about one of their Patrons, Clairvaux, who stated that, 'A Templar Knight is truly a fearless knight, and secure on every side, for his soul is protected by the armour of faith, just as his body is protected by armour of steel. He is thus doubly armed and need not fear either daemon or men.'

"Later, in 1139, Pope Innocent II declared in a 'Papal ball, "The Knights Templar can pass freely through any border, owed no taxes, and were subject to no one's authority except that of the pope."

"That's impresswive." Said Hughes de Payeus.

"I'm also pleased you're so well read, Peter, but gentlemen, we really do need to move on," said Francis. "We have a long way to go and much yet to do."

Chapter Twenty-Two

The journey back to London was uneventful. That was fortunate, Peter thought, since it meant nobody was likely to know of their intentions. Also, he was able to use the time to acquaint himself with the two knights, Hugh and Godfrey.

Godfrey spoke with very high regard about Hugh. He told Peter that Hugh had the reputation of being a great knight and prided himself in his strict observance of the five points of chivalry. In every aspect of his life Hugh was the pinnacle of humility, piety, integrity, loyalty and honesty. However, he did tend to disobey orders, although he also had a tremendous resolve to get, when instructed, assignments completed and would fight to his death to guard his faith and his friends. Other than that, he had a wonderful sense of humour and was afraid of nothing.

When Peter later asked Hugh about Godfrey, strangely, he got an almost identical description. The only difference, it seemed, was that Godfrey was rather more responsible and had a somewhat more serious disposition.

The two knights seemed to get on well. They both very much had a great respect for each other. Godfrey, with his deeper sense of responsibility, was a stabilizing influence for Hugh and Hugh's best traits appealed to Godfrey whom at times, wished he could have been more like his friend. He wished, Peter sensed, to be a little more rebellious and less disciplined, and even to sometimes have a more relaxed approach to the world.

Amalialad waited in the hotel reception for Peter and his new travelling friends.

Peter smiled widely when he saw Amalialad and warmly shook his hand.

"Boy, I'm glad to be back, Amalialad. I've missed you, old chap."

Amalialad smiled.

"I've missed you too, Peter. How was the trip back?" Amalialad asked.

"Great, there were no hiccups on the way, if that's what you mean. Quite a pleasant journey actually."

"Let's talk further upstairs, gentlemen." Amalialad led the way up the stairs to a large suite of rooms.

Seated at a large dining table were Tara, Ben and Chodon.

Although they were given a warm welcome, Peter immediately sensed something was not quite right and suspected something urgent needed to be said and so he quickly sat down at the far end of the table, and invited Francis, Hugh and Godfrey to do likewise.

"Good friends," Amalialad said, "much has happened over the last twenty-four hours. Those of us waiting here have been fully aware of everything you've recently experienced. Luckily this was relayed to me telepathically from Lopsang" Amalialad looked sympathetically at each person who'd just arrived. "Everything you've suffered. And I'm so very sorry for your loss. I can only imagine the grief you must feel. And I know that no words I say can even get close to describe the emotions you've experienced or have now. However, as you know, events could have been worse. Fortunately, Lopsang was able to communicate with one of the cardinals, who was able to warn the rest, so they were able to escape through a secretly concealed side door to safety. I'm happy to tell you that they're now back, safely accommodated in the Vatican."

"Thank you, Amalialad. That's such an enormous relief to us all," Francis said.

Peter wondered how it was possible for Lopsang to get a message to the pope in such a short time. From the moment he and Francis had walked out of there, they would've only had seconds to get out of the chapel. Puzzling he thought but then 'God walked in mysterious way.' He'd perhaps dwell on it more later.

"My friends, I now have grave news. While you've been away, we have investigated many strange incidents which have been reported to us by the Opus Dei and by Lopsang and his fellow monks. Most of these incidents have been identified as originating from Scotland, in an area in and around the

Cairngorms, more specifically to a small village called Braemar. And yesterday, our worst fears were confirmed. There's an unnatural black cloud formation above the area. And it's growing. We can only come to one conclusion. The dark forces are beginning to mass.

"And we must go and investigate. The whole area has been cloaked by some inexplicable, demonic source. We can't even use the astral plane to penetrate it. But we must find out what's happening. It's crucial we find out, so our only option now is to travel by conventional means. It won't be easy. This area is not linked by any roads, so the only access is by a small, narrow path up the side of the mountain. Although we feel that they'll be closely guarded by Shadow Runts and their demonic allies and used by them to expand further outwards into the rest of Scotland."

"So," Ben interrupted, "are you saying we should all travel there together to reconnoiter the area, as it were, and expect not to be noticed?"

"No, Ben," Amalialad said. "Expect to be noticed but pray that we're not. They will outnumber us, so we would be unwise to allow ourselves to be seen. Well there's nothing more we can do here so we will meet again at Braemar Lodge Hotel."

"I understand," Ben answered. Thinking it could turn out badly, he made a mental decision to stay close to Tara. This was going to be dangerous and he didn't want

Chodon saw Tara and nodded in acknowledgement and smiled back.

"We leave at six tomorrow morning," Amalialad said. "So, may I suggest you all eat and get to know each other then get an early night. Peter, before you go, may I speak with you, please?" The rest of the group stood up and left for the restaurant on the ground floor.

"Of course, you may."

"Wonderful. If you follow me, Peter, I'd like to talk more."

Amalialad led Peter to an adjoining, small, sparsely furnished room.

"Please sit down, Peter." Amalialad gestured to the sofa. "I'm aware of most of the events you experienced and before I ask you to give me your own account of what happened, I'd like you to know how very proud I am to have you by our side, supporting us in our struggle, at great danger to yourself. Your bravery was impressive. Thank you, my good friend."

Peter swallowed hard, embarrassed.

"Thank you, Amalialad. Your praise is much appreciated, and I feel humbled and very honoured, but really it wasn't that bad. Your appreciation is much appreciated." Amalialad smiled again. Then Peter told him what had happened in Paris.

Amalialad listened carefully, without interruption. At times he raised his eyebrows in surprise, but he said nothing until Peter had finished.

Peter passed a small box to Amalialad. Amalialad looked closely at it then placed it in his trouser pocket without comment.

"Peter, the world moves in mysterious ways. My whole being hates the idea of physical violence and abuse. The idea of hurting any living thing is abhorrent to me and goes against everything I believe in. Even though, as my friend Lopsang reminded me recently, we're fighting the dead, it doesn't feel right. A man once said, 'to protect the peace we must prepare for war' and I think that's what we must do now. We must destroy an evil that this world has never encountered before. To protect everything that is good we must first fight and defeat that which is evil and be ready to die." Peter nodded and continued to listen.

"We think the enemy is using a disused church for its base. The church has been in the small, Scotttish village of Tarbet for decades but the place is so isolated and the weather so bad in the winter that it was eventually left to rack and ruin. Later it came to be used as a bunk house for travelers. It's an ideal base for Satan and his forces, since the exploitation of such a sacred dwelling enhances his power. We can expect to find it completely desecrated. The church is a symbol for goodness, love and peace and wherever these are overcome, it's a victory for Satan. I think what we're facing now is the first battle. I don't think it's just a scouting force. Satan is in a hurry to vanquish all of mankind and he doesn't want to allow us time to prepare, so he's sending a force of legions to test us. I don't know how many. But there are six thousand in a legion. Each legion is led by a demon, and, depending on which daemon, the number of legions they're in control of will vary. It could be anything between nine and one hundred."

"Bloody hell." cried Peter, "You mean to say we could potentially be facing one hundred legions? That's six hundred thousand demonic entities."

"No. If only that were so. I'm saying that if all the daemons were to arrive led by Satan himself, we might be facing over forty million malevolent lost souls."

Peter reflected on this. "Let's hope you're wrong and it's a small scouting group."

"Indeed, my good friend, let's pray that is the case, because if it isn't…"

"Then our chances are not good."

"So, what's the plan?" Peter asked.

Amalialad told Peter that only Lopsang and Ben knew the plan. Once he'd told Peter, then if any of the four of them were killed, at least someone else would know the plan. But not everyone in the group could know of it, in case they were captured, tortured, and talked. Amalialad just hoped at least one of the four survived.

Peter was then told it was too risky for the whole group to travel together and he'd need to lead a second group on a separate journey, but not to Tarbet.

"Peter, I need you, Francis, and the knights to do something of crucial importance. It will be another arduous task, even more dangerous than the one you've just returned from. But I have no choice and the outcome of our main battle ahead will rely on the success of it."

Peter swallowed hard.

"When I saw Francis and the two knights arrive with you, Peter," said Amalialad. "I knew that the task I'm now giving was ordained. I can't really explain so that you'd fully understand, Peter, but the knights will be the key to your success. Francis will travel with you once again. When you go downstairs to eat, I'll talk to him. We'll be talking until the early hours so don't expect him until late morning, just before you leave. I'll need his help in organising the military corps of the Opus Dei. There will be a lot of fighting ahead so I'll need their support. I've organized six groups in all for our mission."

Peter wondered who the six groups were but didn't bother to ask. He knew if he needed to know then Amalialad would have told him.

"So, what is our task?" Peter asked.

Amalialad looked at Peter with sadness in his eyes.

"Peter, I'm asking the impossible of you. I'm asking you to find what hundreds of academics and religious scholars have tried to do but failed. Even in decades of searching, they have failed. I'm asking you to find the most powerful and divine sought-after holy relic that has ever existed. Peter, you must find it within one month and I expect you to fail. But I hope with all my heart, and I pray with every molecule of my being, to the forfeit of my own soul, if necessary, that you succeed."

"So, what is it we're to find?"

Chapter Twenty-Three

"I need you to find the Ark of the Covenant."

"Wow, that's not an easy task. I'm not even sure it exists."

Peter knew that the Ark of the Covenant was supposed to be a huge golden chest which contained two sacred gold tablets inscribed with the Ten Commandments. But more importantly, he knew it was renowned for its supernatural ability to create storms, produce divine fire, destroy buildings and city walls and wipe out armies. It was supposedly able to summon angels and call for the presence of God himself. It could be very useful, assuming, of course, it really existed. He knew that there were several theories about where it could be found but searches had been unsuccessful. If he had such a short time frame he'd really need to know where the actual hiding place was. Somewhere he'd read about the Knights Templar having something to do with the Ark at some point in history and he hoped that perhaps his friends could throw some light on the subject. He'd ask them that night.

"Do you know where to look, old boy?"

"My friend, I wish I knew but I don't. I could guess but that's all it would be, and it may lead you to the wrong place. I've even tried using the astral plane to find it but the plane does not show the whereabouts of divine relics. For some reason they are invisible to our searches. I think if they are not meant to be found then they won't be."

"Well, wouldn't that assumption apply to us, too? In which case we wouldn't be able to find it either."

"That's very probable, my friend, I'm sorry. I said your mission was impossible but sometimes the impossible is made possible and I'm hoping for a miracle. As I said, the knights are the key to your success. Talk to them. I'm hoping that you will find the answers." Peter nodded and hoped so too. "Go and eat, my friend. Enjoy what little time you have left here tonight with your friends. Then tomorrow you can start your journey on a full stomach and with an alert mind."

The others were already half way through their meals, but all greeted Peter as he came in. Peter simply smiled and then sat down at the far end of the table. His mind was fixed on the complexities of the task ahead. He had some ideas but decided to consult Hugh and Godfrey in the morning about their viability. However, knowing he must eat before the journey the next day Peter broke away from his thoughts. He ordered some food, ate quickly, made his excuses and retired to his room. He needed to just relax and calmly collect his thoughts. It might, he considered, be the last opportunity in a while to do so. He reflected on what Amalialad told him during their conversation.

"You have a special skill of perception, my friend. This ability will protect you in some perilous situations ahead. Your heightened senses will enable you to be much more aware of your surroundings than the others. You will soon even, as you develop this ability, be able to hear the grass being trodden by small creatures, a mile away. You will be able to hear the distant movement of mice as they scurry through the corn and smell the scent of flowers in the distance, even when the wind is moving away from you, and you will be able to feel the moisture in the air before the pending rain."

"But how could you possibly know this?"

"It seems, Peter, that there are some things that, from time to time, enter my thoughts, which I know to be true. Is this a gift which I have? No, not always, since the revelations I get aren't always pleasant ones, but they come from the very core of my being and I just know their authenticity. However, my good friend, it's for you to accept what I tell you or not."

It was indeed quite a revelation, Peter thought. He was aware his senses were good but he'd had no idea he had the potential to harness this to such a degree. But the realisation was comforting and he was excited. He eagerly looked forward to using his new-found skills and decided he'd spend as much time as possible in practicing and developing them. As he imagined using them, he slowly drifted into a deep sleep.

Fast asleep, Peter wasn't aware of the dark grey eyes, staring in at him through the small bedroom window.

Chapter Twenty-Four

The ring tones screeched loudly, and Ben awoke with a start. It had just turned 7 a.m. He reached over and turned off the alarm on his mobile phone. He was sweating profusely.

He'd just woken from the most terrible night terror he could ever remember having. But it was worse than that, he'd felt it was also a premonition. If so, he was about to be involved in a deadly battle against the most hideous and cruelest creatures one could ever imagine. And the outcome he saw was death. Ben tried to convince himself that it was just a bad dream and put the experience to the back of his mind. But it lingered, lurking in his subconscious.

Amalialad had given him instructions to travel to Braemar, a small village situated in the centre of the Cairngorms National Park. Tara and Chodon would accompany him. Amalialad would be monitoring and travelling with other groups. Ben was simply informed that there would be others, like them, who'd be rendezvousing later near Braemar.

Tara had booked three tickets to Edinburgh, so they'd need to be at Heathrow Airport by about 11 a.m. to be in good time to catch the 2:20 p.m. flight. From there they'd hire a car and travel to Braemar. It all, she thought, seemed straightforward.

Peter met Hugh and Godfrey in the reception area.

Simultaneously, both Hugh and Godfrey looked at each other in shock. Peter noticed their expressions immediately but decided to wait for one of them to speak first.

"I'm sorry," Hugh said. "But Godfrey and I were aware that this day would eventually come, although we weren't looking forward to it."

"What do you mean?" Peter asked.

Hugh and Godfrey looked at each other again. Peter observed a slight nod from Godfrey towards his friend before Hugh answered.

"We know where the Ark of the Covenant is hidden."

Peter stared at the two knights, trying to collect his thoughts.

Ben interrupted them with a tray of coffees. Although, the airport departure lounge was very busy Peter, Hugh and Godfrey, eventually sat, across the table opposite Ben and the girls.

"Bloody thing, it's useless!" Ben remarked in frustration. "I can never open these packets. I'm sure they purposefully see me coming and give me the ones with no slits at the side." The girls laughed.

"Here!" Tara said. She took the small packet of powdered milk away from Ben. "Let me do it. You just need a little more patience." With ease she opened it and poured its contents into Ben's cup.

"Ah, you're a typical man." Chodon chuckled.

Ben started laughing too. He felt happy that the girls could laugh at such trivial things. It enabled them to momentarily forget about the danger ahead.

"So, the hire car will be waiting for us at the airport then?" asked Ben.

"For the third time, yes, Ben," said Tara.

"Great. I'm sorry, but I'm just trying to make sure that our journey goes as smoothly as possible."

"I understand, but don't worry."

Suddenly, they were all interrupted by the voice coming from the airport lounge Tannoy. There would be an hour's delay. They later found out that the delay was due to an unusually large congestion of traffic going into Edinburgh airport. and they eventually walked into the terminal arrival section at 5:15 p.m., nearly two hours later instead of the estimated one. All were frustrated but they then decided to waste no further time but to find the Hertz Customer Service desk. Eventually, the receptionist called them over.

"I'm sorry, miss, but our records show you cancelled this booking just over an hour ago, so we allocated the vehicle to somebody else, only two minutes ago in fact. The cancellation was authorised since the caller could provide the booking number and date of booking and we did then, as our policy dictates, wait the necessary hour before selling it on. The person also gave your name and date of birth. We had no reason to assume it wasn't genuine, miss, I'm so sorry."

"I knew it!" Ben said. "It's just too much to expect for anything to run smoothly isn't it?" He knew his frustration wouldn't help, but he was the only one who knew of the scheduled 8 p.m. meeting at the hotel. The knowledge of the meeting was given on a need to know basis and only one, in this case, Ben, needed to know, to lead the others there. And it was crucial they made it.

"Well, have you got another vehicle available?" asked Tara. She knew it was pointless arguing with the receptionist since she was rushed off her feet and could only make sense on what showed up on her computer screen. But two things deeply concerned Tara. She was the only one who'd kept the details of the vehicle booking. She hadn't even shown anybody else the paper confirmation. And her date of birth hadn't been on the booking slip. So how had this person known?

"Ah, yes you're very lucky. We've just had another cancellation. Very unusual."

At least they now had a car, thought Ben. That was the first bit of good news they'd had in a while.

But Ben was wrong again.

Chapter Twenty-Five

Peter was astounded. "What? Are you certain? Where is it?"

"I understand your excitement, Peter, but before we tell you, you need to understand the historical background to this and what you're facing. Those few who are aware of the whereabouts of the Ark are always in deep peril. We immediately put your life and those of your family at great risk. You would be threatened by everything that is evil. You would be sought after by the most sadistic and malicious of the dark forces. They'd torture you to the point of death to retrieve the information you have. They have no morals and are devoid of all emotion. They'd retrieve, by the worst torture imaginable, any information you have then kill you without a second thought, since they excel in slaughter and death. They are mindless men and women who desire only money for their depravity. So, Peter, please take your time to consider the consequences carefully before asking us."

"I understand your concerns, my friends, but I have no family left to worry about. They were all killed in an air accident seven years ago." Peter paused momentarily as he remembered waking up that morning to the radio alarm clock. He found himself listening to the headline news about the crash. The broadcaster had said that all the passengers were killed as the plane plunged into the side of a mountain over the Himalayas. Evidently, an unexpected freezing weather front appeared which had interfered with the satellite communication systems. Consequently, the pilot found he was flying blind and crashed. Peter's parents and younger sister were all on board. The only saving grace of that memory was that they'd died instantly. Until he met Amalialad life really hadn't been that important to him. He'd simply worked each day to survive. However, he was always determined to be positive, humorous and true to himself. He then faced Hugh directly and continued.

"I thank you for your warning. And I've already made promises that have attracted many of the dark forces you speak of, as you know. So please tell me of the whereabouts so that we can defeat this demonic scourge."

"I had no doubt of your answer Peter, but I was duty bound to ask," said Hugh.

"Of course, my friend, I understand that. Your commitment to duty is honorable and I respect you for that."

"Ok, I'll let Godfrey tell the story. He is more eloquent in such things and his memory is much clearer than mine."

"During the first ten years of the Knights Templars' existence," said Godfrey, "my predecessors spent most of the time digging under the Temple Mount, so we knew precisely the layout of tunnels and secret chambers established there, however, we were not privy to what was eventually stored there. Only the temple priests at the time had this information. Consequently, the knights of the Sepulchre were given the task, decades later, in 1867, to re-excavate the tunnels. However, we were still surprised to uncover tunnels which extended vertically from the Al Aqsa mosque. The tunnels stretched out for over twenty-five meters then spread even further, under the Dome of the Rock, which was the site of Solomon's Temple. In one of these tunnels we discovered a small secret chamber. The door was extremely well camouflaged with the tunnel wall. We wouldn't have discovered it but for one of our brothers who'd felt a strong urge to look in that direction and noticed a small speck of light coming from under the door. It took five men to open the door. But then suddenly the earth shook, and a mass of bright, pulsating light came from nowhere and shone fiercely outwards. The brothers screamed as they became completely blinded, but at that moment of blindness, their pain mysteriously left them, and they felt what they described at the time as, 'a beautiful, spiritual peace and oneness with God'. They instantly, at that moment, knew of their future roles. From that moment they were the Bearers of the Ark of the Covenant. As others entered, one of the blinded brothers called out to warn them not to touch the Ark which was in the center of the room. The Bearer quickly explained how only he and his other four blinded Bearers could touch it and that for others to do so would mean instant blindness and everlasting pain or even death. He then smiled in awe as he described how the love of God had entered his soul and went on to explain that each of them held no anger at what happened to them but, quite the contrary, described their experiences as being honorable and humbling. It was then solely their task to carry the Ark wherever it needed to go." Godfrey paused momentarily to collect his thoughts before moving on. "The months ahead, Peter, proved this prophecy to be true. A remarkable man named Ralph de Sudely was our leader at the time and with his careful strategy and painstaking planning the Ark slowly made its way across many lands to England. Ralph de Sudely brought it back to his estate in Herdewyke in Warwickshire. As you know our Order was brutally disbanded by Pope Clement V in 1312. The scheming King Phillip of France had convinced the pope that the Templars had committed foul acts of depravity and that they'd robbed people of their money and possessions. Consequently, the Pope, because his election was strongly supported by the king, reluctantly decided to disband the Order. But that's another story

Peter and Hugh looked at each other but said nothing. Godfrey had quietly drifted off into thought midway through speech and they noticed tears on the side of his cheeks.

Godfrey coughed before speaking again. "Ah, hmm, now, where was I? Ah, yes. Well, the Ark remained hidden at his estate for many years. Later, the Templars were ordered to take it to Roslyn Chapel in Scotland for safe keeping. The owner, hmm, I think it was someone from one of the McDonalds' clans, had built a secret underground tunnel to store it in. However, in 1210, our brothers received another order to redirect the Ark further north to Glamis Castle instead. Evidently a change of mind had directed that the tunnel which was specially made to hide the Ark was to be used instead for something else. We later found out that a Holy Relic of almost equal importance was to be placed there. However, at that time we had no idea what that was."

"Ah, yes, Godfrey," Peter said "Dan Brown wrote that book, The Da Vinci Code. It was a bestseller and the movie which followed was an enormous success too. I believe he suggested that the Holy Grail may be hidden at Roslyn Chapel?"

"Indeed, he did, and it may well have been. But so was the Ark of the Covenant meant to be there and indeed was there for a time," said Godfrey. "But it was thought that a scholar might be able to follow the clues hidden within the sculptures and paintings throughout the chapel and its grounds and would likely discover its hiding place. So, it was decided to move it quickly elsewhere. As I say, to Glamis Castle in Angus, Scotland.

"The earl had a secret chamber which he allowed us to use for its hiding place and promised that only he, his heir and benefactor would know of its existence and they all swore an oath of secrecy. Today, that oath still holds but the estate is now owned by John Bowes-Lyon, nineteenth Earl of Strathmore. And today the estate is open to the public, so getting in, finding and taking the Ark, is not going to be an easy task, my friends. We can't afford to arouse any suspicion."

"Well, how did you get the Ark there in the first place? Did you organize a diversion of some sort to get it past the staff and visitors?" asked Peter.

"Yes, we did, a large fire was started and although it did get rather out of hand, hmm," Godfrey briefly paused to recollect, "and more damage was done than we'd wished for... well, the task was accomplished successfully."

"Ah," said Hugh, "it's said that history repeats itself. Let's just use the same ploy."

"A great idea!" said Peter.

"I must agree," said Godfrey. "It will require careful planning, of course, but it could work."

"We'd need to study the layout of the castle and the estate," said Hugh.

"No problem," said Peter. "We should be able to get them from the local library or even the local university archives."

"Ok, so let's look at the details of the Ark more carefully too, so we can work out a way of transporting it to the Cairngorms," said Hugh.

They agreed to book a hotel in Forfar, which was only about five miles from Glamis Castle where they'd spend time their working out a plan of action. They could talk about the basics along the way. Peter suggested they got a flight to Edinburgh and then hired a vehicle from there to take them on to Forfar. But then he strangely felt something odd. His body began to shiver for no apparent reason and he felt quite uncomfortable without being able to pin point the reason. He sensed it was a warning of some kind. He knew that Lopsang and Amalialad had ways of communicating somehow in this way and wondered if they had anything to do with it. To be on the safe side, he suggested that Hugh and Godfrey hire a separate vehicle and travel a different route. Then, if for some reason either party were attacked, the other could continue with the plan.

Peter used his iPad to find the hotel, it was only about 116km to Forfar and he estimated it should take about one and half hours by car. He suggested Hugh and Godfrey take a different route and meet them at the hotel later. Even though they were on the same flight he suggested that they pretend not to know each other, and everyone agreed it was a good idea. Shortly after, they wished each other good luck then separated and went their own ways.

Peter booked everything online. And their flight to Edinburgh was due from Heathrow in four hours, at 4:30 p.m.

Later, after collecting their bags, they walked together into the arrivals lounge. An Avis Hire representative, carrying a small banner with Peter's name on it, met them there. Hugh had spotted him first and gestured to the others to walk towards the man. He was about average height with brown hair. He wore the Avis company blazer with a large yellow and black logo on his left breast pocket and a bright white shirt with a black and yellow striped tie. A big grin seemed to be fixed to his round face. This must have been a company policy Peter thought, chuckling.

"Goo., good morn., good morning, gent., gentlemen."

"Good morning. Where shall I sign?" Peter asked the representative. The man produced a clip board with a sheet of paper for Peter to sign.

"Just show me where the vehicle is, and we'll be on our jolly old way." The man understood that Peter was trying to avoid any further embarrassment on his behalf, by speaking, and simply gave Peter the car keys and led him to the vehicle. As they walked out of the terminal the representative gestured to the right. They all looked in that direction and noticed a small parking area with about four cars each boot large enough to hold their luggage. The man walked over to one of the vehicles, a large Volvo, pointeded to the car and left waving goodbye. The friends understood and smiled, waving back at the same time. Peter unlocked the car and they all got in. He'd especially asked for this vehicle because he used to own one and knew it handled well. He also knew it was solid, unstoppable, comfortable and dependable. They decided to set off immediately to get clear of the airport and agreed to head straight for the Stag Hotel.

But everything did not run smoothly.

Chapter twenty-six

Ben set the GPS for the Braemar Lodge Hotel. It was situated on the edge of Braemar village in Aberdeen shire, fifty-eight miles west of Aberdeen in the heart of the Cairngorms National Park. Ben noted that as well as Braemar Castle it was also close to Balmoral Castle in Royal Deeside. He glanced at his watch. It was 5:35 p.m. He knew he'd have to drive fast to get there in time for the meeting. Amalialad hadn't said much to him other than he should be very cautious and, if possible, not to stop for anyone on the way. Ben had the feeling at the time that Amalialad wanted to say more.

Ben knew dark forces were afoot. Amalialad had explained how strange sightings and mysterious occurrences had been reported by the residents, tourists and members of the Opus Dei who were working in the area, throughout the small villages in and surrounding the Cairngorms. Unrecognizable creatures and inexplicable sounds had been reported. The incidents had spread and were now even happening in broad daylight. That could only mean one thing, Ben guessed. The creatures were no longer worried about being seen because their numbers were growing and so was their confidence. Before moving off he switched on the GPS and typed in the coordinates of the hotel. The live visual which appeared showed a bird's eye view of the hotel and the surrounding grounds. Ben relaxed. He couldn't see anything out of place. But something just didn't feel right. He must be getting paranoid, he thought and dismissed it. He spoke to the girls.

"Ok, we're off ladies. Just check your essentials." Tara and Chodon felt the wooden crosses which were discreetly hung from their necks. The crosses had been blessed earlier with holy water by a personal close friend of Tara's father who also happened to be a priest. They then checked their small, black string pouches, which were in their purses, to make sure the rock salt was still dry inside. Tara looked at Chodon who nodded her acknowledgement.

"Everything's fine here," said Tara.

"Wonderful!" said Ben. He meant it too. Natural salt was more effective than any man-made weapon could ever be. He knew pure, natural salt repelled any demonic force. Salt had always been used as a preservative and natural anesthetic which has always been used as a purifying agent in folk magic. In many religions too, salt was used for baptisms. In Catholicism, Ben knew, for he had experienced it during his own baptism, salt was put on the lips of a child during the ceremony as a symbol of wisdom. For now, Ben was simply happy that he could drive straight to the hotel without fear of any psychic attack. An attack from any one of the dark entities lurking outside would threaten their mission. The salt and crosses would deter them.

Not far to go now, Ben thought, as he glanced at the digital milometer on his dashboard. They were only about six miles from the village of Braemar. Then, unexpectedly, Ben felt a sudden loss in acceleration. He put his foot down harder on the throttle, but it wouldn't respond. The car just spluttered aggressively and came to a grinding halt.

"Oh, shit!"

The girls sat bolt upright.

"What's happened?" asked Tara.

"We've broken down. I don't understand it. I know the car was fully checked out before we had it, and this make of vehicle rarely breaks down. This is very puzzling."

"But we have broken down?"

"Yes. Stay in the car. I'm going to look at the engine and try to work out why."

"No," said Tara. "I'm coming with you. Someone needs to watch your back. You know it makes sense"

Ben knew she meant it. She was so feisty and independent. But wasn't it that part of her character which attracted him to her in the first place, he thought. It hurt him. He knew that whatever he said or did, she would go her own way. She'd make her own final decisions. It was painful for him. He knew he'd be devastated if anything ever happened to her. His world would totally collapse, and his grief would be eternal. He loved her so very much. The churning he felt in his stomach whenever he thought of her, when she was away from him, was a constant reminder of just how much he missed her when she wasn't around.

"Ok. I understand. I'm sorry. You're right." He popped the hood and they both got out to look. The engine hadn't overheated, which was weird. He carefully checked the rest of the engine. Very strange, he thought. Nothing seemed out of place. Everything seemed fine to him. But then he leaned forward, further into the engine area and felt the fuel lines. He stepped back, bewildered.

"What is it, Ben?" Tara asked. Ben looked at her in dismay.

"That's impossible!"

"Why, what have you seen?"

"The fuel lines are frozen solid."

"What? How could that have happened?"

"I don't know. There's no possible earthly explanation for it. They should be very warm, even hot, yet they're frozen."

"Ben!"

"What?"

"You said no earthly explanation!" said Tara slowly.

"Oh, no! Hurry, Tara, get back into the car." Tara hastily climbed into the back as Ben closed the door behind her. He pulled a pouch out of his front pocket and immediately poured the contents around the vehicle. He then got into the vehicle himself. Ben had allowed a space of a meter from the salt circle to the vehicle. He hoped that would be enough. It was seconds later when they first heard the shrieking sounds coming from the trees, and saw five gruesome creatures, led by a tall, disfigured nighthawk, hobbling towards them into the clearing. The creatures came to an abrupt halt at the edge of the salt circle but some, more eager creatures began to shriek fiercely. They quickly stepped back. Then suddenly the creatures started howling, like a choir singing in unison, their high piercing sounds echoing across the woodlands and surrounding area. More creatures arrived, and it became obvious to everyone sitting, frightened, inside the car, that the creatures' high piercing noises were signals to beckon others.

Ben switched on the GPS and used its phone application to ring Amalialad. But there was no signal. He got out his mobile phone and tried ringing him again. But, once again there was no signal. No sounds at all. The lines were completely dead.

"The salt will protect us from those monsters, so don't worry," said Tara.

Chodon smiled. "I'm not afraid." she said.

"Surely they'll give up soon?" asked Tara. But, unusually, Ben said nothing, and Tara knew then that something was wrong.

"Ok, Ben, tell me, what is it?"

"What?"

"Don't try to play clever with me, Ben. We've had this argument before. You're not telling us something. Now what is it?"

"Um, well. Er..." Ben said. At that moment he looked out of the window.

"Oh my God!"

"What now?" asked Tara.

"The creatures are counting the grains of salt. That's what I was worried about."

"Why, the salt will protect us, won't it?" she asked.

"It will," said Ben. "That is, unless, according to folklore, the daemon manages to count precisely every single grain of salt. If it does, it can pass through."

"But that's impossible, surely?" said Tara. "Isn't it?"

"Well, normally, yes, virtually impossible. That's because normally, a lot more salt would be used for this type of protection."

"But?" asked Tara, emphasizing the word. "What else are you not telling us?"

"Hmm, unfortunately, I didn't have that much salt in my pouch and so the salt wasn't as much as I'd liked. I'd have used a couple of buckets full if only I'd had that much."

"So, how long have we got then, do you think, before one of the creatures counts the grains and gets through to us?" said Tara.

"Ah, well, if they have enough creatures, I'd say we've got about eight hours. But that's a conservative estimate."

"I see, so we may even have about ten hours, is that right?"

"Yes, that's right."

"Ah well, that's much better, isn't it?" said Tara.

"I'm sorry, Tara. But I'm not perfect. I had to act quickly."

"I'm sorry, Ben. It's not your fault. I'm sure I'd have made the same mistake myself. I'm just a little tired."

"You never need to apologize to me, Tara. It's completely understandable how you feel. For what it's worth, I think you're one of the bravest people I've ever had the honour to know. We'll get out of this scrape ok, so just don't worry. Have you contacted Amalialad yet?"

"Yes, but only a few seconds ago. Something was blocking my thoughts. Anyway, he's on his way but he says he's not able to astral project now for fear of raising the alarm to any dark entities roaming around the astral plane. Some can sense activity on that plane and distinguish between good and evil. He says he can't risk losing the main battle ahead through an error of judgement."

"Ok, that's logical. Anyway, I'm sure he'll be here soon." But once again Ben had a most uncomfortable feeling that Amalialad wouldn't make it in time.

Chapter Twenty-Seven

Amalialad had stayed on at the hotel. Lopsang had visited him soon after and they sat in Amalialad's room drinking iced water as the calming scent from the Tibetan incense Amalialad had lit a few minutes earlier wafted invisibly around them. Amalialad had sensed Lopsang had been keeping a watch on some of the proceedings earlier from the astral plane. He didn't mind. Having a guardian angel at hand, especially in these dark days, felt reassuring.

"The news doesn't get any better, Your Holiness." Amalialad had long since given up on asking Lopsang to call him Amalialad. In any case they'd always met in private so nobody else was at hand to listen in. He was also aware that Lopsang would always wear a special amulet around his neck when they met, which he knew would ward off any efforts from any uninvited visitors, good or evil, who tried to listen in or observe them from the astral or any other plane.

"They're coming," said Lopsang, sadly. "And we have very little time to finish our preparations. At this moment we don't know how many, but the sightings have dramatically increased. As expected, they've sent out a scouting group of fiendish creatures including hob goblins, pixies, and shadow warriors led by frenzied Nighthawks and they're brutally killing anything that gets in their way. These devilish creatures are now stronger than ever before, and they've been committing the most diabolical acts. And what worries me most is that they're not concerned about being seen. This led us to suspect a demon from the higher realm is behind their movements. Like most generals in charge of their forces he remains watching, but at bay, looking no doubt from a safe vantage point ready to lead the first, and perhaps, if we can't stop them, the final battle which will destroy all of mankind."

"Hmm, a daemon, you say?" asked Amalialad.

"I know what you're about to ask, but we don't know who the daemon is."

"That's unfortunate," said Amalialad. He knew, as he'd briefly explained to Peter earlier, that depending on which daemon was leading them, the outcome of the battle may be indicated, since each daaemon had control of several legions. If it was a daemon controlling a hundred legions then they'd have very little hope of defeating them since they'd be facing over 600,000 soldiers, that's 600,000 demonic creatures. And not the ordinary creatures that were sent to roam and spy either, but they would be the darkest, vicious and most frightening entities with almost double the strength of the average creature or human. They were in fact humans who've been possessed by their host demon, and depending on which daemon that is, so reflects their strength, determination and ferocity.

"We can only hope it's a daemon of lower rank. A demon with only a few legions under his command," said Lopsang.

"Yes, of course. But the fewest number of legions are with Cimeies, the ruler of all spirits in Africa, and he has twenty legions under his command."

Lopsang sighed.

"Yes, that's true. And even if it were so, that's 60,000 soldiers of Satan's forces, can we even defeat that many?" Amalialad asked.

"Your Holiness," he looked directly at Amalialad, "that's why we need you. We don't have the answers."

"Why do you think they're here, in one of the remotest areas of Scotland?" asked Amalialad. He suspected why but wondered if Lopsang had reached a different conclusion.

"My fellow monks, high Lamas and I, together with leaders of other denominations, have studied the reports very carefully and we've come to the same conclusion. Firstly, it's obvious that Satan has breached a portal into our world. That's how the creatures have so easily crept into it. We are all here, as you know, because we linked most of the sightings around the Cairngorms. But the Cairngorms are huge, and we needed to define the precise point where this port hole may be."

"Well, I think I know," said Amalialad. Lopsang looked up at him in surprise.

"Really, master? Where would that be?" Lopsang asked, hardly able to contain his excitement. He was surprised at what Amalialad said, since he and his peers had spent ages trying to identify a place within the Cairngorms where the portal might be, but in vain. Even though he and his fellow monks had travelled the width and breadth of the bulk of the astral plane, virtually across the whole area, looking for anything unusual, they had been unsuccessful. Apart from the occasional appearance of the odd mountaineer trekking the mountain peaks, there was no activity at all.

"Ben Macdul," said Amalialad simply. "We'll find the portal at the peak of Ben Macdul." Lopsang looked at him incredulously.

"How can that be? We searched thoroughly and apart from the occasional climber, we saw nothing unusual," said Lopsang. Amalialad smiled.

"My friend, as you well know, more than most, the demon is cunning and deceitful. For over a hundred years this daemon has guarded the peaks of Ben Macdul, delegating one of his lieutenants to guard the area. We now know he chose a loyal soldier with special skills. A demonic creature charged with striking terror into anybody or anything that got too close to their portal. Although, if possible, the creature would avoid actual killing, in order not to attract too much attention. The task, after all, was to protect by deterring, not to attract."

"But why didn't we spot him during our search?" asked Lopsang. Amalialad smiled warmly at his friend again.

"We know how cunning the demon can be. Well, he's equally very clever. The soldier he chose, as I just mentioned, has special abilities. One special skill this one has, is that whenever he chooses, he's able to cloak himself against being observed, just like your amulet hides us from observers, this creature can sense the presence of goodness as some of us can also sense the presence of evil when it's around. Further, unlike most of the legions' soldiers who have a thirst for human blood and thrive on killing and the debauchery of it, this entity can completely control its emotions and urges. It's extremely loyal and the creature's orders take precedence over everything else. It will carry them out, if necessary, 'til time eternal, to get them done. And since, as we all know, we can never destroy these beings completely, we can only banish them back to Hell, our task is that much harder."

"I'm stunned, yet relieved that you've found the whereabouts of the portal," said Lopsang. "So, we can now find and block the portal."

"No, we mustn't do that yet. The lieutenant guarding the portal would immediately raise the alarm if he sees a build up of our forces," said Amalialad.

"So, what are we to do?" asked Lopsang.

"We must deal with the lieutenant of course," answered Amalialad.

"You mean banish him?" asked Lopsang.

"Yes, banish him. It'll be our only way to get through the portal. We have no choice." Lopsang nodded. He understood.

"How will you recognize him?"

"That's easy. He's over twenty feet tall and covered in dark wiry hair."

"How do you know that?"

"Because he's been guarding that place for hundreds of years and has often been seen by trekkers in that area. As I said, it's able to spread fear and panic into anybody who gets too close to the portal. It can telepathically project signals to a person's brain to scare them away. If it so wished, it could easily drive a person insane. Its name is Ferlie Mor, but people in the area know it as the Old Grey Man of Ben Macdul. It has become a popular legend in the area."

"This part of the puzzle may now have been solved, Lopsang, but something else still disturbs me greatly," said Amalialad.

"What's that?" asked Lopsang.

"Why is the gathering here? Why have the demonic forces chosen such a remote part of the Scottish Highlands to pitch their battle? What's the daemon's real target?" said Amalialad, although the remark was directed more to himself than to Lopsang.

Suddenly, the whole room shook.

"Get out, your Holiness! You must run quickly," shouted Lopsang as he tightly clutched his chest and cringed in pain. "Please, I beg you – run, run!"

Amalialad didn't question the command. Too much was at stake. He felt sick to his stomach that he hadn't stayed to find out what the threat was and help his friend, but he just knew the risk was too great and the urgency from Lopsang came from the core of his being. With lightning speed, Amalialad ran to the door, opened it and, without consideration, jumped over the banister to the hallway below, a drop of twelve feet. On landing, an instinctive involuntary reaction came into play. Amalialad felt that something friendly was physically guiding him. He rapidly spun and turned to his right, then jumped five feet into the air and dived, head first, through an open window. He tried to think on his feet. What the hell was after him? Was Lopsang ok? Who was helping him? No time to think about that now. He rolled twice as he hit the pavement and found his feet instinctively; he then sprang up and swiftly propelled himself forward into another run. Five minutes later he found himself completely lost and facing a small, terraced house in a narrow, side street. Above the door was a simple sign which read 'Chapel'. Amalialad sensed it was a safe place for him and walked in. And two things registered in his thoughts as he did so. He'd failed to help Lopsang and he'd also just let Ben, Tara and Chodon down, his closest friends, when he'd known that they were in desperate need of help and that now, due to his failure to be there, he'd cost his friends their lives.

And what's more he too may now be walking straight into a trap.

Chapter Twenty-Eight

For most of the journey, Peter followed the same route as Ben but veered off at Perth and headed along the M90 towards Forfar. It was a pleasant journey with some spectacular views of the highlands and rugged coastline. And the weather was just perfect, with a clear blue sky and bright sunshine.

"Did you manage to contact Tara?" Peter asked Francis.

"No, for some reason I'm just not getting through."

"Hmm, they may be out of range. The signal must be erratic occasionally up here," answered Peter. "I was hoping, that if they weren't too far from us, and they were running in good time, we could briefly meet up, but it seems unlikely now. Never mind, I'll try calling later."

As if on cue, a blanket of black clouds gathered overhead.

"There's a storm brewing, Peter, can you see it?"

"Yes, that's very unusual. The weather forecast earlier promised fine weather for the next two days." Peter slowed the car down and pulled over to the side of the road. As he stepped out of the car a fiercely cold wind blew against him and he sensed a gradual build-up of static around him. Although at that moment the storm was at bay, it was about to break. The air was thick and oppressive. And Francis, he now agreed, was correct in his assessment. It was going to be a huge storm. Peter decided to get straight back into the car and drive fast. He thought they may just make it to the hotel before the storm broke.

"You're right, Francis. It's going to be big."

"Huh, when do they ever get the weather right?" Francis asked.

"Well, just the same, it's unusual."

They were only a mile away from the hotel, just on the outskirts of Forfar, when the air around them suddenly thickened. Peter sensed it wasn't fog. Neither was it natural. Francis sat up straight.

"This is weird, isn't it?" Francis said.

"It's very weird. Stay alert. I'm not sure what we're facing here," Peter said. He was very concerned then and his instincts told him that danger was ahead, so he focused his senses.

Then the sky went black and the storm broke. And in that same moment Peter heard the distant shrieks. They sent a cold shiver down his spine and he felt thankful that Francis couldn't hear them yet. He knew they weren't human. He knew they had to act quickly, and when, a moment later, an inner sense of foreboding suddenly swelled up inside him, he also knew they were about to face something big, devilishly big.

"Get out!" Peter shouted. "Get out fast!"

Francis's reflexes were spectacularly fast, and he was out of the door running away from the vehicle before Peter even finished speaking. Peter was on Francis' heels, then past him, within seconds.

"Follow me!" But Francis didn't need prompting. He noticed Peter was carrying a large, thick, cotton sack, and he shivered. He knew exactly what was in it and what it was for, so he ran even faster.

As they reached the first few houses at the outer edge of the town, the shrieks became louder and more aggressive. But now they mingled with other ear-piercing, wolf-like howls. The creatures were coming, and Peter felt that whatever type they were, they were most definitely baying for blood. Francis also heard them. They came to a sudden standstill just outside a deserted building on the very periphery of the town. Peter's mind was spinning, sizing up their options. He knew he had to think quickly.

"In here, Francis!" he cried out. He ran up to a front door which someone had left slightly ajar and pushed it. It opened. Thank God, it was unlocked, he thought. They then heard the noises outside getting louder, and getting much, much closer.

"We've only got seconds!" shouted Peter. "I'll secure the inside windows, if you salt the floor."

"Ok," said Francis. He grabbed the sack from Peter, pulled out his knife from its leather sheath, which was attached to his belt, slashed open the knot at the top of the sack and spread the rock salt as evenly as possible around the inner walls of the ground floor. He then ran upstairs and spread another layer of salt around the first-floor landing so that it also sealed all bedroom doors.

The house was completely empty of furnishings, so Francis simply spilled the salt directly onto the wooden floorboards. He was very careful not to allow any gaps at all in the salt line. To do so would have meant death and damnation. Peter had spread salt around the windows.

It was then that the banging on the doors started. Luckily the doors were solid oak and were sturdy.

The terrifying noises outside gradually increased. Then they became louder still. It was frightening, and a growing sense of panic began to encroach upon them both. The horrific sounds erupted into one loud, screeching crescendo. Then it just stopped, and an eerie silence blanketed the whole area.

"That's strange," whispered Francis. "I wonder why they've gone quiet."

"I can only guess," Peter replied. As the silence came over them, Peter felt mild pulpatations in his head mingled with what he could only describe as perpetual static. They reminded Peter of a badly-tuned radio.

"I think the creatures need to be silent to pick up telepathic communications," said Peter.

"Really?" Francis was amazed that the creatures could do that. But he was even more surprised that Peter somehow knew. However, he decided not to ask about it. Some things, he thought, were best unsaid, and in any case, his faith in God told him there was a reason for everything and as far as he was concerned, they were all directed by God.

Francis had his knife ready. From a casual glance it just looked like a plain knife one could buy from any hardware store. But it was special. It had been given to him by the pope two years earlier. The pope had told him he'd blessed it and had simply asked him to keep it safe. Even though he thought it was a strange request, of course he didn't question it. Francis later discovered that the six-inch blade was made of a rare titanium alloy and the knife's hilt was made of bone. Which bone, he didn't know, but it was light in weight, comfortable to hold and the blade never needed sharpening. It was sharper than any razor. Francis would spend hours dropping cotton pieces onto the blade and watching them slice in two. He'd only once touched the blade, very delicately with his forefinger, to test it. He had pierced his skin. The blood ran from his forefinger to form a puddle on the floor.

"Can you see anything?" asked Francis. Peter was peering out of the lounge bay window.

"Yes. They're the most foul and diabolical creatures I've ever seen, and my skin is cringing at the sight of them. I couldn't even dream up such gruesome monstrosities. I'm quite serious, Francis, when I say the devil himself must have spawned them."

"I see." He carefully considered whether he really did wish to see them.

"That's very strange," Peter muttered. "They're now all moving in slow motion."

"Um, it's puzzling. I think we need to look at our options, Peter," Francis said. "They're limited, aren't they?

"Well, I think we're going to have to stay here tonight anyway. It's too dark out there, so it'll be too dangerous. We'd have no way of finding our way around. Said Peter.

"I agree. The salt sealing should stop them from coming in so it ought to be safe enough here, although it's very cold. Also, once this storm clears, we may get a signal, so we can call for help."

As Francis spoke, Peter could hear the pitter patter of the first drops of rain. Wonderful, he thought, it might send the creatures running for cover. Not because they'd get wet but there were salty elements in the rain itself which would cause them pain. Then the rain got heavier. They both looked out of the window. The creatures had gone. But the downfall got worse and they could see from the torchlight that there were heavy drops, the size of small coins, splattering the roof and grounds around them. They watched, intrigued, as the deluge continued to stream down. Powerful thunderclaps followed, splitting the blackness above and ripping the clouds apart, opening a window of light. Lightning blazed in quick strikes, as if strategically attacking the ground around them. Peter thought he could hear cries of pain as the strikes pounded the ground outside. It continued for over an hour. Then as quickly as the storm came, it vanished and with it the blackness and, finally, the normal, tranquil night sky returned. Peter and Francis continued to look out of the window for signs of movement. But there were none. Although they were sure that they were safe and could probably escape and reach the hotel, they decided to wait 'til daylight. They agreed it would be much safer and, in any case, they needed to sleep. They were both mentally and physically exhausted. They agreed to sleep in shifts so that one of them could stay on guard. They were facing a clever and deceitful foe and didn't dare risk being careless.

Daylight started sneaking through the window at about five the next morning. Francis was staring out at the scorched ground just beyond the walls of the house. He could make out some of the scattered, circular patches of black spots from the lightning. It just wasn't natural, he thought, it was extremely rare for such ferocity. But, more than that, it looked as if the strikes were calculated. Peter stirred awake.

"Do you see any movement?" he asked.

"Ah, good morning, Peter. No, everything seems ok."

"Wonderful. Let's get out of here, shall we?" Peter asked. "We can make our way to the hotel."

"Great. The first thing I'm going to do is have a hot shower. Then I'll order breakfast, with lots of tea. Then I need to make some calls."

"That sounds like a brilliant plan, my friend. After that we need to discuss strategies and formulate a plan of action. I hope Hugh and Godfrey are ok."

As they left the house, Peter raised his hand to cover his nose and mouth.

"Bloody hell, it stinks out here. Can't you smell it?"

"No," replied Francis.

He took a couple of deep sniffs. "I still can't smell anything."

They continued to walk down the pathway. Peter suddenly stopped and stooped down to look closely at one of the scorch marks. That's when the smell hit Francis too.

"Phew! That really stinks. I wonder what caused it? It can't just be the smell of burning?"

"What do you think it is?" Peter stared at Francis and waited for the realization to sink in.

"Of course. It's the creatures."

"Precisely." said Peter. There were far more than either of them had anticipated, of various shapes and sizes. But then the same thought struck them both and they looked at each other and smiled. It had now become obvious to both. They had help from a Higher Realm.

"God moves in mysterious ways," said Francis.

"Yes, he does," agreed Peter.

But then he wondered, what exactly was it that helped them? The thought played heavily on his mind.

Chapter Twenty-Nine

Ben silently cursed. Seven hours had passed and there was no sign of Amalialad. He knew there'd be a good reason for his absence and guessed that some type of emergency had cropped up. If that were the case, he hoped Amalialad would deal with it. But their situation was becoming desperate.

"They only have a few centimeters of thickness of salt left to count," shouted Tara. "What do you suggest we do, Ben?"

"Has anyone else got any ideas?" Ben asked. He hoped one of them could find a solution, but he also needed time to think. He had the crux of one but needed more time to work it out.

"Could we somehow distract one of the creatures doing the counting? The distraction may make it forget the last number it counted, and they'd all have to start the count again, wouldn't they?" said Chodon.

"That's a good idea but I see two possible problems," said Tara. "The first is that the creature may not forget the last number they counted and, of course, we can't afford to risk that. Secondly, like me, some may have the ability to communicate by telepathy. This means other creatures will know what the count is, so they would remind the creature. Otherwise, it would have been a good idea."

"That's true. I hadn't considered that." said Chodon.

"Well, be proud of yourself. You're the only one that's come up with an idea," said Tara, as she looked steely-eyed at Ben.

Ben felt her gaze on the back of his neck. He decided it was best not to turn around at that moment and pretended he didn't know that the remark was directed towards him.

"Not much time left!" shouted Tara. Ben was still looking away from her, still pretending he hadn't heard her. Then suddenly the shrieks started up again. This time they were much louder.

"It's not looking good, is it, Ben?" Tara was scared. Ben knew she needed reassurance, but he felt he had none left to give. He knew the end was near, and they had just minutes to live.

"Since we started this mission it's never looked good, has it, Tara? But we've always strived, no matter what, against all the odds. And we got through. So, remain strong and steadfast. This is no ordinary battle we face and while it may feel like the outcome is inevitable, it isn't. But know this, if we do die today, we do so to help save all mankind as well as those we love and cherish. I'll be beside you both until my last breath. But we're not there yet."

"Thank you, Ben," Tara said. "Thank you for everything." Then she quickly brightened. "I've just had a message from Amalialad. He's on his way. He said he'll be fifteen minutes. He then blurted a few thoughts I couldn't quite grasp and said he'll explain later. I sensed he needed all his energy to get here in time, so I didn't ask questions."

"Damn it!" said Ben again as Tara finished speaking, and as he looked out to see the final grains of salt being counted. "That's fantastic, but I think we're out of time." They became silent as their thoughts raced. They were each desperately thinking of a way to survive an extra twelve minutes. Then abruptly, Ben, eyes wide, looked at both girls. "There may be a way. Quickly, give me your knives and salt pouches." Without question, they hurriedly handed them to him.

"But you still won't have enough salt to complete a circle around the car." Chodon said. It had just dawned on her what Ben had in mind. "There won't be enough to complete the circle."

"Trust me, Chodon. I know it's a long shot, but it may work. It could give us the time we need. Firstly, please hold your knives out for me." Ben then carefully poured some liquid over the blades from a bottle he'd stored in the dashboard of the car. "I've covered the knives with holy water. And if anything, evil touches them, it will suffer chronic burning and excruciating pain. On the count of three I want you to open your doors and follow me. There are only five creatures within our immediate vicinity, so we should be ok. I'm going to run a small distance outside our salt circle then I'm going to abruptly stop. I want you to hack and slash out at anything which comes near you as you run. When you reach me, huddle up." Ben started counting. As he did so, Tara took a final glance out of the window and saw that the salt had disappeared. Her heart raced. The creatures had counted the final few grains and their screaming reached an almost impossible pitch, a final crescendo. Then, with their nail-encrusted clubs held outwards and with their jagged fangs proudly displayed, the creatures raced towards them.

"Three!" Ben shouted.

Ben and Chodon raced out, followed by Tara. At that same moment, in a vicious frenzy, the first of the gruesome creatures broke into the opposite side of the vehicle and with long, wart-encrusted, scrawny arms and vicious, venom-tipped claws, they ripped open the leather fabric of the seats as they charged after them. Ben came to an abrupt halt about two hundred meters beyond the car. It was the precise spot he'd headed for. In front of him was a tall, wide-girthed oak tree. He quickly loosened the string from the first pouch he'd been tightly grasping and hurriedly spread the salt in a two-meter diameter circle around the tree. Ben thought the tree would be useful for some protection from behind. The salt from the single pouch was not enough to complete the ring so he rapidly repeated the process using the salt in the second pouch which he'd also carried and kept in his side pocket. Ben knew the circle was thin and that the salt he'd dispensed would only give them about twenty minutes if the creatures started counting the grains again, but he hoped it would give them enough time until Amalialad arrived. The girls had caught up and stood close, knives at the ready, as the first of the crazed creatures came hurtling towards them. Shrieking loudly, it came to an abrupt halt just inches from the salt.

Seeing this, the other creatures quickly slowed. Then they all edged cautiously forward. Ben noticed the first few were shadowrunts but because of their varying deformities, they were difficult to distinguish from some of the other creatures. The Shadow Runts began to sniff loudly, and Ben realized they could smell the salt. One of them bravely edged further forwards and stopped just beyond the circle. Ben had his knife out at the ready. He didn't expect it to try and break through the circle, but he knew he couldn't leave anything to chance. He knew there was a possibility of the creature's death should it foolishly touch the salt. He knew from all his research that it would then mean, by all folklore and most accounts from the scriptures, its instant banishment from the earth plane and into another which was said to be worse than hell itself. It was, evidently, a place where banished creatures would suffer existences of eternal torture. So, Ben considered, it was unlikely it could be trusted because even if its own natural instincts of self-protection were threatened and it wished to retreat, its demon master may have a different plan in mind which could involve purposely sending it forwards, into the salt, and possibly, to its death. Ben could think of one good reason why its demon master would do so, but he was startled to see the hunched-back monstrosity move and crouch over the salt. It then stretched out one of its scrawny arms to touch it.

Ben was ready and about to strike out with his knife when suddenly the creature hissed loudly and jumped back in pain. And it didn't return to the others but painstakingly reached out and picked up a single grain of salt. It hissed and screeched out in agony as it did so. The pain must have been excruciating. But this was what Ben had suspected might happen and knew it was the demon's agenda - the demon which was now in control of the creature's actions. Ben was still astonished to see the creature repeating the procedure. Then the other four creatures joined it and they too were now all stretching their arms out and howling in agony.as they tried desperately to remove and count the grains. Ben realized then that this was the daemon's strategy. It didn't matter how many creatures got injured or killed - they were dispensable. He understood that the daemon must have had one objective. It wanted to destroy them. And at any cost.

"They're counting the grains again!" said Tara.

"Yes, they are but we can stop them." And Ben struck the scrawny arms with his knife as they attempted to extract more grains. Tara and Chodon joined him and the creatures hissed and shrieked as the knives cut, thrust and burnt into their flesh and bones. But even though they were suffering tremendous pain and their bodies were cut deeply, with limbs hanging loosely at their sides, they continued to count. Then, for no apparent reason, they abruptly stopped and limped off to the shelter of trees.

"It looks like they've stopped to dress their wounds," Ben told the girls, as he peered into the distance at the creatures.

"But I couldn't believe it, Ben, they were in tremendous pain yet still they snatched the grains." Tara looked puzzled.

"I suspect they had no choice. I think the daemon forced them to do it regardless of their suffering," Ben said. "Do you mean, they would continue to count even though their limbs are cut to shreds?" asked Tara.

"Yes. They'll count until every appendage is cut off completely. In short, they will work until the grains kill them or they kill us." said Ben. "I reckon they know our mission and they're determined to destroy us."

Tara looked at Ben.

"That's shocking!" said Tara.

"How long have we got?"

"Well, if Amalialad is true to his word, and he usually is, we have fourteen minutes."

"We should be ok then," said Tara. "I count twelve of them. It should take the creatures at least thirty minutes once they start counting again."

"Hmm, perhaps you're right. Let's hope so."

"Why don't you agree?"

Ben silently cursed himself.

"No, Tara, I do agree. It's just that..."

"What, Ben? What do you mean by 'just that'?"

"Look!" Ben said, pointing towards the trees. They saw more creatures streaming out. "I was about to say that very soon there may be more than ten. And, now it seems I was right, the demon has sent more to assist."

"Oh, my God," cried Tara. There were at least fifty of them. Suddenly, dizziness overcame her, and she sensed a stirring of pure evil shadow the core of her soul. Then she felt the worst splitting headache ever. Her hands shot up to hold the sides of her head as the pain became almost unbearable. She thought her head would explode. And the words she heard next, frightened her rigid.

"We're coming for you, bitch!" The words echoed hauntingly through her mind and Tara felt herself losing consciousness. But then, from somewhere very distant, another voice broke through.

"Stay strong, Tara. You must stay strong" Amalialad's voice pierced through and entered her mind.

Ben was still watching the creatures and hadn't noticed Tara slump down to her knees. However, on hearing Amalialad's voice, Tara swiftly picked up her knife, which had slipped out of her hand earlier, stood back up and, with a steel sense of reinforced vigour, braced herself ready to fight.

They came. With blood curdling cries, the creatures charged towards them and the ground shook as their feet pounded forwards. They came very fast and the defenders knew they weren't going to stop.

"Stand firm and knives at the ready!" Ben said. The girls stood, rooted to the ground and stared intently at the oncoming mass of hideous entities. They were terrified, but each had a powerful inner strength, a determined resolve and a deep-seated stubbornness. They weren't going to be killed without a fight.

Strangely, at that moment, Ben's thoughts weren't on the impending clash, just moments away, but instead on the words Amalialad had once told him about reincarnation.

And since he expected to be killed very shortly, he hoped that reincarnation might mean that he'd meet and fall in love with Tara again in the next life.

The creatures were almost upon them and Ben was suddenly jolted back to reality. And he and the girls dropped to the ground.

Chapter Thirty

Amalialad found himself walking on cushions of white clouds and looking down on an ocean of crystal blue water. An overpowering sense of tranquility and peace came over him and he felt that he didn't want to leave the place. Then the most gentle and serene voice he'd ever heard broke his thoughts.

"Be at peace, Your Holiness. Nothing can harm you here. You deserve to rest a while." The words could only be described as magical and instantly flooded Amalialad's body with a gentle caressing of pure peace and a perfect contentment. He wanted to stay in the place for ever. He turned to face the speaker.

As he did so he immediately sensed a man of tremendous strength and fortitude, but most of all, a man of peace. The aura he saw of the smiling, serene face sitting in front of him was familiar but at that moment he couldn't remember where he'd seen it before.

"Master?" Amalialad said. He wondered if this man was a former tutor of his.

The Fourth Panchen Lama, Lopsang Chokyi Gyalsten, the Great Scholar, spoke again.

"Please, don't struggle to remember me, Your Holiness, we haven't met 'til now, but our spiritual lineage will always be connected. I am your tulko."

Amalialad was suddenly overwhelmed with emotion. He couldn't hold the tears back and it felt natural to just let them flow. At that moment he knew as much about the man standing in front of him as the man knew himself. The man was his tulko. He was his rebirth. He, Amalialad, was the reincarnation of the man who was sitting calmly in front of him. The man was mildly amused as he studied Amalialad's face. He knew Amalialad was slowly coming to terms with the reality of his existence. He knew that everything that was missing in Amalialad's mind about his past life memories had now been fully restored. The Pencham Lama also felt a tremendous sense of pride and happiness that

Amalialad had become such a humble man of almost perfect character and one who had, in a short time, achieved such accomplishments He knew Amalialad would eventually surpass even his own strengths and abilities and the wisdom which Amalialad would eventually gain would be vast.

"I am here to aid you, Your Holiness," said the Pencham Lama. But Amalialad noticed sadness in his tone. "I know what you've been through, Your Holiness, and I'm aware of the great challenges ahead of you. I've known about them from the first day my soul entered your body. Here, I'm in a higher realm, beyond the astral plane, in an elemental state of existence. I reached the state of enlightenment and could have settled for eternal rest in the very highest realm but I decided to help you and others to achieve the same enlightenment on the earth plane and so I became a tulko for you. It's been an honour and already you've exceeded all my expectations. But you still have further to travel. Your struggle will become far more arduous than any man has had to contend with before. But the enemy is strong, and their numbers are huge. Your Holiness," the man sighed, "it greatly saddens me to say it's likely you'll fail and suffer the most diabolical death." But Amalialad smiled.

"Great Scholar, I remember now, it was you who taught us that 'death is not to be feared by one who has, with love and compassion, lived wisely'. And I have always endeavoured to do that."

"Certainly, I'm glad you remembered that." The Pencham Lama smiled widely. He didn't want to praise Amalialad too much. Even though Amalialad was still only twenty-four, he didn't want to influence a potential trait of arrogance in him which in turn, he knew, could lure Amalialad into insecurity and that could be his eventual death knell, and the end of all that was good in the world.

"You will shortly be facing the most ferocious and fearsome battle that's ever occurred on Earth. You will be fighting the most fiendish daemons in the devil's army. I know you've worked this out for yourself, but I feel I need to remind you that if you fight only ten legions of daemons your chances of surviving are remote. However, if you're up against any more than that..." the Pencham Lama paused for a moment. "Well, let's hope not, eh? I'm sorry, Your Holiness, but I'm unable to help you much in this battle. However, I may be able to aid you in a small way. Nearly twenty years ago I summoned all the dabdobs that had ever lived. The dabdobs were warrior monks that lived among us in Central Tibet. I suspect it is a surprise to you because, as you know, Buddhists don't hold with violence and war. However, the dabdobs were an exception. At times, I'm sad to say, a necessary exception. They were our protectors when disorder broke out. They were monks but seen as outcasts by most because of their aggressive and violent nature. They lived discreetly within the larger monasteries but would be called upon by authorities to help with security when large events took place, such as our annual Great Prayer Festival. They would spend most days practicing their fighting skills and became the most feared warriors in Tibet. I selected these monks because of their fighting skills. I knew then that a great calamity of some kind would eventually face the earth, but at that time I didn't know when that would be. The dabdobs are honourable and will act as personal body guards for you and your friends in the days ahead. I didn't force them, they all volunteered after I'd explained the circumstances. Most are still progressing through the stages of Karma but because of the mistakes they've been responsible for during their first lives of injuring and killing. Most of them have many rebirths ahead before reaching enlightenment. However, they know that your life is one of crucial importance and that their own destinies depend entirely on the outcome of your success in the battle ahead. If you lose this coming battle, we will all be thrown into the depths of Hell itself. So, when you return shortly back to the Earth plane, Your Holiness, they will be waiting for you. But they will be invisible and guarding you from the shadows, coming to your aid only when necessary. They will possess all the intelligence and skills they'd developed during their lifetimes and you will recognize them by the key characteristics they've always had, the locks of hair behind their ears, the pieces of red cloth worn above their elbows and their eye shadow."

"Thank you, Great Scholar, any aid in this fight will be most welcome." Amalialad vaguely remembered the name dabdobs, but not from his present life. He remembered them also being referred to as Fighting Monks and Athlete Monks and many monks used to speak of their unbelievable speed and agility in their displays of sword and knife fighting. The Warrior Monks, as he knew them, had a great passion for fighting and even their practice sessions often resulted in serious injuries and death. He remembered too that the warriors had great pride in their order and wore their own distinguished unique dresses, as well as the other distinguishing features which the Great Scholar had highlighted. Amalialad also knew that their eye shadow was used to help them appear fiercer in battle. The warriors were also known, he remembered, for carrying a huge key in a strap as a weapon as well as a discreet knife or small sword hidden somewhere on their person, and in archery they excelled. Further, he remembered, their vision was fine-tuned by the application of a special ointment, its content most secret. In battle, they were the elite of the elite.

"How will I recognise them, Great Scholar?"

"Ah." The, Great Scholar smiled widely again. "You are the Dalai Lama, you will know them when they are there. They are linked to your spirit and you will recognise their auras. You must leave here now, Your Holiness. This place is but a partial paradise for those that finally achieve enlightenment. But it will tempt you to stay if you don't leave now since it recognises that you're close to achieving enlightenment and therefore it's affinity with you will grow stronger. I sense you have already become attracted to it and that you don't wish to leave. However, your time here is not now. You have much to do on the earth plane. You have friends now in desperate need of your help. You must go to them. May Buddha guide you. We will meet again."

Amalialad didn't have a chance to answer. In an instant, he found himself standing back outside the chapel door. Amalialad looked at his watch and realised he'd only been absent for one minute. He wasn't surprised. He understood that time could be distorted when traveling on the higher planes. While still pondering, his thoughts were abruptly interrupted by the sound of screeching tyres. Amalialad's reaction was instant and he looked sharply to his right towards the noise and saw the striking red and silver streaks of a Mercedes Benz SLS heading fast towards him. He instinctively jumped back, pressing his body hard against the door of the chapel, allowing the vehicle to pass by. But it screeched to a halt just in front of him. As it did so, the burning stench from the rubber tyres wafted into his nostrils.

"Get in, quickly!" A male voice shouted from the open window of the Mercedes. "Lopsang says we haven't got long." Dazed, but suddenly sensing he was not in danger, Amalialad opened the nearest door and jumped into the front seat. The time to ask questions, he thought, would be later.

"I'm sorry about that, Amalialad, but time is of the essence. I received a message from Lopsang a few minutes ago. He asked me to collect you from here and to tell you that he's fine but will explain things to you later." A flood of relief came over Amalialad on hearing the news. He felt guilty about leaving Lopsang in grave peril and was curious as to how Lopsang had escaped. As he'd left him, he'd felt a very powerful malevolence in the room. Nothing could have pleased him more at that moment than knowing that his good friend was still alive.

"My name's Joseph," said the driver and it was in that moment that Amalialad realized the driver was a member of the Opus Dei. Joseph smiled.

"It's an honour to meet you." Amalialad smiled back, then took a small piece of paper out of his pocket and handed it to Joseph. "This is urgent, Joseph. Can you please put these coordinates into your GPS system and get there as quickly as you can? I have friends there whose lives are in immediate danger. Can you communicate with the other members?"

"Yes, Your Holiness."

"That's good. We may need their help very soon." Amalialad's was now focusing intently on how to save Ben and the girls.

"Ah, before I forget, Your Holiness, Lopsang gave me some items to give to you. He simply said you'd left them behind."

Amalialad knew he was referring to the knife, his stick and the Bible. And it was a relief. He knew he'd need them in the days ahead.

"Thank you, Joseph, and in future can you please call me Amalialad and not refer to me as Your Holiness. I'm incognito."

"Of course, but if you don't mind, I'll refer to you as 'sir' since Amalialad is, I feel, too informal and I'd feel 'sir' at least allowed for a modicum of respect."

"Ok, I understand, that's fine."

"And may I say, sir, it will always be an honour and a pleasure to serve you. Now, sir, would you kindly put your seatbelt on, we'll be going as soon as you've done so."

And as Amalialad clicked the seatbelt into the locking mechanism the car screeched and abruptly sped forwards.

"How long will it take to get to Heathrow Airport?"

"Probably faster than you think, sir. We're firstly travelling to a small private helipad just a mile away. Sir, Douglas Montague-Herbert has his own banking business in the center of Chelsea. He's one of us, sir. The building has its own helipad. We're heading there and depending on traffic we should be there in about ten minutes, and Heathrow not long after that."

"Ah, I see. Wonderful," said Amalialad. He prayed for Buddha's blessing and good weather. He then focused intently on Tara and his thoughts traveled to her.

After parking the Mercedes in the middle of the road, outside the Commercial Bank of Ireland, Joseph hurriedly got out the vehicle then raced around to Amalialad's door and opened it.

"We get out here, sir. Please follow me." Amalialad glanced around and saw others racing towards them. He suspected they were all members of the Opus Dei and, carrying his own bags, he followed Joseph into the bank's reception hall, where he saw Joseph, whom, as he walked by, casually tossed the keys to the female receptionist. She was smiling at Joseph and caught the keys with ease.

"Take care of the car please, will you, Susan? Is the copter ready?" Joseph asked. Then he winked and smiled.

"Yes, Mr Benson. It's as you like it, whirling and ready."

"Fantastic." Amalialad smiled at the banter and then turned, noticing that another ten men dressed in army fatigues had joined them. They bowed their heads towards Amalialad, then followed Joseph into an elevator. On the twenty first-floor they got out and headed towards the helipad. As they got closer, the pilot started the engine; the noise from the rotating blades was deafening. Within a few seconds of leaving the elevator they were all safely inside the helicopter.

"We have to travel over four hundred miles Joseph, so will this helicopter manage that ok without refueling?" asked Amalialad.

"No problem, sir, you're sitting in an Airbus EC175. This model is top of its range and can travel five hundred and ninety seven nautical miles without refueling. It also holds sixteen passengers, so don't worry about your friends, who we'll be picking up later. It can also do a speed of one hundred and fifty knots which is about one hundred and eighty miles an hour. We'll be close to that speed. Our ETA is in two hours and forty minutes."

"Thanks, Joseph. That's very reassuring."

The flight went smoothly and Amalialad brought them all up to date with the recent events. He then asked the two generals present for their advice on the best military strategy to be implemented after landing and, after several ideas were discussed, they eventually formulated a plan. It incorporated a few options; this flexibility was crucial because nobody knew exactly what events would have occurred since their last communication.

"ETA is just fifteen minutes, gentleman," said Joseph. The men changed into camouflaged overalls and checked their knives and belts. Amalialad guessed that they left it till now to change in order to look less conspicuous earlier. It was important they didn't attract too much attention. He noticed that the belts held long heavy iron keys. He also noticed a set of eleven leather quivers, each carrying about ten arrows, standing in the corner of the helicopter. They looked as if they were designed to fit into the belts and on closer scrutiny, he also noticed clip attachments next to the hanging keys where, supposedly, the quivers fitted. He tried to telepathically send a message to Tara telling her they'd be fifteen minutes. He'd just finished relaying it when he felt a massive surge of electrical energy piercing his head. He instantly jumped up as the shock of the force violently shook his body. Joseph rushed to his side to support him but Amalialad quickly regained control.

"Are you ok, sir?" asked Joseph.

"Yes, I'm fine now. Thank you, Joseph."

"If you don't mind me asking, sir, what caused it?"

"It was a telepathic attack from our enemy with a message for me." Amalialad wouldn't forget the sinister voice which had relayed the message. It was inhuman, and its malevolence was chilling.

"What was the message, sir?"

"You're too late and we're coming!"

Chapter Thirty-One

Lopsang felt the invisible, cold, scrawny claws around his throat. They weren't sharp, but they were very strong, and they were throttling him. His chest heaved as he instinctively tried to break free. He tried to steal the claws away from his throat, but no matter how hard he tried, his hands simply passed through the claws. The claws had no physical mass, yet he felt them, and the increasing pain continued to shoot through his throat and chest cavity. He was beginning to choke. Desperate for breath, he tried one final time to release the grip. With all the energy his withered body could muster, he tried to push the claws aside. But it was useless, and he found himself losing consciousness - slipping away. His vision was fading, and blackness was creeping in. He thought about Amalialad and, in his dying thoughts, he gave a silent prayer for him.

Then suddenly the claws lost their grip and, though he struggled, he eventually managed to open his eyes to see the whole area lit up by an enormous, phosphorous, warm glow slowly spreading out to fill the whole room. It appears it was cleansing everything in its path. However, Lopsang wasn't scared. He'd sensed a peaceful and calming presence in the room and, miraculously, felt much better.

Then telepathically, the Watcher spoke.

"I know you sense me, Lopsang but please be at peace. I am here to help you, not to harm you."

"I sense that. And far from being afraid I feel strongly protected. What is your real name, Watcher?"

"My name is Michael. I'm a messenger of God."

"Are you also known as the Archangel Michael, the healer and protector?"

"I have been known by those names."

"Thank you for saving me."

"It is my duty, and your calling is not yet due. You will be needed in times ahead."

"Can you tell me what it was that attacked me?" asked Lopsang.

"The daemon, Berith, known by humans as the Daemon of Wrath, tried to suffocate you. I felt his presence here, less than one of your seconds ago, and rushed to help. He leads twenty-six legions, if that's the information you desire."

"Oh No! That's too many!" shouted. Lopsang.

"I assure you it's the truth. And that's not including his War Mounts who possess brutal strength and special abilities of their own."

"No, forgive me. I don't doubt it, I'm certain it's true. What I meant was, that's too many for us to even contemplate defeating. Our numbers are relatively few." Lopsang lowered his head in sadness. After a few moments, he looked up at the Watcher.

"Forgive me; I'm extremely fortunate that you arrived in time to save me. Thank you again. By telling me this you have given me information which could help my friends to develop a strategy to defeat the devil's army. Although how they could possibly do it now, only God knows." Then he looked back at the Watcher.

"I've heard of the daemon, Berith. Isn't he supposed to ride a red horse?"

"Yes, he rides a red horse, twenty hands high."

"That's huge. Are you here to help us in our battle?"

"I hope to be, but nothing is certain. Yet even I cannot do as much as you may think I can. When the Darkness comes, we are all in peril. But you sense this, Lopsang, don't you? You are aware we need the support of many, but only one holds the key to the outcome of the battle."

Lopsang nodded. He did know.

"Yes, Michael, the prophecies are clear on that but we both know that we still need God on our side."

"It's as you say; only God knows. Normally, as His messenger, I'd know His plans too, but on this matter, I do not. I believe even God has not made a final decision about the outcome of this battle you refer to. I'm sorry, but this means I'm also unable to help further. My instructions come directly from

God. What I've done for you today is from my own volition, but I cannot promise any further help."

"I think I understand," said Lopsang sadly. He knew that the behavior of humanity had caused this war and that they now needed to resolve it.

"May God bless you, Lopsang." The last words were sincere but faded as they were spoken and Lopsang knew the Watcher had gone. He tried to telepathically communicate with Amalialad but for some reason the signal didn't get through. He knew he might be worrying unduly, but he was also hoping to get an update on the situation. But then he reconsidered, he wouldn't try contacting Amalialad again; it would be a distraction, which Amalialad couldn't afford. Lopsang decided to rest. As he lay on the bed, beginning to drift off into sleep, his thoughts were abruptly broken by one of the Monk Warriors, who had been sent to help Amalialad. Following a brief exchange, Lopsang drifted off into a deep sleep.

And, for now at least, Lopsang was content.

Chapter Thirty-Two

Lying face down, Ben felt helpless as the Shadow Runts, leading the daemon onslaught, raced in at the three of them. He could hear their aggressive grunts and smell their stench. Then, suddenly, bullets pounded inches above him, skimming his head, to tear straight into the thick, stinking flesh of the daemon horde.

"You must stay face down!" shouted Tara, as the barrage from the guns continued. She'd got the warning from Amalialad a split second earlier and had just managed to shriek out the warning to Ben and Chodon before the bullets flew.

Then, mysteriously, one by one the daemons fell, the shooting abruptly stopped and there was silence. The scene, as the daemons fell, reminded Ben of dominoes - as the daemons were shot they crashed into one another, each toppling against the one in front to fall to the ground. But Ben was bewildered. He knew that bullets were normally useless against the daemons and wondered why they were now able to kill them. As Ben looked on, he also noticed that arrows were used too. And all, on this occasion, were equally effective in the killing. Ben was stunned to see that each arrow perfectly pierced the heart of its daemon target. And when he looked more closely, he couldn't see any loose arrows lying around. All had perfectly hit their target. As he looked out at the mass of flesh and bone strewn over a hundred meters in front of him, he saw that not one daemon had survived.

"Quickly, run to the helicopter!" Amalialad appeared at Ben's side. He had a muddy face and was dressed in camouflage. Ben was startled and nearly cracked a joke, but knew it wasn't the time for jokes. With Amalialad were twelve others, all dressed similarly, and, strangely, Ben thought, all carrying large, plastic containers. But he had no time to think further and, with the girls, ran as fast as he could to the helicopter. The strong wind created by the swirling blades nearly knocked them off their feet, but they managed to quickly steady themselves and scramble up into the helicopter. As they entered, they passed two more soldiers who were standing, machine guns in their hands, at either side of the cabin entrance.

"Hurry!" shouted one of the soldiers. "We need to leave ASAP."

Before stepping into the helicopter, Ben had quickly glanced back and saw Amalialad and the other men pouring liquid over the bodies. It then occurred to him, as he saw the bodies instantly flare up, that they were dousing the daemons with holy water. Of course, he thought, and mentally chastised himself for not recognizing the reasons for the containers earlier. He then entered the helicopter. A soldier, who introduced himself as Lieutenant Simon Peterson, directed him to a seat between Tara and Chodon. The others hurriedly entered a minute later, and the doors immediately closed.

"Go! Go! Go!" shouted the second soldier who had been guarding the entrance, and the helicopter lifted off as the final clicks of the seat belts were heard. Amalialad glanced over at Tara as he settled into his seat.

"Are you ok?"

"I'm fine now, thanks, Amalialad, but it was touch and go."

"I know, I'm sorry. It was touch and go for me too."

During the flight Amalialad explained to everyone what had happened to him earlier. It was crucial that they were all brought up to date with events.

"Before I left my hotel earlier today, Lopsang, whom everyone here knows, and I were attacked by a powerful daemon." Some eyebrows were raised but most simply nodded in acknowledgement. They'd all heard a lot, too, about Amalialad and none of them were in any doubt about the truth of his words.

"ETA for Braemar Lodge Hotel is ten minutes," said the pilot.

While they were waiting to land, Ben turned to Amalialad.

"Arrows and bullets don't normally have any impact on the daemons, so how were yours able to kill them? I was amazed at the accuracy of your archers. Not one arrow missed its target. Every arrow was true. It was astonishing. But even so, like the bullets, the arrows should have had no effect on the daemons. We all know that man-made weapons are useless against them, yet the daemons were destroyed. Why?"

Amalialad smiled. "It was simple, Ben, and if you gave it more thought you'd soon arrive at the answer. I arranged for manufacturing of special, intensive, salt-tipped arrows and bullets. It was the intense salted tip which killed them so easily. Then we poured holy water over them."

"Of course. It's as you say, a simple idea but tremendously effective."

"That's usually the case, my friend." Amalialad answered. "Even now, as we're speaking, we have over a thousand men and women capping arrows, bullets, swords and knives with rock salt. They'll be vital in helping us fight in the battle ahead."

"Fantastic! But how did you recruit so many people so quickly, especially since some would be asking awkward questions?"

"Ah, well, you can thank Francis for that. All the people volunteering to do this are trusted members of the Opus Dei."

"Then, my friend, not all is lost. If our fighting strategies are equally inspirational, then there is some light at the end of the tunnel."

"It's a good start, as you say, but we're going to need lots more of it if we stand any chance of defeating the daemons.

"Well, how many is that?" asked Ben.

"Well, I envisage about ten legions, which is fifty thousand daemons."

"Wow, that's a lot. What could it be then?"

"Millions! It could be millions."

Chapter Thirty-Three

Ben quietly pondered on those words until Amalialad broke the silence.

"I've booked an additional five log cabins to the two you've already booked."

"That's fine. How many more guests are you expecting, then?"

"Well, if all goes according to plan, about ten more. We need to negotiate a plan of attack in more detail and that will mean discussing strategies. Presently, I'm not sure of our numbers but what's even more crucial, as I said to you, is that I've got no real idea of the numbers we're facing yet. Lopsang is one of the guests and he says he has some very important information about possible numbers, and of course, we're all desperate to know. I've been pacing up and down during the last few hours, speculating. But that's useless. Unfortunately, we dare't risk communicating by conventional means, so I'm using telepathy, even though there are some, who are uninvited, with the ability to listen in to my telepathic signals, I can usually sense them, I must take the risk. Most of the information I send is of course most secret, so we must all be extremely vigilant."

"I see. Is there anything more I can do for you?"

"Just be there as you've always been, Ben. You've been by my side and watched out for me ever since I've known you. Nobody could be more loyal, and your loyalty has been faultless. I consider you my rock and I trust you completely and I know I can rely on you always for strength and resolve." Amalialad looked directly at Ben when he spoke. Ben blushed with embarrassment.

"Thank you, I'm now unusually speechless."

"Ah, then this is a rare moment, my friend." Amalialad laughed.

"We'll be landing shortly, Ben, and when we do, I'd like you, Joseph and Lopsang to share a cabin with me. Tara and Chodon will also share a cabin and the rest I've yet to allocate."

"That's fine by me." said Ben. The voice of the pilot came through, requesting the fastening of seatbelts. They were about to land.

They landed on the vast lawn in the center of the log cabins. As they climbed down, they all stared at their surroundings in amazement. The scenery was spectacular. The backdrop of trees behind the cabins included a scattering of tall Scots Pine and Jupiter tress and beyond these was the mountain range. With their bright snowcapped tops and jagged outcrops, it was one of the most beautiful views they'd ever seen.

Tara and Chodon volunteered to walk to the hotel so they could register their arrival and collect the keys to the cabins.

"Is everything ok?" he asked.

"Perfectly," Tara answered. Then she looked at Chodon and they both burst out laughing. Amalialad smiled.

"Well, it's good to see you're both happy."

When Ben saw the girls giggling, he felt a tinge of jealousy. He guessed there might be a few young male guests they'd seen but then he quickly shoved those thoughts aside.

"The decor in the hotel is awe-inspiring," said Chodon.

"It certainly is," said Tara. "They've got some fine antique furnishings. Some must be over three hundred years old. It's no wonder this hotel has many awards on display. We noticed too that it's extremely busy. There are obviously a lot of guests staying here and there are also quite a few cars parked at the side and at the rear of the hotel. I counted about three hundred altogether. And there were eight guests checking in as we left. Strangely though, they all seemed to be men on their own."

The girls looked at each other and Ben thought that he saw a glint in their eyes.

"Perhaps there's a function here tonight or within the next day or two?" said Tara.

"Well, that's wonderful," Amalialad said. "But we need to get inside the cabins before it gets too dark. This time of year, this area is renowned for becoming blanketed with fog within minutes."

"OK," said Tara, as she and Chodon walked towards their cabin.

"We need to meet later, so if you both come to our cabin in an hour, that should give you a chance to freshen up and eat first. You should find the fridge and cupboards well stocked with food," Amalialad said, as he, Ben and Joseph, walked towards their own cabin. The others had already been given the same information and left for their cabins earlier.

"That sounds good. See you soon, then," said Tara.

"Wow!" said Joseph, as he entered the centre cabin. "This looks first class."

The cabin was furnished to a high standard.

"So, we have an hour to shower and eat," said Mal.

"Ok," Joseph said. "I'll cook us something while you two take your showers."

After showering, the three of them sat down and ate the pasta Joseph had quickly cooked.

"That was really delicious," said Amalialad.

"Yes, it was," said Ben.

A little later, the loud knocking on their cabin door came of no surprise to Amalialad.

He opened the door to a tall man, standing in front of him. The man grinned broadly and reached out to shake Amalialad's hand.

"Hello once again, my friend." From the first time Amalialad had met the man, a few days earlier, he'd warmed to him.

"I'm very happy you arrived here safely," Amalialad said. Then he turned to face the others. "Gentleman, I'd like to introduce you to Colonel Andrew Sinclair. He's second in command to Francis of the Opus Dei and one of the most experienced strategists in the British army."

"Ah, forget the formalities Just call me Andy, ok?"

They all chuckled as they warmly greeted Andy. They immediately felt at ease with him. There was another knock and Tara and Chodon came in.

"Hi, ladies, your timing is impeccable," said Amalialad, who then introduced them to Andy.

"Good afternoon," Andy said. "It's an honour to meet you both, although I do believe I'm at an advantage, since Amalialad has told me lots about you both already." Then he added. "All most complimentary, of course."

"I've given Andy the background on everything that's happened so far." Amalialad said. "I'm expecting Lopsang here shortly too. He's been waylaid but promises to be here soon. I've just received some coded information by text from him but I'm waiting for more. Until we receive that information, we cannot even consider developing our strategy. Lopsang knows the name of the daemon who is leading the invasion."

"Hopefully it's a daemon from the lower rankings," said Chodon.

"Yes. Within the hierarchy of daemons, the lower the ranking the less legions they will have under their control. We know that the daemon Bael, for instance, has sixty-six legions. This means if he was leading, we'd be facing an army of three hundred and ninety-six thousand soldiers from hell. This number would be virtually impossible to defeat since each daemon soldier has the strength of two men or more. Let's pray we get a lower ranking daemon in charge."

Suddenly, there were shouts and shrieks from outside. Amalialad rushed to the door.

What he saw made him sick to the stomach.

Chapter Thirty-Four

Peter and Francis arrived at the Stag Hotel in Forfar at precisely 6:00 a.m. Their car had miraculously started up when they reached it, so they drove straight to the hotel. When they arrived, they could see Hugh and Godfrey standing inside, peering out of two bay windows. Their faces lit up with relief as he and Francis stepped out of the car.

As they walked towards the hotel entrance, the doors suddenly opened, and Hugh ran out to greet them.

"What happened to you? Are you both ok?"

"We're fine now, thanks, Hugh. Let's go inside we can explain everything to you," Peter said.

"Yes, of course. Forgive my manners. Let's go in." Hugh said. And he led the way into the hotel.

Godfrey stepped forward to greet them with the keys to their rooms.

"I'm so happy you both got here safely. I've already checked you both in, so don't worry about that. You must go to your rooms now and freshen up. Perhaps, afterwards, you'll both join us for breakfast. Anyway, God bless, you're both safe now."

Peter suddenly felt drained as he entered his room and the sight of the large bed was inviting. It hadn't helped that the brass number plate on his bedroom door was loose and hung downwards. It had taken him ten minutes to find room number nine. He'd discovered that the brass number on his door was loose and so passed by it earlier, seeing it as room six. He could have so easily headed directly for the bed and fallen asleep but instead he quickly showered, put on fresh clothes and left to join his friends for breakfast. After all, he was also famished, and he felt it would have been rude not to join them since both Hugh and Godfrey were so eager to hear what had happened. Peter felt they should be updated as soon as possible.

Peter left his room not long after entering it and walked down into the dining area.

Hugh and Godfrey stood up to greet him. "Are you sure you're ok, Peter?" said Godfrey.

Peter raised a smile. "I'm fine, seriously, but I appreciate your concern."

"Ah, that's good," said Hugh, and he beckoned over the waiter.

Peter ordered his breakfast then slowly explained to the others what had happened.

"That's extremely concerning," said Hugh. "We're all aware that we're facing satanic forces that are determined to stop us. They will stop at nothing to do this. We need to be on our guard at all times."

"You're right, of course," said Peter. "That reminds me, we need to restock our salt sacks and water cont..." Peter abruptly broke off as he suddenly sniffed a most pungent stench. "Phew, can you smell that?" His friends looked confused.

"No, I'm sorry," Hugh replied, looking puzzled.

"I can't either, I'm afraid," said Godfrey.

Peter was suddenly distracted by a strong urge to look out of the bay window. He quickly walked over and peered out. He could only see two teenagers in hoodies talking with each other in the car park. As he focused on them, they looked up at him, and Peter jumped back in horror. Both boys had pitch black eyes and gazed fixedly back at him. He noticed how slender and pale they both looked. They each wore dark jeans and their hoodies were ragged. But then, in those few brief moments, Peter sensed a most malevolent evil and a feeling of overwhelming dread and fear. His hands started to shake, and he heard a multitude of strange voices inside his head. He was feeling faint and sickly when he realized something very dark and sinister was attempting to invade his body.

"Please let us in. We are hungry and lost. Can you give us just a little food, please?" one of the boys pleaded. As the words were spoken Peter felt a physical tug pulling him towards the main door, and he felt a lingering sadness for the boys and the urge to let the boys in grew stronger. He must open the door for them, and he walked towards it. Then he felt someone pushing him.

"Be gone, daemon!" Godfrey shouted, as he pushed Peter to one side and raised his small iron cross at the boys outside. With smug smiles on their faces, the boys slowly walked away.

"What were they?" asked Peter, as he stirred awake.

"If I'm right, they're known as black-eyed kids or Bek," said Godfrey. "I've never met them before, but I know people who have. They have entirely solid black eyes, hence their name, and they wander the earth spreading ill will and personal doom. If you'd given them permission to enter and let them in, your soul would have been taken from you. I'm surprised they're here in such a public place; they usually wander in deserted and abandoned areas. Apart from their solid black eyes, they can usually be identified by their pale or bluish tinted skin, like that of a corpse, and they normally speak with an eloquence well beyond their age. Many believe that the Bek are the spirits of lost and disturbed children who were killed, when alive, due to the evil acts they committed. When you stare back directly at their eyes it's said they're able to use some level of mind control. What's more, they don't just possess your soul like most entities, they destroy it completely and send it into the abyss. You were lucky, Peter."

"So, I wonder why they risked coming here in broad daylight," Hugh said.

"It's simple and I'm a complete fool," Peter replied. "The daemon is sending everything it has to stop or waylay us. I should have been far more alert. I knew something didn't feel right when I first saw the boys and should have realized immediately. Gentleman, please don't make the same mistake as me. The evil is rising, and we can expect other challenges from the Devil's army." Hugh and Godfrey solemnly nodded quietly in agreement.

They agreed to spend the rest of the day going over their plan to find the missing secret chamber, which was hidden somewhere in the depths of Glamis Castle. An elderly member of the Opus Dei who worked at the castle had provided details of where he thought the chamber was hidden. But the three weren't certain that the reasons for his suspicions could justify their search there. Further, if caught, they needed an acceptable excuse for being there. Eventually they decided they had no choice. Time was of the essence and they had nothing else to go on. They used their smartphones to look at the layout of the castle and formulate a plan. Godfrey then made some phone calls to confirm their ticket bookings into the castle and Hugh finally contacted Amalialad to update him on events so far. He also contacted what he vaguely described as 'other sources.' At that point Francis came down and they quickly updated him.

"I'm so sorry, gentlemen, but as soon as I got into my room and sat down to relax for a few minutes, I drifted off to sleep."

Everyone smiled.

It was midnight when they finally went to their beds.

Hugh woke up about two hours later to the sounds of scratching at his bedroom door. He wandered over to the door to listen more closely. He was sharing his room with Godfrey, who was still fast asleep, so he decided not to disturb him. The scratching sound increased as he got closer to the door. He wasn't prepared to open the door on his own, so he decided to wake Godfrey. He'd need Godfrey's back up just in case they'd be facing another entity. Before turning to wake Godfrey, Hugh thought he could make out voices over the sound of the scratching. So, he decided to put his ear close to the door to try to hear what was being said. He leaned closer.

Then an arm whiplashed through the solid door and grabbed him by the throat.

Before passing out, Hugh's final vision was that of five, scrawny, bloodied fingers with long, sharpened nails, then his throat was ripped mercilessly apart.

Chapter thirty-Five

Twenty minutes later Godfrey shook Hugh awake.

"Wake up, Hugh. Come on, don't be so lazy, we've got about an hour before we leave, and I'd like some breakfast before we go." Hugh stirred awake slowly.

"I had the worst nightmare I can remember. It seemed so real."

"Well, tell me later, but for now just get yourself washed and dressed, ok, I'm starving."

"Yeah, yeah, ok, hold your horses. I'm getting up now." Hugh shook his head and wiped the sleep from his eyes. But he felt uncomfortable. He simply didn't feel right. He walked to the shower, stepped out of his shorts and walked into the shower cubicle. As he looked in the mirror his heart almost stopped. The shock brought the nightmare back. His right hand shot up to feel the side of his neck. There were no doubts that the deep scratch marks on his neck were real.

When Godfrey heard about Hugh's nightmare and saw the wounds on his friend's neck, he was stunned. "It's inexplicable," he said. "Were you wearing your cross during the night?"

"Of course, I never take it off, not even when I bath or shower."

"Then you are most fortunate, because that cross, blessed by the pope himself, will shield you from anything evil. I'd suggest that whatever entity did this to you was a very powerful one. However, if you hadn't worn the cross you would be dead. You would have been killed within your dream and not woken up. It was the cross that saved you."

"Yes, I think you're right. Let's go and join Peter and Francis for breakfast. I'm sure they'll be intrigued about what happened to me and they may have other ideas about it."

At breakfast, Peter couldn't help sensing the nervous tension emulating from Hugh and Godfrey, but he decided that they would speak when they were good and ready.

"Hugh was attacked in his sleep last night." Godfrey looked directly at Peter, then Francis, as he spoke. Both looked at Hugh. They could then see the scratch marks on his neck.

"What happened?" Francis asked. Then Hugh explained.

"I think Godfrey could be right in his analysis. But I'd also seriously consider something else. The energy surge needed to cause that wound to Hugh's neck from within his dream state would have had to be huge. I think it could have been manipulated by a small group of entities working together and consolidating their power through one of them to create the power surge. But I've never heard of it before, it's just a theory," Peter said.

"Nor have I. But it makes sense," Godfrey said. "We need to find out the name of the daemon or entities behind this or I suspect they'll continue attacking us while we sleep. We need to eradicate them."

"You're right. We can't afford to rest while this threat is over us," Francis said. "We need to trap it or banish it."

"But how would we do that?" Hugh asked.

"We trap them in a séance," Francis suggested.

"We could do that, but I don't think we have to. I have a strong feeling that whatever it was will return tonight, possessing even more power. I think it's been commanded to stop us. And it, or they, will come to do that tonight," Peter said. His friends stared at him in amazement.

"When you say stop us…" asked Hugh.

"Destroy us," said Peter flatly. There was a brief pause while his words sunk in. Then Godfrey spoke.

"Why would they suddenly possess more power and why would they return so soon? Surely, they'd know we would be more prepared tonight?"

Suddenly, Francis stood up.

"It's obvious gentleman. Today is the thirty-first of October."

"Of course, how remiss of me not to realize that," Godfrey said. "Today is All Hallows' Eve, otherwise known as Halloween. For witches and ghouls, tonight is party night. On this night, evil will be stronger than ever."

"That's why, gentlemen, we have another busy day. We must prepare," Peter said.

"What do you want us to do, Peter?" Hugh asked. Peter explained, and they agreed to meet later that evening in Peter's room.

They met at 8 p.m. that evening. Peter was just packing away some coloured pens and iron crosses when Hugh and Godfrey walked in.

"Hi, Peter, we managed to get more rock salt but with winter approaching they charged us double the normal cost," Hugh said.

"Well, although we can question their ethics, it's worth it to us, Hugh."

"Please sit down everyone," Francis said. "If we're attacked again, we're going to use the Devil's trap to bind the entity in the centre of the room. When we've done this, Godfrey will read out a text in Latin which should send the demon or entity straight back to hell. You must be strong. Make sure you hold your iron crosses which I blessed earlier with holy water. They will offer protection too. Keep the salt pouches on your person. They may be needed. The entities are clever. We should expect them at midnight when their power is strongest but they're cunning and could come at any time to surprise us. From now on we must be quiet, not a single word to be spoken, and very patient. We have three hours till midnight. May god bless us all."

Then, except for the slow, monotonous ticking from the small wooden clock set up high on the wall, there was silence.

The waiting seemed to go on forever and, of course, Peter began to doubt if anything would happen. He looked at his friends who were quiet and still and regretted not having learnt to meditate properly himself. They seemed to welcome the waiting as an opportunity to pray and be silent. Peter's senses were on high alert and it was at 11:45 p.m. that he decided to wake the others. Surprisingly, they all opened their eyes just before he touched them. But ten minutes passed, and nothing had happened. Peter started having doubts about whether anything would happen. Then four more very slow minutes passed by, and there was only one minute to go till midnight. He noticed all eyes were fixated on the clock. It was, he thought, the longest minute of his life. But the second hand didn't quite make the next minute before the Peter's intervention.

"They're here!" He sensed there was no more need for quiet. They were now being attacked.

In horror, they all looked up to see three, haggard, old women fly swiftly through the door to the centre of the room. As they flew past, he could see, by looking at the mirror in front of him, that they were not solid forms but rather three transparent outlines all wearing long shabby, creased skirts which flowed as they flew backwards and forwards across the room. Then he cringed as he noticed their long, knotted, dirty grey hair swaying to and fro as together, in garbled voices, they cackled loudly. It sent a chill down Peter's spine. The temperature dropped rapidly, and the haggard, wrinkled, wart-ridden faces of the old woman, slowly, very slowly, turned to face them. An instinct told him not to look around but in the reflection in the mirror Peter could see their black piercing eyes abruptly flare up.

"They're witches! Don't look at their eyes!" Francis shouted. "They'll turn you to stone!"

It was too late.

Chapter thirty-six

Slumped over one of the Warrior Monk's shoulders, Lopsang's bloodied torso swung precariously in the air. A preliminary effort had been made to stem the blood flow by one of the Warrior Monks, but the old torn shirts used were not enough. As Amalialad ran over to him, Lopsang was still coughing heavily and losing a lot of blood.

"Hurry lay him down on the bed," Amalialad said. He noticed further wounds in Lopsang's side, and a deep gaping wound which ran across his stomach. He knew then that Lopsang's condition was far more serious than he'd first thought and looked over at the Warrior Monk who'd brought him in. The Warrior returned the gaze with a gentle shake of his head and Amalialad understood. Lopsang was dying. Amalialad knew that very few could survive such a serious stomach wound but Lopsang had also lost a lot of blood, too much blood to be able to save him. Tara and Chodon ran forward to help patch up the wounds. They brought with them bandages, ointments and towels, and, although Amalialad knew they could do little to help, it would at least allow a little comfort in Lopsang's final minutes. Lopsang started breathing heavily in short bursts and Amalialad stepped closer to his side.

"Lopsang, can you hear me?" It was heartbreaking to see him like this. However, Amalialad reminded himself of the terrific responsibility they all had and that it was vital to get any information from Lopsang that he could, to improve their chances of success in their battle ahead. Tara saw Amalialad looking at Lopsang and knew his dilemma.

"It's hard, Amalialad, isn't it? But you're doing the right thing. We're going to give him some morphine now. So that should ease the pain for him. It'll make him more comfortable."

At that moment Lopsang opened his eyes and looked up at Amalialad.

"Please, Your Holiness, don't worry about me. You have the world to save and we shall meet again one day. Please come closer." Amalialad quietly did so. "I have little energy to raise my voice." Lopsang was weak, and he began to stutter. Amalialad leaned forward to listen more closely, but then, without warning, Lopsang's body violently jerked up and he coughed and spluttered until finally his whole body went into a spasm. Instinctively, Amalialad held Lopsang closely. It was an attempt to both restrain and comfort him in his last moments. Lopsang was not only Amalialad's mentor but he had also become a very close friend. Indeed, a father figure. Amalialad struggled to understand why the fates were so cruel. Then without warning, he felt a sudden flurry of emotion building up inside of him. He felt full of fury and frustration mixed with a heavy sadness. Then a deep sense of hopelessness overcame him, and he looked up at the ceiling.

"Why?" he cried out. "Why do you now forsake us?" He collapsed to his knees. And for a few minutes it was quiet in the cabin.

Ben saw Amalialad drop down and swallow hard. He then quietly walked over to sit on the floor beside him. He put his arm around Amalialad's shoulders and held him close. Nothing was said. He just needed to be there for his friend.

Tara felt Amalialad's pain and couldn't stop the flow of tears which streamed down her cheeks. She then felt the twisting and churning of her stomach and a tremendous confusion pounding inside her head and wondered whether Amalialad could cope with the responsibility he'd been given. After all, the worst was yet to come and Amalialad had been let down badly. Until that moment, all their hopes had been pinned on Lopsang providing crucial information about the daemons which could help them win the coming battle. But that hope had now been extinguished.

Minutes passed until Amalialad got up. He slowly walked over to the Warrior Monk.

"Thank you, my friend. I think your name is John, isn't it?"

"Well, yes, Your Holine… I'm sorry, I mean, sir."

"Can you please sit down with me and tell me precisely what you saw?"

"Yes, of course, sir. We were keeping watch on the compound, particularly around the log cabins and the hotel, when we heard a vehicle skidding then screeching to a halt. The mist had blanketed the whole area, so we couldn't see anything. The security cameras became effectively obsolete and even the flood lights proved useless and so we had to rely on the microphones which were strategically positioned outside to establish what was happening. We could, however, from inside our cabin, smell a distinct burning odour which must have wafted in through an open, front window and we guessed it must have come from the vehicle's tyres. Then we heard three doors closing and from the footsteps we heard, we estimated that three people had got out from the vehicle. We heard them running hard, racing towards us. One set of steps was much slower, and we guessed it would have come from someone less physically fit. Seconds later we heard shrieks and grunts, and the heavy padding of feet. Then this was followed by scratching sounds, so we guessed they were being chased by the daemon creatures. These daemons were trying desperately hard to stop the runners. Just as the mist was clearing, we saw the two faster runners stop in their tracks. They just turned around, withdrew their knives and ran directly into the raging creatures. It was a suicidal move and they'd have known the outcome. I guessed they thought their actions would have given the last man, whom I now know was Lopsang, the time to get to the safety of a cabin. Indeed, it would have done, but unfortunately Lopsang slipped and fell and in so doing he lost the vital few seconds he needed to get to safety. As soon as the mist lifted we saw what was happening and launched our arrows, killing many of the daemon creatures running towards him. Then five of us raced forward to help Lopsang, to hopefully bring him back in before the creatures reached him. Unfortunately, they got to him at the same time and, even though we fought hard to protect him, we failed. Four of my brothers were killed and unfortunately Lopsang was badly injured. However, I managed to finally drag him back to the safety of your cabin. I surmised he may have had some important information for you." At that point, John looked at Amalialad with sadness. "And I could see that time was short." Amalialad understood and John continued. "As I ran back with him, I tried to stem the blood which I'd seen flowing from his stomach, but I'm afraid it was of little use. The flow was just too heavy. I'm sorry he died. I sensed he was a good man."

"I'm so sorry for your loss, John. I know whatever I say right now won't take away the aching pain you must feel. Your friends sacrificed their lives to save the rest of mankind. No man can be braver or more courageous than that. And there is no greater cause to die for."

"Thank you, sir. Your words have helped me more than you'll ever know."

Tara walked over to Amalialad with Lopsang's medallion which she'd just removed from the monk's neck.

"I thought perhaps you might like this, Amalialad. I'm sure Lopsang would want you to look after it." Amalialad smiled at Tara.

"Thank you, Tara. That's very thoughtful. I'll always treasure it."

Amalialad vividly remembered his third visit to the temple when Lopsang first showed him the medallion he wore. The medallion depicted the Mandala symbol of the Five Wisdom Buddhas. He'd explained that each of the Buddhas embodied various aspects of enlightenment and that the medallion aided him in his meditation. Amalialad looked closely at the silver medallion. He was fascinated by its intricate detail. Then as he turned it over carefully his attention was drawn to a strange looking script. It was only a single word, but it seemed out of place. So he looked closer. And fell back in astonishment. On the closer inspection, it had become evident that the word had only recently been poorly engraved. But the letters could be read. And they read: B..E..R..I..T.. H. Amalialad closed his eyes and let his thoughts drift. "Wherever you are, my friend, thank you for this." Amalialad had guessed that Lopsang had written the word on his medallion knowing that should anything happen to him, it would be given to Amalialad. Berith was the daemon, the Duke of Hell, and he had twenty-six legions. Amalialad remembered that Berith, also referred to as the Demonic Red Soldier, usually rode a red horse and had a demonic army of 130,000 soldiers. As his thoughts drifted further, the others in the room did not disturb him.

It was hours later when Amalialad finally aroused from his trance state. He looked around and noticed the others had already retired, so he made a mental note to apologise to them in the morning. He realised that the trance state he'd just fallen into was far deeper than he'd ever experienced before and that the clarity of the visions was more focused than any others he'd had. He then remembered the medallion and felt it now hanging around his neck and he knew why.

They all met for breakfast at 7 a.m. Chodon was first up and was cooking omelets for everyone. Tara was helping her. When he walked in, Ben and Joseph were talking at the table. Amalialad was pleased to see that everything appeared normal. However, he knew they all felt devastated about Lopsang's death and the killing of some of their newly-found allies, the Monk warriors, but that they were determined not to allow it to affect their focusing on the vital work ahead. Their grief had to be put on hold.

Amalialad called a meeting and an hour later Ben, Tara, Chodon, Joseph and John sat with him around the dining table.

"Thank you for joining me so promptly my friends. I know that with the tragic deaths of our friends, and the grief we suffer, how extremely difficult it is right now to concentrate on the battle ahead. But we must. I know that Lopsang and the Warriors would wish it. And we need to show that their deaths were not in vain. I'm not going to refer to them again until our mission is completed. Except for one thing. As you know, before he died, Lopsang was unable to talk to me about the daemon we're facing and so all seemed lost but that now is not the case." The others looked up in surprise and waited for Amalialad to continue. "Lopsang left his medallion for me to find, which I wear now." Amalialad took it off his neck to show them. "Lopsang cleverly managed to inscribe one word on the back of it. I think he did it knowing that something may happen to him. That word is Berith."

"Was he referring to the daemon, Lord Berith, also known as Baal?" Joseph asked.

"Yes, Joseph. He is also the Great Duke of Hell, the demon of slaughter and blasphemy. And Berith is very cunning, deceitful, powerful and terrible and he has twenty-six legions of demons under his command. Beware, he can appear as a soldier dressed in red, riding a massive red horse and wearing a golden crown on his head. It is said his skin is red too. But I must warn you further, when you see him you will be awestruck and frightened, perhaps even near to the point of death, and if you have a weak heart it may kill you. Berith also has a black aura of pure evil which sends out an esoteric energy of tremendous strength. If you give in to it, it will send you mad. I'm sorry to be so blunt but you must all be aware of what you're facing. There will be no recriminations, my friends, if any of you wish to return home and spend your last days with your families. You would do so with my blessing and sincere thanks for your help and bravery which you've all admirably demonstrated so far."

Ben looked at the others and could see their mild looks of surprise. He knew that, just like him, none of them would even consider the idea of leaving. They were all brothers now, committed to giving their lives for each other and humanity itself if necessary. Nobody was leaving. Ben knew that his friends were simply surprised that Amalialad had even suggested it.

"I'm sure I'm speaking for us all, Amalialad," Ben said, "when I tell you we're all staying." As Amalialad looked around, he saw all heads nodding in confirmation and a wave of pride swept through him.

"Thank you." Amalialad knew that if not all, then many of them were likely to be slaughtered. But he dismissed the thought from his mind.

"So, what's next then, Amalialad?" Ben said.

"Well, firstly, we secure this area, including the hotel, which incidentally belongs to Lord Kitchener, another active member of the Opus Dei. This compound will be our operations centre and so must be protected. Presently, staying inside the hotel are more than three hundred members of the Opus Dei who've been especially chosen for this operation. Many include Special Forces who've been given special ministerial leave to assist us here."

"Ah, so that's why the hotel was so busy yesterday," Tara said. "Now it's all fitting together." She smiled.

"Correct," Amalialad said. "There is a small army task force in the hotel responsible for securing this whole area. They are all familiar with warfare techniques and are the best in their field."

"Won't we attract attention from the police?" Tara asked.

"Francis assured me a few days ago that we won't. He just said, 'everything has been arranged' and I didn't question him."

"Ah, I see. That's a relief," Tara said.

"But we are vastly outnumbered and if all twenty-six legions march against us all at once, our position will be difficult."

Ben noticed the daunted expressions on the faces of everyone present, so he spoke again.

"So, what do you propose?"

"Well, it's plain what we have to do. The challenge, however, is in doing it. We have to block and seal the portal which brings the demon's army through to the earth plane."

"Wow! And how do you suggest we do that?"

"Well, Ben, we first need to find the Big Grey Man, known locally in Gaelic as Fear Liath Mhor."

"Who? What?" Ben asked. "Did you say a big grey man?"

"Yes, I did, and he's about twenty feet tall with a body completely covered with long, grey, wiry hair."

Chapter Thirty-Seven

Amalialad went on to explain that the Big Grey Man lived at the top of the Cairngorm mountain of Ben Macdhui, the second highest peak in Scotland. In local folklore the creature was known for decades, but it was the famous mountaineer Professor Norman Collie who, in 1889, first brought it to national attention with the first recorded encounter. He claimed to have heard the beast following him as he trekked back down from the cairn. For every three steps he took, he claimed he heard the creature take one.

He described, at a meeting of the Cairngorm Club in 1925, how he was terrified and that he'd never return there. Many trekkers of the mountain had since claimed to have seen a huge ape-like, misty figure accompanied by strange noises and feelings of extreme panic and dread.

"It's my view," said Amalialad, "that this creature is guarding something on the mountain and if anyone gets too close to it, it'll scare them away. Although it hasn't physically harmed anyone, I think that's because it doesn't want to attract attention from officials, since that would mean a thorough investigation of the area which may lead to what it's protecting.

"So now we need to search that mountain area to try and track the creature and to find possible locations where a portal may be hidden and where hundreds of daemons could hide. With us, I'm bringing along five Special Air Service officers who've had extensive experience of this type of terrain. I suspect we'll find the portal in one of the deep corries which litter the mountainside. A corrie would be an ideal hiding place and would probably provide enough space for at least a legion of daemons at a time to assemble. We'll take pictures of the whole area and I've arranged an aerial photographer to take photos. He should be circling that area as we speak. While we're away, other groups will be travelling to meet us here on our return. We'll be leaving in about two hours and you need to pack for up to four days. Oh, and by the way, I hope you all like camping in the snow." He smiled to himself, for he knew Ben hated the cold.

They all met at 10 a.m. outside the log cabin. The officers all wore army issue, fleece jackets over dark, woollen jumpers. They arrived outside the cabin in two dark blue Toyota Land Cruisers. Both vehicles had tinted windows and seated eight.

Everyone placed a duffel bag of personal belongings into the boots of the vehicles. Amalialad had explained earlier that any other special clothing and equipment which would be needed would later be supplied to them. They returned to the cabin for a final meeting.

"Thank you, once again, everyone for meeting us back here on time," Amalialad said. "I'd like to first introduce you to, and pass you over to, Commander Colonel Jackson." The colonel smiled and slowly looked around at his audience.

"We shall be travelling together in two groups to our starting point, which will be at the Linn of Dee car park. From there we shall continue to our first main path in Glen Lui. We'll follow this up-glen for a few kilometres until we reach an old house, which is used as the mountain rescue post, at Derry Lodge. We'll talk once more when we arrive. But from there it's about two hours' trek to the car park and then another hour's trekking to the rescue post. We should arrive there at about twelve hundred hours. You will follow our leadership without question. If I say jump, you jump. Do you understand this?" The colonel eyed each one of the men seated, including his own.

"Yes, sir!" the colonel's men said loudly, in unison. The others also nodded their agreement. Everyone knew their lives depended on following orders, but they felt uncomfortable. They weren't used to the formal military rhetoric

"Ben, Joseph, Simon. Tara, Chodon, John and Sergeant Willis will travel with Amalialad's group in vehicle one. The rest of you will travel with me. Any questions?" There were none.

The road to the Lyn of Dee was rugged and winding.

They pulled into the car park at 10:45 a.m. They parked in two private bays near the customer service kiosk in the centre of the car park. The kiosk had two discreet security cameras, hidden in the recess of the tiled roofing, which overlooked the car park, including their vehicles.

The colonel and his group exited their vehicle first. After getting out, they collected their belongings. Apart from their heavy duty, waterproof, duffel bags, the officers also took out larger bags which held other essential equipment. Joseph observed them with interest and guessed the larger bags weighed at least thirty kilograms. They must have been carrying a total weight of fifty kilograms, he thought, as he saw them briskly walking away towards the start of the track for Derry Lodge.

They were, as they looked around at the area before walking, all awestruck by the spectacular scenery. They started the march along the forest track in the lower part of the glen. They passed through old native Scottish pines and a variety of colourful shrubs and bushes which grew at the sides of the track. The fresh scents wafted from the vegetation and smelt like expensive cologne. They reminded Joseph of walking into a perfumery store.

Halfway to Derry Lodge they came across a rather impressive building and decided to break for snacks. The views from the building, which looked like an old shooting lodge were impressive, like the ones they'd seen at the start of the Glen Lui track. Amalialad paused silently and was suddenly overcome by a spiritual aura of peace and tranquility. There was, he sensed with relief, no evil here. But they still had a tough trek ahead. Within seconds he sensed a dark foreboding.

"Do you remember much about your former life as Warrior Monk?" Ben asked John.

John smiled.

"Yes, I remember most of it and carry the guilt of what I did then with me today." He paused. "We all do."

"I understand, but surely you shouldn't have to carry the guilt from a past life to this one?"

"Well, of course we must. We pass eventually into a new life in order to learn and pay for the mistakes from our past lives and so our Karma will either develop or deteriorate until we reach the state of enlightenment-perfection."

"Well, how many lives will that take?"

"Well, that depends on the individual. You see, each life still gives us free choices. We can choose to follow goodness or be tempted by negativity or evil. If one chose the latter, then the journey to enlightenment would take much longer."

"Were you aware of all this in your last life?" Ben wondered how anyone could choose the way of evil knowing that their journey would take so much longer.

"In all our lives we are still human, Ben. As such we sometimes make split second decisions without giving enough thought to the consequences. I was very vulnerable and young when the high lamas at our monastery gave me the chance to train as a Monk Warrior. I felt it an honour, as did most of my brethren Warriors. We weren't aware of the evil we were doing since we obeyed the orders of our masters without question. As far as we were concerned, those we killed were evil. We had no idea of the corruption that some of our masters possessed. Further, our training was brutal, and our lives were threatened if we disobeyed. Our days were spent in extensive training, fine tuning our combat skills and working on fighting strategies until we became the most terrifying warriors the country had ever known, and, I'm now ashamed to say, committing every type of atrocity you could ever conceivably think of to achieve our goal and please our masters."

"I'm sorry, John, but I think the whole group feels safer with you and your fellow Warriors."

"Thank you, Ben. I choose to be here today to defend the good against the growing evil. There is, I think, in all men, a line which they can cross, which cuts through their hearts, when choosing either the road to goodness or evil and I truly believe that most opt for goodness. And if that is the case then goodness will triumph."

"Well, John, let's hope you're right." At that moment Amalialad called his group over to talk with them.

They all sat around an old pine table which had been there for years, used by picnickers visiting the lodge.

"Well, it's been wonderful so far hasn't it?"

"The most fantastic views I think I've ever seen," Tara replied.

"And the smells from the trees and plants are just stunning. The exercise felt good too," Chodon said.

Then Amalialad spoke again.

"But of course, you know why we're here." They all nodded again, looking less cheerful.

"The Big Grey Man we seek could be anywhere or nowhere. Sightings of him have occurred from this point onwards, so we all need to be extremely vigilant. Report anything unusual and take nothing for granted. I'm sorry, but no conversations en-route either, I'm afraid, you need to keenly focus all your senses on the search. We need to be aware of anything which may seem unusual or out of place. If it's what I think it is, then somewhere ahead, we're likely facing an extremely cunning and dangerous creature. A daemon of immense power. When we reach Glen Luibeg, the Colonel's group will be taking a different route. They're travelling a longer route to get to the summit. We felt that by dividing the groups we'll have a better chance of both finding the creature and increasing the chance of at least one group achieving our objective. If any of the groups spot the creature, we'll send up a flare to warn the other group as well contacting each other by mobile or radio phone. Now, the signal's very good up here so contact shouldn't be a problem. However, if for any reason no contact can be made, we'll meet at the summit later. I'm afraid when we part, we'll have a little extra essential equipment to carry, but don't worry, the colonels' men won't be passing that on to us until we divide up. Ok," Amalialad glanced outside, "the colonel's group is leaving now so let's go. But as I said, no chatting and stay alert." They then followed Amalialad and continued along the main track, past the mountain rescue building, until they came to the Derry Burn footbridge. Once again, the views were dazzling. On the far side of the bridge they turned left across the flats. Then the changes began. The path became extremely boggy and they started struggling to negotiate the track. It got worse as they trudged ahead towards Glen Luibeg. They noticed the colonel's group had stopped just ahead at a fork in the path and realised that this was the place where the groups would split up. Except for the colonel's group, they were exhausted. It became obvious to Ben as he looked at the other group that they were extremely fit, much fitter than him anyway. He was also reminded then, as he saw some of the Colonels men take off some of their duffel bags and placing them on a dry area of ground nearby, of the extra load they would each have to carry. He seriously wondered if he'd cope.

The colonel walked over to Amalialad.

"This is where we part, my friend. Good luck. If we hear from you by phone or flare, we'll get to you in a jiffy, rest assured."

"I know you will. May your God be with you, Tom." They shook hands firmly.

Groaning silently to himself, Ben picked up his extra load. The rest of the men did the same, but Tara and Chodon were not given additional luggage to carry and even though the two protested Amalialad had made the decision. Amalialad shared the load by picking up the heaviest bag. An hour into the trek he turned to the others to speak. He could see they were already tired and would soon need to rest.

"Not far ahead should be an ideal place to rest and camp for the night. There should be a fresh stream and a dry place to shelter there." Amalialad hoped that the research he'd read about the area and the maps he carried were correct. After a ten-minute rest, they walked on.

But as Amalialad took just a single step forward he found himself suddenly enveloped in a heavy blanket of mist. Struggling to orientate himself, he felt a demonic malevolence in the air. But he realized it too late; it was a trap!

Chapter thirty-eight

Godfrey looked directly into their eyes as he shrieked with pain. It was agonizing. He then felt an excruciating, increasing tightness flow through his body and the last words, which he'd barely heard, was Francis's warning. But he knew it was then too late. Every molecule in his body, from his toes to the top of his head, were slowly turning to stone and his last frightening memory was looking down to see two solid, concrete legs.

Peter looked over with horror and wondered if he was hallucinating. Hugh was also stunned at what he'd witnessed and, shrieking in frustration and anger, ran to help his friend. But his attempts to help were in vain. "No! It's what they want. They want to distract us. We must focus on trapping them before we get turned to stone too. Quickly, Peter. Resist their influence." Francis shook him. "You must help me coax them to the centre of the room. We must get them into the circle."

Peter's mind spun. The garbled sounds of the witches somehow subdued his consciousness and he felt himself gently slipping into sleep. But then the words from Amalialad days ago drifted quickly into his thoughts. 'You have a higher sense of perception than most people be sure to use it.' With that memory, something snapped in Peter's head and he swiftly brushed aside the witches' mind control effects and ran to the centre of the circle. Then, with Francis, he tried to beckon the witches to follow. And follow they did.

"Now get out of this circle, Peter. Hurry up!" Francis said.

And Peter quickly left the circle. His reflexes were extraordinary and once outside the circle he pulled his cross from his pocket and held it, face up and straight out, at the witches. And, like a statue, unmoving, he held his ground.

"Well done. Now stand still, Peter," Francis said. "Whatever happens, say and do nothing. They may try to trick you but ignore them. It's absolutely crucial you stand steadfast and true." The words from Francis sunk in and Peter stood stock still. Then, inexplicably, Peter's awareness heightened dramatically, and he began to translate the Latin words which Francis started reciting. Peter recognised some of the words from the 'Rite of the Exorcism' which was taken from King Solomon's Book of Magic, about the Key of Solomon. Peter knew it to be one of the most popular grimoires which dated back to the fourteenth century. And the strange circular drawing, inscribed by Francis earlier with chalk on the floor was, Francis had informed him, called The Devil's Trap. Peter knew it to be one of the most powerful traps for daemons. It consisted of circles and pentagons filled with Latin words and strange symbols and Francis positioned himself in front of the screaming witches which had now become mysteriously trapped inside the circle. Peter listened intently to the words. They had a haunting, mystical chill about them and he sensed a tremendous power resonating from Francis's voice, as he eloquently emphasised each word of the rite.

"Exorcizamus te, omnis immundus spiritis, omnis satanic potestas, omnis incursion infernalis adversarii, omnis legio, omni congregation et secta diabolica..."

Suddenly, fiercely, the witches sneered and growled. Then, as if in a fit, they thrashed their bodies powerfully against the floor, and in an instant and without warning, they sharply jumped up and raced for the edge of the circle. And Peter realized, almost too late, they were heading directly towards him.

But he remained stubbornly still.

Then, just half a meter away from him, they crashed hard against what could only be described as an invisible wall. Peter's eyes were closed but he'd perceived their every movement and he could smell the nauseating stench from the demonic presence as his heart raced and the adrenalin surged through his body. Peter guessed that the entities were testing him, studying his resolve. They knew, as he did, that a forcefield, which Francis had initiated earlier with his spell, was there and they were trapped inside it. The act was a ploy to test him. But why?

As Francis continued reading, Peter, along with him, translated the rest of the rite.

"We exorcise you, every impure spirit, every satanic power, every incursion of the infernal

Therefore, accursed dragon and every diabolical legion, we adjure you."

"Revenge, revenge we want. We from Forfar want the revenge," cackled one of the entities. The voice was hideously slurred, and Peter sensed their pain as they struggled to speak. He was puzzled. Why did they want to talk when it meant bearing such excruciating pain? And their talk of revenge? About what?

Francis continued with his recital.

"Cease to deceive human creatures and refrain from giving to them the poison of eternal damnation.

Begone Satan, inventor and master of all deceit, enemy of man's salvation,

Humble yourself under the mighty hand of God, tremble and flee when we invoke the holy and Terrible Name which causes hell to tremble

From the snares of the devil, deliver us, O Lord.

We exorcise you, every impure spirit, every satanic power, every incursion of the infernal adversary, every legion, every congregation and diabolical sect

Therefore, accursed dragon and every diabolical legion, we adjure you...Cease to deceive human creatures, and give to them the poison the poison of eternal damnation

That thy Church may serve Thee in secure liberty secure, we ask Thee hear us."

As the last words were spoken, the witches collapsed in a heap on the floor. Hugh was still grief-stricken at the loss of his friend and had drifted off into a deep sleep, but he was just beginning to come around. He soon grasped what was happening in the room and the shock of what he saw quickly stirred him to action. He jumped up with his cross in his hand and held it out towards the sneering witches slumped on the floor.

"Begone! daemon witches of Forfar," Hugh shouted. "Revenge you may be granted, but you have committed a bigger sin. You have allied yourselves with the dark forces of Lucifer himself to enact your revenge. That is unacceptable. You shall now be sent back to the pits of Hell, banished for all eternity." Then, just after Francis finished his ritual, Hugh took out a small bottle from his trouser pocket and poured the liquid over the witches. Instantly, the bodies exploded and the only remains of where they'd lain were large blackened scorch marks covered with a dirty, brown ash. And writhing within the ash were three large black maggots. Then the smell hit them, an awful stench which rapidly spread throughout the room. Everyone covered their noses. The disgusting smell was almost unbearable, and Peter felt that such a diabolical stench could only stem from something evil. For a few moments they continued to gaze in amazement at the stain of malevolence left on the floor but then, mysteriously, a tremendous glow of white light entered and lit the whole room. It was so bright that the three of them had to cover their eyes to avoid its ferocious intensity. But equally mystifying, within a few seconds the light swiftly disappeared, and they stood, stunned, and awestruck. Moments later, when they looked back at the floor, to their utter surprise, there was nothing there. Not a single mark. Even the drawing of the Devil's trap had gone, and they were left staring once again, confused and in utter bewilderment at what they'd just witnessed. Peter wondered if it was to do with the spell Francis had cast and, indeed, Hugh too glanced towards Francis for answers. Francis suspected what they were thinking.

"There's nothing to tell you my friends, only that the devil's work here has been cleansed." Hugh and Peter nodded slightly. But neither had a clue as to what had happened and why it had happened.

"I'm so very sorry about Godfrey. He was a most loyal and courageous knight," Peter said, solemnly.

"Indeed, there were none braver," Francis said.

"He was my best friend," Hugh replied. His head hung low. "He'll be forever in my thoughts on calm and happy days and never forgotten while I breathe air." Francis then gave a blessing to their friend, starting and finishing with the sign of the cross. Peter closed his eyes and remained still, simply repeating the sign of the cross in unison with Hugh.

"How did you know the creatures were witches?" Peter asked Hugh.

"I saw their memories in a dream, albeit several years ago. I'd visualised a terrible witch hunt carried out here in Forfar nearly four hundred years ago. A group of women were falsely accused of witchcraft by the town council of that time. In that dream I felt their torture and suffering. Even their families were painfully tortured and put to death. Most were killed by drowning. Since that time those women have wandered the earth in deep torment but with a single desire. Revenge! Since their deaths they have systematically haunted and terrified other women and to wreak revenge on men. What happened to them was shameful, but they shouldn't have taken out their revenge on innocent people. They sought havoc wherever they roamed, and many people have been literally terrified to death by them. As I said, one may initially have had sympathy for them since they were innocent, but they chose to commit the biggest sin of all. Their evil desires increased and later they freely joined Lucifer's army to obtain more power and to enact their revenge. The moment they made that choice, their fate was sealed."

"I understand," Peter said. "But I don't think it was a coincidence that those witches joined the dark forces. I think Lucifer, the devil himself, purposely recruited them. Every person living has a conscience which intrinsically identifies the lines of good and bad within our souls. If you like, we all understand what's right and wrong. But, over the centuries I think some of these lines have become blurred. And I think this is because of the manipulation of people by the devil's minions who are wandering amongst us all and growing at a tremendous rate. I suspect these women only turned to the dark side because of the cruelty to them while alive. Gentleman, our battle ahead will be far more arduous now than we could ever have imagined. We must now focus on finding and bringing the Ark of the Covenant to Amalialad, at Braemar. The odds are drastically against us and we're now one brave man down." Peter then looked slowly at Francis and Hugh. He sensed no fear there, but instead, a determination and a deep, steadfast resolve to get the job done, whatever the cost. Or to die trying.

Chapter thirty-nine

The demonic energy was powerful and Amalialad felt he'd been kicked hard in the stomach. Then he felt something heavy wrap itself around his neck. And tighten. He could just make out a massive arm as he struggled to breathe and tried desperately to loosen the grip with his hands. In vain he kept trying, but sensed it was useless and soon felt a dizziness overcoming him. He knew if he passed out there'd be no hope for him. Then he heard a gruff voice in his head. 'Just give in and relax. Don't fight it. You'll be ok.' Amalialad wasn't fooled. He recognised the daemon's voice. But the power it unleashed was awesome and he knew he couldn't hold it off much longer. He tried to free himself, but it was futile. He felt himself weakening. He knew he was on the very edge of losing consciousness. He was also dimly aware that if he passed out now, he'd never awaken again. Amalialad tried one more time to break free and mustered up every fibre of energy from his physical body, from the core of his being and from the deepest depths of his soul. But it would be his last attempt, and he knew it. He knew he'd die if he failed. But worse, he knew he'd become an eternal slave to the daemon in Hell if he didn't try. So, finally, with his consciousness rapidly ebbing away, with enormous effort and tremendous determination, with his mind he moulded every single molecule of energy together into a ball of enormous light and threw it around the invisible arm. And for an instant the brutal grip finally broke, but an instant was enough for Amalialad and with lightning speed he spun around and sent the flaming ball swirling again. Up and down and around it spun and again it went hurling around and around until the tremendous energy surge cleared the heavy mist encircling him and he felt the malevolence in the air fade away. And with it he heard some fading final words from the daemon filter through. 'When you, Dondrom, boy leader of Tibet, face me again it will be different. I will destroy you and all your human kind. But your death will be slow and so very painful. I will personally take you back to the deepest depths of hell with me and watch as your skin slowly burns to a crisp. And then down to the bones. Oh. So unimaginably excruciatingly unbearable it will be. And then I shall watch you heal again. And when it heals, I shall watch it burn to a crisp once more. And so, in perpetuity this will continue burning then healing, burning then healing, until your soul cries out to serve me' The daemon then laughed, and as it faded, its hideous sound echoed through the air.

Amalialad staggered to the ground. He was thoroughly exhausted, drained and his heart was weak. Then as he looked up, he noticed that the ball of light he'd thrown was almost extinguished. With a final effort, Amalialad telepathically pulled back the last residual threads of the energy and focused them on his heart. It was his only hope. He then remained completely still, in a self-hypnotic state, until finally he felt his heart start pumping normally again. In that time, he hadn't noticed Ben running to him.

"Are you ok?" Ben asked. Amalialad stirred. Then he slowly turned and looked up at Ben. Ben jolted back in horror. Amalialad looked twenty years older.

"Ah, Ben, we must return to Braemar Lodge. We have vital work to do lest this battle be lost." Amalialad spoke softly. His voice was very weak. Ben, still in shock at seeing his friend in such a poor state, simply nodded. This was not the time for questions, he thought. It was a time for action. Ben let Amalialad rest while he rushed back and gave instructions to the rest, to pack up and be ready, at a moment's notice.

Amalialad still looked haggard as moments later he approached Ben.

"I need to get back to the lodge as quickly as possible," he said. Ben turned to Amalialad and saw the deep worry lines on his brow and knew something very serious had occurred.

"What's happened?"

"Let's just say that the enemy have just used their best weapon. And we have been truly fooled."

"What weapon have they used?"

"Trickery! My friend, deceit at its best. We have been tricked and the tables have been, yet again, twisted and turned against us. Unless we act quickly this battle is lost!"

Chapter forty

Glamis Castle was just six miles from Forfar and they reached the entrance gate to the castle grounds within fifteen minutes. No hold ups. Some luck at last, Peter thought as he slowed to a halt at the entrance. He quickly paid their fees then slowly drove on through the wide entrance and into the expansive grounds. Then a flickering thought crossed his mind. There was no traffic around. But it only briefly flickered, so he didn't dwell on it. And it didn't raise any concerns. The grounds were spectacular, and Peter reflected on what he'd recently read about Glamis Castle. It was renowned to be the most beautiful castle in Britain. He stared, totally enthralled, at the beauty of the grounds and at the mass of bright colours which flashed past him as the myriad of flowers, primarily rhododendrons and azaleas, scattered abundantly along the driveway and across the vast pristine green lawns, went by.

The main entrance to the castle was stunning to look at and the time, effort and craftsmanship that had gone into building was incredible. But the towers in front of the castle were the most impressive part of its structure and were breathtaking to look at. Francis had arranged to meet Simon, the senior tour guide and a loyal member of the Opus Dei. Peter negotiated the final few yards into the staff car park, where Simon had suggested they parked.

Five minutes later, Simon opened the door to greet them.

"I'm glad you all managed to get here safely, gentlemen. It's an honour to meet you." He stretched his hand out to Hugh, then to Francis and then to Peter. And that, Peter thought, was his first mistake. Francis looked surprised too and knew something was wrong.

As a member of the Opus Dei he should have recognised Francis immediately and greeted him first and foremost with his formal title. His second mistake was wearing the ring of the Opus Dei upside down. The ring bore the crest of the Opus Dei - a simple cross encircled by a circle. But his ring was put on his finger incorrectly and showed the cross to be inverted. A loyal member of the Opus Dei would never have made this error. It would have been a sacrilege. Francis glanced towards Peter. He was wondering if Peter had noticed his concern. He had, and Peter discreetly nodded his acknowledgement. Peter knew they still needed to get inside to the small chapel as arranged and that they still needed the imposter's help to do that before directly confronting him, and as they entered, he just hoped the imposter had no more surprises waiting for them. His feeling was that other surprises wouldn't come until later, after the imposter had acquired more information about their intentions for visiting the castle. Francis had only told Simon that they were there to do some historical research on behalf of the Opus Dei.

Simon led them through the doorway into a small reception area. Then, smiling broadly, he turned to face them.

"Francis has told me about your visit and, of course, I'll do all I can to help."

"Thank you, Simon. Perhaps you'd take us on a general sightseeing tour first, so we can get a feeling for the place and of course see some of the amazing rooms which we've heard of and read so much about."

"It'll be my pleasure. Please follow me and we can talk along the way."

As they entered the first room, the imposter began talking again.

"As we walk through the castle and all its majestic rooms, it may very well remind you of any museum. However, every painting, and every piece of furnishing and each tiny detail you see along the way will show you that this is not a museum but an amazingly incredible family home that has witnessed..." and so Simon went on.

Peter whispered in Hugh's ear to follow closely behind Simon while he conferred with Francis but told him he'd explain more to him later. Nevertheless, Peter knew his conversation with Francis had to be discreet and brief. He didn't want to attract any suspicion from the imposter even though he seemed to be utterly focused on his tour script. Of course, Peter knew they'd all done a lot of research about the castle themselves and probably knew as much, if not more, about its interior as the imposter but he needed this time to talk with Francis and to decide on their next move.

"I meant to ask," whispered Francis, "why do we need to go to the chapel? Is that where the Ark is hidden?"

"I don't think so but it's where I hope to find the answer to that question."

"Ah, is there some sort of hidden document there you need to find?"

"No, no document."

Francis looked at Peter, perplexed.

"Then, if you don't mind me asking, why would you need to visit the chapel?"

"I hope to talk to the most beautiful lady who ever lived. She was a lady who beheld beauty in her heart, body and soul. She was a lady who had the most impeccable character. She was a lady without blemish. Indeed, she was braver than any man and she was tortured and killed in the most tragic circumstances." Peter spoke from the heart and Francis noticed the lump in his friend's throat as he saw him swallowing hard. He wondered too whether he saw his friend's eyes water.

"Ah, I see."

"I'm sorry, Francis. I should have explained before now but, crucially, I had to arrange a specific time to get here and I didn't want any delays. Of course, you have the right to ask any questions you wish but, please, let me first briefly explain my thoughts and what I know about how I think we can find out where the Ark is hidden. It may answer some of them."

"Thank you, Peter. I'd appreciate that."

"As I said, the circumstances were tragic. It was four hundred years ago when the Sixth Lord of Glamis married Janet Douglas. They had a son, John, and lived a very peaceful and happy family life. That is until Lord Glamis died. Lady Janet was born into the Douglas clan and her brother was the stepfather of King James the Fifth. King James hated the Douglas Clan and so when Lord Glamis died, he sought advantage to carry out a vendetta against

Lady Jane. Finally, using lies, deceit and torture he managed to falsely convict Lady Janet of being a witch. But a witch who'd plotted to kill him. Consequently, he managed to convince others and get her and her son imprisoned in the dungeons of Edinburgh castle. Everyone that knew her suspected that the allegations were totally unfounded but there was little they could do. In fact, Lady Jane was known to be one of the kindest, caring and respectable women that ever lived. Eventually, on July seventeenth, 1537, then virtually blind from being imprisoned for so long, Lady Janet Glamis was burned at Edinburgh castle. She was, as I said, a most beautiful woman in her prime yet she courageously endured her torture and pain in silence. Some say she was a symbol of goodness itself, you might say, a saintly woman. She is known in Glamis Castle as the Grey Lady. But to me she was the most wonderful, loving and caring person one could ever wish to meet. She really was goodness incarnate."

Francis looked at Peter in astonishment.

"You somehow knew her personally? But that's impossible! She's been dead for nearly four hundred years!"

Peter stared directly at Francis. His eyes were red from straining to hold back the tears.

"Not quite, my friend. She came back. She was my dearest and most precious. She was my soul mate. She was my wife for fifteen years. She came back."

Chapter forty-one

They set a hard pace and reached Braemar Lodge within half the time it had taken to reach the peak. Amalialad was focused on getting into the communications room which was in a back room of the lodge. He had many to contact and he knew the signal was strongest there, despite the harsh weather outside. Without explanation he'd hurriedly left Ben and the rest of the group. There were ten technicians sitting behind monitors and three other office staff casually walking around. When Amalialad walked in they all glanced towards him. Amalialad smiled broadly and then spoke. His words were strong and forceful yet not intimidating. They reflected an urgency that everyone listening understood and when he'd finished, they all knew they had to work harder than they'd ever done before. Almost immediately, the room was a hive of activity. Secretaries and typists pounded the keyboards on their laptops and computers. Voices were raised in urgent tones as information and instructions were speedily disseminated from inside the room and out across the globe. They were now in Category One.

Ben sat at a table with Tara, Chodon and Daniel, one of the Opus Dei commanders named.

"I have enormous respect for your friend, Amalialad, Ben," said Daniel. "He has, for someone so young, proven to be both wise and brave, yet he always seems so calm about what's happening around him and unafraid of the dangers ahead. That concerns me a little."

"Sometimes the strongest among us smile through adversity and pain, but they cry and shed their tears in the shadows. They take on heavy responsibilities and in doing so they must sometimes live long periods in secrecy and fight battles very few know about. Such is the nature of their work. Amalialad is special and one of these rare individuals. You need not concern yourself, Daniel. There is nobody else alive today that could take on the measure and overcome the perils we face." Daniel nodded in satisfaction. He'd also developed a huge respect for Ben and wholeheartedly trusted his opinion. But second thoughts fleeted through Daniel's mind when the whole cottage shook moments later. The attack was unexpected and the fetid stench which blew through the open windows gave the hideous creatures away. Everyone had heard the stories about trolls. They weren't just fairytale characters from children's books. They formed a crucial part of the daemons' legions. It was said that they usually led the battles. They were the strongest creatures ever to roam the earth. With their thick leather skins, which no ordinary bullets could ever pierce, their large, deformed heads, whose mouths contained over a hundred sharp, serrated teeth, each tooth six inches long, and whose body frame stood an average height of seven feet, they were not to be easily reckoned with. Further, their arms were pure muscle and their clawed hands could rip open any creature's belly in seconds. They were empowered with enormous strength. But they had weaknesses too. Their enemies knew in advance of their coming since they were easily recognized from a distance by their foul smell. Most described the smell as being five times stronger and fouler than any skunks. Their vision too was weak and blurred, which was, evidently, due to some rare genetic defect. They were also cumbersome and slow, and their intelligence was low. And Ben was relying on this.

Salivating heavily at the thought of eating human flesh, the trolls trudged defiantly towards the lodge.

Chapter forty-two

"You mean this is the same woman that supposedly haunts the chapel? The same ghost whose seat, it is said, has never been used by anyone since her death?" Francis said. "And now you're telling me, she was also your wife?"

"Precisely."

In his research about the castle Francis had read about how a grey lady haunted both the chapel and the clock tower. It was said that inside the chapel, where she'd often been reported to have been seen sitting, nobody since her death was ever allowed to sit in the seat she'd occupied. Even now, when the chapel was no longer open to the public, and only family ceremonies were conducted, nobody could use the seat.

"I'm so sorry, Peter, but I really am lost for words. My deepest sorrow of course for your loss but I'd have a problem questioning my own sanity if I automatically accepted what you've told me. If we hadn't experienced so many strange and inexplicable events already together, I'd have to advise you to seek some sort of psychological help yet in my heart I strangely know that what you're telling me is the truth. But assuming that's so, how can she help us if she's no longer alive?"

"Francis, you will find my next statement even more difficult to accept but I ask you, as a close friend, to do so. If you have doubts, I'd ask you to put them to Amalialad later since he will confirm what I say next. Gloria, my wife, was the reincarnation of Lady Douglas."

Francis was dumbstruck.

"At first I had no idea. It wasn't until the very end, when Gloria was only hours from death, that she told me something very strange. I didn't take much notice at the time because I was so overcome with the thought of her dying and because my concern was for the immense pain she was suffering. Also, I thought she may have been a little delirious because of the high dosage of painkilling drugs she was taking."

"What did she say?"

"She said, 'My dearest Peter. Always remember I love you so very much and that our love for each other will always exist. For true love can never be taken away, not even by death. There is a reason to our lives, my darling, and to our passing but trust me, we will meet again. Remember too, just as we have shared our love and lives together, so we have shared everything else too and we shall continue to do so. I love you, Peter. I'll always love you so very, very much'." Peter remembered then how Gloria's bright smile lit up the tears which glistened as they streamed gently down her cheeks. Then her eyes closed, and she was still. But at that very moment he felt his body fill with a warm glow. He then felt a surge of enormous emotion, which he could only describe as pure love and affection, flow through his entire body. And this was followed by a distinct odour of lavender which he quickly recognized as Gloria's favourite perfume. He then remembered wishing for the feelings to remain with him forever, but he knew they were all given to him as loving, farewell gifts, and wouldn't linger for long.

It was only after meeting up with Amalialad and listening to him talking about reincarnation and how he was supposed to be the fourteenth Dalai Lama, that Peter began to wonder more about Gloria's words. She seemed to know so much more about life than he did, and she mentioned continuing to share things. It was puzzling. And when Amalialad asked him to go to Glamis Castle, his research brought up some strange happenings that had evidently taken place there and when he'd read about the Grey Lady, he'd suddenly felt the same surge of love flow through him, and with it too, the same smell of lavender. He knew his keen sense of perception was far stronger than most, but at that moment he knew, without question, it was a message from Gloria.

"On further investigating, I discovered that the portraits of Lady Janet Douglas drawn at that time were identical to Gloria. You can imagine how shocked I was at such a discovery, but what's more, their birthdays were also the same, although of course years apart. One could argue that this was pure coincidence but every sense in my body tells me I'm right. I believe they both had the same souls which lived two separate lives. Now I know this seems ridiculous, Francis, but I'm hoping, if I'm right, that the Grey Lady will be able to tell me where the Ark is hidden."

"What?" said Francis, trying not to raise his voice. "I'm sorry, Peter, but this is all too much to take in. I really don't know what to say. I need time to digest all this."

Peter couldn't help smiling at Francis's reaction. He had half-expected it and was himself not sure if what he intended to do would work or yield any positive results. But he knew that to any sane individual the whole idea must seem preposterous. For him, it was another gut feeling. But his feelings had so far proven to be reliable, and, like Amalialad had told him, his sense of perception was most remarkable, and he should depend on it more often. He had, and during the last few days he'd practiced and vastly improved his channeling skills. Indeed, his hearing had now become so acute that he could clearly listen in to conversations fifteen meters away. Suddenly, Peter's thoughts were interrupted as he noticed the imposter turning back to look at his three guests.

Francis stood next to Hugh while the imposter spoke Then, Francis silently signaled to Hugh to go to Peter. Francis then observed Peter whispering into Hugh's ear before both caught back up with him. As they did so the imposter, once again, turned towards them.

"So, are there any questions, gentlemen?" the imposter asked.

"Yes," Peter answered. "Who are you?"

"Pardon?" But his face lost its paleness and he began to shake.

"Who are you? You're not Simon, the person we arranged to meet. So where is he and who are you?"

Hugh positioned himself behind the imposter. It had the desired effect and, feeling intimidated, the imposter replied.

"I was just told to show a small group of three gentlemen around today because a colleague was ill. That's all. I swear it."

"What else?" Peter said.

"What do you mean?" Hugh put an arm on the imposter's shoulder. The gesture was taken, as it was meant to, as a threat.

The imposter quickly decided that the five hundred pound he's been offered wasn't worth the potential injuries he may suffer if he didn't explain himself, so he blurted out the whole story.

He explained that it was his day off, but he'd got a call to say a replacement for the day was needed because one of the tour guides was ill. So, when they offered him the money, he'd jumped at the chance to fill in. All he had to do was to wear a silly religious type of ring and pretend his name was Simon. Easy-peasy, he'd thought, and, for so much, he hadn't questioned their motives, although now, on reflection, he wished he had.

"Will he be ok?" Francis asked.

"He'll be fine. He'll just be unconscious for a short while. Don't worry, I'll hide him away somewhere safe for now. He'll be out for at least an hour, but I'll tie him up too. He won't be found until the morning."

"Ok, that's fine," Peter said. "Thanks, Hugh."

"That's what I'm here for, my friend. The guide mentioned he was told to lead us all out to the courtyard. That'll be a trap, right?"

"Yes, that's for sure, but I was hoping we could avoid the attackers. Their numbers will be high and so our chances of defeating them would be very slim. However, they can't afford to let us escape from here. There's too much at stake for them, including their lives, I'm sure, if they failed to deal with us. I think it's come to, either we die here, or they die here."

"If we avoid them and escape, how would they die?" Hugh asked, puzzled.

"Other daemons would be instructed to kill them instantly for their failings. You know how brutal Daemon Lords are, their anger would be enormous. If the creatures that come to the courtyard fail in their task to stop us, the punishment for them would be cruel and agonizing deaths. Firstly, they would suffer unimaginable torture. Simply killing them would be a godsend, but we both know, Daemon Lords never entertain god-sends."

"Of course, you're right," Hugh said. Then as he quietly reflected on what Peter had said, he lifted the imposter's body, put it over his shoulder and carried it away.

"Ah, Hugh, just hold on a moment, please," Peter called after him. He walked over to the imposter's hanging body and searched his pockets. He pulled out a cell phone and some loose change. There was nothing else. He replaced the change. "This is what I'm after. Thank you, Hugh."

"It's a pleasure." Said Hugh. Then, effortlessly, he walked off again with the imposter's body swaying against his back.

"Don't you have a phone?" Francis asked.

"Yes, but it's always good to have a spare, right?"

"Hmm, I suppose so," Francis said, but he thought it odd nevertheless.

"What time do you make it, Francis?" Francis glanced at his watch.

"It's exactly eleven thirty."

"Thanks." Peter altered his watch slightly to correlate the times. "Now, Francis, do you mind waiting here for Hugh? He should be back shortly, only I want to walk ahead to check the layout."

"Of course, but be careful. You know we're more vulnerable now on our own."

"I understand, but time is limited, and we must find the chapel. I have a plan of the castle and I want to check it out. It's crucial we get to the chapel as fast as possible. That's where I feel sure we're find our answers. I'm going to check out the wing of the castle where the chapel is supposed to be located."

"OK, good luck. We'll wait here for you, then."

Peter hadn't been entirely honest with Francis. He knew his friend was perfectly right. For him to wander off on his own at such a time was foolhardy. However, he had a good reason. While talking with Francis earlier he'd felt an icy cold chill pass through him. It was a deathly chill he'd felt once before. Peter shivered again as he remembered. He hadn't mentioned it to Francis because they'd had enough horror to contend with at the time, but he'd experienced it in the deserted house he and Francis were locked up in while escaping the demonic creatures surrounding them. Peter felt something was stalking him and now it was time to face it, but without endangering Hugh and Francis.

His perception was of a dark demonic creature with a single mission - to kill him. He guessed it would be a strong adversary and although he wasn't surprised, he was scared. The malevolence he felt in the chills was frightening and for the first time he had doubts about surviving. He knew he'd undertaken a key part in the fight to defeat the dark forces and his continued success was crucial in defeating the enemy, so it was of no surprise that the enemy would seek him out, and remove him, someone who was a key annoyance to them, from the picture.

   He hoped the route he took was the one which would lead him to the chapel. He'd remembered the layout of the castle perfectly. About six corridors ahead and a few twists and turns and he'd be there. The sound from his footsteps was heavily cushioned by the thickly-carpeted walkways and he perceived there was no other person around. His perception skills were now getting much stronger. It was quiet but eerily quiet and as he walked further, he suddenly felt something was waiting ahead of him. What was waiting was not human. He sensed it was lurking in the shadows ahead, ready to pounce, as he walked close by. Peter walked on regardless. He knew he had to face whatever it was at some time or another and right then he just wanted it dealt with. It was ten minutes later when Peter passed a sign with the words St. Michaels on it that his hopes brightened. St. Michaels was the name of the chapel. Then, as he turned into the final corridor, he saw the door to the chapel directly ahead of him. But he felt again the familiar, haunting and deadly chill pass through him and stopped abruptly in his tracks. He stood stock still, almost frozen to the spot yet his body still, involuntary, shook with uncontrollable fear. He focused as best he could straight ahead and watched in horror as a dark, grey, shimmering mass, of what looked like jelly, manifested in front of him. And the chill became colder and colder. Peter felt his fingers stiffen. He was gradually freezing to death. Peter focused once again, much harder this time and mustered up the strength to put his right hand into his pocket. What must have been seconds seemed like hours before he managed to withdraw the rock salt pouch and open the lace to reveal the contents inside. He could barely move now, and the biting cold had numbed his whole body. But with one last desperate surge of willpower, he jerkily stepped forward and threw his arm around, releasing the salt from its pouch. The salt flew across the short space and traveled through the air to land on the demonic mass of jelly. It had no distinct shape. It just shimmered and grew as it pushed in and out of different shapes as it continued to move forward. And the salt had no effect. Peter felt sickened and slumped to the floor. The salt was useless against it, but why? Peter thought hard. That's impossible. Salt would always deflect any evil. He glanced again at the monstrosity. He was astonished to find it was still growing in shape and strength. And it was still moving forward. Then, abruptly, he felt his consciousness slipping away. He tried to control it and focus but it was useless. He just couldn't think straight. Was this the end for him? The thought flashed through his mind. Then at the edge of his sense of awareness, he thought he heard a faint voice and with what little sense of consciousness he had left, Peter listened carefully to try and catch the faint words.

"You're destroying yourself, Peter. What you see are your own fears which have grown and culminated into an entity of your own making. Fear not and you will overcome."

The mass grew to fill the width and height of the corridor, then it started to trudge slowly forward. It was now just a few feet from him. Then, without warning, a decaying, foul stench filled the air and Peter immediately tried to cover his nose. But he couldn't. His arms were now frozen to his side. The smell became unbearable. It reminded him of death and he thought now of his own. Was he to die now by being frozen or suffocated? Even thinking was a strain until finally Peter sensed the last ebb of life force leave his body. Peter's final thoughts pondered on the angelic voice that just visited him. Then a memory hit him. How could he have missed it, and an abrupt surge of overwhelming anger aroused him to consciousness. It was anger at his stupidity. It suddenly all made sense to him. Of course, the salt had no effect. He wasn't fighting a demonic entity as such but a monster far worse. He was fighting his own fears. He remembered, since the age of three he had had a deep fear of the cold. He remembered it started after he'd wandered out into the night during a fierce snow storm. He'd had no real concept of the danger at the time but wanted to catch up with his cat which had run out of the house. He vaguely remembered getting lost, then the biting cold. It was painful, and he became petrified when he found he suddenly couldn't move his limbs. He vividly remembered the excruciating pain in his fingertips and crying out for his mother. They found him passed out in the heavy snow an hour later. They said he was very lucky to survive and that he'd developed some frostbite on his fingers. From that day, a day he'd decided to completely forget about, the phobia had begun, and although since then he'd coped, there was always a deep undercurrent of fear of snow and ice which remained dormant, deep inside his subconscious mind. Similarly, his fear of the smell of decay started years later. He was twelve when he'd decided to take the shortcut from school by crossing the local marshlands to get home. He'd been chatting longer than he'd thought to a girl in his class whom he'd become very attracted to, and only realized the time two hours later. His mother, when it came to dinner, was a stickler for punctuality and got very upset if they were not all eating together. He remembered it was a very sunny day and so he knew the area he had to cross would have dried up, which would make the short cut safer. However, he was about half way across when the nauseating stench of decay had hit him. And when he looked ahead, he saw a mass of black flies encircling a small mound of soil. He'd hesitated before he very cautiously stepped towards it. He was a little uncomfortable since he'd heard stories of all sorts of strange and hideous creatures which wandered the marshlands and his fertile imagination went into overdrive. Perhaps, he'd thought, it could be an injured cat or a massive snake ready to throw itself at him. He knew that an injured animal could quite easily attack if it felt cornered. His uncle had told him that. Then abruptly Peter stepped back in sheer horror. What he saw in front of him was far worse than he'd ever imagined. It was a man's body with its head almost chewed completely off. The sinews of muscle stretching tightly from its neck just held the head on to the body. Dried blood had adhered to the skin and torn muscle tissue. The eyes were missing from the open sockets in the head and the teeth were all scattered about and where the mouth used to be. And the stench got worse as the growing mass of flies flew from the body and invaded his own nostrils and incessantly buzzed around his head. Peter felt his legs give way as a surge of nausea swept through him. It was impossible, he knew then, to prevent the sickly liquid from his guts spouting out of his mouth. The memory of that incident stayed with him and whenever the smell of decay was around, Peter would shudder and shake uncontrollably. He now understood why. The other fear he carried with him was the cry of the Banshee. Peter had first heard it as a young thirteen-year-old. He was watching a film one Halloween called 'The Cry of the Banshee'. He'd found the shrieking howl unbelievably scary and shuddered violently with fear since then, whenever he heard it. He could never understand why but kept the fear to himself, managing to quietly control the effect it had on him.

It was a clever ploy by the enemy to find out about and manipulate his fears. He knew they must have intruded into his unconsciousness during the nights while he slept to find out what they were and then somehow compound and intensify their effects on him to scare him literally to near death, otherwise he'd have perceived their presence. Peter opened his eyes and glanced at his monster, which was now just a few feet away but trudging closer towards him. But he was no longer afraid. He just smiled and marched confidently forward to meet the dark monstrosity. The mass, in its final attempt to scare Peter, began to wail. A high, shrieking, ghoulish sound erupted from its dark form and exploded in the air around him. Then, as Peter looked to see the mess left behind, he saw nothing there. There was absolutely no indication that the entity had ever existed. Peter laughed in further scorn at what they'd tried to do to him, and then he shouted, "Be gone! I fear you no more."

And the Watcher smiled faintly as it lurked in the shadow. Its help wasn't needed after all. Perhaps, it thought, the humans had a chance after all.

Chapter forty-three

The ground continued to shake, and books flew violently from the shelves, striking most of those in the room as everyone dived for cover and grabbed for their weapons. And the trolls continued to thunder forward towards them. And as they got closer the cabins shook more.

"I'd say they're about two hundred meters away and coming in fast," Daniel shouted to Ben. "Any suggestions?"

Ben's heart raced as his adrenalin increased, and his mind went into overdrive. He knew he had to evaluate the situation rapidly and come up with answers.

Tara and Chodon acted quickly too. Simultaneously, they made brief eye contact. They knew they had the same idea, and both rushed out of the cottage. Ben guessed they'd gone to find the best vantage point, to get a better understanding of what was happening.

"Quickly, smear your faces and put your camouflage on. Take your night binoculars, a spade and collect as many explosives and smoke grenades as possible. Then, on my command, get ready to leave," Ben said.

Moments later, Chodon and Tara came back and gave Ben a brief appraisal of what they'd seen. Ben couldn't help but admire their calmness, discipline and strength of resolve. But he felt a tinge of sadness to see the innocence which Tara had had when they first met, slowly erode.

"The ground at the rear is our safest bet. There are trees and shrubs to hide us. A small vale of trees beyond this will also provide us with an escape route if needed. But we only have three minutes."

"Thanks, Tara." Ben turned towards the others. "Ok, follow me." Everyone followed Ben out of the cottage and they all ran to the safety of the trees at the back of the cottage. "Ok, dig your own hiding holes behind these mounds of grass then get ready to throw your smoke grenades at my command. You have two minutes." They all sped into action. It was fortunate the soil was soft, and all were ready and waiting within the allocated time. Then abruptly, like a fierce, volcanic quake, the ground shook more aggressively as the trolls, jaws open wide, pounded forward. Only meters away and their black, globular eyes could be seen. The stench was overwhelming, and everyone held their breath while they hurriedly fitted their face masks. Puffs of stagnant air blew out of the trolls' twisted grey nostrils. Then a terrifying noise broke loose from their mouths and, in a crazed frenzy, they raced faster forward to claim their prize.

"Now!" Ben shouted, and as hard as they could, everyone threw a smoke grenade into the rushing mob of trolls. Thick, white smoke bellowed out from the ground and quickly rose upwards and outwards to cover and the attackers.

"Go!" Ben shouted, and this time they all ran to take cover within the canopy of trees behind them. The trolls, blinded by the smoke, began to trip over and in to each other. They fell bawling loudly, many in excruciating pain as their ankles, arms and legs sprained and broke.

"Now!" Ben cried out. This time he screamed louder so that everyone could hear him above the howling from the screeching trolls. But this time each person threw a grenade into the mass of trolls in front then quickly ran back further into the safety of the trees behind them. They waited as the last of the explosives blasted. Then, as haunting quiet settled around them, from the cover of the trees, Ben shouted once more.

"Again!" And while the creatures were in disarray, they all ran forward and threw more grenades into the belly of the remaining trolls, then ran back again into the safe cover of the trees. As they reached them, once again, the grenades exploded. Ben turned to look around at the results of their own attack and felt a sudden pang of guilt and even sympathy for the trolls. They had no chance, he thought. They'd walked straight into a simple trap. Body parts were scattered unceremoniously across the ground in front and to the side of them. Mangled bones, hanging gristle and yellow fluid oozed from the now motionless bodies. Only one bemused, injured troll stood erect at the rear of his dead comrades. It made no sound but simply looked around dazed and confused. Then with a fierce roar and with all the breath and energy it could muster, it suddenly charged angrily straight at Ben.

But a loud shot ran out in the air. And the troll fell to the ground.

Ben looked beyond the dead troll to the open grounds in front of Braemar Lodge. Kneeling about a hundred meters away was a soldier holding a rifle. The soldier stood up and walked slowly towards Ben. As he approached, Ben recognized the SAS insignia on the arm of the soldier's jacket. It was an amazingly accurate shot and Ben now knew why. The soldier was from Special Forces.

"Hope you didn't mind me intruding in your operation?" the soldier asked, smiling. "I've been watching the scene for the past few minutes and tried to help earlier but my bullets had no effect on the things. They just bounced off."

"Yeah," Ben returned the smile. "They're called Trolls and ordinary bullets will have no effect on them unless you manage to shoot at their eyes. But obviously one worked in the end. Did you use some sort of special rifle? I don't recognize the one you're holding but it looks heavy. And thanks, your help was most welcome. I can now live to tell the tale. My name's Ben and I'm extremely pleased to meet you, sergeant." The sergeant smiled broadly and reached out to take Ben's hand.

"Likewise, Ben. My name's Thomas. And you're completely correct in your assumption. When my bullets initially had no effect, I guessed the trolls' hides were too tough, so I went back and exchanged my weapon for a .905-calibre rifle. It fires rounds at 2,100 feet per second and is the most powerful rifle in the world."

"Wow! That's some weapon."

"Well, Ben, it did the trick, huh?"

"It certainly did. Thanks again."

"No Ben, it's me who should be thanking you. I met Amalialad inside. He's an amazing character and seems to have such a natural empathy with people. Everyone seemed to warm to the guy. There's something strange but good about him. Couldn't put my finger on it, if you know what I mean. And, wow, what an amazing strategist. He spoke highly of you and your group. Now I understand why. We can't afford to lose you. It was Amalialad who assigned me to come out here on watch. I'm glad he did. I suspect he had a suspicion something like this may happen. Anyway, I must get back to report what's happened here if that's ok by you. We need to be ready in case of any more surprises."

"Of course," Ben replied. He watched as Thomas turned swiftly and ran back towards the Lodge. He pondered on what Thomas had said about Amalialad and smiled to himself. Hmm, he thought, if only he knew the half of it.

Tara walked up to him.

"Any update from Amalialad?" Ben asked. He had seen Tara concentrating earlier and guessed she'd been communicating telepathically with Amalialad.

"Yes, but he just said well done and he'd be out to talk to us shortly. It was well done, too, Ben. The manoeuvre you executed was brilliant. I'm so proud of you." Tara gently kissed him on the cheek. "You're my hero." She walked off towards the cottage. Ben felt embarrassed and knew he'd turned bright red. She did that on purpose, he thought. She knew how he'd feel. He saw her reach the cabin door and turn to face him before entering. He saw the wide smile on her face as she'd also seen his betraying red cheeks.

Fortunately, when the trolls had realized the occupants had fled, they bypassed the cabin. Their keen sense of smell had signified nobody was inside, so they just continued to the rear.

The four of them had entered and sat down at the small table. Although a little disheveled, they were all fine. Ben explained that Amalialad would be with them shortly and suggested it would be an ideal time to break for coffee and rest while waiting. Ben first thanked them all for such brilliant support and bravery. It was tempting, he thought, to run a lot deeper into the forest rather than face a small army of fearsome trolls. Yet he knew his comrades would have fought till they died on their feet.

Amalialad walked in a few minutes later. He walked from one to the other and shook their hands thanking each of them for their courage and success in destroying the trolls. Then he sat down at the table and invited them all to join him.

"You've all done extremely well and everyone here at the lodge owe their lives to you for saving the day. The troll attack was completely unexpected. We knew some sort of attack was imminent, but we didn't expect it to be carried out so quickly. We were expecting it within a timeframe of ten to fifteen hours not twenty minutes after our arrival. They knew we were rushing back here. It seems it was coincidental that they would have got the information at about the same time I'd told you all my decision to return. On my way back here, I personally checked that we weren't followed which can only lead me to one conclusion."

"We have a traitor among us?" Ben said sadly.

"Yes. We have an informant." Everyone instinctively looked at each other in shock at the realization.

"That would also explain the attack on you in the mist, since nobody could have possibly guessed we would pass there. The attacker was expecting you," Ben said.

"I think so, Ben," Amalialad said.

"Have you any idea who it is?" Ben asked.

"Absolutely none at this stage, it mystifies me. It's obvious though that the person is very clever and highly cunning. Now, especially, we all need to be highly focused on what we say and do. And if anyone has any ideas about who this informant is, please see me. And, may I stress, only me." Amalialad's tone emphasized his words strongly. "With respect to everyone else, security is vital if we're to find our traitor."

Everyone nodded in agreement.

"What's the plan now?" Chodon asked.

"We have to attack them before they attack us again," Amalialad said. "Hopefully, no troll managed to escape to inform the others about what happened here. Anyway, we will now be moving out at first light. You have the rest of the day to prepare. Fortunately, the weather has changed in our favour and the snow has melted but it's still cold. The strategies have been discussed and I will inform you of what we intend to do just before we do it. I'm sorry, but we have a traitor among us and so everything now will be done on a need to know basis. Ben, if I could have a moment with you outside, I'd be grateful."

"Yes, of course." Ben followed Amalialad outside. Amalialad gestured to Ben to follow him to the side of the cabin, so they were out of earshot of the others inside.

"Of course," Amalialad said, after they'd walked a few meters away from the cabin, "I'd trust you and others with my life, but I need to be seen to be doing things fairly and so I'm only confiding in you, my friend. After a careful analysis of what's happened so far and information which we've gleaned from various agencies, we're certain we know the precise whereabouts of the enemy's headquarters. It's not far from the point we reached on the mountain earlier; it's a peak called the Devil's Point. We need to get there quick, and, if possible, armed with the element of surprise. Don't get me wrong, after their failed attack, they'll know we'll be coming, but they don't know when. We'll be taking a huge risk. Some will say that what we're doing is crazy. Maybe. But we're out of options, my friend, and for now, it's do or die and we must take the avantage while we can. We don't know what we'll be facing but I suspect their forces will be much stronger than we first thought. For this battle I've sought help from every conceivable source. I'm sorry but I haven't heard from Peter for two days, so I must assume the worst, although I hope to God, I'm wrong. I really like the guy and his new companion very much."

"I liked them all too. They've become very close, so I hope you're wrong."

"I hope you're right."

Ben's group arrived at the command base which was situated on a large plateau just behind Devils Point at 6 a.m. the following morning. The army helicopter touched down quickly on the mobile pad then speedily dispatched marines before returning to pick up another group. From this vantage point, as far as the eyes could see, the whole area was buzzing with activity. Every conceivable type of army transport was flying backwards and forwards. Ben knew the army operated assault transport helicopters in medium and heavy classes and he could see them all there busily carrying out their duties. The medium transport helicopters were most apparent. They transported large cargoes. Sometimes that might be transporting a platoon of infantry or tanks and other military vehicles and equipment either internally or towed or under slung. Ben saw at least ten in the air at once and marveled at the pilots' maneuvering skills. In the distance, he recognized a heavy lift helicopter and knew it must have been carrying more troops and other small armored fighting vehicles. As it got closer, he recognized it to be the CH 47 Chinook, which was known to be one of the most efficient and reliable military helicopters in existence.

Ben stepped off the pad and jumped onto an area of flat ground just beyond it. His friends followed, and they all gathered together beside one of fifty army tents set up earlier and ready for immediate occupation. Before entering the tent, Ben noticed another group of about twenty assault helicopters standing by behind a rocky outcrop about a hundred meters in the distance. They were all covered in camouflage netting, ready to take off at a moment's notice. Ben stood in awe for a moment, admiring the efficiency displayed by the army units. He knew that the SAS had the main control of this battle theater, so he wasn't too surprised. He took his binoculars out of his rucksack, carefully adjusted its focus and looked further out. Beyond the assault helicopters he could just make out about two hundred tanks.

"Remarkable, isn't it?" Ben hadn't noticed Sergeant Thomas come up to him. He quietly chastised himself for not being aware of the approach. He was slipping, and he couldn't afford to lose focus. His life and those of the others were all potentially at risk if he failed them in any way. He'd been too focused on the activities around him and should have been aware of Thomas's approach.

"It certainly is, sergeant. Good to see you again. I'm just admiring the scene. Those tanks in the distance, are they the latest Leopard 3A7 series?"

"Well done. You have excellent vision and are very knowledgeable. Those tanks were only fully developed last year and have been in service for just six months. We've only invested in the best. This area is very isolated, so it meant utilizing the most efficient vehicles to get maximum use. For protection, firepower and accuracy this little baby's the best. What you see from this standpoint is just one tenth of the firepower we have and we're still bringing more in. Hmm, I won't bother asking where you got your information from. It's obvious you have been given a high classification protocol." Ben didn't answer but changed the subject.

"What's the intelligence on our enemy?"

"Well, thank goodness, right now, all seems quiet. We have small teams, discreetly carrying out sorties around the Devil's Point. We've got an eight window to set up and every second of that time is crucial. We only have a few contingents. Amalialad is running something a little more in clandestine, but that's ok. He's also commanded everyone to carry some strange items. God knows why. We've all been told to expect to face some weird creatures, and if we do, the earplugs he's asked us to carry may be needed, although what earplugs will do to help only God knows. Anyway, that's fine by me."

Never a truer word said, thought Ben. God knows.

"You can rest assured, sergeant, if we win this battle, whatever Amalialad has asked you to do or is organizing right now, his instructions will be our saving grace." Ben smiled reassuringly at Thomas.

"My gut tells me you're probably right, Ben." Ben smiled again. He knew he was.

"Well, with the weaponry we have here, we shouldn't need any help. And we have some of our most experienced veterans and combat soldiers." Thomas beamed with pride and confidence.

"I hope you're right." But, deep down, Ben had some serious doubts.

Tara and Chodon stepped out from the tent and joined Ben and Thomas. They all looked out across the large plateau in front of them. About four miles in front of them they could see the base of the mountain known as Devil's Point. The land area in between mainly contained grass and dark, rocky outcrops with the occasional scattered shrubs. To the right, about a mile away, they saw a solitary, small lake. Soldiers were quickly carrying out, what seemed to Ben, last minute manoeuvres and mechanical tests on military vehicles. Officers could be seen instructing their platoons and doing final exercises as well as checking their rifles and other weapons and equipment. It seemed now that it was just a waiting game.

"So, you think we're ready?" Tara asked Thomas.

"Yes, ma'am, we're as ready as we'll ever be and I'm happy to see you again."

"Thank you, sergeant. I'm pleased to see you too."

Thomas grinned.

"How have you ...." Then, abruptly, Tara stopped talking, and her face went ashen. They all looked at her.

"What is it?" Ben asked.

"It's started. They're coming." The message in her head was clear. Alarmed, she looked up at Ben.

"Don't worry." Ben could see something had scared her. "It'll be ok."

"But you don't understand. There must be over a million of them!"

Chapter forty-four

The corridor in which Peter now stood was rarely used. It was hidden away in the rear wing of the castle. He stood in front of a large oak door which led into a small chapel. Peter walked to the door and started to turn the large iron handle.

"Peter!" Francis called out to him from the opposite end of the corridor. "Are you OK?"

Peter turned and smiled at Francis. He also noticed Hugh, who was standing behind Francis, looking concerned. "I'm sorry. Have I been gone long?" Francis tried to hide his surprise at the question but answered.

"Well, let's just say that after about half an hour we became concerned about you and decided to look for you."

"Ah, that long, huh?" Peter said. He hadn't realized that he'd been away so long. "I'm so sorry, old chaps, but you might say that something came up. I'll explain later, but time's important now. We need to hurry."

"That's why we hurried after you. While waiting for you, Hugh did a bit of scouting around. He thinks he heard sounds coming from the courtyard area. He thinks they sounded like the rumblings of the shadow warriors."

"Goodness, you just reminded me, I'd forgot." Peter pulled the imposter's mobile phone from his pocket and quickly sent a text message. "That should stall them for a few more minutes. I've texted that I'll be at the courtyard door in twenty minutes. I'd told them one of the guests needed an urgent toilet break."

"Hmm, let's pray the ploy works," Francis said.

Peter pulled the door towards him. It was heavy, but slowly opened, and they entered the chapel. He then pushed the big door shut and slid the large steel bolt across from the inside, ensuring they were safely locked in. As he turned back around again, he was amazed by the sudden feeling of peace and tranquility he felt. He was drawn by the warmth of sunlight on his face and looked up. As he did so he noticed how the sun light split as it passed through three large rectangular windows and threw out arcs of bright reds and oranges across the room. It looked and felt so spiritual. He felt humbled.

"What a truly holy place this is," Hugh said.

"Truly, it is," Francis said, as he looked around in awe. The ceiling and walls were covered with the superb paintings of Jacob De Witt. Francis remembered seeing most of the Dutch painter's works in a book he'd read the previous summer while visiting the Vatican's library. The paintings included 'Our Lord's Life' and 'Apostles' and Francis stood quite still for a moment, mesmerized at their detail and quality.

Peter focused more on the layout of the chapel's furnishings and observed that wooden chairs were set out in rows facing the raised alter and chapel area. They numbered forty-six in all. He also observed two other doors inside and wondered where they led to.

"OK, my friends, you know why we're here." Peter didn't like to break up their obvious pleasure in looking at the paintings but unless they very soon found what they came for the consequences were unimaginable.

"Where do you suggest we start looking, Peter?" Hugh asked. "It's only a small chapel but there are potentially hundreds of possible secret hideaways."

"Right now, I need your silence for a few minutes, gentlemn. I've come here with an idea in mind which I'm desperately hoping will work, but it will require great concentration on my part if it's going to." Then Peter closed his eyes and started his breathing exercises. Within a few seconds his heart rate dropped and his whole body relaxed. Peter had done this hundreds of times now and soon he was able to reach the theta state of inner peace. All other concerns left him as his mind sought her out. Then he reached out to her. You said you'd always be with me. Please my dearest, love, be with me now. Peter immediately felt himself being gently pulled forward and felt compelled to open his eyes. His gaze, for no apparent reason, rested on a chair at the very back of the chapel. It was the last wooden chair in the back row. It was on the far right as he faced the altar. He walked over to the chair, and as he got closer, he felt a strong urge to sit in it, but before doing so he glanced down and was surprised to find that, unlike the other chairs, this one had rarely been used. The seat was like new. There were no scuff marks or creases on the material nor any small scratch marks which one would expect after decades of use. It was most odd he thought but then gave it no more concern. He had other things on his mind. Then as Peter sat down, his world changed once again. He felt a warm glow flow through his body as, simultaneously, a fragrance of pure lavender entered his nostrils. But more wonderful than that, he felt such love and affection overwhelm him and he knew his love, Gloria, was with him again. Overcome with emotion Peter sent his thoughts to her.

"Oh, my darling, how I've missed you. My mind has been consumed with the constant thought of you and the pain of missing you has grown daily. I thought it should lessen with time. It's what everyone says, but it didn't. Life without you has been almost unbearable. Without you I only plough on, contending with the sleepless nights and coping with the depressive days, to fulfil a promise I made to a dear friend. But once that promise has been made, I plan to be with you once again." Gloria felt his pain and wondered if he knew her own pain was worse. Her frustration was even more unimaginable than his. But this was not the time for selfish thoughts. She knew Peter had a vital mission ahead of him and his fate was bound by the outcome of that. His fate would be their fate but even more than that it would be the fate of all humanity. It was the Love that existed in all worlds and all planes of existence. It was the fate for all Love that had ever existed. She knew Peter must move quickly to protect it and all that was dear. He must see it through to the end. Peter heard the echoes of her words in his mind. My dearest, Peter, with all my heart I believe that when Love is real it will find a way back and when you've done what you must do, we will be together again for ever. 'Til then our hearts will yearn for each other and we must endure the pain. I can sense the darkness spreading. It even encroaches here. So, you must go now and help your friends. They need you. I don't know the outcome my love, nobody does, but I do know you must hurry right now for any hope of achieving what must be done. So go with God's speed! I can help a little. Under this chair, on the base of its right leg, is a button you must press. It will show you the way." Then Peter felt Gloria's presence fade and the last echoes of her voice melt away.

"Wake up, Peter. Wake up." Peter felt himself being shaken and opened his eyes to see Francis's concerned face. "Are you ok?"

"Yes, I'm fine. What's wrong?"

"We must leave here. There's banging on the door."

"Ah, Ok." Peter quickly jumped up and whispered instructions.

"Please, both of you come here." Peter then lifted the chair and pressed the button which he found hidden inside the base of the chair's leg. He held it still and watched while the flooring beneath it began to part.

"Hugh, what can you see down there?" Hugh stepped forward and kneeled by the opening.

"Wow! There's a stone stairway leading downwards. Hold on a moment." Hugh pulled a small torch from his pocket and shone it down the hole. "I can see a floor about ten meters down, but that's all."

"Ok, hurry, I'd like both of you to go down. I'll be just behind you." Suddenly, the banging on the chapel door got louder and they could hear the metal lock as it took the strain. They all knew the lock wouldn't last long.

Although wary of the slippery steps, Hugh and Francis hurried down the stone stairway. They both knew that just one careless slip could lead to a fatal drop onto the hard bed of stone flooring below. After Hugh and Francis descended, Peter pressed the button again and the floor started to close back together. Then, just as he took the first two steps in a single stride, and just before the floorboards closed, he heard the chapel door give way and the creatures break through. He raced down the steps to join his friends.

"Thank God you're ok," Hugh said. "We heard a loud bang and thought you'd fallen."

"No, I'm fine but our uninvited guests have arrived," Peter said. "We have very little time."

"Why, do you think they'll find the sliding panel?"

"Ordinarily, I'd say no. It's too well hidden. But they have supernatural forces on their side and sooner or later they'll be descending these steps."

"You're right, but do you have any idea where the Ark is hidden?" Hugh asked hopefully.

"If you mean, do I know precisely where, no, I don't. You might just say I'm following a hunch."

"A hunch! Peter is that all?" asked Hugh, a little surprised.

"Well. It's a strong hunch."

Francis, who had stood by quietly listening, gazed upwards.

"God help us" he said, as he simultaneously gave the sign of the cross.

"Follow me," Peter said. "This air's musty and it's beginning to block my nose. I'm hoping there'll be some ventilation ahead." There was only one direction to take and Peter led the way. There was no lighting in the tunnel. It was pitch black. However, all three had brought out their torches. They walked on briskly, with Peter leading, though he was wary of any potential dangers ahead. None of them voiced their fears as they walked on, but all thought about them. But the one question they all concerned themselves about was, would they meet the challenge and defeat the evil that threatened human existence?

As they walked slowly down the tunnel, they noticed the passages branching off both left and right. Francis momentarily stopped to look down one of them but could only make out an endless blackness. However, he felt a stronger dampness in the air and a deeper foreboding. However, he decided to keep quiet. It was probably just his imagination anyway, he thought, and shrugged it off.

Peter really had no idea where the Ark was specifically hidden. All he had was an overwhelming sense of mental perception, a powerful sense of intuition, that it was hidden somewhere within the castle. And as he walked further into the heart of the tunnel that sense grew. As he passed each side he focused heavily, for a sign of some sort, to indicate the Ark's whereabouts. The Ark had tremendous energy and power. It was, after all, representing God himself. But he felt nothing.

"Thank you, Peter. I can show you the way from here." Peter turned around in surprise to see Hugh standing, smiling before him.

"What do you mean? You think you know the way? But you've never set foot in this chapel building before, never mind this tunnel. How could you possibly know?"

"No, that's true, Peter, but I will be shown the way, my friend." Both Peter and Francis were shocked at the calm way Hugh had spoken to them.

"How do you know where to find it, Hugh?" Francis said.

"Because, my friend, it has always been my destiny." Francis and Peter stood completely still and looked at Hugh. They waited for him to explain.

"From the moment I was ordained as a knight it was my destiny to live, find and guard the Ark of the Covenant. To this end I was sanctified by the pope to do so. Only he knew of my destiny. That's how it was meant to be. I am now the only living being who can safely look upon the Ark, without its protective covering, without being killed." Hugh looked away briefly as he said this, and Peter noticed the sadness in his face. Then Hugh continued talking. "Godfrey was another, but as we all know, God bless him, he didn't make it. Only those who are sanctified for the purpose can be safe when looking upon it. For it is as though looking upon Christ himself. Those before me have said that there are no fitting words in our language that could ever describe the beauty and splendour of the Ark. However, apart from the chosen guardians, the Ark can only be seen by those from Heaven. The last humans that tried, as I know Francis and probably you too, Peter, are aware, were the Beth-Shemesh, and the four Angels of God, who still stand protecting the Ark, slew more than fifty thousand people who dared look upon it. My friends, to prevent your own destruction, I now need to take the lead."

"I didn't see this coming," said Peter.

"I'm sorry for the deception, Peter, but if you think about the situation I was in a little more, I know you will understand. I had no choice. There was no weakness on your part. It was all God's will. On this occasion, your rare perception skills were neutralised, so when trying to use them to find the Ark, you were unsuccessful. Finding the Ark was my mission. However, your fate, my friend, is far more challenging than mine. For, after I find it, it is you who must somehow complete the impossible. To win the final battle you need to somehow transport and use the Ark at Devil's Point."

"Perhaps," said Francis, "and I have no idea how we are going to do it but at least when we find the Ark, that will be half the challenge met." Hugh suddenly looked sad and gazed downwards before speaking.

"What's wrong Hugh?" Francis asked.

"Ah, it's nothing. I just feel so overwhelmed at being so close to finding the Ark."

"Well, we can understand that, my friend. I'd never have guessed you had such a huge secret. It must have been such a heavy burden on you."

Hugh smiled. "More than you know, my friend, but it's an enormous relief to me now that you all know. I felt I was betraying you in keeping the secret."

"You had no choice. I'm sure we'd have done the same if the roles were reversed. So, Hugh, where do we go from here?" Francis asked.

"Please, follow me." Hugh walked confidently to the next tunnel which branched off to the right of the main corridor. Peter and Francis had no clue as to why Hugh chose that direction. There was nothing there to indicate a signal or direction, as far as they were concerned, neither could they sense anything that suggested something was special about it; they were simply walking into a black tunnel. However, Hugh was transfixed on a bright white ball of soft light which floated just in front of his eyes. As he followed it he felt a soothing warmth circulate inside his head and realized that all his worries and concerns, the doubts of achieving his quest, had completely left him. Instead he felt a renewal of inner strength flow through his body and he knew at that moment, he was about to accomplish his destiny. The others sensed a swift, unnatural change in the air and intuitively looked towards Hugh. Stock still, they stood in awe of him as a bright, shimmering, white light encircled him.

Hugh spoke softly to them.

"Don't worry, my friends. We are all quite safe. Please follow me but don't touch anything."

Chapter forty-five

The ground shook violently as the mountain in front of them suddenly split in two. Its sides cracked loudly as its centre slowly gouged outwards against the rocky terrain in front. And then a fierce storm blew from inside the bowels of the mountain and blasted out, like a cork from its bottle after being violently shaken, spewing its contents. And the still air was shattered.

Thomas, and those around him, stumbled forward, barely managing to keep their balance. Eventually, they looked on in horror as they saw a mass of black figures running towards them. In the distance they seemed like tiny, black, matchstick men. Running with them were smaller, green figures and, although they resembled each other in shape, the green figures were much more agile and quicker on their feet. As they came closer, everyone could see they were horribly deformed. Some soldiers were sickened at the sight and involuntarily stepped back in horror. The creatures floundered forward. Their arms continuously waved up and down as they wielded their vicious weapons. Thomas stood still as he looked on, totally dumbfounded at the unbelievable spectacle of horror he saw in front of him. And their numbers were overwhelming. Even though he was a strong army veteran with significant battle experience, he shook to his core. This was surreal. He was bewildered at the prospect of facing supernatural entities and just hoped he'd quickly acclimatize to fighting his new adversaries. As the creatures got closer, Thomas could see their sharply clawed, black, hairy hands. They were frantically waving and slashing, even inadvertently, in their frenzy, cutting off the arms and injuring body parts of their own comrades. On closer scrutiny, Thomas observed how the creatures seemed to be mesmerized in some way. It was if they were being controlled by someone else watching on. The creatures' crazy frenzy continued as they marched forward, but, noticed Thomas, their movements were predictable, like Zombies marching forward without a mind of their own. His army could easily slaughter them in this state, so why were they sent? They were just like cattle fodder, so what was the point? Then, suddenly, he saw the creatures straighten up. It was as if they'd abruptly been reprogrammed and given a new set of instructions. The creatures seemed now to be looking ahead with more foresight, a new strategy. Then, swiftly, they ran forward. Thomas was surprised at the rapid change in strategy. The creatures' actions were, he felt, premeditated. They ran faster, silently at first, then with unexpected speed and in complete unison, they screeched loudly, like banshees from hell. Unbeknown to Thomas, that's exactly what many of them were. And the banshees ran faster still.

"They're Banshees, Shadow Runts and Goblins!" Ben said. "Be careful. They're all cunning and extremely dangerous and their weapons will probably be tipped with poison. There's no known antidote! Sergeant, you must quickly pass the word around. Everyone must wear their leather gloves and protect as much of their body as possible from the attackers' weapons. And beware the Banshees - be careful of their sharp claws and don't look directly into their eyes. They'll literally scare you to death. If that should happen, your soul will be instantly snatched away into the pits of Hell."

And the screeching got louder. And louder. It reached ninety decibels and their ears started to ache. Ben quickly realised what was happening and shouted an alert to Thomas.

"Put your earplugs in, Thomas, then signal the message to everyone else." Thomas acknowledged the instruction and reacted fast.

He ran to a control station nearby and stood on the top platform. He gave hand signals which were quickly relayed to the next station and the signals were passed on from one station to another. Within three minutes every soldier got the message, and all were wearing gloves and helmets and earplugs and were ready to fight. Then they waited for any creatures who should break through the heavily defended steel barrage which stood firmly grounded, twenty yards away, in front of their base camp. And in front of the barrage were the heavy tanks and behind those were the machine gun batteries. To the left and right, lifting off loudly, were assault helicopter gunships.

The massive tanks boomed first as they fired at will. Their missiles, on target, exploded in rapid succession. And they destroyed the bulk of the first wave of creatures. Jagged, torn and shredded bones and blood-soaked sinews of muscle flew. Most of the creatures that escaped the blasts were mowed down by sniper fire and the few still left standing looked up aimlessly in confusion. They'd never been beaten before. They didn't realise that the bullets used by the army had been covered with a rock salt mix, thereby making the demonic creatures' normal immunity obsolete. The soldiers hadn't realized this either. The bullets and missiles had been secretly prepared days earlier. It was highly classified, and only the prime minister, the minister of defence and the commander in chief of operations knew of it besides Amalialad, Ben and Tara.

Amalialad watched the events take place from high up on a mountain adjacent to Devil's Point. He looked down to see the movements across the vast plateau below as well as observing the base of Devil's Point.

"So far, so good, eh, Amalialad?" the commander in chief of operations, Colonel Reginald Jackson, said enthusiastically as they watched the second wave of the enemy being annihilated by the tank division and support troops. But Amalialad was very quiet.

"What's wrong?" the colonel asked.

Amalialad looked up in alarm.

"We've been completely duped! This has been far too easy. We've been knocking the creatures down like we would ducks at a funfair rifle range. Like the ducks, these creatures aren't given the chance to fight back. I've been so stupid. We've been so very cleverly tricked. You're using the standard, flanking manoeuvre to attack, am I right, colonel?"

"Yes, we thought it to be the most effective."

"Well, with respect," Amalialad said, "look and think again!"

The colonel looked more closely and then sharply stood up.

"Oh, my God."

Every soldier knew about the flanking manoeuvre. It was an attack focusing on all sides of the enemy's position. In this case, it meant that the whole mountain at Devil's Point had been surrounded, including from above by aerial stealth drones and assault helicopters, so that there was nowhere for the enemy to escape to. They were completely locked in. It was a siege, until the enemy either tried to fight their way out or surrender. But the enemy's position may not have only been inside this mountain at Devil's Point. The enemy may also have well-fortified base positions inside the other mountains surrounding that one, and them. With horror, the colonel understood. The consequences of such an error could be catastrophic. Their positions could quickly be reversed and they themselves could effectively be ambushed and annihilated in a short, sharp and swift attack. They could be destroyed within minutes, and the game would be over. At that precise moment of realization, they both saw another daemonic horde racing out from the bowels of Devil's Point. Amalialad and the colonel looked at each other in shock. They knew then that their worst fears were realized. Others from their own army, thinking they'd dealt with the enemy, would now come to try to defend them. They would come fast, not knowing that the earlier attack on them was a ruse and that they were heading straight into an ambush. Colonel Jackson quickly swung around to give a counter command to his lieutenant. But it was too late.

Chapter forty-six

Their worst fears were confirmed moments later. Telepathically, Amalialad had just sent the alert to Tara when, almost simultaneously, two Shadow Runts jumped down towards him from a rocky outcrop just above his camouflaged tent. Luckily, he'd sensed their presence a moment before they sprang, and he reacted at lightning speed. Amalialad's reflexes were uncannily fast and his skills went into action instantaneously. As the rusted, nail-riddled club hammers swung fiercely through the air, Amalialad twisted and ducked clear so that two of them, although initially on target and set to crack his skull, narrowly missed. But the menacing hammers, wielded by the ghoulish, gibbering Goblins, continued to whistle loudly as they flashed by. Backwards and forwards, they ploughed through the air as they completed their arcs. Amalialad's mind raced and he leapt again into action. His right arm shot out and he grabbed the muscular, wart-infested elbow of his attacker and pulled it ferociously from its socket. Then he threw the creature off the precipice down onto the stony ground twenty meters below. Not fazed by that, the second runt brought his hammer back up and, with a mighty strength, bore it straight back down towards Amalialad's head. But in an instant Amalialad snatched his oak staff from its leather sheath and twisted around swiftly to face the creature's hammer head on. Amalialad held his staff tightly, waiting for the inevitable clash. He waited for the tremendous reverberation which was sure to follow. But it didn't come. He felt and heard nothing. And then it occurred to him; it wasn't an ordinary oak staff he had. It had been passed down the centuries to him by his ancestors. Amalialad didn't understand why but knew that somehow his staff had a special strength of its own. It had just cut clean through the opposing hammer like a sharp knife through soft cheese, and he'd felt nothing as it did so. Amalialad now understood why the wooden staff was left for him. But his brief pondering was quickly broken by the sounds of loud shrieks and the clashing of swords close by. Amalialad raced around the narrow ledge towards the clamour, but he then stood back in shock as he saw the gruesome carnage spread out in front of him. Bloodied, broken, muscle-torn bodies scattered the ground around him. From both sides' corpses blanketed the area. He saw trolls, Shadow Runts and goblins as well his own soldiers lying close by. He knew, in just one glance, that his own men had been ambushed and overwhelmed by the enemies' numbers. His men hadn't stood a chance. He also knew it was then too late for anyone to do anything for any of them, so he rushed on forward. As he turned another sharp bend, he had no time to think further of the horror he'd just seen. But his pace increased rapidly as he noticed the colonel, just a few yards in front of him, struggling desperately to overcome a massive troll, and he needed help quickly. Amalialad could see that the troll was far stronger than the colonel, who'd obviously been fighting off others and now looked exhausted. He was now using up his last reserves of energy and it was only a matter of time before he fell. Moments later, the troll grabbed a hammer from its belt. The colonel, now helpless, sapped of all his strength, waited for the inevitable fatal blow. The troll, relishing the moment, very slowly raised his arm and stared hard at the colonel's head. The head he was about to smash to pieces. Then, with a sudden loud screech, it brought its arm down hard to beat the exhausted colonel to death. Amalialad knew that the blow from the troll's hammer would be fatal, just as he knew that he'd never make the run to block the blow in time. And as the hammer was brought down, Amalialad saw the colonel fleetingly glance his way. Their eyes met and Amalialad saw the colonel's final look of sadness and resignation. The colonel knew his time had come. And Amalialad's heart sank.

Amalialad focused with every spark of energy he could muster. He could feel the left side of his head heat up as his brain, now almost at bursting point, gathered every single atom of kinetic energy from his body, until it could take no more. And it was then, at last, with a single final, focused thought, Amalialad directed his energy straight towards the troll's arm. He held it for a microsecond, then let it go.

Just centimeters from the colonel's skull, the troll's arm was torn away from its body and was propelled backwards. And the creatures' hammer disintegrated.

The troll, shrieking in agony, fell to the ground. Its arm lay bloodied and limp at its side. The colonel struggled shakily to his feet, then clumsily he withdrew his side arm from his belt, aimed slowly, and shot the creature clean through the forehead.

Amalialad said nothing. Now was not the time for words. He knew the colonel was in shock. He simply walked over and sat down on the ground beside him. The colonel cradled his face in his bloodied hands and wept quietly. Amalialad knew that the colonel had a young family he'd not seen for two months and would likely never see again. The future must look hopeless. Amalialad gently put his arm around the colonel's shoulder and for the next few minutes sat quietly with him.

Chapter forty-seven

Peter heard the new calm and gentleness in Hugh's voice, but there was also a strange energy surge around him. It didn't surprise Peter. He'd watched Hugh search for purpose in his life. He'd perceived that he had some grand destiny. And looking at him, Peter felt that Hugh was fully aware of what that destiny would be.

Hugh led them further along the damp and murky corridor. Peter could only just make out Hugh's form as he ran ahead of them. His enthusiasm to reach the place, however, was understandable.

Around the next bend, Peter felt a strong breeze against his face. Three steps further, he stopped in amazement, looking up at a vast cavern. The others bumped into him with mild curses, then fell silent.

In front of them was a sight few had seen, a sight they'd only read about. For some, it was a biblical message of hope. For others it was just another myth, a legend.

The Ark of the Covenant stood in the centre of the cavern. Nothing about it looked spectacular. There were no bright, shimmering lights or shooting stars. But they all felt an overwhelming surge of peace and spiritual cleansing that touched their very souls.

They were standing in the presence of the Lord, in the holiest of all sacred places. Francis fell to his knees in prayer and Hugh turned quickly to whisper,

"Don't come any closer. Your lives would be at risk." Peter remembered a passage from the Bible stating that should anyone come too close to the Ark of the Covenant, they would be killed instantly. Only a high priest on Yom Kippur - the Hebrew day of atonement - could be in the presence of the Ark and live. He wondered why they weren't already dead.

Hugh kneeled in front of the Ark and began praying in what sounded like Hebrew. Just over two feet in height and width, and three feet long, the box was made of acacia wood with a lid of pure gold. Two gold cherubim faced each other above their outspread wings, which formed the throne of God. The Ark itself was God's footstool. Gold rings on the corners of the Ark allowed staves to be passed through the Ark so it could then be carried by the Levites, the only Hebrew tribe allowed to do so. Next to the Ark, on a small acacia table, was a folded blue cloth used to cover the Ark when it was carried.

The Ark had been lost for more than two thousand and six hundred years and was last kept in Solomon's temple in Jerusalem. How did it get to Scotland? But more importantly, why? Peter turned and saw Hugh whispering to Francis, who turned deathly pale as tears flowed from his eyes. Peter turned away quickly.

Then Hugh approached Peter. He looked distraught, and Peter felt fearful for the first time in ages.

"I'm so sorry, my friend, but there's no easy way to say this. I'm afraid you will not be getting the support you were hoping for. The Ark will not be used to help humanity again."

A chill ran down Peter's spine.

Chapter forty-eight

Ben shuddered in fear as four huge explosions simultaneously accompanied his vision of a rapidly changing landscape. It was surreal, and Ben's heart raced. Four giant mountains surrounding them rose and split in two, revealing thousands of clambering daemon creatures racing to the sides and down the mountains towards them. He saw a troop of SAS commandoes rushing forward and firing their MP5A3 submachine guns as they met the leading group of creatures head on. They'd broken away from their hidden reconnaissance positions to stem the flow of the surprise attack, and although they quickly dealt with the first surge, Ben estimated they must have mown down sixty creatures within a second. He knew that, with just fifteen in a troop, even though they were among the best fighting soldiers in the world, they'd soon be overwhelmed by numbers. Ben remembered Amalialad telling him that the SAS had seconded eight troops to help. That was half of their entire contingent. Each troop, led by a captain, was given important positions of responsibility. Ben was glad that the captains had the authority to change tactics should they feel the need. He had no doubt that that was exactly what the remaining captains would do. And reflecting on earlier, he thought that Tara had had good reason to be terrified of what she saw. He was looking at just a part of that scene. Ben lowered his binoculars and ran over to Tara, who had slept for almost two hours since her vision but had begun to stir. Thomas was still nearby.

"Now you're back here, I need to go, Ben. Four mountains have suddenly opened, spilling out thousands of the creatures. We've been ambushed from all sides, and I'm afraid it doesn't look good."

"You're right, but we must play with what we've got. Can you get a message to RAF command?"

"Yes."

Ben scribbled some notes on a scrap piece of paper and handed it to Thomas.

"Then send this message. It might give us a little time."

"Will do. Take care, Ben. I hope we'll meet again."

Then Thomas sped off.

"What's happening?" asked Tara.

"You've seen it already. It's not good, and we need to get undercover. Quickly!" "Where's Chodon?" said Ben.

"I don't know, I've been asleep, remember?" said Tara.

"Hmm, that's strange. Well, I hope she's ok."

"Don't worry, she can look after herself. Anyway, I've just had a message from Amalialad. He says he's on his way back to us."

"Great! Thank God he's safe. And we need him now more than ever. Where do we meet?"

But Tara's answer was drowned out by the noise of several aircraft buzzing overhead.

"Ok, the fun begins. Quickly, we need to head for the station."

Station six was one of nine control stations set up around Devil's Point

As Ben and Tara reached the entrance, they were greeted by a stocky commando, holding a rifle, with a serious expression on his face.

"ID please and I would appreciate you being quick. We have one minute to get inside." Ben knew why but didn't have time to explain to Tara.

As they entered, the boom went off. The time was exactly 4:30 p.m. Exactly as planned. And the control station shook violently. Everyone was on the floor. Most managed to stabilize themselves with their hands but some were thrown sideways and found it more difficult. Ben and Tara gripped onto two rails, normally used for rucksacks. When the reverberations stopped, Ben was the first to rush forward to the window to see the devastation. Ohers quickly got to their feet and joined him. Ben knew that what they'd see today would be ingrained in their memories for the rest of their lives. Most gasped in fear as the massive mushroom cloud hung over the mountain. Ben knew, although they felt the shockwave, at five miles away, they were just within the safety range of its blast. For the initial few minutes, from their vantage point, they stared in disbelief at the cloud. More than an hour passed snd they used the time to sleep. Then the clouds began to clear, and they could just see a mass of grey as swirls of smoke massed above the ground. And it was just moments later they saw the horrific results. On and around the mountain, the snow had gone and the whole area was laid bare, flattened to scorched ground, and thousands of burnt bodies lay scattered across it, though most now were no more than cinder patches. Everyone watching was in shock - mesmerized and silenced by the scene. But this was eventually broken by a cheer.

"For God's sake, Ben, what happened?" Tara gasped.

"Well, I suspect HQ took up my suggestion and used the MOAB to destroy the areas around the surrounding mountain ranges."

"What's the MOAB?" asked Tara.

"It's a Massive Ordnance Air Blast."

"What? What the hell is that? Come on, Ben, in layman's terms please." Tara knew that Ben was well read up on Military weapons. He'd a lways had a strong interest in the history of warfare.

"Well, to put it simply, apart from our nuclear arsenal, it's the biggest bomb we have. It's a demolition bomb designed for a surface blast that creates a shockwave, as opposed to a penetrating bomb which burrows into a target. Considering the massive force we're facing, we really had no choice. It's probably the only weapon we have that can help us defeat these creatures."

"That big?"

"Well, you've just seen for yourself the damage it can do. It's packed with 8.48 tons of H6 explosive material and its shockwave can cover a hundred and fifty meters and reach into underground caves and tunnel systems. In this case it was perfect for our needs. It reached far into the depths of the mountain crater. I don't expect anything to have survived the blast."

"Wow, who would have devised such a destructive device?"

"Actually, the Americans did."

"Amazing, but will it do the trick?"

"If you mean will it destroy all the creatures, I hope so. Certainly, around this mountain. The MOAB is a concussion bomb, meaning that it's designed to detonate before it hits the ground, to create a shockwave of up to a hundred and fifty meters."

"Weren't we lucky to have such a bomb close by?"

"Yes, we were. Evidently, we have an air force base near. Top secret location. The problem wasn't the bomb but the aircraft which carries it. Guided by GPS the MOAB can only be dropped from a C-130 transport plane. We were lucky they had one at RAF Lossiemouth."

"How do you know all this?"

"I've been getting text updates from Thomas."

"No, I guessed that. I mean how come you know so much about the bomb. The MOAB, as you call it?"

"Ah well, that comes from my interest in American presidents. One of the most controversial presidents the US ever had was Donald Trump, and he took the unprecedented step, in 2017, of dropping the MOAB on Syria."

"I see. Yes, I remember reading about that."

"Most people would have. But we still have some big problems, Tara."

"Are there four of them?"

"Indeed, we still have four more mountains to deal with. All hiding thousands of those creatures."

"Well, we can just bomb them too, right?"

"If we had the bombs, yes. But evidently, we can only get hold of three more."

"So, what do we do about the last mountain?"

"We attack with more conventional weapons and fight them."

"Can we defeat them, Ben?"

"Of course, we can. It will take very careful and well-coordinated planning, but we can do it."

The other people in the room began to relax. Everyone knew that there were many more creatures, but most had little doubt that other bombs would take care of them too.

The door opened, and, to Ben's relief, Amalialad stepped through.

"Welcome, my friend. You're very welcome indeed. We..." But Ben's speech was violently interrupted as Tara snatched a gun from an officer's sheath, aimed it at Amalialad and shot him directly in the centre of his forehead.

Chapter forty-nine

"Please, Hugh, is there anything you can do?" Peter asked. "You of all people know that most of mankind are truly loving and Godly. Should we all suffer for the sake of the few who seek the evil ways? I know that God is forgiving so can He forgive us now and offer us another, final chance? Hugh, please. There must be something you can do."

Hugh had tears streaming from his eyes as he spoke again. "You think I haven't tried, Peter? I begged Him to help you. They've allowed evil to step in and He remains adamant. I'm so very…"

He stopped talking and Peter could see he was suddenly communicating with someone.

"Somebody else has come forward to help but I cannot divulge who. And I've staked my life on that, so please don't ask."

"Oh, thank you, Hugh, that's fantastic, I promise we won't fail."

"He will allow you to use the Ark, but it would be down to you to transport it to where you desire its help."

"But you know that's impossible, Hugh. The Ark needs to be carried over a hundred miles and there is now only Francis and I left here. Apart from that, we have at least two hundred creatures outside this building right now baying for our blood. So as soon as we step out, we'll be slaughtered. He knows this, doesn't He?"

"Of course, He does, Peter."

"Great, well, what did He say?" asked Peter.

"He said, you either will or will not find a way."

"How are we supposed to do that?"

Hugh lowered his head. "I'm so sorry, Peter."

"Thank you, Hugh. We know you've done all you can. You must go now and do what you must do." Then Peter walked over to Hugh and hugged him tightly. They clung on quietly, for a few brief moments. Then Francis, who was listening nearby, stepped in and did the same. Hugh had been a brother and good friend for years. He'd miss him tremendously. No more words were said as they stepped away from each other.

Francis, spoke. "What now?"

And Peter laughed.

"That's strange."

"What is?" asked Francis.

"Well, I was going to ask you the same question."

That moment of light relief was loudly interrupted by a raucous cacophony along the side corridor of the tunnel.

"Oh no, not already."

"What is it?" asked Francis.

"Probably our worst nightmare, Francis."

"What do you mean?"

"They've found us."

"You mean…"

"Exactly that, Francis. They've found us. I'd say they'll be here in about a minute."

"I'm sorry, Peter, I know you've done everything you can, and I want you to know that it's been a great pleasure and an honour to know you."

"Likewise, my friend." And as the first of the howling creatures turned, jaws wide open and fangs bare, Peter flinched. Strangely, his last thoughts reflected on what Hugh had said to him.

"You either will or will not find a way."

Chapter fifty

Tara met Ben's gaze.

"It's not what you think! That's not Amalialad. It was a shapeshifter."

"What?" "Ok, that means there'll be more. Wait here." Ben opened the door cautiously. Slumped unceremoniously on the front steps was the body of the guard. His throat was slit from ear to ear. Ben quickly stepped back into the eerie silence. All eyes were on him.

Ben said nothing but put in a call to Thomas.

"Code B35572C. Can you clarify?"

"Clarified. Code T29978M," answered Thomas.

Ben checked his watch to clarify the coding and when he saw it matched Thomas's full name and rank, he continued.

"We have a strategic Code 630, Thomas. I repeat Code 630. Can you confirm?"

"Confirmed. Take care."

"You too."

"You told him about the shapeshifter?" asked Tara.

"Yes. He'll alert every tent and control station. I just hope it's not too late."

"What do you mean?"

"Well, I can only assume you knew that the shapeshifter wasn't Amalialad because you were telepathically in touch with Amalialad himself moments before the bogus one walked in. Am I right?"

"Yes. Amalialad said he'd been held up and would be here in half an hour. And I sensed the malevolence in the intruder as soon as he stepped in."

"Exactly. Others don't have such talents."

"Oh, my God. You mean…"

"Precisely. A shifter could become any recognisable officer, and with the right weapon, without being challenged, just walk into his station or tent and kill everyone inside."

"What can we do?"

"What I've just done. It's now down to Thomas. But, Tara, our enemy is cunning. They would have carefully planned this." Tara grew pale.

The officers in the room were still quiet, waiting for some sort of explanation from Ben. He explained the circumstances quickly.

"How will we know it's a shapeshifter and not the real person?" an officer asked.

"You can't, unless you have time to capture and interrogate it for at least an hour. These shifters would have researched their hosts carefully. They will probably know more about them than you do. You need to set up a password identity system to distinguish yourselves from any intruders. And if anyone should suddenly go missing, change the passwords. Because if they're captured, they will talk."

Ben turned back to Tara, just as Amalialad walked in.

Ben hesitated.

"Ah, lost your sense of humour, Ben? You normally have something nice to say when we meet. Don't worry, it's really me."

Ben relaxed.

"You have every reason to be cautious," said Amalialad. "In fact, now nobody can be too cautious. And may I say you've been doing a great job so far. I've been told of your leadership qualities. And a wonderful suggestion about using the MOAB. Would you believe it, nobody else had considered it? Anyway, thank you, Ben." Tara walked over at that moment with a small tray carrying three coffees. "I need to talk further with you both but let's just walk over to the corner of the room. I think we'd have a little more privacy over there." Amalialad said. Then the three of them walked over to the far corner and sat down.

"I'm sorry I'm late but much has happened, and I've just come from a meeting with Thomas and other key senior commandoes. It's not good. But, thanks to Ben's idea, we did surprise and hit the enemy hard with the MOABs. Four of the mountain bases have been virtually wiped out and the marines have estimated a kill rate of eighteen thousand. The devastation has been enormous." Amalialad looked closely at Tara and Ben as he continued. "Tara has kept me updated, Ben, and unfortunately you were right again in another situation. Thirty-six control stations and over three hundred tents have been completely destroyed because of the infiltration by shapeshifters."

"Oh, my God," Said Tara.

"You couldn't have done any more, Ben. The information you gave Thomas helped him prevent the destruction of all our bases and tents. He managed to alert the security of the other stations and tents in time for them to repel the shapeshifters. Those commandoes left alive now owe their lives to your quick thinking."

"That's true, Ben. I'm really proud of what you've done," said Tara.

"Thank you. So, what's the plan now, Amalialad?"

"Well, to put everything in a new perspective, we now have a battle-ready force of nearly three thousand, but almost two hundred of them have been assigned to medical and care duties for those injured from the shifters' attacks. We've had to improvise in making more stretchers and temporary medic units, including two specialist psychological trauma stations. The effect of seeing and dealing with daemons and shapeshifters have taken their toll and we've had to bring in four more psychological counsellors and that means releasing more commandoes to them, which we're desperately short of now."

"I see." Ben looked Amalialad in the eyes.

"But what's the worst news?"

There was an uncomfortable pause. Then Amalialad looked directly back at him.

"We estimate an enemy force of at least five thousand but potentially a lot more."

"What do you mean, potentially? asked Tara. "How many could it be?"

"Twenty-eight thousand."

"We don't have a chance, do we?" Ben said.

"Oh, we have a chance, Ben."

"You mean if we only end up facing five thousand? And even then, what are the odds we can beat them? After all, we're still vastly outnumbered by nearly two to one?"

"Well, I admit a little luck is needed. And of course, lots of moral support from my cheerful friends."

"Hmm."

"We have a strategy I'd like to go through with you both. But our forces mean to use the best method of defence tomorrow at dawn."

"What's that?" asked Tara.

"Attack!"

Chapter fifty-one

They doubled the guard, and every shelter, including the tents, control stations and working bases, followed the instruction which came through as a Priority One.

Thomas was waiting for Amalialad at the steps of control station number sixteen, which was about a kilometer further on from the one they'd just left behind. Thomas had sent a light All-Terrain Vehicle to collect them. When they arrived at the station, Thomas stepped forward and insisted in helping Tara from the vehicle.

"It's a pleasure to see you again, Tara, even under such bleak circumstances."

"Likewise, Thomas, and thank you."

"I've asked you all here because I'd like your advice on the security of the layout we have. We're dealing with an unusual foe and I don't know of anyone more clued up on what we're facing than you lot. I thought if I show you all around you can then advise us on ways in which we can improve the set up."

"Of course, it'll be a pleasure," Amalialad said.

The tents were spread out in rows of twenty and Zone sixteen had fifteen rows. Each tent had a sergeant in charge and accommodated ten soldiers. And every four tents had a captain for overall responsibility. Ben noticed that there was also some larger canvas shelters that he suspected were used for stores. To one side of these, though set back further for safety, were ammunition stores.

After walking up and down the rows, randomly entering different tents on route, they finished back at the control station. The tents were set up primarily for sleeping.

Thomas had arranged for ten captains to join them in the control station. It was, he'd earlier instructed them, their individual responsibilities to relay any information they'd be given by him, directly to their men. As they entered everyone was seated around a rectangular table. Thomas had reserved seats for his friends, with himself and Amalialad seated at the top of the table, nearest the entrance. It became quiet and everyone became immediately attentive as Thomas and his guests sat down. Then Thomas got up to speak.

"Thank you all for attending and for your patience. It seems we're a few minutes late. I've already given you all a quick briefing for the reason of this meeting and now I'd like to hand you straight over to Amalialad."

Amalialad stood.

"Good morning, everyone. I'd firstly like to start by saying how extremely sad I am for the loss of your comrades yesterday. It was tragic. We were all taken by surprise by creatures known as shapeshifters. They are probably the most dangerous of our foes because they can masquerade as anything, human or animal, without you knowing it. If you do have reason to doubt someone and you have time to question them, you may catch them out. However, that's still doubtful. But you have all been given passwords to identify each other so please use these. The shapeshifters have no knowledge of them.

"But what if a shapeshifter does find out and manages to masquerade as one of us? said Ben.

"Then we're seriously compromised. I'm afraid time is against us, so we just must hope and pray that they don't." Amalialad gave Ben a look of resignation then continued.

"Next, I'd like to say how very impressed I was with the dedication and professionalism I've just observed in my brief tour of your encampment and that it's an honour to serve with you all." There were satisfied nods of approval at this before Amalialad continued. "Ladies and gentlemen, I'll come to the point. We are here to fight off the most evil and hideous creatures you will ever come across or dream about. For many of you, until recently, this may have seemed somewhat surreal but take it from me, this is serious and very real. But we are now fighting for our lives, your family's lives and the rest of humanity. We're fighting for everything you hold dear and love. The odds, I'm afraid, are heavily stacked against us and for many of us it will be our last fight. But we can reduce those odds by being smart. As you know, we are fighting creatures which are, in every conceivable way, evil. This means our main weapon is everything which is deemed good. Not necessarily by you, since it's likely if you hold an atheistic belief, you're not likely to hold much faith in the cross or the Bible defending you. No, but the important thing to remember is that the creatures you face do believe and fear these things and they will be weakened by them. So, my first piece of advice is to make sure you carry these items everywhere you go, and I mean, everywhere. All these items, which incidentally have been blessed with holy water, have been allocated to your tents; make sure everyone gets them. Also, and I know Major Thomas has told you, but all your bullets and missiles have been heavily coated with rock salt. Without this coating your bullets and missiles would be obsolete. This salt is a real defene against evil and the first thing I suggest you all do, if you haven't done so yet, is to circle your tents and other shelters with this. No evil creature will step over this line."

A few eyebrows were raised at this but Amalialad continued. "Major Thomas has arranged for two extra personel to be allocated to each tent. I can only tell you that these individuals have both the knowledge and skills which will help you stay alive and defeat these creatures." Ben knew he referred to the Opus Dei and the Monk Warriors. He also knew that it was probably going to be their advice which got most of them through the battle. He hoped they'd all listen, since he was also aware, among the lower ranks, of some deep skepticism. He understood how far-fetched everything they were being told must seem, but there was no time left to convince them. They either accepted what they were told or they, most likely, would die. Amalialad then finished. "Well, my friends, we are now to fight what could be our final battle. But it will be side by side, as friends, indeed much more, as brothers in arms. Now before we part, I'd like each of you to quickly just sign and give me the details of the numbers under your command."

Amalialad waited for the document to be returned.

Ben thought it odd that he should require such details now; surely, they could be collected by someone later and, in any case, he thought, they'd only just collected the same information when they walked around the encampment earlier.

The loud, piercing screech of pain made everyone jump. All eyes were on a female officer who'd just signed the document. Angrily, she threw the pen and document to the floor then jumped backwards and snarled. And then she changed shape. Within seconds, she had changed into a hideous black-horned creature with a distorted, fat face and jagged fangs and her whole body became scaled. Like that of a lizard, thought Ben, and he watched in horror as her sharp red, bloodshot, eyes focused. They focused hard, solely on Amalialad. But only Ben, from his vantage point, could see her smooth fingers change to claws. Claws which held a sharp black knife. Ben leapt forward. His judo skills came in handy once again as he flew, and with his left foot, just after she raised her arm up to throw the poisoned blade, he kicked the knife from her clawed hand. The creature turned to face him. Ben had safely landed on his feet just a few feet away from her, but he expected her response and as he landed, he twisted fast and to her right, behind her, and once again he charged, this time at her spine. For a split second the creature became disorientated and couldn't see him. Her eyes glared hard at everyone staring at her and the officers stepped back in horror. This was new to them and most of them felt helpless without their sidearms, which had been confiscated earlier when they entered. But suddenly, Ben reacted, and the crack was loud as his right foot connected and smashed the shapeshifter's spine in two. The sound was chilling, and even Tara shrieked. The creature instantly changed into a puff of black ash and as the ash hit the floor it too changed and became a black, oily stain. And the room was filled with an obnoxious pungent stench of decay.

"Thank you, Ben," Amalialad said calmly. "Well, now you know what we're facing, are there any questions?" But there were none. Most were still stunned by what they had just witnessed.

"We plan to attack in three days. We have one mountain left virtually unscathed, which holds at least five thousand creatures. We will be training and rehearsing the strategy in the next two days. It's not long so use the time effectively. In the meantime, beware, stay focused and alert. The enemy seem to have a sixth sense and may very well be aware of something afoot at our end."

At that moment the door opened and Colonel Johnson, with his arm still in a sling, walked in. He went over to Thomas and whispered in his ear. Thomas turned to face the audience.

"We've just received some urgent intelligence. The creatures are gathering in force at the base of the mountain, so the time's been changed. I'm sorry, you'll now only have today to plan. We march tomorrow."

Amalialad noticed the nervousness in Thomas's body language as he spoke. That was unusual. Nothing would normally stir him. Amalialad went over to him.

"What else?" Amalialad whispered.

"There are at least another three thousand creatures." Amalialad raised his eyebrows at that. "It seems many escaped from the other mountains to this last one through underground tunnels which linked them all together. We had absolutely no idea. Our aircraft would normally have detected them, but it seems the creatures had some sort of cloaking device which hid them from the planes." Amalialad was at a loss.

"Ok, well, we have a lot to do. So, we meet here again tonight at twenty hundred hours to go over our strategy, is that right?"

"That's right," Thomas said, surprised that Amalialad hadn't reacted to what he'd just been told. Hmm he thought, nothing seemed to faze his friend, and felt more confident to know that Amalialad was with them.

Chapter fifty-two

Amalialad, Ben, Tara, and Chodon were allocated a three-room tent a few meters away from the station. Like the others, it just contained the bare minimum. Amalialad had just updated the group on the information Thomas had given him.

"Is anything going our way?" Ben asked.

"We got our own tent, didn't we?" Tara answered, smiling.

"Great," Ben said.

"Well, I'm sorry, but there's nothing we can do about that," Amalialad said. "But we can make sure we put the best strategy in place to increase our chances. We're badly outnumbered but we have more reason to win this battle than they do and together, I think, we're much smarter." As they considered that they heard colonel Johnson call out for their attention from outside the tent. Ben drew down the zipper at the entrance.

"CJ2568," said the colonel.

"Ah, yes, thanks, colonel, come in."

"Well, aren't you going to check it?"

"Already have. I know yours off by heart," said Ben

Colonel Johnson walked over to Amalialad.

"Sorry, I couldn't talk to you earlier, Amalialad."

"Please, say no more. I completely understand."

"Well, anyway, thanks for saving my life. I don't remember thanking you earlier. I'm afraid I was somewhat traumatized."

"Well, it's no more than you'd have done for me. I'm just happy you're ok. How are your family, did you have a chance to talk?" The colonel raised a brief smile.

"Yes, a very long chat. Thanks."

"Any further updates, colonel?"

"Yes, many of the tents are being visited by banshees and ghouls. I checked what they were by the list you gave me."

"Any of the men killed?"

"None yet. That's strange isn't it?"

"No, not in this case."

"What do you mean?"

"Well, forgive me, but have you seen any of these two creatures yet?"

"No."

"I thought not, because if you had you'd have a tale to tell. The sight of the creatures you've seen so far is awesome, isn't it?"

"Yes, they're the ugliest scum I've ever seen."

"So far. But if you'd seen either the ghoul or the banshee it's likely they'd either scare you literally to death or at the very least render you helpless and quivering like a frightened child and wishing for your mother. You would probably spend the next few years in therapy. And that, my good friend, is exactly their plan. To render our army useless."

"My advice would be to set up a total no go zone in the encampment overnight and if they hear anything trying to enter their tents, they shoot to kill. Meantime, all men must remain as inactive as possible, with their eyes covered and guns at the ready, inside their tents until sunrise. These two creatures are nocturnal, so they will only come out at night. If anyone must move, they should verbally let the others know, to avoid being shot. Fortunately, both creatures are extremely noisy." The colonel was relaying the message to all the captains before Amalialad had even finished speaking.

"I'm wondering what to do about our meeting tonight," he said.

"I suggest you cancel it. Do you have a new strategy in light of what has happened?"

"None yet. We had intended to devise a surprise attack tomorrow, but it seems they've beaten us to it. They're now gathering their forces and I suspect they could very well march this way as soon as it gets light."

"Hmm, I have an idea."

"What is it?"

"I'll let you know when I return. I should be no more than an hour."

"But you know we have a curfew."

Amalialad had already drifted off to sleep.

"Don't worry," Ben said. "He doesn't need to go out. He's astral projecting." The colonel looked puzzled.

"He's what?"

"Sit down and I'll explain," Ben said, smiling.

Chapter fifty-three

Amalialad stirred.

"How are you feeling?" Ben asked.

"Well, touch and go at first but I managed to accomplish what I intended to do, and I've got a plan."

"That's great," said the colonel.

"What's the plan then?" asked Tara.

"Well, basically, the creature's journey is vulnerable to attack from us if we use the Teutoburg Forest strategy. Have you heard of it, colonel? It's been well documented as one of the most brilliant plans of attack carried out by Arminius, a Romanised German."

"It does ring a bell; did he ambush Romans or something like that?"

"Indeed, he did. In 9AD, Varus, the Roman governor of Germania, was lured into an ambush by Arminius. The governor led three legions through the forest to suppress a Germanic revolt. But when his twenty thousand men were stretched out along the route, Arminius took advantage and attacked with his much smaller warrior army. Varus's men struggled on for days until they made a final stand at Kalkriese Hill, just north of what we now know as Osnabruck. The defeat here wasn't just physical but also psychological. It was extremely embarrassing for Rome, especially since Arminious's tribesman were wild barbarians. Carrying out their plan demanded patience and careful sitting and coordination which totally dismissed the notion that they were wild barbarians."

"Wow. Arminius was clever," Ben said

"Anyway, I just flew over the whole area and noticed the obvious track, along a river bank, which they're highly likely to take. This track runs by a mountain side, one of a group of mountains known around here as the Angels' Peaks. And I've sited strategic positions along the route, ideal for ambush."

"What if they don't take that route? What if they actually consider being ambushed while marching that way?" Ben asked.

"Then everyone, we're buggered. But I'm betting they're over confident right now. They far outnumber us, and I don't think that, in their arrogance, they would have even contemplated the idea that we would try to attack them. So, colonel, have you got the maps of the area? We have some planning to do."

The plan took hours, but once it was done, it was communicated by phone to the other leading commando officers, including the SAS units who'd be responsible for leading the assaults. The colonel received a secured text confirmation from the general himself, who was based at the SAS headquarters in Herefordshire, simply stating. Looks good, go ahead at your discretion - we're all rooting for you. God speed. We've sent most equipment you asked for but not enough time or appropriate transport to deliver it all.

"Ok, that's it then," the colonel announced with some relief. "We leave at first light. As we planned, the SAS groups, accompanied by fifty veteran commandoes and, of course, as you also advised earlier, a man from the Opus Dei and Warrior Monks, will each be given a map reference identifying their ambush sites along the mountainside. They'll no doubt use rapid attack and withdrawal tactics. Our best scouts will investigate the specific locations and study the terrain before the contingents arrive. In that way they can feed back any potential difficulties like rock falls, but also suitable hiding spots and even, as you pointed out, should the creatures have been clever enough to consider what we're doing, any explosive devices or traps. Have I mentioned everything?"

"They need to expect surprises, even from above. Alertness will be the key to success here. After the first attack the creatures will expect more. The first one must count." said Amalialad.

"I agree, that's why we have two hundred heavily-armed men carrying that one out. And we'll be constantly buzzing them from the air. We'll have a continual rota of fighter planes firing down at them. If, as you calculated, they can only travel two creatures abreast on large stretches of their journey, they're going to be caught with their pants down."

"Let's hope so," Ben said. "It's about time something worked for us."

"Ok," said Amalialad. "I'll continue to scout overhead and keep you abreast of activities. Ben and Tara, as agreed I want you both to help organize the home defence. There'll be tanks, cannons, machine gun turrets and more and I want you two to make sure nothing seems out of place. You both have a depth of initiative which is rare. But Tara, I also need you to be in constant telepathic communication with me. If anything goes wrong, it will be down to you to get any messages from me passed on."

"Understood. But be careful, you know you're taking a risk flying so close to the daemons."

"I understand your concern Tara, and I love you for it, but stop worrying. I've exactly worked out my parameters and won't go any nearer to the enemy than I need to."

"Ok."

"Fine," said the colonel, "then I'll suggest we all get some rest and wish everyone a good night."

Chapter fifty-four

The deafening screeches woke Ben with a start. It sounded as if they came from somewhere inside the tent. But they abruptly stopped, and he couldn't hear any more or see anything. He noticed that the others were still asleep and wondered why. It was disturbing, and he felt himself perspiring, but, with an effort, he calmly collected his thoughts. From the cacophony of screeches and wails he'd just heard, he guessed there was a banshee nearbye. But then, without warning, another sound came which wasn't loud at all, in fact it was quite eloquent and relaxed. However, it was the most haunting and terrifying sound that Ben had ever heard, and it swept throughout his physical body and deep into the furthest recesses of his mind, almost into his soul.

"Oh, you are frightened of just one banshee, Benjamin? But I have thousands more of them to introduce you to. And, of course, so many other little friends who are most eager to meet you. But, please forgive my manners. You will, of course, first join me for lunch in my fiery little pit. Your painful demise will stir your appetite for sure and I can introduce you to the others afterwards." Then the voice changed, from calm to bloodcurdling. Ben started shaking violently. And the horrific vision of the bottomless pit entered his thoughts. But then suddenly he heard, deep in the back of his mind, an almost imperceptible whisper. 'Grasp the cross.' And, even though he felt totally exhausted, he somehow summoned the strength to very slowly reach out, slide a hand down his neck chain, until he touched his hanging cross, and gripped it hard. And as he did so, he woke with a terrific start. His forehead and palms were dripping with perspiration and his top shirt was soaking wet. Tara and Amalialad were awake.

"Are you ok, Ben? Tara whispered.

"I'm fine now, thanks. I just had a bad dream, that's all." Ben knew by the look on Amalialad's face that he'd guessed that there was something more to it than that, so it was no surprise when he later found himself alone with Amalialad that he was asked the question.

"What happened in your dream, Ben?" And Ben explained.

Amalialad sighed. "I thought as much. The daemons are now desperate. They're doing everything they can to destroy us. That cross around your neck saved you but if your personal strength of will and resolve was weaker you would not have grasped the cross. However, it was the rubbing of salt on the cross which forced the daemon to release its deadly influence on you. You were lucky, Ben. But if this happens again, can you please let me know immediately. We all need to be aware when these attacks take place, ok?"

"Of course, you're right. I just didn't want to scare anyone more than they are already." Amalialad smiled.

"I knew why you didn't explain what happened fully, Ben, but don't you see, we all need to be frightened, very frightened. It will keep our adrenalin flowing. We're not helping each other by hiding the truth about what we face. Lives can only be saved by understanding the strength of the opposition." Ben nodded. He knew Amalialad was right.

Everyone stepped out of their shelters at dawn. This was the day. And the nervousness was apparent. When the breakfast bell rang the food was taken up quickly and each found an area to sit and eat. While eating, most talked.

"Have they left?" Amalialad asked the colonel.

"Yes, exactly on time, ten key groups. They'll be scattered along the mountainous ridge parallel with the river path of the route the creatures will hopefully take and our own heavy equipment, including the bulk of our force, will be waiting to meet those who make it through. The marines here, in our own zone, will form the rearguard and will be getting into position shortly."

"We can only hope that our calculations turn out right." Amalialad said, sensing the concern in the colonel's voice.

"Indeed. Well, we had drones arrive yesterday, and I have one now hovering over the gathering enemy forces. I expect to get an update on their movement any time now." His phone buzzed.

"Wonderful," the Colonel said over the phone. "Keep me regularly updated." He turned towards Amalialad.

"So far, so good, my friend. The creatures have started to march and have taken the river path along the range of Mountains, range, as we'd hoped for."

"Great. That's a big relief and the first mistake they've made. Our first hope has been met but we have a long way to go and more challenges yet to face. Some will be unexpected, so we must be ready to meet anything which attacks us."

"I'm afraid you're right. I've just had a message through. There are more than eight thousand creatures on the march. That's even more than we'd anticipated, and we still don't know the full number."

"That is a concern. Is it possible to get a drone into their mountain fortress? Otherwise, I'll have to risk flying down there myself."

"That's not a good idea, Amalialad. I've heard Ben advising you not to get too close to the creatures for risk of detection by the daemons. I also know from what you've said that travelling the astral plane is very risky if daemons are close by. So, what chance do you have if there are thousands still occupying the fortress? And, unfortunately, the entrance is too tight for any of our drones to get in. It's covered with a steel like mesh, so nothing would get through without alerting them."

"Hmm."

"Please, Amalialad, we could really do with your help right now, so don't risk anything stupid."

"Is the first strike position ready and in place?"

"Yes, it's about three miles in from their main fortress. It's now just a matter of waiting, but it seems each creature has a lot to carry, so by the time we attack, they should be fairly exhausted, and it should be dark."

The colonel's phone rang again.

"The first wave has attacked."

Chapter fifty-five

The synchronization was perfect, and the four detonation switches were pushed simultaneously. Seconds later, the massive explosions rocked the side of the mountain and the avalanche of jagged rocks, which had unceremoniously been torn away from the solid stone face, pounded down heavily towards the unsuspecting creatures. Through his night binoculars, Captain Hennessey saw the beaded eyes of the creatures glare upwards in shock. They'd decided to attack the supply train at the rear end of the marching force to instill as much mayhem as possible and to destroy the key load of heavy weapons and other supplies. Also, the captain knew that their actions would block the path and make it almost impossible for the creatures to turn around and go back to the fortress or return to find an alternative route. He had thirty veteran marines and nine more SAS commandos as well as one warrior monk and a soldier of the Opus Dei in his contingent. He knew he could rely on his own soldiers but had, surprisingly, also found the warrior and Opus Dei member useful. The Monk Warrior, using his bow, and without binoculars, silently took out two lead creature scouts, who were scouring the side of the mountain. The trackers must have been at least fifty meters out. The Opus Dei member had given him and his group some important tips to defend themselves against the supernatural, especially in closely armed combat. Agility and speed were paramount so unfortunately no heavy weapons could be brought along with them. However, each man, including the warrior, held state of the art, lightweight, repeatable rifles which they now had pointing directly at the creatures below, and as the dust cleared, the sound of forty repeating rifle shots added to the cacophony of noise around them. The creatures fell one by one as the bullets hit their targets. Captain Hennessey counted about four hundred dead during the time that the creatures ran for cover. Still left, he noticed, was one creature whose pack had obviously got caught up in the side of what looked like a type of wheel and another who was being dragged and bounced around by what looked like a horse creature of some sort. But in all he estimated about a thousand dead plus casualties. They'd been there for precisely four minutes when he gave the order to expedite, and as he silently ran from the place, he pressed the red button on his phone.

The signal was received almost instantly by Captain Morrison who, with his own equally efficient contingent, was waiting a further two miles down the river path. He received a signal green which meant everything was going according to plan. Had it been a red signal he knew they'd have to abort and get away from where he was damn quickly. As the massive explosions triggered a second avalanche, the creatures below him were completely taken by surprise. This operation was almost identical to the first and equally successful with over eight hundred dead creatures and many injured.

Two miles ahead the third contingent lay patiently in waiting.

But this time the creatures were ready for them and a dozen troll scouts were sent ahead. The creatures below walked cautiously against the side of the mountain, each one carrying a protective shield above its head. The third contingent waited as the creatures walked by, and from their camouflaged rafts they threw the grenades. The creatures bodies lay completely exposed to the river side of the path and they were, yet again, taken completely by surprise. Before the sound of the explosions drifted away, forty rifles began to rattle, and more creatures fell to the ground. They were helpless. But disciplined and on cue, the marine contingent stopped firing and left the scene. It was a slaughter and over a thousand had been killed. As he left with his men, the captain pressed the red button on his phone.

But the creatures were now prepared to tackle an attack from either side and sent their most vicious and skilled creatures to the front of the line. The attack did come, as anticipated, two hours later. But, once again, they were cleverly outmaneuvered and completely taken by surprise, to find themselves bombarded by gun fire from the air. The bullets rained down on them continuously. It was totally unexpected, and they had no way of dealing with it. Then, rocks from the mountainside suddenly fell on top of them. And as Lieutenant Jackson, the pilot of the first plane, flew over the area for the sixth time, he felt some sympathy for the creatures below. He knew that the avalanches had been brought on by the precision dropping of small cluster bombs onto predetermined points of the mountainside and that anything left standing below would be totally crushed. The F-36 Lightning 111 he was piloting was the most efficient tactical fighter plane in existence. And within ten minutes two of these planes had annihilated two thirds of the creatures left on the path.

Chapter fifty-six

The colonel had just got off his phone and, smiling broadly, he turned to Amalialad.

"A complete success. I've just had a report back. The planes have finished the job and the creatures, with over two thirds taken out, have been stopped completely in their tracks."

The colonel noticed Amalialad's solemn demeanor.

"What's wrong, Amalialad? Aren't you pleased at our success?"

"I'm sorry, colonel. Forgive me. Of course, I'm very happy about the way things have gone so far."

"But?"

"Well, do you remember that when we planned these attacks, you asked why we couldn't send the planes in first and let them wipe out the creatures in one quick strike?"

"Of course. You explained that the planes would have to fly too close to the creature's main mountain fortress where the real power of the higher daemons was likely to be. As such there was too high a risk to the lives of the pilots and loss of the planes."

"That's true. If any of the higher daemons are there, they'd have the power to manipulate the minds of the pilots, in which case they may have simply forced them to either fly into the side of a mountain or, much worse, fly back and fire on their own soldiers causing a horrific number of casualties. We couldn't take that risk."

"Yes, I understood that and agreed with you."

Amalialad looked at the colonel and remained quiet.

"Oh, no. We've been duped, haven't we?" the colonel said with alarm.

"I think so. I suspect that there are at least two higher daemons at the mountain fortress already who've purposely arranged the charade of the creatures attacking our position, knowing that the creatures would eventually be killed or stopped. They've never cared about the welfare of the creatures. They've always simply been a means to an end and in this case, in my opinion, purely to gain more time, they've sacrificed thousands of them."

"More time for what?"

"More time to get help. To get more support from the higher daemons and their legions. If they do that, colonel, there will be no more hope for any of us. It will be the end." As Amalialad finished speaking, a lieutenant walked in with an urgent message for the colonel. The colonel read it and sighed.

"Can you share it with me?" Amalialad asked. "It's a note from General Howardson. He says,

Well done so far. But what's all this nonsense about the planes being prevented from attacking the fortress because the minds of the pilots might be influenced by some supernatural attack. My pilots are the best. This is utter balderdash! Get them to attack asap. That's an order.

"I'm sorry, Amalialad, I emphasized in writing the danger of such an action and since I hadn't heard back from him, I assumed he'd accepted my advice."

"It's not your fault, colonel. I suspected this might happen but desperately hoped it wouldn't. The general is of the old school and finds it difficult to accept the reality of what we're facing here. Obviously, you must do as ordered, but if you do, can your computers override the pilots' control of the planes?"

"Well, that's unusual, but yes."

"Good, because if the pilot's minds are manipulated, you'll need to take over."

"I dread the thought, but you're right. Any other advice?"

"Only that all the military need to be ready and waiting before you send the planes. If we're correct in our thinking, when the planes attack, not only may it badly backfire and affect the pilot's minds, but we may well provoke a full-scale attack by the higher daemons themselves. They're angered easily."

"What does that mean?"

"Hell will break out. Literally"

Chapter fifty-seven

The intensity of the roar was unfathomable and even with earplugs, many ear drums were ruptured. Within seconds medics were racing backwards and forwards with stretchers to those affected. The big cannons were fired at the daemon as it raced across the sky, but they had no effect. The attack was sudden, and all those that looked skywards towards the source of the sound were stunned by the sight. They were now facing a higher daemon. Most trembled. A few collapsed. Their minds couldn't accept the reality of what they'd seen, and they'd become completely confused, which ultimately caused black outs. Amalialad stood looking up in quiet contemplation. Ben realised that what he saw didn't seem to faze him. But Amalialad knew the daemon's name. His university studies about the supernatural and demonology had taught him the descriptions and characters of all the daemons. He remembered this daemon well as its vivid illustration in the Book Grimoire was unforgettable and what he now saw, flying swiftly across the sky, almost perfectly matched it. The daemon looked like a soldier dressed in red. It had a large golden crown on its head and rode a huge red horse which, with tremendous speed, hurled two and fro, zig-zagging across and high in the sky, above the basecamps scattered below.

What can he do to us? Ben wrote the question on a white board with a red Sharpie and showed it to Amalialad, who, in turn, took the board and pen and wrote his answer beneath.

Well, not much more than he's done already. The daemon's name is Berith. He's already incapacitated over a thousand of our men and women by rupturing their ear drums and if it wasn't for the ear plugs, we're all wearing, we'd all be writhing around in agony on the ground. But he's also here to intimidate and spy on us. Amalialad then passed the board back to Ben and he read the words along with Tara and the colonel. Then the colonel wrote:

Berith seems too quick for our guns.

Amalialad wrote:

No, it's not that. The daemon is also a master of illusion. Now, to your men, he seems quite close, but in fact he is much further away than you think, and well out of range of any of your guns. He's testing us, finding out what weapons we have and if there's anything he needs to fear.

The colonel responded with:

Can you tell me any more about this Berith?

Amalialad wrote:

He was also known as the Duke of Hell and governed 26 legions. He is also called Beel and Bolfri by the necromancers. He is supposed to have the knowledge of past, present and future events and can turn metals into gold, so is also known as the Daemon of the Alchemists.

The knowledge suddenly alarmed the colonel and seconds later, what Amalialad had written had quickly sunk in with everyone. Then to Tara, who read his thoughts, he spoke.

"Oh, my God! No wonder Berith didn't wait for reinforcements. It feels confident enough to destroy us all without help and since the roar didn't render everyone helpless, it intends to turn everything into gold."

Tara's thoughts frantically came through. "What can we do?"

"Nothing." With sorrow and deep resignation Amalialad sank to his knees. "There is absolutely nothing more we can do." As she communicated with Amalialad, Tara wrote the telepathic messages down on a small white board for Ben to read. Tara and Ben looked at each other in surprise. Amalialad always had an answer. Then in a split second of silence they looked at each other as the realization stuck in. Then they hugged. They wanted to be close to each other if these were to be their last moments. No words were said, they just held on tightly to each other.

Chapter fifty-eight

The colonel reached the top of the ridge. After catching his breath, he viewed the scene below. Everything seemed normal and there was no sign of the Berith. He breathed a sigh of relief. It seemed, for now at least, Berith had gone. But he contacted Thomas and warned him about possible consequences should the daemon return.

"That's not good," was Thomas' response.

No, it bloody well wasn't good. The colonel thought.

"It certainly isn't." The colonel said. "And we have no answers. There's nothing more we can do."

There was a short pause before Thomas spoke.

"We can hope, colonel. Recently we've been surrounded by so many amazing, miraculous things. So, we can at least hope for one more miracle to save the day."

The colonel brightened a little. Thomas would make a wise leader one day, he thought, if they survived this.

"Indeed, we can."

But within seconds that hope started to diminish. As the colonel, through his binoculars, perused the activity below, he suddenly stepped back in horror.

Thomas senses something amiss.

"What's wrong?" Thomas asked.

"Use your binoculars from your position and look out. What do you see?" the colonel answered, as he, shakily, lowered his own pair.

"I'm sorry, colonel." In the far distance, barely recognizable, Thomas saw a group of five figures frozen in mid stride and, close by them, a stationary, golden tank. Both knew then that their worst fears had come true. Berith was once again roaming the skies above, changing everything to gold.

"Why are you sorry?" asked the colonel.

"Because, sir, I offered hope when, realistically, there was none."

"You're an excellent officer, Thomas, one of the best, and it's been a pleasure serving with you."

"Thank you, sir."

After making a quick call to Amalialad and several of the commanding officers, both put their earplugs in and waited.

Amalialad walked to a more solitary space and sat. He closed off all his external thoughts, calmed down to the theta level and let his mind wander. He was searching the astral plains for help. For answers. He was about to give up when he thought he heard the faint sound of a voice, so he focused harder on the source of the sound. He'd also felt a tug on his physical body but decided to investigate the voice before waking. It was still very faint but Amalialad recognized the gentle tone as the voice of Lopsang and sent his thoughts out to him. Is that you, Lopsang?

Yes, Amalialad. But there is no time to linger. Then, Lopsang's voice broke up You m... us t use the ..r in ...Lopsang's voice abruptly trailed off. And another tug at his physical body woke him..

"Wake up, you must wake up, Amalialad." Ben and Tara together were pushing and pulling his arms and legs. Amalialad opened his eyes.

Ben spoke first.

"Berith's started turning everything to gold! I've just taken a call from the colonel. I think he's just about given up. He sincerely thanked us for our help and bravery and then abruptly told me he had to make more calls before cutting the phone off."

"Ok, you must help me solve a puzzle."

"What? We haven't got time for puzzles. As we speak, Berith is turning everything, including our own men and women, to gold."

"Exactly, so the quicker we can solve the puzzle, the quicker we can stop this cursed daemon."

Amalialad quickly explained what had happened.

"I heard the voice, too," Tara said.

"What did you hear?"

"I clearly heard Lopsang tell you to use the ring."

"That's what I thought he said. But I couldn't quite make out the word ring. Lopsang's voice sounded muffled towards the end."

"The ring?" asked Ben. "Oh. I'm sorry, but until now I didn't give it much thought."

"About what?" Amalialad asked.

"Well, when I heard you passing on knowledge about Berith to the colonel it crossed my mind that you may have left something out, but I wasn't sure and knowing you're rarely inaccurate, I kept quiet."

"What is it, Ben?" Tara asked.

"Well, as you know, demonology wasn't my subject but occasionally I'd read parts of your textbooks, whenever I had to wait around for you, and I think I read something about Berith being controlled by a ring."

"Of course. Well done, Ben. How could I have forgotten such a crucial detail? The words you read were written by a prominent researcher of demonology, Colin de Plancy, in 1863." Ben and Tara looked at each in other and once again spoke the same words simultaneously.

"Solomon's ring!"

"Indeed." Amalialad reached into a secret pocket, which he'd had specially sewn into all his trousers, and pulled out a small plastic zip up pouch. He withdrew a small, brown box.

"How will you use it to control the daemon?" Ben asked.

"When the time comes the words will flow," Tara said.

Amalialad and Ben looked at Tara in astonishment.

"Where did you get those words from, Tara?" Ben asked.

"From Lopsang, of course."

"Why didn't you mention that earlier?" said Ben.

"Because I didn't remember it then. For some reason it only entered my head after you'd asked Amalialad the question of how to use the ring."

Then suddenly and loudly, Amalialad pushed Tara and Ben abruptly to one side. As they both fell, they twisted their gaze to look up.

The daemon Berith was flying directly towards Amalialad. They pushed their earplugs hard into their lobes, rapidly clutched their Bibles and crosses, and helplessly stared up at the daemon.

"It is you I seek," Berith roared and pointed the head of his mount straight at Amalialad.

Gripping the ring, Amalialad looked directly back at the daemon and spoke. There was power in his voice.

"With this ring of Solomon, I now control you, Berith, or Beel, or any other name you are known by. This sacred, holy ring that commands all daemons now commands you. From the Testament of Solomon, the ancient manuscript, written by King Solomon himself and whose petitions and commands are endorsed by the Archangel Michael, I now command you, Berith, to ride directly to the bottomless pit of hell. There you shall remain in damnation for all eternity. Go now!"

Ben, looking on in fright, remembered later seeing the startled, red, grizzled face of Berith cringe in agony before its mount turned around swiftly and disappeared.

For a while, nobody spoke, as the reality of what happened took time to register. Then Ben broke the silence.

"Wow! Did that really just happen?" Amalialad, with his eyes now closed, was in deep thought and Tara, strangely, was silently upset. Her tears made Ben feel uncomfortable.

"What's wrong?" he asked, and Tara wiped her eyes and looked up at him.

"If you focus more on that question, Ben, you'll know the answer." And she went silent again, while Ben racked his brains for an answer.

"Of course, I'm so sorry. You must think I'm so selfish, Tara, but I truly don't mean to be. But you never know, perhaps, not all the people were turned to gold. Chodon, wherever she is, Thomas, Joshua and the colonel may be ok."

"They're all ok," Amalialad said. And Tara sat up sharply. How do you know that?

"The colonel and Thomas told us they saw it happening with their own eyes," Ben said.

"Yes, they did."

"Well? What do you mean?" Tara asked.

"What they saw was an illusion. A most deceitful illusion. Berith could only turn metals into gold, but not people. But he was also known for being able to project illusions."

"Thank God!" Tara said.

"Indeed, Tara, indeed." Amalialad responded.

They all met up with the colonel and Thomas later at the main base encampment. The greetings were heartfelt and warm, and the excitement was mutual as they shook hands and hugged each other. The colonel explained that most of the army defence force were safe although there were over three hundred fatalities and more than fifteen hundred injuries, mostly due to ruptured ear lobes. Their medics, he told them, were rushed off their feet.

The colonel explained that their biggest logistical task was in removing the domestic and military equipment as much of it had been turned into gold. Leaving Tara and Ben to explain how he had destroyed Berith, Amalialad wandered off, explaining that his body was aching and needed a little exercising. But the truth was, he was worried. He knew that the other higher daemons would eventually come for him and, if that happened, even with the army, he wouldn't stand a chance. To eventually end this, he'd have to plan a strategy to defeat the daemon, Abaddon the Destroyer, Lucifer's second in command, and, finally, Lucifer himself. They were the leaders, the daemons in control, and if they could be banished from the earth, the rest of the higher daemons would be dragged down with them. But no matter how much he focused, he had no answers, the challenge was too much, the task was impossible.

"Everything, ok?" Tara asked. She'd read some of his troubled thoughts and concerned, she'd followed Amalialad.

"Yes, fine. Thank you. I was just relaxing."

"You know you can share your thoughts with me, don't you?"

"Ah, were you reading my thoughts?"

"No, of course not. But I sensed you were troubled over something. I could tell they were private. But you know, you can share them. Sometimes it helps."

"Thanks, Tara. I appreciate that and if I feel the need, I won't hesitate to come to you." Amalialad smiled warmly. The colonel approached, and Tara left them to talk.

"I've done as you've suggested. Our trackers are out looking for signs of enemy activity and our frontlines are on alert. But I'm not sure how much more the men can take. Because of the weight of the gold our heavy equipment is now virtually restricted to performing from stationary positions and the psychological effect of what they've seen has taken its toll. Even some of my best veterans are nervous, which could seriously compromise their performance in battle. From my experience it would normally take two or three tours of Iran or Afghanistan to bring such symptoms on." The colonel looked quietly at Amalialad after he'd spoken. He wasn't sure why he had so much faith in a twenty-two-year-old kid, still studying at university, but he knew there was something very special about Amalialad. He had an intelligence and abilities far beyond his years and, as far as the colonel was concerned, if his help meant overcoming the enemy, that was good enough.

Amalialad looked at the colonel with sadness.

"I'm truly sorry, colonel, we're in very unusual times. In fact, the worst that humanity will ever have to face, for if we fail now, that's the end. Not, I think, the end of man, for the daemons will rule and they'll need something to control, but it will be the end of true love and kindness and goodness, as we know it, and it will be the beginning of anarchy and chaos. There will be greed and constant fighting and warring. There will be little charity, but rape, murder, hunger and thirst will be commonplace, and suicide will be prevalent. The strong will overcome the weak and evil will inherit the earth. You see, olonel, we have all brought this upon ourselves. Our attitudes, the way we've lived, shunning and turning our backs to the dire needs of others instead of supporting the hungry and thirsty and desperate souls of others, turning to conflict instead of searching for peace. We are generally too busy with our own agendas to care for others. And therefore, we are where we are now, and if some truly amazing miracle gets us out of this mess, we must change." The lecture was heartfelt, and the colonel suddenly felt a pang of guilt. He was glad of the interruption when his phone rang.

"Calm down, soldier!" The colonel was firm. "You have a strategy, so follow it. Why didn't Captain Thomas ring me? Ok, I see. Well, I'll be there in ten."

He turned to Amalialad.

"Evidently, we're being attacked by thousands of locusts, causing all sorts of problems, and Captain Thomas has left to lead an investigation into a report from one of the trackers. Over a thousand monstrosities, none of which we've seen before, are heading our way. Do we have any respite?" The last question was said in frustration, but both knew it wasn't a question and both knew the answer to it. While the colonel was speaking Amalialad also got a telepathic link from Tara. She described the monstrosities in more detail. Amalialad was now certain who they were all facing and spoke quietly to himself.

"So, Abaddon, Duke of Hell, Destroyer, and King of the Locusts, as well as your insects, you've also brought the Daevas to help you. Could you not manage our downfall without them? Hmm, what are you afraid of?" Amalialad then reflected on what he knew about the Daevas. He remembered they came from Persian mythology. They were probably the most notorious of all daemons and the personification of every imaginable evil. They each looked horrific and no two looked alike. Seeing such an army of them approaching would prompt even the staunchest of men to turn and run. And with that last thought Amalialad felt it prudent to push on faster. He needed to be there at the front of the defence force.

Chapter fifty-nine

The colonel seemed to have positioned his men and military machinery sensibly and, as Amalialad arrived and swiftly inspected the lineup, there was little he could fault. But where were the locusts? The colonel explained that they had been spotted earlier from a distance but had since, it seemed, disappeared. What was Abaddon up to? But in the meantime, there was a more vital concern. The Daevas were marching towards them and their ETA was forty-three minutes.

The tanks stretched out over two hundred meters along the front line. Cannons were positioned at the sides, but all weapons were facing the front. Line by line, one hundred meters behind the tanks, were the specialists in standing machine-gun fire. These took up two lines. The first line would shoot then duck down, allowing the second line to continue firing over their heads; five meters behind these were the rifleman including some of the best sharpshooters in the army. They were in lines of two hundred and strategically positioned so that when the first line released their load of ten shots, the next line would take over, while they reloaded. Finally, behind these stood the main core of the army, the SAS, the Monk Warriors, the Opus Dei and other commandos and marines. They chose not to stand in their own isolated groups but instead to be mixed up, amongst each other, standing and supporting each other side by side. They were all combat ready. Waiting. And they were all, if necessary, prepared to die.

The colonel asked Amalialad to stand with him on a high, rocky ridge nearby and help him overlook the movement and activity below, while Ben and Tara had volunteered to help secure the HQ Station, which held two key administrative and computer personnel. This stood about fifty meters from the colonel's and Amalialad's position on the ridge.

Captain Thomas heard them first. He stood ahead of his combat commandos, at the centre of the front line. The march wasn't rhythmic, like most troop movements, but rugged, unsteady and thumping loud. It reminded him of several drunk soldiers walking home from a raucous party, but these steps were much heavier, and shook the ground. At last, as they came into view, Thomas could understand why he heard what he did. They were the most hideous monstrosities. Not even in his worst nightmares, and he'd had some bad ones, had he seen anything so frightening. For a split second he felt like running away. They were all different in shape but seemed to have one thing in common. All their limbs were molded together, he presumed, from parts taken from other macabre creatures. Some had twisted horns and old leather hides with long, elephant-type ears and hippos feet. And their arms looked like they'd been taken from bear-like creatures. And so, it went on. But one thing was for certain, he thought. All came from Hell.

Abruptly, the cannons roared, and the tanks fired and for the next few minutes, under the blanket of the dense, grey, stinking smoke, which soon covered the marching daevas, there was mayhem. But still the guns continued firing until, almost out of ammunition, the order was given to stop.

And there was left in the air an unnatural silence. Nobody spoke. The lines of commandos behind Thomas were still standing and kneeling, remaining tightly to their positions, but gripping their weapons more tightly, partly, Thomas suspected, to hide their trembling hands. Otherwise they were stock still, alert and waiting. Then suddenly, the smoke cleared.

And five thousand daevas were left, frozen to the spot. But those that had been killed, Thomas estimated over two thousand, had vanished. Only black spots remained as evidence of their existence. Then suddenly, the daevas left frozen started to move. They roared, stood up high on their limbs and ran forward at the lines. It could have been comical but for the seriousness of the situation. The daevas clumsily, but determined and clutching spiked clubs and iron mallets, came running forward.

The machine gun fire was explosive. Each man in the front row had a magazine in his gun containing four hundred bullets, and in rapid succession, from one hundred and fifty men, sixty thousand bullets sprayed forward in less than one minute. But the daevas were very strong. When the firing had stopped, there were about two thousand daevas still standing, frozen still once again, and as before, except for the black spots, the dead and injured had disappeared.

Even before the daevas started to move, the riflemen fired at them quickly in rapid succession. The first line fired then ducked down to reload while those standing behind fired, and so on. Once the first two rows ran out of ammunition the next two rows would continue. This allowed the first front two rows of men to run quickly around and behind the back of the lines, get more ammunition, reload again, then quickly get back into place to continue the firing. It was exhausting. But it worked. And within minutes the daevas had all disappeared.

"Jolly good!" the colonel shouted. But Amalialad was quiet. "What's wrong?" the colonel asked.

"It was too easy. I think Abaddon is playing games with us."

"Oh, come on, give our side some credit. We simply had superior weapons and good strategies. In this instance the daemons didn't stand a chance."

"Well, colonel, I hope you're right, but don't you wonder why they were sent in the first place? Horrific and intimidating as they were, with our weaponry, there was no way that they'd get within breathing distance of us."

The colonel paused to think before speaking.

"A diversion?"

"That's what I'm thinking."

Then suddenly in the near distance they saw a rapidly growing black sky moving towards them.

"Clouds don't move that fast," the colonel shouted as, with the black sky, came an increasing sound of humming.

"Get your umbrella out and put your earplugs back in," Amalialad shouted. "The locusts are here." The colonel did so and then knelt on the ground, so that one knee was forward and the other flat to the ground and held out his umbrella. Millions of locusts were flying low towards them, and the colonel hoped both the umbrella and his strength would hold. He closed his eyes. And prayed.

They pounded hard at him, hundreds at a time, smashing and squashing themselves against his umbrella. It continued for almost an hour. Twice he almost lost his hold as the massive swarm passed over and around him. He was thoroughly exhausted at the end of the onslaught and was surprised that the locusts weren't more aggressive. But no, they'd simply flown into him because of their sheer numbers, as they passed through. Then finally, they'd left, and the light returned, together with the silence.

But the silence felt uncannily, unnaturally wrong. They opened their eyes at the same time and both looked up. What they saw was, in all its definitions, soul destroying.

Chapter sixty

The most powerful daemons in existence were hovering above them. The very daemons that, with Lucifer, (now known as the devil or Satan) had been thrown out of heaven after losing their battle with the Archangel Michael and his angels. Amalialad realized at that moment how cleverly Abaddon had deceived them. Both the daevas and the locusts sent against them were diversionary tactics to allow for the other higher, more powerful, daemons to join him. How could he have been so stupid not to have understood the deception sooner? Amalialad recognized all of them. With Abaddon, hovering in midair, was Azazel, the goat-eyed daemon. The Jewish texts portrayed Azazel as the daemon responsible for teaching people to make weapons of destruction and cosmetics. Next to him was the notorious Beelzebub, one of the seven Princes of Hell. Resembling a giant housefly, he hovered backwards and forwards, to and fro, carrying a bow and, on his back, a quiver of arrows. To his right hovered Malphas, the mighty president of hell and the second in command to the devil himself, and one of the most frightening daemons anyone could lay their eyes upon. It was said he was deceitful and cunning and would promise anything for a blood sacrifice. Next to him was Asmodeus, the daemon of lust. It is said that he spent millions of years in Hell before coming to earth and becoming king of the earthly spirits.

In all, more than thirty daemons poised above them. All carrying bows and quivers of arrows. All still and looking down. Amalialad guessed they were waiting for the signal from Abaddon to attack them. Amalialad knew he had no more tricks up his sleeve to defeat them and that, like a young fawn facing a wild tiger, their days were numbered, but still, he thought, he still wouldn't be quitting without a good fight. The colonel looked on. He thought as Amalialad did and was waiting for the right time to press the red button on his radio, for his own attack. Then Amalialad looked directly at Abaddon. Abaddon scoffed at the affront of the human and looked down at them all with a contemptuous, cold glare before fixing his gaze and moving closer to Amalialad. Much closer, as his neck suddenly sprung forward, over a hundred meters, to abruptly stop within a few inches of Amalialad's face. Amalialad shuddered but held his ground. But he genuinely thought that Abaddon meant to bite his head clean off. But something had forced Abaddon to abruptly stop. A last moment's reconsideration of its intention to kill him, Amalialad thought. Why? Then Abaddon spoke.

"You are as insignificant as the worms in your stagnant soils." Surprisingly, Abaddon spoke eloquently and calmly. But then, with a hoarser voice, he bellowed loudly. "Yet you dare to think you had a chance to defeat me. Indeed, to defeat us all. We Angels, whose sole purpose has been to come to earth to help and support mankind. You are demented!" The daemons' breath stank, and his voice was deafening but Amalialad gave no indication of his feelings and continued to hold his ground.

"So, your master is too busy elsewhere to support you?" Perhaps, he didn't think you that important?" Amalialad said. He had noticed that the devil himself was missing. If he could distract the daemons long enough, he thought, the colonel could give the signal to fire first. If so, there was a slim hope some of them could escape.

"I have no master! And I'm now bored with your interference and insolence." And it was at that moment that Amalialad noticed the almost indiscernible feint by Abaddon to his daemons. "It's time to die." And before Abaddon completed the sentence, Amalialad discreetly signaled the colonel who, in turn, pressed his red button. So, as the daemons started to raise their bows, the cannons roared, the tanks fired, the rifleman discharged their weapons and the Monk Warriors shot their arrows. And pandemonium broke out.

Amalialad dived to the ground, rolled over rapidly a few times and then ran fast towards the cover of a previously prepared hideout. The colonel was already inside, giving quick instructions on his radio. The colonel was flustered as he hastily spoke to Amalialad.

"Our weapons have been virtually ineffective and almost a quarter of our men are dead. We initially managed to disorientate the daemons but that's all. Their arrows are flying at us non-stop and every one of them is reaching its target." Before Amalialad could respond, the colonel answered another incoming call.

"What, more monsters? I don't believe this." He turned, in almost despair, to Amalialad.

"Now it seems we've got another lot of monsters heading towards us about two kilometers away. I'm told they're carrying some sort of weapon. Any suggestions?" Amalialad could see the colonel was desperate.

"Yes, I have. Get ready to celebrate." The colonel looked at Amalialad with total dismay. The poor chap's gone crazy, he thought. But Amalialad continued. speaking. "Peter, you son of a gun. Please, colonel help me lift the entrance slab, we need to peek outside."

"I don't think that's a good idea right now." said the colonel, now concerned about Amalialad's mental state.

"Look, I know how it must look, but I'm ok. Really, I am. Please trust me, Colonel." Then together they slowly moved the slab and looked up. They glared upwards in amazement as they saw the last two flaming arrows fly through the sky and pierce the hearts of Abaddon and Beelzebub.

"How did you know?" said the colonel.

"Tara told me." said Amalialad.

"Ah, say no more."

Ben and Peter were excitedly chatting to each other about the events when the colonel and Amalialad walked into the cabin. Amalialad, surprisingly, hugged Peter. "Well done, my friend. I'm sorry, but I'd given up on you. What happened? We can see you brought the Ark and some other friends but how have you accomplished the impossible?"

Peter cheerfully related the events of the last few days, about how Hugh discovered his destiny and remained with the Ark, although he said they could meet him soon enough as he was with the Ark at that moment, which wasn't too far away. Peter then stated how, like them, he'd thought he and Francis would be killed by the creatures but how at the very last moment he remembered to call out for the Djinns, who then not only came to his aid instantly by destroying the creatures, but also then continued to carry the Ark to them.

Then, to Tara's great relief, Chodon walked into the hut and embraced her. And it was at that moment that Ben felt something was very wrong. As they embraced, Chodon took out a knife from her belt and pushed it hard, to the hilt, into Tara's heart.

"No!" Ben cried out. Then, pushing people aside, he ran at Chodon.. He swung his own knife, viciously up and down towards her. He was just a second away from stabbing her in the heart. But Chodon was ready for him, and suddenly twisted around, sharply blocked his arm and knocked the knife from his hand. She then aimed her own knife at Ben's heart.

But it didn't quite meet its mark. Another knife plunged into her back killed her an instant before. Amalialad discreetly pulled it back out as she fell and then caught Ben as he continued to propel himself forward. Ben was delirious and grief-stricken, so Amalialad gently eased him down to the floor and asked everyone, except Peter and theCcolonel, to leave the hut. Then he spoke.

"I'm so sorry, Ben." Then Amalialad turned to face Peter and spoke softly.

"Please, take care of him for me." Then he pointed at Chodon's dead body. "This was not Chodon, but a shapeshifter. I'm afraid that in the excitement we let our guards down. I'm to blame for that. But I think I may know who was responsible and I intend to deal with it."

"Can I help you with that?" Peter asked.

"No, my friend, you've done plenty already and I'd like you here with Ben. In any case, I must do this alone."

"Ok, if you insist, then I promise I'll take good care of Ben and everything here until you get back. Oh, by the way, I don't know what he meant by it, but Francis asked me to tell you that he'd done as you asked."

"Thanks, Peter." Amalialad packed a few things into a duffle bag and left the hut. Waiting just outside was the colonel. "I think we've said sorry to each other many times these last few days but truly I really am sorry about Tara. I knew she was very close to you and in the little time I knew her, I got to like her very much."

"Thank you, colonel. That means a lot." Then there was a short pause while Amalialad thought of Tara. He'd miss her tremendously. But he had to get going if he was to meet his nemesis on time.

"I've got a favour to ask."

"Name it." said the colonel.

"Can I borrow your fastest vehicle?"

"Of course." He then called over one of his lieutenants stationed outside the hut and gave him some instructions. Ten minutes later, an almost new FV108 Scimitar was driven up to them.

"I think this'll do the job. There are a few weapons in the back you might need, and…"

"And, what?"

"It's not gold." The colonel laughed. "It was the only vehicle stored undercover, below ground when Berith turned our vehicles to gold." They both laughed. Then Amalialad threw his rucksack into the back of the vehicle and jumped into the driver's seat before turning around to face the colonel again.

"Thank you," Amalialad said with conviction.

"It's a pleasure. Are we likely to meet again?"

"I hope so, colonel. I really do hope so."

Chapter sixty-one

Alexander Lindsay, the 4th Earl of Crawford, also popularly referred to as Earl Beardie, because of the large beard he'd always worn, sat at the top of the small circular table. He'd proved to be a cruel, pompous, evil man and an avid gambler. With him were four others who had agreed to play poker with him even though it was the Sabbath. They met annually at the same time, midnight, and played for four hours. The same visitor also interrupted their play with a request to join the game at 3 a.m. and was always invited to do so. And this tradition had now been going on, in a secret room, tucked away in the West Tower of Glamis Castle, for four hundred and ten years. The event was to be repeated for eternity and each time, as far as the players were concerned, it was a new and exciting game. And so, once again on a Sunday morning in 2026, there was a knock on the door at precisely 3 a.m. The stranger, having permission form the earl, walked in. He wore a long black cloak and kept his face in shadow. However, he spoke most eloquently, and with an air of authority.

"Forgive my intrusion, but I hoped, of course with your kindest permission, that I may join your lordship in your friendly game?" The stranger then bowed in a gesture of respect and sat down at the spare place left at the table.

It was exactly the moment Amalialad was patiently waiting for and from his position on the table, he spoke.

"Welcome Satan, to our game." Amalialad spoke calmly. And Satan, momentarily, looked startled.

"Ahh, it's the boy from Tibet. You have made a big mistake coming here."

"It's you, Satan, I'm afraid, who has made the big mistake." Then Amalialad got up and moved quickly around to the back of Satan's chair. The devil tried hard to move but mysteriously couldn't and became very angry. However, Amalialad ignored him, took a container from his pocket and quickly poured rock salt at the back of Satan's chair. It soon joined up with the rest of the salt which was spread around the table and chairsearlier, to complete the circle. And the circle of salt was inside the hectogram, known as the devil's trap, a similar one to that used by Peter and his companions to trap the witches, but this trap was enhanced with extra symbols and chants to ensure the power necessary to trap Satan. Satan suddenly found himself completely trapped. He struggled and looked directly at Amalialad. His eyes suddenly grew, and glowed blood red and his voice became taut, as his anger and frustration grew, but then it quickly changed again to a loud croaky and deeply penetrating sound. Amalialad felt something attempting to probe inside his head. But he focused hard and holding up his Bible, and gripping his cross tightly, he managed to build a wall of resistance against Satan's attempts to control him. Amalialad knew that all the circle could do for now was physically restrain Satan. But his goal was to banish him from earth. He knew if he could do that then humanity had a chance. He knew that without Satan daemons would still exist within the world, but they'd be much weaker and if goodness had once again started to overcome evil, as he hoped now, otherwise, he thought, why would God have allowed the Ark to assist them, then they had a chance. He wasn't a Christian but a Buddhist, but he had faith and believed in the power of the Christian symbols and knew that if the daemons feared them and God himself, that was all that mattered.

Suddenly, the other players disappeared, and Satan grew. Changed. He became the fallen angel once again. The Archangel who was at one time on God's right-hand side, then known as Lucifer, the morning star, the bringing of light. When he was thrown out of Heaven by the Archangel Michael and his Angels in losing the final battle with God, he took on his daemonic shape. The shape which was now hideously growing and becoming more grotesque as each additional scale of its huge, thick, twisted and shiny, red carcass grew. And so, it got bigger. It got huge. Until standing in front of Amalialad was the massive red dragon. And as Amalialad looked on, chilled to the bone by what he was witnessing, the dragon's mouth opened wide to display its gigantic, razor sharp teeth. It then whipped around its enormous, red tail which lashed hard against the force field of the circle, but to no avail. No daemon could ever escape the power of the circle. The dragon opened its mouth wide, bearing its sharp twelve-inch gritted, salivating teeth and then shot out rapid puffs of smoke and short, bright streams of burning gas from its nostrils. Amalialad began to have second thoughts. The very thought of it made him tremble to the core and he knew he'd have to muster every single fibre of energy in his mind and body to fight and stave off its power, to overcome this dragon, to conquer the devil. That's why he couldn't believe what he suddenly saw materializing in front of him. The dragon grew and grew until it took up the entire space, from the floor to the ceiling and from side to side, and Amalialad wondered whether he was hallucinating when he noticed an almost imperceptible shudder at the side of the circle. Then, without warning, the dragon turned its massive head around toward him. It scraped against the edge of the force field as its cramped body ploughed its way around towards Amalialad, and its bloodshot, red eyes, zoomed in, pushing hard against the invisible force of the circle and, with its face distraught as it tried to push harder against it, it came level with him. Somehow, Amalialad stood his ground, even when, moments later, a booming, guttural, voice broke through and entered his head.

"You know I'll be out of here soon, Tibet boy. There is nothing that can hold me. You have stood in my way for too long already. But I have sympathy for you and will allow you to leave here without physically harming you if you release me right now."

Amalialad knew the devil's cunning. He was, after all, the master of lies and deceit, so instead of linking his thoughts directly, thereby risking losing control of his mind, he projected them onto a white screen for the devil to read. He knew if he could keep the daemon an hour in the circle it would then be banished from earth to his own home in the bottomless pit. So far it had been in the circle fifty minutes.

"It's tempting, how do I know I can trust you?"

"But of course, you can trust me. Didn't you notice I wasn't supporting Abaddon or the other evil daemons who attacked you? As I told you I'm only here to help you. Its obvious others have lied to you about my intentions. I can understand why you believe them; probably, if I were you, I would too. But human, I'm not here to physically harm you." It sounded convincing. But, of course, Amalialad knew, like all gamblers, the devil was addicted and had an important appointment at a poker game to keep.

Five more minutes passed by.

"Hmm, that's true. Can I have a few minutes to ponder it?"

"Of course. Nobody can ever accuse me of not being patient. You have three minutes."

Amalialad needed four but accepted the three. He'd hoped he would be able to delay the devil by at least another minute after the three had run out.

But the devil was conspiring himself. And he only needed three minutes to escape the circle.

"It's a trap, Amalialad. Move back. You have two minutes." It was a telepathic link from Lopsang.

Amalialad crept back to the corner of the room, where earlier he'd left his small rucksack. He crouched down and prepared to implement his backup plan.

It was exactly three minutes later when the forcefield ruptured and, with an almighty roar from the dragon, the whole room shook, as it stepped out of the circle and into the room.

It was do or die now for Amalialad, as he withdrew his ivory knife and stick from the duffle bag, then put his ivory-handled knife into his side sheath, which was fitted to his waist belt, and, after that, having unscrewed the walnut knob of his stick, grabbed the top of it and pulled out a silver sword. The sword was a mystery. The only thing known about it was that it had been passed down through the centuries from the Fourth Phanem Lama himself, the wisest and leading of all Dalai Lamas. But its biggest mystery was that its metal was unknown. It fitted perfectly in his hand. Then, just as the dragon pounced, he rapidly twisted and ducked, so that the teeth of the dragon snapped together, narrowly failing to snap his head off. Swiftly, Amalialad back flipped to the side and dived down and rolled around to the back of the dragon and, with his sword, struck its tail, slicing it in two. Screeching, the dragon reeled back in pain, but its momentum continued as it spun back around again, and it charged a second time at Amalialad. This time, as it surged forward, vicious flames gushed forth from its open mouth and reached out to engulf Amalialad. But instinctively Amalialad swiftly turned around, so that his flame resistant, padded jacket took the brunt of the flaming surge, and then he quickly flipped sideways. He rolled forwards, away from the dragon, turned again and jumped to his feet. It was then, as he saw the dragon changing shape, and he saw other heads beginning to grow, that he realized his fatal mistake, and remembered the text from the Book of Revelation. He remembered the time when Satan and his Dark Angels were thrown out of Heaven down to earth by the Archangel Michael. He reflected on the text which described how Satan had first appeared in the sky.

And another sign appeared in Heaven, behold, a great, fiery red dragon having seven heads and ten horns, and seven diadems on his heads.

How could he have forgotten such crucial information? He quietly cursed himself. It was somewhat ironic, he thought, even the daemons couldn't have sealed a worse fate for him than this. To fight a fierce, fiery flaming dragon with one head was bad enough, but to face one with seven heads, ten horns and seven diadems was quite another thing. Most would say impossible and he agreed with them, but he was here now, with one task in mind. To destroy Satan. And even if he should fail, he would at least die trying.

Amalialad stared in amazement as the transformation took place. This was the moment, where only one head had grown, where the dragon was most vulnerable and so, after quickly testing the sharpness of his sword on his shirt, which cut it more smoothly than cutting butter, Amalialad fixed his mental strategy to memory.

Then he flew. Skillfully, in a smooth but rapid flow, he waved his sword back by his side and then, as swift as an arrow, he brought his sword around in an arc movement and cut the first head clean off, but before landing back on his feet, still in midair, Amalialad pulled his sword back and around, swept it out wide and sliced off the second head. And the dragon roared in rage and immense agony, but it still managed to lash out sharply with its injured tail and catch Amalialad's stomach as he leapt off it.

    Amalialad fell to the ground and quickly crawled to the corner, next to his rucksack. He was hurting. It was excruciating, and he knew at once it wasn't just a normal wound. As his heart pumped and his blood flowed, so his eyes began to dim, and he found it difficult to focus. Eventually his thoughts became more muddled and confusing. But there was too much at stake; he had to keep going. While still suffering enduring pain, the dragon was momentarily disorientated. This gave Amalialad a little time so, with grit and determination, he reached inside his bag for bandages. He knew he had to do the best he could to stem the blood flowing from his stomach. His fingers searched around but there was nothing inside. Nothing that is except for what felt like a very small box. He'd felt sure he'd packed bandages but with everything all happening at once over the past few days, he may well have forgotten. Then he remembered. He pulled the box out of the sack. It was the silver box Peter had given to him days ago. Amalialad fought hard to remember. There was something about only when there seems to be no hope left. Then he heard movement behind him. He knew if he turned around the dragon would be aware that he was conscious, still alive. Amalialad noticed the brass tag fixed on to the outside of his bag and, very stealthily, with his hands out of sight from the dragon, he lifted that part of the bag to the side and carefully peeked at the reflection. The dragon was perusing its injuries and leaned to its side to look closer to where one of its heads used to be. Amalialad jerked in shock. Through the reflection he could just make out the numbers '999' marked on the dragon's neck. Then, further realization came to him. A code? Something about a code. He looked at the box more closely, and there, molded to one side of it, was a three-digit lock. Amalialad put in the numbers 999 and pulled the top up to open it. But, nothing. It remained tightly closed. Fading away, as the blood continued to seep from his body, Amalialad knew his time was almost up. Satan wins, he thought. But as he said Satan's name, he remembered the number 666. Of course, the actual number was 666. Quickly Amalialad put 666 into the lock and the box sprung open. Inside was an old silver ring and Amalialad lifted it up and held it close. His vision was very poor now and he had difficulty reading the small inscription on the side of the ring. It was in Latin, but he could just about understand it. When all hope seems lost I Solomon alloweth the bearer of this ring to command.

It was then that the dragon, with its five heads, ten horns and seven diadems roared and raced forward to stamp out the intruder's life and torture its soul forever.

However, Amalialad heard it coming and knew this would be it. So, with one final burst of energy, he held the ring up high and pointed it towards the racing dragon. Then he shouted out at the top of his voice,

"With the power given to me by Solomon, I now command you, Satan, to be banished from this place and go to the bottomless pit for all millennium."

As Amalialad lost consciousness he wondered where he'd got the words from.

And hidden in the corner of the room, the Watcher, both intrigued and in awe of the young human, looked on. He was glad he hadn't had to intervene. The boy deserved his win. He'd just told him what to say to Satan at the end. After all, the Watcher thought, it was he who, on behalf of God, had, two thousand years ago, given Solomon the power to command daemons.

Chapter sixty-two

One week later at a hospital in London

Amalialad pulled the cord at the side of his bed. He only had to wait a few seconds before a nurse in a bright blue uniform rushed in.

"Ah, we're awake at last, are we? You've been asleep for a week. A brief coma but I'm glad to see you're ok now. You must be hungry."

"Yes, starving."

"Well, we've got some stew and dumplings. Will that be ok? And a nice cup of tea now, if you fancy one?"

"Perfect," said Amalialad.

"Great, and please be careful when you're moving around. Your stomach has healed now but you need to take it easy still, ok?"

"Of course, nurse and thank you very much. And no sugar in my tea please. Just milk."

"I don't know, you men, you like to be waited on hand and foot, don't you?" Then she smiled again at Amalialad and left.

The nurse returned with the tea ten minutes later.

"There yer go, sir. I hope it's to yer liking?"

"That's fine, thanks."

It was soon after that Amalialad heard a knock on his door.

"Come in." A doctor came walking in. He smiled. "The nurse told me you were awake and that you seemed to be in good spirits. Jolly good, that's always a good sign. My name's Dr Goodwin and I'm most pleased to meet you. As you're now aware, you've been in a coma for a week, which of course is not surprising considering what you've been through and the massive loss of blood you'd suffered. But anyway, I checked you over yesterday and your stomach wound has healed perfectly, albeit for a large scar, which I'm afraid we couldn't help. You had quite a large wound."

"I very much appreciate all the hard work you've done, Doctor. I gather this must be a private hospital or clinic so can you please just invoice me, and I'll settle it."

"Ah, that won't be necessary sir, if I tell you that this hospital belongs to the Opus Dei, I think you'll understand why. I've been instructed to treat you like royalty and to offer you anything you need. Everything is paid for."

"Well, again thank you, doctor. When can I leave?"

"Well, I suppose, as long as you take it easy on your stomach for a few days, there's nothing stopping you leaving now."

"Fantastic. But please, don't get me wrong, your nurse is wonderful and I'm sure the stew and dumplings are wonderful too, but I'll get dressed now and go." The doctor laughed.

"Ok, I can't say I blame you. In your shoes I'd no doubt do the same. But just one more important thing." The doctor handed an envelope to Amalialad. "I was given this to pass on to you. Ah, and we've added some medication which you should take to help with any pain you may suffer. Goodbye, sir."

Amalialad saw that the envelope he had been given had no name for whom it was intended yet it had one of the most important seals in the world on it, that of the pope. Amalialad carefully opened the letter. It was written by hand, in pen and ink and in the old English script.

Dearest Amalialad,

Words that exist do not give enough justice to show the amount of indebtedness this world owes to you. For what you've done is more than remarkable and the bravery you've shown in carrying it out was something which no man should expect another man to endure. But you did so, and from the bottom of our hearts and the depths of our souls, here in the Vatican, and from the pope, whom especially asked me to convey his love and thanks, we wish you always Godspeed and our life long prayers. Further, the pope wished to reassure you that we have changed our ways dramatically now, for the better,

Now, I need to bring you up to date on a few things. Just after you had finished your fight with Satan I was given a message in my sleep instructing me to return immediately to the secret room and it was there where I found your body. Obviously, I then quickly made the necessary arrangements for you to be cared for. Consequently, you will have woken up, and hopefully are now healing well, in one of our best clinics we have. No one there knows your name since we felt it prudent to keep it hidden, until you make your decision on what direction in life to pursue. Further, except for those that need to know, nobody that experienced the last few days' events will ever remember them. It was felt by the messenger, although he did leave the decision to us, that the knowledge of what we now know and the experiences we had would, if all knew, cause massive, widespread panic. Therefore, after a long counsel with the cardinals, the pope agreed. However, it was also agreed that if you wish you can still tell those whose memory of the events we have removed, and we will then of course back up the information you give them. The last message, also from the messenger is for you. He said: 'As long as the inscription fits you have two opportunities for its use. Think carefully and you will use it wisely'

Finally, Amalialad, I have arranged for new shoes and clothing to be left for you, as well as a little money, until you get yourself organized, and a small thank you gift. I hope one day to meet you again.

Your good friend,
Francis.

PS. Once this letter has been opened for five minutes, the ink will vanish. Not a miracle, I'm afraid, but purely scientific. Evidently, once the air gets to the ink, which is made of a special chemical, it has a brief life span.

Amalialad smiled to himself. He knew exactly what he must do next. He hurriedly got dressed. When he put his shoes on, he found a key fob hidden inside one of them. He then left the room and walked down a long corridor which led to the reception and then went out into the car park. He pressed the button on the key fob and heard an answering beep and the lights of a red Subaru came on.

Evidently, Francis had updated Ben and Peter on Amalialad's progress and so along the way, when Amalialad stopped at a restaurant for a quick break, he made a call to both, asking them to meet him later that day at the Holiday Inn hotel in Brent Cross.

Ben and Peter were sitting chatting when Amalialad walked in. They didn't notice him and so he crept up behind them.

"Where's my coffee then?" he asked. And they both turned around in surprise.

"Amalialad, it's great to see you." Peter rushed around the table to give his friend a brief hug. And Ben did the same.

"I've missed you," he said.

"And I've missed you too, Ben. I'm so sorry I couldn't be here for you."

"That's ok, Amalialad I know if you could have been here, then you would have been." Then Ben managed a smile. "Anyway, we knew you were still busy saving the world, didn't we, Peter?"

"Indeed, always. Let's order the coffees, shall we?"

"That's a great idea," said Amalialad. "Can you order four? I'm expecting someone else."

While Peter ordered the coffees at the bar Ben had a chance to talk more with Amalialad.

"I've arranged the funeral for Thursday, next week. I hope you can make it?" said Ben, sadly. Before Amalialad could reply, Peter returned with the coffees.

Suddenly, the room grew silent as everyone turned to look at the woman who had just walked in. She was dressed in a soft black, Pia Michi velvet gown, with a fine golden necklace and black, high-heeled shoes.

Peter was standing, open mouthed. Ben looked up and what he saw knocked him senseless.

"What the ..." Peter put a hand over his mouth and stopped him from saying more.

"Listen, my friend. For now, ask no questions. Just accept that sometimes miracles happen, and, my God, if anyone deserves one it's you. Just accept and enjoy the rest of your lives together." Ben got up and rushed over towards Tara, who opened her arms. Tears of joy streamed down Ben's cheeks, but he was so overcome with emotion that no words would come from his lips.

Amalialad and Peter had lots to catch up on and so they discreetly moved to a more private lounge, leaving Ben and Tara to catch up. Amalialad quickly established that Peter still retained his memory of the events and had been told by Francis the importance of keeping the past events secret. Ben remembered everything too.

"So, Peter, what will you be doing next?" Amalialad asked.

"Well, there's the matter of a few artifacts to be returned."

"Oh, of course, I'm so sorry Peter. I'd completely forgotten."

"You've had enough to deal with, don't worry about it. I've got everything in hand."

"As you always have, my friend. You know I could never have managed any of this without you, don't you?"

"Ah, hogwash. You would have coped somehow. You know, my friend, you really are special. I'm not sure why and I don't envy you - too much expectation and responsibility can be put on you. But if you want my help on your own quest now, I'd be happy to help as soon as I've dealt with the artefacts."

"You've been a true friend, Peter, but I'll be ok."

"Well, the offer's always there. I'll be leaving early in the morning, so I'll say my farewells now."

"Ah, before you go, Peter. I've been asked to give you this." Amalialad pulled out an envelope from his pocket and handed it over.

"What's this?" Peter asked, as he opened the envelope. He looked at Amalialad.

"Wow. A cheque for £100,000. This isn't necessary."

"Oh, yes, it is. And so, the Vatican should pay it to you."

"The Vatican, you say? Hmm, in that case I'll consider my arm twisted and I'll accept it. Goodbye, Amalialad, look after yourself."

"You too, Peter, take care."

Ben and Tara were up, bright and early and drinking coffee as Amalialad walked into the dining room at 8 a.m. He was so happy to see them both laughing and enjoying each other's company.

When the time came to use the ring in the mortuary, he had felt a moment of indecision. But it was short-lived. Since the messenger, whom he now knew was the Archangel Michael, had, in essence, condoned his intention to bring Tara back to life, then he felt even more justified. For Tara and Ben, Amalialad knew there would have been no hope for a future together, but for the intervention of God, through Michael, and through Solomon with the help of the ring. It certainly had been, he thought, the right decision.

"Good morning. You look wonderful together."

"Good morning, Amalialad," Ben said.

"Thank you so much for all you've done for us, Amalialad." Tara smiled widely as she stood up and walked over and hugged him.

"Well, thank you, and I'd like to say a big thank you to you two. Without your help I'd have failed."

Ben flushed with embarrassment. Tara smiled.

"Thank you, Amalialad."

"I'll be leaving shortly, perhaps you'll both walk down to the car with me?"

"Of course."

They walked down to the car park together.

"Wow, lovely car," Ben said. "If you had more time, I might have persuaded you to let me take it for a spin."

"Well, the car's yours, Ben." Amalialad handed over the documents and the keys. "It's no good for where I'm going."

"What? You're joking. Are you sure? It must have cost a bomb."

Amalialad laughed.

"Well, probably, but it was a gift to me, which I'm giving to my best friend."

Ben beamed again, with pride.

"Thank you, Amalialad. But what about university? Aren't you finishing your last year?"

"Ah, it slipped my memory. We've both been awarded honorary degrees." Amalialad said it as casually as if he were talking about the weather and Tara knew he was teasing Ben.

Ben's eyes nearly popped as he jumped up in the air and waved his arms around with joy.

He embraced Amalialad again.

"Before you leave, one question. How in the hell did we win? The odds were so tremendously against us."

Amalialad smiled.

"Peter kept the Crown of Thorns safe. That may help answer your question."

"Hmm, I see. So, the legend about whichever army held the Crown of Thorns would win their battles is true?"

Amalialad just smiled.

"Take good care, Amalialad, you know where we are if you want our help," Ben said.

"Of course, I do. Thank you, but please, both of you, promise me you will enjoy the rest of your lives together, and don't forget to invite me to your wedding next August."

"What?" Ben said.

But a BMW with tinted windows drew up and laughing, Amalialad stepped inside and, within seconds, sped off.

"What's this about a wedding?" Ben asked Tara.

"Oh, didn't I tell you? We're getting married in August. Are you happy with that?"

"Well yes, of course. But I wished you'd asked me before telling anybody else."

"Ben, do you think I'd do that? Amalialad was very naughty, he'd read my mind."

"Ahh, typical."

"Do you think we'll really see him again?" Tara asked, as they both walked hand in hand back to the hotel.

"Oh," said Ben, "I've a funny feeling we will."